NEW STORIES
FROM THE SOUTH

The Year's Best, 1998

The editor wishes to thank Kathy Pories,
whose taste, skill, and tact are essential
to this anthology.

Edited by
Shannon Ravenel

---

with a preface by Padgett Powell

NEW STORIES
FROM THE SOUTH

The Year's Best, 1998

Algonquin Books of Chapel Hill

Published by
ALGONQUIN BOOKS OF CHAPEL HILL
Post Office Box 2225
Chapel Hill, North Carolina 27515-2225

a division of
WORKMAN PUBLISHING
708 Broadway
New York, New York 10003

ISSN 0897–9073
ISBN 1–56512–219–4

CONTENTS

Editor's Note: *Two years ago, after writing eleven prefaces to this annual anthology, I came to realize that a single preface writer has a limited store of fresh arguments for reading, relishing, and celebrating the yearly crop of outstanding short fiction being written in and about the American South. There are, of course, many more arguments than mine to be made. And who better to make them than those who believe in them most? Thus we now turn to the short story writers themselves—one of each year's contributors is invited to introduce the collection. As Robert Olen Butler's inaugural guest preface to the 1997 volume and Padgett Powell's preface to this one prove, there is indeed more to say and more to learn about the short story, Southern or otherwise.* —Shannon Ravenel

PREFACE: WHAT SOUTHERN LITERATURE IS

A mule runs through Durham. There is something on his back, on fire. Memaw gives chase, with a broom, with which she attempts to whap out the fire on the mule. The mule keeps running. The fire appears to be fueled by paper of some sort, in a saddlebag or satchel tied on the mule. There is of course a measure of presumption in crediting Memaw with trying to put out the fire; it is difficult for the innocent witness to know that she is not just beating the mule, or hoping to, and that the mule happens to be on fire, and that that does not affect Memaw one way or another. But we have it on private authority, our own, that Memaw is attempting to save the paper, not gratuitously beat the mule, or even punitively beat the mule. Memaw is not a mule beater.

The paper is Memaw's money, perhaps (our private authority accedes this is likely), which money Pawpaw has strapped onto his getaway mount, perhaps (our private authority credits him with strapping the satchel on, but hesitates to characterize his sitting the mule as he is as a deliberate, intelligent attempt to actually "get away"; that is to say, we are a little out on a limb when we call the mule, as we brazenly do, the mount on which he hoped to get away, and might have, had he not, as he sat the plodding mule, carelessly dumped the lit contents of the bowl of his corncob pipe over his shoulder into the satchel on the mule's back, thereby setting the fire and setting the mule into a motion more vigorous than a plod. A mule in a motion more vigorous than a plod with a fire on its back attracts more attention than etc.).

Memaw, we have it on private authority, solid, was initially, with her broom, after Pawpaw himself, before he set fire to the satchel behind him, so the argument that Pawpaw might have effected a clean getaway without the attention-getting extras of a trotting mule on fire is somewhat compromised. Memaw, with her broom, has merely changed course; she wants, now, to prevent her money's burning more than Pawpaw's leaving, though should Pawpaw get away with the money unburnt, she presumably loses it all the same. That loss, of unburnt money, might prove temporary: unburnt money is recoverable, sometimes, if the thieves are not vigilant of their spoils, if the police are vigilant of their responsibilities, if good citizens who find money are honest and return it, etc. But burnt money is not recoverable, except in certain technical cases involving banks and demonstrable currency destruction and mint regulations allowing issue of new currency to replace the old, which cases Memaw would be surprised to hear about. And it is arguable that, were she indeed whapping Pawpaw and not the fire behind him, her object might not be to prevent his leaving but to accelerate it.

So Memaw is now whapping not the immediate person of Pawpaw but the fire behind him. It is not to be determined if Pawpaw fully apprehends the situation. He may think Memaw's consistent failure to strike *him* with the broom is a function of her indextrous skill with the broom used in this uncustomary manner. We are unable, even with the considerable intelligence available from our private authority, to hazard whether he knows the area to his immediate rear is in flames. Why Memaw would prefer to extinguish the fire rather than annul his escape or punish him for it is almost certainly beyond the zone of his ken. We have this on solid private authority, our own, our own *army* of private authority, in which we hold considerable rank. Pawpaw is holding his seat, careful to keep his clean corncob pipe from the reach of Memaw's broom, errant or not. Were the pipe to be knocked from his hand, either by a clean swipe that lofted it into the woods or by a glancing blow that put it in the dirt at the mule's hustling feet, he would dismount to retrieve the pipe and thereby quit his escape. It is likely that Memaw and the burning mule would continue, leaving him there inspecting his pipe for damage.

The mule is an intellectual among mules, and probably among the people around him, but we, the people around him—intellectuals among people, or not, as per our test scores, our universities and degrees therefrom, and our disposition to observe public broadcasting, and with the entire army of private authority we command —can not know what he knows. It is improbable that he knows of Pawpaw's betrayal, of Memaw's hurt rage, of the accidental nature of the fire, of the denominations of the currency, of the improbable chance that among the money are dear letters to Memaw before she was Memaw that she does not want Pawpaw to discover, even after he has left her and might be presumed to be no longer jealous of her romantic affairs. It is not certain that he, the mule, knows his back, or something altogether too close to his back, is on fire. It is certain, beyond articulated speculation, that he senses his back is hot and that the kind of noise and the kinds of colors which make him hot and nervous when he is too near them are on his back. He has elected to flee, or is compelled to flee. Nervousness puts him in a predisposition to flee. A woman with a broom, a two-legger with any sort of prominent waving appendage coming at him, puts him in full disposition to flee, which he does, which increases the unnerving noises and colors and heat on his back, confirming him in the rectitude of this course of action, notwithstanding certain physical arguments, which he has almost certainly never heard and might or might not comprehend were he to hear them, that he'd be better off standing still.

That is Memaw's position: If the bastard would just stand still, she could save him *and* the money. She could get Lonnie Sickle's

letters out of the money, get the money out of the bag, then get
Pawpaw, as he stupidly yet sits the mule guarding his pipe, which
she could verily whap into the woods with one shot, and then get
Pawpaw and the mule on down the road, where they are fool
enough to think they want to go. She knows the mule is not fool
enough to want to go down the road—the mule would appear to
be a faultless fellow until caught up in human malfeasance and
crossfire and dithered by it; plus, he is on fire—but she is going to
uncharitably link him to Pawpaw during the inexact thinking that
prevails during domestic opera of this sort. This is precisely the kind
of inexact thinking in which it does not occur to one that burnt
money can be replaced at a bank under certain technical circumstances which make one nervous to speculate upon in the event that
the money concerned is one's own. But now that the army of our
private authority has revealed the further intelligence—which we
suspect it could have revealed sooner were relations between us, the
rank, and it, the file, better—of the existence of personal letters also
in the satchel, we know that the money was never Memaw's first
concern in her zealous whapping of the fire on the mule. And we
know that Memaw, no matter how inexact her thinking during
domestic opera of this sort, is not inclined to think that letters, like
money, can be replaced, under certain technical circumstances, after
they are burnt. Letters of the sort she is protecting now, in fact, are
themselves but the thinnest substitute for, papery vestiges of, the
irreplaceable tender emotions they recall, tender emotions she held
and that held her in a state of rapt euphoria some thirty years ago,
emotions she can but vaguely recollect when she holds the letters
in her rare few moments of calm, tired tranquility. She and Lonnie
Sickle are only nineteen years old, they kiss without the nuisances
of whiskey and whiskers and malodorous thrusting, without the
complications of bearing children, and Lonnie Sickle has not yet
been found with the pitchfork tine through his heart.

Pawpaw is, in contrast to Lonnie Sickle in this recollected tender tranquility and in the loud, mean, prevailing domestic opera

which surrounds her small tranquilities like a flood tide, a piece of shit what thinks it won World War II and thereby earned the right to be every kind of shitass it is possible to be on Earth, and then some, if there is any then some. This, his single-handed winning of WWII, is inextricably and inexplicably a function of his people's collective losing of the Civil War eighty years before.

Memaw did not become Memaw until she allowed herself to be linked to Pawpaw via a civil ceremony during the postwar frenzy of imprudent coupling that wrought more harm to the country, she now thinks, than Hirohito and Hitler combined. She had a normal name and was normal herself. She was Sally, and a fond uncle would call her Salamander, which now, against Memaw, sounds charming. And Pawpaw had been Henry Stiles until two minutes after the ceremony when people seemed to come out of the woods and the woodwork all calling him Pawpaw and her nothing, ignoring her for a full two years, it seems, until slowly addressing her, tentatively at first but then unerringly, as Memaw. She was powerless to stop this phenomenon; it was not unlike a slow, rising tide, unnoticed until it is too late to escape. There she had been, first on a wide, isolated silent mudflat of wedding-gift Tupperware and their VFW mortgage, and then in a sudden full sea of *Memaw* and only a thin horizon of sky and water around her. It stunned her to hear "Memaw makes the best cornbread," stunned her into hearing it again and again, and then Sally was never heard of or from again, and she was not a Salamander but a Hellbender.

We have it from the army of private authority that dogs love Memaw. Two dogs are, in fact, at her heels as she herself dogs the heels of the mule, of which dogging she is tiring, and Pawpaw — who dropped his pipe and voluntarily quit the mule to retrieve it, having grown complacent with his surmise that his pipe is unhurt — is in an awkward amalgam of embarrassment and fatigue and uncertainty as to what to do now. Memaw is between him and his burning getaway mule, and he is more winded than Memaw and the mule, so that the matter of his skirting around Memaw and overtaking the mule himself is out of the question. He is somewhat concerned—even the innocent witness can deduce this, by the nervous motions of his feet when she turns occasionally to glare at him and point one long finger at him—that Memaw will desist pursuit of the burning mule and come after him, which will put him in the face-losing position of having to retreat. Keeping his distance, as he is, he has had occasion to pick up pieces of charred currency and an envelope with a cancelled stamp on it dated 1943, which he knows was the war because he knows (first to bloom in his troubled brain at this moment, this is to say) of the 1943 steel penny, a copper-conservation thing owing to the war, which he knows (second to bloom) he was in, which he knows (third) because he won it. The letter is addressed to Sally Palmer in a handwriting not his own—

The question What is Southern literature?, were it not asked perpetually by so many persons presumably not uninterested in knowing the answer, would seem to be a question profoundly uninteresting. It is more the answers to the question, as numerous and every bit as eager, that tire. Most of them mention, in a holy let-you-in-on-a-secret way, the *human* heart. The present author would rather swallow NPR political doctrine than endure, and certainly rather than issue, the old verities lecture.

The man who I think made that phrase—the old verities—fresh, before it was famous, is William Faulkner. Here is Mr. Faulkner's quintessential line: "Well, Kernel, they mought have kilt us, but they ain't whupped us yit, air they?" This is spoken by Wash Jones, one of the poor men who it is now said did the fighting, to Sutpen, one of the rich men whose war it is now said it was. It is the answer to the tired question.

The literature of the South is full of people running around admitting or denying their whippedness. The blend of this confession and denial can be complex—and you can have the less interesting stark extremes of all denial, all confession—but finally that is the key: the people have been whipped, and whipped good.

This is why, in real life, as my daughter puts it, the dog fight—at which one party will not be beaten, on pain of death, and one will—is a distinctly Southern thing, excepting anomalous Boston, where they also, curiously, last turned over school buses. Blacks, when not inhabiting their own literature, stand by, visible or not, in begrudging or bemused witness of this variable posture of the whipped white man.

Integrity is to be seen in the denial of whippedness. "Does one's integrity ever lie in what he is not able to do?" Flannery O'Connor, Juno to Faulkner's Jupiter, asked in this regard (if it is tenable that Hazel Motes is whipped by Jesus). "I think," she said, "that usually it does."

Pawpaw, in his estimate, has never been whipped and, trust me, never will be. Memaw knows better. To the stricken look on Pawpaw's face, when she snatches her letter from him, she says, "All the snow in the world don't change the color of the pine needles, does it, Henry?"

Pawpaw says, "Who?"

PUBLISHER'S NOTE

The stories reprinted in *New Stories from the South: The Year's Best, 1998* were selected from American short stories published in magazines issued between January and December 1997. Shannon Ravenel annually consults a list of ninety-nine nationally distributed American periodicals and makes her choices for this anthology based on criteria that include original publication first-serially in magazine form and publication as short stories. Direct submissions are not considered.

NEW STORIES
FROM THE SOUTH

The Year's Best, 1998

Josh Russell

YELLOW JACK

(from *Epoch*)

Plate 1—*Louis Jacques Mandé Robin*, 1860.
Half-plate daguerreotype.

It is a mystery why those chronicling the history of photography have chosen to obscure the name of Augustus Robin. The assistant of L.J.M. Daguerre (after whom the subject of this portrait was named) was not only the first American Daguerreotypist, setting up his studio in New Orleans, but also the first man to publicly display daguerreotypes, possibly as early as November of 1838. That this date precedes Daguerre's official announcement of 19 August 1839 may be explained by the fact that Robin and Daguerre had been working together on the invention in Paris. After a spat, Robin left the city with one of the earliest cameras and as many of the silvered brass plates as his luggage could hold. In short, he stole the invention which Monsieur Daguerre would later claim as his alone. Whether out of an odd feeling of respect for the European rights to the miracle that would lead Paul Delaroche to declare on the event of its announcement, "From today, painting is dead!" or whether out of fear of prosecution, Augustus Robin made his way to New Orleans via sail. There he and his marvel were warmly received by the French community and the city at large.

In reaction to the hubbub that arose when Daguerre presented his camera and its shimmering trapped moments to the Académies des Sciences et des Beaux-Arts, the New Orleans *Bee* replied, "It is no great surprise that the Europeans are aflutter about a miracle we have had for these many months. Once again America stands at the forefront of Science and Art."

Robin flourished in the '40s and early '50s as a portraitist as well as a landscape photographer. (For an example of his landscape work see Pl. 185—*Trees Being Felled Near Lake Pontchartrain to Combat the Yellow Fever.*) It was not only novelty and the vanity of New Orleanians that led to his success. During the yellow fever epidemics that annually plagued the city in the mid-1800s it was not at all uncommon for doctors to recommend that the very ill be transported to Robin's studio so that a last image could be made as a memento for their loved ones. In just four months of 1853, the worst summer of yellow fever the city ever saw, Robin reported to a *Daily Tropic* columnist the photographing of over four hundred terminally ill and recently-deceased fever victims.

The Civil War brought a boon to the field of photography. Soldiers on their way to battle would often stop in a gallery to have portraits taken for families or sweethearts, and Robin's richly appointed studio was one of the city's finest. Soon the Federal blockade of the Port of New Orleans scarcened supplies, driving up prices, and Robin's days, as well as those of the daguerreotype, were numbered.

Although he attempted to discredit in paid advertisements the ambrotype, the tin or ferrotype, and the calotype as cheap and tawdry imitations of the noble, more expensive daguerreotype, he was eventually driven out of business. When examined now, Robin's death in 1863 was clearly the result of his work in the field. Because of his constant contact with the mercury vapor used to develop daguerreotype images he had lost all of his teeth and was mad for the final three years of his life. He was known to wander the wharves along the Mississippi day and night, and on the morning of October 23rd, 1863, his body was pulled from the river.

This portrait of his youngest son holds the only known image of Augustus Robin, his right hand. It rests gently on the infant Louis' head, steadying the child before the lens.

Plate 2—*Nude Male Standing Before a Shuttered Window,* c. 1838–39.
Plate 3—*Nude Female on a Couch,* c. 1838–39.
Plate 4—*Nude Female Out-of-Doors,* c. 1838–39.
Ninth-plate daguerreotypes.

This narrow span of dates can be assigned to these three plates because of their size and the fact that they appear to have never been cased. A ninth-plate daguerreotype barely fills the palm. Robin may have brought these small 2 × 2.5–inch plates with him from Paris where they were extremely popular. He never again uses the ninth-plate; the 2.75 × 3.25–inch sixth was the smallest available in his studio. In 1840 Robin began placing his daguerreotypes in the same types of cases in which miniaturist painters placed their small portraits and landscapes. (For a discussion on cases see Pl. 10 —*Still Life of Daguerreian's Tools.*) These silver-coated copper plates have aged considerably because they were not protected—all are spotted from dust and moisture and faded by the sun; Pl. 2 bears teeth marks on its upper righthand edge.

The dates assigned to these four plates can also be proven when the subjects and style are examined. Robin was yet to experience the rigid confines of style and the prudish morals of commercial art, and the unfiltered light and unembarrassed camera angles he utilizes are inspired and free.

In Pl. 3 the slightly plump female form brings to mind Rubens. She reclines on a couch, the plate's deterioration oddly kind: her eyes are clear and her face unflawed while the photographed settee's fabric looks as bad as the true settee's upholstery must if it still exists. Time has also left a bowl of papayas and grapes unblemished. Even in the silvery gray tones of the daguerreotype the fruit looks ripe.

In Pl. 4 the young model's flowing blond hair and the carpet of flowers on which she poses mimic Jean Honoré Fragonard. She looks like a nymph beneath her crown of black-eyed Susans. This plate, sadly, shows how the elements can destroy a daguerreotype. Sunlight has harshly faded much of the image. Only the subject's left breast, left shoulder, and head retain their original clarity.

The man lit by stripes of sun sneaking in through louvered shutters in Pl. 2 has the hair and muscle tension of Michelangelo's David. Here too we can see the changes that can occur when a plate is unprotected. Aside from the teeth marks, Pl. 2 has incurred many scuffs and scratches. The effect the highly polished surface once gave is lost because of this damage; the man looks out of focus. Even so, his regal pose and unabashed nudity are remarkable.

The nude disappears from Robin's work for thirteen years marked by brilliant art managed within the narrow bounds of making a living. When it reappears, his wife, ironically, provides the return to the nude (see Pl. 93).

Plate 5—*Girl on a Rocking Horse,* c. 1839–1842.
Plate 6—*Man with Sideburns,* c. 1839–1842.
Plate 7—*An Old Couple,* c. 1843–1848.
Plate 8—*Dog Posed Begging on Chair,* 1845.
Quarter-plate daguerreotypes.

The portrait is democratic, the only quality required of the sitter being the purse to pay the portraitist. The daguerreotype made posing for a likeness more accessible, the price even cheaper than that charged by an inept painter. (Robin's rates as listed in a print ad of 1848 were as follows: "Whole plate—Four Dollars, half plate—Two Dollars Fifty Cents, quarter plate—One Dollar, sixth plate—Seventy-Five Cents, lockets, charms, brooches, &tc.— Negotiable.")

True, these inexpensively attained portraits made many happy, but this bargain also put art into the hands of people who did not think of it as such. Oil paintings hang above fireplaces for generations while daguerreotypes are viewed as part of the effluvium of a life lived in the 1800s—like stereo card viewers and worm-tunneled croquet mallets—to be discarded when cleaning out attics.

These plates of three unknown human subjects and one unknown pet are an excellent example of this tendency. They were found in an antique shop in the French Quarter, a flea market in Arabi, and a junk shop in Grosse Tete. Pl. 5 is a marvelous example of Robin's artistry. The child looks unposed on her horse even though she would have had to remain still for the photograph. Pls. 6 and 7 have the formal stiffness many people wanted in their portraits; Pl. 8 is a lively contradiction. Now common in snapshots, animals were rarely the subjects of early photographs. When they do appear it is rare that they are as well-focused as is this hound.

The most saddening thought occasioned by the discovery of these Robin masterpieces in a two-for-a-dollar shoe box is that the works that remain may be far inferior to those produced by the genius. Who can say that Augustus' greatest art was not stupidly lost or destroyed by those who were unable to recognize its wonder?

Plate 9— *Orion Wagasuc, Mayor of New Orleans,* c. 1848–53. Imperial-plate daguerreotype.

Augustus Robin was the premier portraitist in New Orleans almost from the moment of his arrival in the winter of 1838. Despite the leporine proliferation of other studios and daguerreians, he was recognized as the master of heliographic arts for many years. Robin's clientele included the city's elite and wealthy, as evinced by this example, which is both unusually large and lavishly framed. (The ring on Wagasuc's left hand, added after the plate had left Robin's studio, is of gold leaf with a diamond sliver set in a groove gouged into the plate's surface.)

Wagasuc's pose and props—a law book and a cane with an ornate horse head handle—are not unusual. The daguerreotype took from classic portraiture a love and respect for icons: Soldiers held pistols and sabers, mothers their young, the schoolteacher leaned against Greek pillars, the young lover clutched flowers and gazed drunkenly on thoughts of his absent *objet d'amour.* Good daguerreotypists provided trunks of hats, sidearms, musical instruments, and great works of literature from which to choose. Robin's prop shop is said to have rivaled that of the opera house.

Almost every English and French newspaper lauded Robin's studio on the corner of Toulouse and Dauphine. The *Daily Tropic* described it as "the city's most lavish. The salon is as deep as the building and appointed with wonderful examples of daguerrin [sic] art, as well as with pleasing specimens of classic Greek sculpture, and busts of Shakespeare and other figures from history and literature . . . it is a wonderful place for the ladies to have their likenesses rendered." The *Bee* agreed, adding that "the expense that Mr. Robin has invested in his rooms is evident both in their appointments and in the finest examples of heliographic art available in New Orleans." The *Daily Picayune* furthered the universal admiration with the simple judgment, "Augustus Robin's studio is near to perfect and his work does credit alike to the operator and the art."

Plate 10— *Still Life of Daguerreian's Tools,* c. 1850–1853. Quarter-plate daguerreotype.

Robin was a zealot in his art, so it is little wonder that he made this still life of his tools. The box camera, the dozen slim-necked bottles, and the trio of shallow dishes hint at a simple procedure for daguerreotypes—the opposite is closer to the truth.

The daguerreotype process was arduous and extremely involved. The silvered copper or brass sheets were prone to tarnish, especially in humid New Orleans, so the first step was painstaking polishing, usually with a spinning buckskin-headed apparatus. Next the shiny plate was suspended over iodine, the vapors uniting with the silver to produce a light-sensitive silver iodine coating. The plate was transferred to the camera, exposed to catch the image of the subject, and then developed by placing it above a dish of heated mercury. The mercury vapors reacted with the exposed silver to produce an image in an amalgam of silver mercury. The image, fixed by immersion in a solution of salt or hyposulfite of soda, was toned with gold chloride to improve color, definition, and permanence.

After it was fixed and toned the image was covered with a sheet of glass, sealed with tape, and mounted in a booklike case with an opaque hinged cover. These cases are to be thanked for many of the dates assigned the plates in this study. Robin's case supplier was Wayne Lauren Wilson & Co. of Boston, a firm still in business and in possession of records over a century old. They provided Robin with cases of morocco and also with thermoplastic "Union cases" (pressed sawdust and resin). All the cases can be dated based on their color. Robin ordered black, oxblood, and brown from 1842 to 1849, and replaced brown with red in 1850. Pl. 10's possible dates are based on its scarlet goat leather cover.

The daguerreotype is delicate; New Orleans' climate is perhaps the worst for such photographs. Humidity pocks faces with tarnish and breaks down the silver and mercury images, sunlight makes figures fade as if the past is tugging at them. Mildew, palmetto bugs, and mice destroy the cases and the sealing tape, exposing the daguerreotype to even more destructive moisture. That the plates in this small study have survived is a wonder for which we have a single sea chest to thank. Many of the daguerreotypes discussed here were discovered in the attic of Robin's former residence at 927 Toulouse Street. They had been placed in a locked trunk and spent almost a century hidden by discarded furniture. The trunk was watertight, intended to hold papers on ocean voyages, and thus many of the plates are in exquisite condition.

Plate 11—*Miss Emily Hulbert,* 1851. Whole-plate daguerreotype.

It was customary in the social set to have one's portrait made every year during the winter season, usually in oil or pastel, and for the less wealthy, in silhouette. If the subject was a prominent bachelor or a marriageable young woman the sitting would often serve as the reason for a fête— a coming-out of both young person and portrait. The daguerreotype portrait was no different; in fact its novelty warranted even more interest than had other forms.

The *Bee* reported that Robin was in attendance at the party in November of 1851 at which Miss Emily Hulbert and her portrait debuted. Robin was unmarried at the time and it is very possible that at the gathering he met the woman who would later become his wife—Vivian Marmu. Miss Hulbert's father, W. O. Hulbert, was New Orleans' most successful sugar broker. Miss Marmu's family was also involved in the sugar trade. Further evidence they may have met at the party is found in the marriage announcement of 28 November 1852, which notes that Vivian and Augustus had been courting for "twelve months, almost to the day."

An amusing note on the party and the photograph appears in Miss Hulbert's book, *Life in New Orleans in the Glory Days* (Smith Bros., 1875). She says of her portrait that "it accentuates each and every imperfection of my countenance. My nose is that of a monster, my chin like a chisel, my eyes like dots. When I complained to Mister Robin, telling him that my face when rendered in pastel was much kinder, he merely smiled and told me, 'My dear, the daguerreotype does not lie.'"

The daguerreotype's appearance in New Orleans was dramatic and exciting; the monied and the poor flocked to exhibitions of Robin's work. The cocktail of art and science that the daguerreotype represented was enticing near midcentury. Even if it did point out strong noses and beady eyes, painters soon found it the preferred medium for the yearly portrait.

The painters' loss of revenue was disastrous and many of them made slapdash attempts at embracing the new technology. It was obtainable via mail-order and from traveling salesmen who offered their services as portraitists, teachers of the new art, and suppliers of the cameras, plates, and other necessities needed to make a living as a daguerreian. An oft-seen advertisement in the *Bee* offered "a complete daguerreotype, with plates and appendages, perfect for a man of leisure, or a wise investor in search of a situation." There was money to be made and by 1852 over a dozen studios were listed in the city registry, an impressive number for a city whose population barely topped 100,000. Many of these studios were operated by artists who had once worked with brush and palette.

Robin's studio was the city's most respected, yet he was not content to allow inferior photographers to go about their business. He denounced them in farcical newspaper advertisements in which they were given silly nicknames. Exhibitions were held at which the work of other daguerreians was presented side by side with Robin's exquisite, superior renderings of the same subjects. If these means did not drive a competitor out of New Orleans, rumors circulated that more dastardly forms of sabotage were employed.

Plates 12, 13, and 14 — *Nuptial Triptych, Dr. and Mrs. Victor Benoit.* Individual portraits, 1851; middle portrait, 1852. Quarter-plate daguerreotypes.

The nuptial triptych was a specialty of Robin's. In advertisements he lauded himself as the form's inventor. It combined two traditional portraits in a specially constructed case—the daguerreotypes exchanged Monday morning after Sunday night proposals, and the formal wedding portrait.

The subjects of these portraits are posed in their individual plates as was the fashion—Young Doctor Benoit holding a volume of Homer, his fingers tangled in the pages, the Soon-to-be Mrs. Benoit chastely clutching the Bible. The wedding portrait is oddly unconventional in that the groom's head is lower than the bride's.

Robin and the Doctor, originally of Boston and educated at Harvard College, soon became friends after meeting in 1851. Benoit, like most learned men of the day, was interested in all technological advances, including the daguerreotype. Robin was famous for his volatile temper and lack of social graces (he is said to have slapped a woman during an opera because she would not stop talking). Despite Robin's hot blood, their friendship bloomed while Benoit studied the art under the master. During the spring of 1853 the *Daily Tropic* reports that there was even a display of the Doctor's landscape views in the Robin studio (a fire consumed the Benoit family home in 1901 and no examples of Victor Benoit's work are believed to have escaped the blaze).

The families often attended social events together; Victor Benoit was attending Vivian when she died in 1853. Ten years later he signed Augustus' death certificates.

Plate 15—*Canal Street at Noontime,* 1851.
Whole-plate daguerreotype.

What was it about the daguerreotype that so delighted people in the mid-1800s? Never before had a moment been trapped so perfectly. Painters were encouraged to work from daguerreotypes, not fussy paid models or subjects too busy to sit again and again for a portrait. Architects were promised benefits from images of great buildings with details unattainable from even the best lithographs—every gargoyle's smile visible, the mortar between each brick discernible. Photography advanced armchair travel beyond written accounts and imperfect sketches to accurate views of the Great Pyramids and the Parthenon.

America was in love with all types of technology, but it was more in love with itself. Like Narcissus' still water, the mirror of the daguerreotype was irresistible. Local scenes, like this one of a busy Canal Street in winter, were more revered than those of other cities or distant lands. Robin's gallery was famous for its wide range of New Orleans subject matter—persons of distinction, buildings under construction, the bustling port, major thoroughfares at noon. The city had suffered a devastating economic crisis in 1837 and with each passing month of regained prosperity its citizens loved it more.

This image of horses and pedestrians swarming Canal Street

was winner of the First Premium Award at the 1851 Agricultural and Mechanics' Association Fair. Even now the image is marvelous — the dark Xs of workmen's suspenders, the blurred legs of horses pulling a river of delivery wagons, the domes of gentlemen's bowlers and the cupolas of ladies' parasols.

The *Bee* said of the photograph, "From a rooftop on Canal and Camp Robin has caught in an eye-blink what New Orleans has again become: a metropolis alive with work and trade, a port where the World brings its goods and leaves with cotton, sugar, and the knowledge that the Crescent City is the Venice of the Americas. We consider Robin's daguerreotype the *ne plus ultra* of excellence in the amazing art which he has brought to us."

Plate 16 — *Francis Marmu, His Wife Charlotte, and Their Daughter Vivian,* 1852.
Half-plate daguerreotype.

Perhaps spurred by the warm reception given Emily Hulbert's portrait, dot eyes or no, the Marmus came to Robin's studio shortly after the New Year.

The family was well known; Mr. Marmu was a city councilman as well as a businessman and his antics were famous at the time. Felix Moissenet relates in his series of pamphlets, *Prose Sketches of Notable New Orleanians,* that Francis Marmu was "a man of great valor. When a black cat one day found its way into the City Building and then breached the defenses of the Council Room, Councilman Marmu was unafraid. He launched a fusillade of inkstands at the invading feline, chasing and cursing it as it attempted to circle and attack his flank. When other Councilmen were struck and splattered by the missiles, and thus awoke from dreams of law and commerce, Mr. Marmu was so wise and quick as to be unharmed by their return fire. He dispatched the cat and made motions that the session be ended. Motion was seconded quickly and the brave man was carried away to a fine meal in commemoration of his thrilling victory."

The portrait's arrangement is odd at first look based on the positioning of the subjects, mother and daughter segregated from the father by a column with an almost indistinguishable daguerreotype portrait set atop it. A possible explanation can be found in the Moissenet pamphlets. In a less sardonic mood he says of the Marmu women, "They are close as sisters, the mother lovely as the child. At the opera, the theatre, or a ball, the two ladies are always to be seen side by side."

Vivian was nineteen when this portrait was taken, an odd age for an attractive, wealthy young woman in 1852 to reach without a husband at her side. She had been betrothed to William Spats, a Newark textile merchant. While visiting the city during the summer of 1851 Spats had met Vivian, proposed, contracted yellow fever, and died. The portrait on the pillar is of him, and the ribbons both mother and daughter wear pinned to their breasts are in remembrance of William, a fact confirmed by Moissenet— "Vivian wore the grosgrain *in memoriam* of William until she replaced it with one for her father, then replaced that with one for her beloved mother."

Plate 17—*Greta Dürtmeer,* 1852. Sixth-plate daguerreotype.
Plate 18—*Memorial Portrait of Georg Dürtmeer,* 1852. Whole-plate daguerreotype.

A news item in the *Daily Picayune* tells the story behind these two daguerreotypes. It reports that Mrs. Dürtmeer went to the Robin studio one May Sunday to keep a portrait appointment. She was served tea and cakes while the camera and plate were readied, then was seated and arranged—neck positioned in the iron rest so that her head would remain still during the exposure, parasol angled against a knee, background adjusted to catch the late morning light. Problems then arose. Mrs. Dürtmeer is, as Pl. 17 proves, a homely woman. Despite the crack Emily Hulbert claimed he made about her portrait, Robin was known by many women as a photographer who could manipulate the camera kindly.

Mrs. Dürtmeer's face was full and heavy, but her head small. Robin knew how to compensate: He raised the camera and had the headrest adjusted so that Mrs. Dürtmeer's head projected before her shoulders. She was annoyed and insulted by the adjustments, and she felt the portrait that she was presented with afterward was not good enough to warrant all of the indignities. She screamed at Robin that he was incompetent; she refused to pay. Robin, the article claims, calmly explained that, "The daguerreotype is a mirror, and if the mirror is held before Medusa . . ?" Unamused by the reference to her lamentable hairdo, she threw the portrait at Robin and stormed out.

She hurried home and recounted the entire debacle to her husband, adding, one assumes, insults and attacks on her purity. Georg Dürtmeer was furious. He equipped himself with a set of pistols and had his wife lead the way back to the studio. According to the article, Robin was suffering through a portrait session with "a brat of English origin" when Dürtmeer crashed in, pushed aside an assistant, and challenged Augustus to a duel. Robin accepted, and the two men exited, walked the five blocks to Canal, crossed to the neutral ground, and prepared.

This is the point at which the article's author, *Picayune* reporter Stanley Roberts, became an active part of the fracas. "I was discussing the season's mildness with a dry goods shopkeeper when a man I knew as the daguerreian Augustus Robin and another man, his shirtfront heaving, pulled pistols and began to step off distances." The reporter was pressed into service as Dürtmeer's second; Robin's assistant provided that service for his boss.

Mrs. Dürtmeer and a small crowd watched as the men stood back-to-back, then paced away from each other—"a pickaninny with a fine voice was paid a penny to count aloud"—then turned and fired. Dürtmeer got off his shot first, but it was wide, striking a horse standing innocently before a milk wagon.

Robin's shot was perfect. Dürtmeer fell dead and his wife "threw herself upon his still corpse." The police arrived and arrested Robin, his assistant, Stanley Roberts (who seems to have enjoyed this occurrence the most), and the child paid to call out numbers. The assistant, one Philip Breson, was charged, for some reason, with loitering, Roberts with the same, the youth for disturbing the peace. All were released when Robin's bookkeeper arrived and paid the fines.

Deciding what exactly Robin's crime was required a day of study. On Monday afternoon he faced the judge to plead guilty to the charge of dueling on a Sunday, an offense surely found in the margin of a document from the century before. He paid twenty dollars and was freed.

He hurried to his studio, gathered a camera, some plates, and his assistant. They made their way to the rooms of Herman Lance, the undertaker to whom Georg Dürtmeer's body had been entrusted. Robin was known by many doctors and undertakers, and surely Herman Lance was a close friend. The connections between the physicians who tended the dying, the photographers who took their memorial portraits, and the men who prepared their bodies for eternal rest is easy to figure. Lance allowed Robin to pose Dürtmeer on a plain cooling board much like the ones upon which slain outlaws were posed after Wild West executions.

That evening Robin rounded up the newspaperman and other witnesses to the duel and paid a visit on the widow Dürtmeer. "He rang the bell and the Widow answered it herself. At the sight of Robin, his arms full of gifts, she sank into a chair. When he pulled from its wrappings the portrait of her husband, her shrieks were grotesque and the entire party hurried for the relative silence of the street. Mr. Robin seemed not to be insulted by his reception, and left all but the portrait on her stairs."

Plate 19—*Memorial Portrait of Francis Marmu,* 1852.
Plate 20—*Mourning Portrait of Charlotte and Vivian Marmu,* 1852.
Half-plate daguerreotypes.

Portraits of the dead seem odd and macabre to the contemporary viewer, but during the mid-nineteenth century they were common and often considered necessary as a means of keeping the deceased in mind. For many the memorial photograph was the only taken of them; even the extremely poor would scrape and borrow to afford a memorial portrait of a loved one. Careful survey of the obituary sections of New Orleans papers of the day has led to the discovery of hundreds and hundreds of memorial images affixed to the doors of crypts in the city's many cemeteries. Time and sunlight have turned a large percentage to tarnished squares. A few daguerreotypes hold faint images of the occupants, but most are mirrors that show the visages of the living.

Francis Marmu would not live to see his only child wed Augustus Robin. He was one of the first victims of yellow fever in the summer of 1852, a light summer of deaths. Only 456 of the city's 147,441 citizens fell victim to the fever. In Pl. 19 Mr. Marmu is seated in a chair, a Bible held loosely in his hands. He looks as if he has slipped into a gentle nap. Such "sleep of death" poses were often seen, especially if the subject was very young or very old. Adolescents, teenagers, and young adults were usually posed in bed or in their coffins, a reflection of the fact that their deaths were more startling and sudden.

Pl. 19 is cased in a black morocco memorial case with an engraved silver funerary mat and silvered outlines. Some memorial cases featured poems, death notices, or letters pinned to velvet facing mat. Mr. Marmu's has a small brooch engraved with the first letters of his name and the names of his wife and daughter.

In Pl. 20 Charlotte and Vivian stand hand-in-hand, both wearing second-stage mourning dresses, a clue that dates this plate as later than Pl. 19. It is likely that the two women were absorbed in the details of Francis Marmu's death and unable to take the time for a portrait until later. In Pl. 20, Vivian holds Pl. 19, making the photograph an odd diptych.

* * *

Plate 21—*Spirit Photograph of Charlotte Marmu Standing Behind Her Daughter Vivian,* 1852.
Plate 22—*Memorial Portrait of Charlotte Marmu,* 1852.
Plate 23—*Mourning Portrait of Vivian Marmu,* 1852.
Half-plate daguerreotypes.

Pl. 21 demonstrates how a master like Robin could transform one of the daguerreotype's shortcomings into a wonderful effect. Mother Marmu appears to be standing ghostlike behind her daughter, watching over the girl from beyond the grave. Such photographs became somewhat common in the late 1860s, but no other examples of this technique are known to exist as early as this one. The ghost image was managed by having the "Spirit" subject move out of the picture before the full exposure elapsed, exploiting the slow speed of the shutter.

Most were made when the subject was soon to become a true ghost. Pl. 22 makes this fact sadly true; Mrs. Marmu followed her husband to the grave in September, also a victim of yellow fever. It was not rare for entire families to be carried away by the fever, common for the older members to be the least able to recover. Orphanages were crowded each summer with young survivors. Vivian's resilience can be explained by this passage from Felix Moissenet's pamphlets: "The Marmus were originally from Massachusetts, a fact neither Francis nor Charlotte let anyone forget. A trip to the Marmu home in the summer months would invariably set the stage for a sermon on Devil Summer and his Hell Fires and Demon Mosquitoes. Vivian was born in New Orleans, and when barely eight she suffered and recovered from a bout of the Fever. Such good luck made her, as well as so many other natives to this fine city, impervious to Mister Jack. Her parents, alas, were not so lucky, and in time the poor child was left without either mother or father."

In Pl. 23 the motherless young woman is stunningly posed. She gazes at the memorial portraits of her mother and father, which stand on a small table at her elbow. Robin's use of light and shade is a marvel. The drape behind Vivian is a range of peaks and valleys, the folds of valleys dark with shadow, the peaks snowcapped with well-directed light. The table's legs guide the eye upward from the dark pool of the carpet to the pale line of the lily, which leads to Vivian.

Plates 24 and 25 — *Wedding Diptych of Vivian Robin*, 1852.
Half-plate daguerreotypes.

Two months after her mother passed, Vivian and Augustus were wed. The *Bee* announcement of 28 November mistakenly states that Robin hailed from Boston, but does manage to spell *daguerreian* and *daguerreotype* correctly, a feat of no small consequence. The couple honeymooned in Savannah, Georgia, returning to New Orleans in time to celebrate the Christmas holidays with the Benoits, who had by then become a small family—Sylvia Benoit gave birth to a girl, Susana, at the end of September. The ever-present Felix Moissenet reports that Vivian and Sylvia spent much time doting on the infant while Victor and Augustus discussed photography and medicine.

This diptych is odd in light of Robin's special nuptial triptychs. In Pl. 24 Vivian smiles happily, her mourning dress replaced by a light frock pinned with the always-present grosgrain; in Pl. 25 Vivian stands in her wedding dress. The pair of daguerreotypes is in a kidskin-bound case once white that has aged to the color of butter. The mats are engraved with the names of the bride and the groom and the cover is embossed with the wedding date. In both pictures Vivian appears happy—in Pl. 25 her face is contorted with joy.

That the only known photograph in which Robin appears is Pl. 1 leads to the belief that he was either possessed of huge quantities of modesty, or of distrust that no one else could capture what he could. These two plates display a master at the height of his art, able to create on a plate of silver and brass memorials that survive more than a century later.

Plates 26–183—*Vivian Robin,* 1852–1853.
Whole-, half-, and quarter-plate daguerreotypes.

Augustus' love of his wife did not fade or flicker as the weeks passed. Between November of 1852 and August of 1853 Robin made at least 177 daguerreotypes of Vivian.

She appears in an assortment of poses and settings. Most are simple and seem unplanned. The Robins lived in a sprawling suite of rooms below the studio and it is easy to imagine Augustus playfully luring his wife before the camera for a quick snapshot. In Pl. 32 Vivian holds a cake as if she's brought it to show her husband and been caught, forever holding it out to him. In Pl. 52 Vivian is dressed for the theater, opera glasses dangling from her hand; in Pl. 31 a servant girl brushes her hair. Pl. 89 is a beautiful study of Vivian looking out a window, her elbow, shoulder, and chin forming a triangle through which sunlight gently pours.

In Pl. 34 she sits on a blanket with a picnic lunch. The fruits, breads, and even the flatware seem carefully placed. The sun is reflected in miniature on the surface of a dish, apples and pears and rolls around it like planets, Vivian in a white dress reclining above the assortment like a Venus made by a connect-the-dots joining of stars.

She was no prude. There are dozens of plates in which Vivian appears nude, her face in shadow or covered with coy masks, but in Pl. 93 she smiles happily, her body bare to the camera lens. Visible is the button of a birthmark on her thigh, a reference point that proves the lady sprawled on the settee and the lady bathing and the lady reflected in the mirror are the same.

Perhaps most touching is Pl. 103. In it Vivian stands dressed in her night clothes, her eyes bleary with sleep, her mouth a groggy smile. Did Augustus wake at her side and need to capture what he saw, hair a dark crown on the pillow, arms akimbo? Or did he have her step naughty steps up the stairwell after they made love one early morning, that sweet smirk fueled by physical love?

She appears alone in every plate, but the eye of the camera is the eye of Robin. He adored her and could offer what others could not: a visible record of his love, of what he loved—cakes, the curve of a knee becoming a thigh, the edge of her eye when she squinted.

The Yellow Jack Plates, 1853:
Plate 184—*The Howard Association.*
Plate 185—*Trees Being Felled Near Lake Pontchartrain to Combat the Yellow Fever.*
Plate 186—*Jason Meyers, A Stone Cutter.*
Half-plate daguerreotypes.

Victor Benoit was a member of the Howard Association, a group of doctors and other citizens that cared for the sick during the yearly yellow fever outbreaks. Pl. 184 shows the thirty members of the Association gathered in June 1853 to discuss the epidemic. The City Council granted the Howards absurdly small amounts of money to be used to help the city's poor, while at the same time the newspapers ridiculed them as doomsayers and panics. Both the Council and the papers wanted to keep the outbreak as hushed as possible. As late as July 15th the *Daily Tropic* was denying the existence of yellow fever in New Orleans. It is easy to understand why—a deserted city holds neither advertisers nor consumers.

In the summer of 1853 Benoit and the Howard Association enlisted Robin to chronicle in daguerreotypes what would be the worst epidemic ever to strike the Crescent City. The city's population at the time was 154,123 and that summer the fever carried away over seven thousand victims, almost one in every twenty inhabitants. These numbers, horrible to begin with, are worse when it's taken into account that as many of the 154,123 as could afford it fled the city for the summer. They left to escape not only the fever, but the oppressive heat and the annoying clouds of mosquitoes, yet to be recognized as the means of fever transmission.

The Doctor published a small volume of observations entitled *Yellow Jack* intended to accompany a group of Robin's plates which were displayed at his studio late in December 1853. Few of these photographs remain. Many may have been in Victor Benoit's possession—he was the executor of Robin's will—and were possibly destroyed in the fire that ravaged the Benoit home in 1901. The plates which remain, combined with the Doctor's tortured accounts, present a passionate example of what may have been the first photojournalism.

Pl. 185 is one of the few surviving examples of Robin's landscape work, and the story that accompanies it is fascinating. In the heat of mid-July, then-mayor Orion Wagasuc took to heart the advice of an English surgeon, John Matthews, who hypothesized that the fever which attacked the city each summer had its root in "some type of insect or organism or flora that inhabits the trees and foliage near the city." He was close. The fever was being transmitted by mosquitoes, but they were just as prevalent, if not more, in the open sewers of New Orleans than among the trees that stood between the city and Lake Pontchartrain. Ignorant of this, the mayor hired work crews and sent them on a mission: Cut down each and every tree.

Robin recorded the supposed salvation of the city's populace by the mayor's quick action. As this plate shows, the daguerreotype process was far from the stop-action now possible with a brief shutter opening and fast film. The trees fall in arcs across the horizon, thirteen falling at once, the entirety of their descents recorded.

The yellow fever went undaunted even after this massive effort, and Wagasuc was not reelected though he ran on a platform that attempted to stress the fact that his family too had fallen victim to the pestilence—his daughter, three-year-old Dorcas, died in October of 1853. (The *Picayune* obituary mentions that Robin photographed her memorial portrait.)

A total of seventeen plates of these blurred trees appeared in the *Yellow Jack* exhibit, more single-subject images than any other Robin showed. After the exhibit failed to rally the city to fight the causes of yellow fever—open sewers, badly maintained streets, et cetera—many of the plates were sold, among them this daguerreotype. Pl. 185 was purchased by mayoral candidate Riley Wilson

Richmond for use in his victorious campaign and has been pre-served as a family heirloom. Our thanks to the Richmonds for its use.

Pl. 186 is the last daguerreotype discussed in *Yellow Jack*. The subject's head is obscured by a cloud of marble chips as he cuts a name into one of 1853's many grave markers. Benoit writes: "Mister Meyers tried to laugh when he judged that the Fever was the best thing for the Undertaker, the Priest and the Stone Cutter, but his mirth gave way to tears. His son Stephan and his wife Roberta both died earlier in the summer, victims of Yellow Jack, and Mister Meyers cut their names into stones."

Plates 187–195—*Progress of Vivian Robin's Pregnancy*, 1852–1853.
Half-plate daguerreotypes.
Plate 196—*Memorial Portrait of Vivian Robin*, 1853.
Whole-plate daguerreotype.

Plates 187–195 continue Augustus' loving record of his wife's short life. Each is simple and similar—the entire frame filled with Vivian's bare stomach, a hand-lettered card recording the date held just below the belly button, the backdrop unpatterned and dark to provide striking definition to her light midriff, which after Pl. 191 enlarges visibly plate by plate.

During the taking of these images Robin was also involved in recording the yellow fever epidemic. Victor Benoit's descriptions of the surviving *Yellow Jack* plates are accurate; one assumes that his talk of fetid shanties in the swamps north of the city, hovels along the riverfront, and the crowded wards of Charity Hospital is also true. The many plates of Robin's wife, these nine especially, surely had their inspiration in the time Robin spent away from her. It must have been heartening for Augustus to return to vital life after a day photographing death, crushing for him to lose Vivian.

In a summer when so many New Orleanians died that news-papers all over the nation began calling the city the Necropolis of the South, it is almost alarming to find that Vivian did not die of yellow fever. Instead she met an end almost as expected as the summer's annual outbreak: childbirth. Victor Benoit was unable to save her. Vivian's obituary notice and the engraving on her tomb are the same: "A Loving Mother Who Sacrificed Herself for Her Child." Her son, Louis Jacques Mandé Robin, lived until he fell victim to yellow fever late in the summer of 1860. Augustus survived him for three years.

This portrait is out of character for Robin. The lighting is bad, the angle odd. Unlike the careful posings in which the dead look as if they are napping peacefully, Vivian's face still retains the pain of her passing.

Plate 197—*Vivian Robin (?) and a Servant Girl,* 1853.
Quarter-plate daguerreotype.

Pl. 197 was found in the Robin sea chest among the many photographs of Vivian Robin, and the servant is the same female who appears brushing her hair in Pl. 31. The figure to the left must be Vivian. Her face has been scratched from the plate, but the tiny black loop of ribbon she wore in memory of her parents is visible between the scars a knife has inflicted on the daguerreotype's silver plating. Clearly the vandalism is deliberate. To alter the plate someone would have had to remove it from its case, cut the tape joining cover sheet to daguerreotype, scratch away the image, then re-tape and replace the damaged plate.

The plate is in a black thermoplastic mourning case of a type not used by Augustus Robin, the only cased daguerreotype found in the chest that is not in a case from the Robin studio. While this might put into question whether this is an example of Augustus' work, the artistry of the daguerreotype dismisses all doubt. Even with the brutal erasure, the plate's remaining images are near-perfect. Both Vivian and the girl hold black kittens, the little cats' silhouettes against the women's light laps.

The case itself provides more mystery: Placing a portrait of two living subjects into a memorial case is very odd. Also queer is the engraving on the silver funerary mat: "Dearest Sydney, You are Remembered." Perhaps Vivian gave the girl this portrait as a gift, and when the young woman died her relations were too poor to afford a memorial portrait. Their only option may have been to alter the plate and place it in a secondhand case.

––––––––––

Josh Russell was born on Thanksgiving Day, 1968. His fiction has appeared in *Denver Quarterly, Epoch,* and the *Southwest Review.* He lives in Nashville with his wife, Kathryn Pratt.

"Yellow Jack" began when I saw a portrait of a disembodied hand steadying an infant's head for a daguerreotype's long exposure. That baby and that hand provided the subject matter for a story in the covertly emotional language of art books. The story took off when I realized that the heyday of daguerreotype-process photography coincided with the worst of the yellow fever epidemics in New Orleans. History hides its lies behind dates and names. "Yellow Jack" is history: some facts about yellow fever and daguerreotypes and New Orleans in the middle 1800s, some lies.

RITA'S MYSTERY

(from *The Oxford American*)

Mayes rose to speak at the A.A. meeting, his first time giving testimony. He said, My name is Mayes Mello and I'm an alcoholic. People applauded. Mayes thought, Well, *maybe* I'm an alcoholic, but it was too late to take it back. He didn't want to disappoint. He had become very impressed with the people who attended the meetings. They were all wondrous. He had something he wanted to tell them, about the power they knew and relied on, and how it was manifested to him.

My wife is Jesus, he said. He chuckled. Just kidding. What I mean is that Rita is like Jesus. She has a quality. She's extraordinary. Yet, my Rita says that no matter what, you cannot plan your life. Did Jesus ever say a thing like that? I don't think so. Jesus understood something other. I don't know that Rita means it; she might be only trying to fit in with all of us unenlightened ones. I mean, even I know that to at least some extent you can plan your life. For instance, if you eat a cake a week, you get fat, so you can plan to get fat that way or you can plan not to. I plan not to, for instance. Or, if I want to know how a metal alloy behaves at sixty below, I drop the temp on that sucker and watch it crack. I'm a cryophysicist, and I'm sitting okay, having gone from high-school science-teaching, through the higher academia—specimen that I was—to practical research of the behavior of mass in the too-cold climates of space. I planned the whole trip. Rita, I should think, ought to respect that.

Jesus said that what you do now determines how you will be later. That's what he meant: to know the future, study today, what goes around comes around, you reap what you sow. I believe that. Anybody just glancing ought to see that it's pure common sense. But Rita, my wife, is like Jesus in that she does everything right instinctively. She is like the Buddhas and bodhisattvas I've read about. She's got a really good heart, is what I mean, and she loves everybody. Even the guy that kidnapped her. That's what I'm trying to get the police to understand. Rita is originally sinless.

She asks what past event, what past present, led to her being abducted, assaulted, and then arrested for public drunkenness—for drunk driving—and caused her picture in the paper, her arrest on television? She was on her way to work, damn it.

She doesn't think anyone believes her. She doesn't blame anyone, really; she understands how it looks. She was drunk, and driving. But she expects people to be charitable, to believe the truth.

I can tell she even suspects me of doubting her because sometimes she cries and she won't let me comfort her. She quotes to me my belief in cause and effect—if she's in trouble, then she caused it—assumes my complete faith in that logic. I admit, I don't understand.

The police, of course, and the D.A. certainly think she's lying. Her lawyer, maybe he believes and maybe he doesn't. He keeps asking her to tell the story again. Did anybody see her in the car with the guy? Did she phone anyone at work before leaving home that morning? Is there anyone—a neighbor, me, the paperboy—who can say that she even intended to go to work, that she's telling the truth? I tell them, yes, she's telling the truth, she intended to go to work.

Still, she's a drinker. All our friends know that. But she's not a drunk. She doesn't get drunk in the morning and miss work. She couldn't keep a job that way, not a teaching job anyway. She's called in a few times and gotten substitutes, but for the flu, like anybody else.

Now the principal is hinting that her calls have had a pattern. Monday morning calls. He's said that maybe now that she's gotten this attention she can get the help she needs.

The head of our library branch, where Rita tells stories to the preschoolers on Saturday mornings, has suggested that she discontinue her visits until this is all straightened out. So she's putting up with this suspicion and betrayal, and she loves and forgives the principal, the librarian, and especially the guy that's done this to her.

If we could just find him, everything would be better.

But Rita only half wants to find him. Certainly, she doesn't like being thought a liar, and it's embarrassing—indeed stunning—being perceived as someone you absolutely are not. But she knows the man is in pain and she would not want to cause him any more. The police aren't even looking for him. When they question her, she tells the same story every time, a little different here and there as she remembers things, forgets things, finds something or other more or less important.

She was just two blocks from home, at the traffic light, and she saw the man approaching in the side mirror. But she didn't think to do anything. Her door was unlocked. Bums are always on the corners, and the only thing different was that he was in her mirror this time, coming up beside the car. That was strange, and when she thought to run the light or lock the door it was too late. He was pushing her over onto the passenger seat. His odor paralyzed her, shocked her, made her cringe. He smelled like excrement. Like excrement and b.o. and rotten teeth. And *he* must have run the light because she realized they were speeding, the world outside the car blurring by.

He wore an unbuttoned blue shirt with green stripes tucked into beltless pants, and the dark skin of his chest was ashy-gray. It was cold that morning and the heater had not yet fully melted the frost on the windows. She had on her coat and gloves, and a knit hat and scarf. His pants were filthy, the color of tobacco, with black stains like grease and white stains like snot. His shoes, badly scuffed wing tips, had no laces, and he didn't have socks on his gray, cracked ankles. He reached inside his shirt and pulled out a gun. It had a short barrel. That's when he looked at her sidelong with huge watery eyes.

"I'll kill you," he said.

"No," she said.

He cursed her viciously, vulgarly.

His stink was so strong it was in her ears. She vomited.

"Looks like you had breakfast," he said, and snorted a laugh.

"Let me out," she said.

"I'll kill you," he said. "Messing up my day with this mess." He shook the gun at her and then put it back in his shirt.

As always, she had flung her purse and briefcase on the back-seat. She wanted to reach back for a tissue from her purse, but she also didn't want to call attention to herself. She thought about his stealing her money and credit cards, and the hassle of cancel-ing everything.

But she was embarrassed by the vomiting, so she reached back. He grabbed her arm and snatched the bag. The car swerved, nearly hit a truck in the next lane, and he caught the wheel and straight-ened. She tried on the spot to remember that truck but couldn't. Immediately it was gone.

The man took from the purse her fat wallet filled with receipts, cards, photos. Then he turned the bag over and flung it around. Pens, makeup, gum, checkbook, and tissue littered the seat and her lap, landed in the pool at her feet.

She wiped her mouth with a tissue, cleaned the dashboard as best she could. She thought about me, she says, and our daughters. She felt sorry for us, who wouldn't know what had happened to her—who'd learn maybe months later that the skeleton found in the distant woods was his missing wife, their missing mother. Black female, mid-to-late fifties. And imagining that made it all seem unreal to her, as if she were predicting the end of a made-up mystery.

* * *

When Rita tells her library stories, you feel as though you are in them. This is because when she tells them, *she* is in them. You sense that in front of her eyes there is a transparent screen on which her tales live and through which she observes her audience. And the audience, through the service of the same transparent screen, observes the tale and the teller. She stands there wearing her caftan, waving her cow-tail switch, and the myth of the origin of sleep awakens, or the story of the clever spider and the palm gourd begins to creep and speak of itself.

Yet she is holding something back from the police and her attorney, and that is why they don't believe her. I do my best to persuade them, to speak without saying what she doesn't want me to say. We differ about what should be known, although even if I could tell everything, my power to persuade would be less than hers.

It has been a month since the mystery. She yelps in her sleep. Usually I wake her as soon as she starts, but once I was in the basement washing a late-night load of clothes when I heard her. She got so loud I was honestly surprised she didn't wake herself. I shake her, is what I do. She stops with a grunt and a whimper. Always, somebody is chasing her. That son of a bitch. Yet, she seems afraid only when sleeping. When awake, she's angry, disappointed, but laughing and forgiving.

I used to say, Rita never meets a stranger. She's become good friends over the phone with the wife of the man who delivered our living-room tables last year when we were redecorating. I don't know how it happened. She'd never seen this woman in person, just some photographs the deliveryman showed her. She served the guy ham sandwiches and tea for lunch and looked at his snapshots, and somehow she's talking to his wife about who knows what. Troubles, it turns out. Their teenage daughter was pregnant. Later, we sent the baby some toys. We gave them some money when the guy had to have a leg artery sewn to his heart, to replace one that was damaged.

She has invited people over at the least provocation. She meets someone from Ontario, for example, where we used to live, gives them our address and tells them to come by anytime, as if we all have so much in common. If she meets someone who is going to Ontario, she gives them our old neighbors' addresses. So far none of these strangers has actually shown up at our door, and I don't know who has visited our old neighbors at my wife's insistence. I tell her it's dangerous to be so open, so giving, so trusting. She thinks I'm saying you're not supposed to like people so much. Maybe I am. She could be inviting over a killer, a robber, a vampire. I should hope that during her kidnapping she did not invite the kidnapper to our home, this man she dreams about.

She told me that after she got sick, when they were out of the traffic, on the outskirts of town, she felt hot and realized that the heater was on full blast. She switched it off and yanked loose her scarf, pulled off her gloves, unbuttoned her coat. She tried to breathe deep but his smells stopped her. She wanted to lower a window, but she looked at the man and realized he would be cold. His knuckles were scabbed, his fingers long and creased. The stubble on his face seemed as stiff and black as brush bristles, some of them ingrown; white, pus-filled bumps dotted his cheek and chin. He was skinny but muscled, like a scavenger animal, a hyena. Hair grew thick down his neck.

He steered the car onto a ramp to the interstate, heading west. As the ramp rose and they sped along the bridge across the river, she gazed out over the top of the town—churches, schools, houses, office buildings. She thought, this is what it's like to die, leaving everything familiar, accelerating, unable to stop.

He didn't kill her, obviously. He drove way out of town, got on some narrow backroad that split fields of dried cornstalks. She tried to talk to him and he cursed her. Cursed her for hours. Around ten, he made her buy bourbon at a rural package store and forced her to drink it with him as they drove empty two-lanes. They drank in a parking lot of an abandoned gas station along some piney country road. The concrete lot was crumbling, tough old winter weeds grizzled in the cracks. She tried not to swallow the liquor, but he held the gun to her throat and ordered her. She swallowed what she dared and then he drank some. They took turns like that. It was a half-gallon bottle. He raised the tilt wheel out of the way, leaned their seats back some.

As I said, Rita knows how to drink. First of all, she made it look like she was swallowing a lot, but she wasn't, and second, alcohol doesn't go straight to her head. She can hold it pretty well. She had a lot by now, though, and it was creeping up on her. She could sense the man was feeling better. It was clear that he relied on alcohol to ease his pain. She was worried he'd get the idea to rape her.

She began to imagine that when he drank, he left some of his pain in the bottle; and that when she drank, she first swallowed his pain away and then breathed in her well-being. That was the exchange—his pain for her health. And he became jollier. He said they were going to drive to Las Vegas, spend her money, and when the money ran out they would use her shining credit. He said she could buy him a house on a lake, in Africa, on Lake Victoria, and what kind of name for an African lake was that?

"What's your name?" she asked.

He let out a breath, let his chin slump to his chest, the bottle between his legs. He told her to get out of the car, and as she did he got out too, came around to her. The wind was whipping—ballooning and flapping his open shirt and molding his pants to his pipe-thin legs.

Straight on, he had a wide face, winglike cheekbones, eyebrows that met in a V in the middle, and beautifully shaped, cold-white lips. He hit her. She ducked and his fist grazed and split her eyebrow. She fell back against the car and he rushed her, groping for her breasts through her coat. She felt nothing much, random and unpleasant pressure, as if drugged and submitting to a foul-smelling search. Then, as if he could not be satisfied, could not make himself felt, he gave up, let his arms go limp as he leaned on her, and breathed into her knit hat.

He rolled off and pushed back, arms pinwheeling like a stumbling cow town drunk. He ran tiptoed away from her but stopped at the corner of the building. He turned and, in an afterthought, pulled his gun and pointed at her with the length of his arms. For seconds he steadied it. Then he backed away and disappeared.

But while he had stood there sighting her, she had seen a radiance about him, a gleaming silver-gold sheen issuing from him like the spiny fins of a phosphorescent fish.

After he was gone, the whole scene was radiant—the tall, dry, pale grass in the ditch across the road, the black, bending pine trees with their silver-needle quills, the disintegrating parking lot, the glowing rust of the gas pumps, the white concrete-block building. She took her glasses from her coat pocket and put them on, to verify what she was seeing. The car was the most beautiful she had seen it, the paint like a clear, green glaze over chrome.

Light was in everything during her drive away from there, during her woozy, disoriented search for a phone booth. She doesn't know how far she drove before she slammed into a tinseled, shimmering tree that seemed to swoon out of the middle of the road. The road itself had seemed as bright and straight as a sheet of glass.

The police believe her bleeding head resulted from the wreck. She wasn't wearing a seat belt.

There is little evidence of the man. There were fingerprints other than hers found on the half-empty bottle but Rita can't remember where they bought it, and the police say the prints could belong to the salesman. They don't match any known criminal's. No distinct suspicious prints anywhere else, not even on the purse, not that the police looked very hard. Nor can she remember where the old gas station is, despite our drives around to look for it.

So, right now, it doesn't look good for Rita legally. She failed big-time on the Breathalyzer test. She won't tell the police about the vision—refusing to be ridiculed for something as powerful as that and sad that it would be received with the knowledge that she was drunk. She was plastered, blitzed, looped. If she had planned it, she says, there would be no suspicion attached. If she had planned it, she would be in control. Nothing, she says, can account for what she's gone through.

But I tell them, for her faith in me and for my faith in her, that she was not injured in the car wreck. That bruise is no steering-wheel mark over her eye. In fact, she remembers something the police could verify. When the state trooper found her she was sitting upright behind the wheel, the front end accordioned, the motor running, and the heater on low. Her eyeglasses were on the floor between her feet, neatly folded, reflecting blue-white light back at her, as if placed there for her, for when she was ready for the whole truth to be revealed, again.

John Holman is a native of North Carolina. He lives in Atlanta, where he teaches in the Creative Writing Program at Georgia State University. He is the author of *Squabble and Other Stories*. *Luminous Mysteries,* a new book of fiction, is forthcoming. His writing has appeared in several magazines and anthologies.

As with a lot of people, the reality of homelessness and death startle me. Happily, notions of faith startle me almost as much. I must have been pretty alarmed when I wrote this. I have a friend who was kidnapped in a way similar to what I have described in the story; however, other than that her account could be and was doubted, I imagined the details of the characters and the adventure.

Mark Richard

MEMORIAL DAY

(from *The Oxford American*)

The boy mistook death for one of the landlady's sons come to collect the rent. Death stood leaning against a tree scraping fresh manure off his shoe with a stick. The boy told death he would have to see his mother about the rent, and death said he was not there to collect the rent.

My brother is real sick, you should come back later, the boy said. Death said he would wait.

They had sent the boy's brother home from the war in a box. When the boy and his mother opened the box, the brother was not inside. Inside the box was a lifesize statue of a woman holding a seashell to her ear. A messenger's pouch hung around the statue's neck. Hide this for me, the note in the pouch read. Love, Brother.

Then came the brother a week later. He was thin and yellow and sorry-looking, too weak to fend off his mother when she struck him, too weak to be held. The mother and the child carried him into the house and put him to bed.

The next morning, a black healer woman walked down the white shell driveway and straight into the house to squeeze the older brother's guts and smell his breath. She looked over her shoulder at the high weeds and the statue box and the bitter, brown gulf beyond and she said This place flood flood flood. Stink, too.

The mother bathed the brother with an alcohol sponge and the black healer woman twisted his spine to break his fever. The brother saw monkeys in the corners of the ceiling that wanted to get him, their mouths full of bloody chattering teeth. The black healer woman and the mother fought with the brother and told the child to Get out! when he came in to tell them that someone was waiting in the yard.

It was not unusual that the child could see death when the mother and the healing woman could not. Once at a church picnic the child had seen Bad Bob Cohen walk through the softball game and past the barbeque tables with a .22 rifle slung barrel down over his shoulder on a piece of twine. The child had watched Bad Bob walk right past where mothers and small children were splashing on the riverbank, had watched Bad Bob reach up and select two sturdy vines to climb up, and Bad Bob had turned and looked at the child, feeling him seeing him, and Bad Bob had nodded because they both knew that Bad Bob was invisible, and then later when the deputy and the road agents came to the picnic looking for Bob no one had seen him and no one would have believed the child if he had said he had, so he said nothing. Also, one Easter, the child had seen an angel.

Tell them they have to wait, the mother said. The rent's not due until tomorrow.

You have to wait, the child told death sitting in a tree. Death ate a fortune cookie from his pocket. His lips moved while he read the fortune to himself.

I'll come back tomorrow, death said finally, jumping down from the tree.

The black healer woman stood on the porch and said she would keep death from the doorstep as long as they had faith in Christ Jesus Our Savior and a little put-away money to cover her expenses coming down the long white broken shell driveway to their house. Death, that day, was wearing white pants and a white dinner jacket, a small, furled yellow cocktail umbrella buttonholed in his lapel. There were three good scratches across death's cheek from the beautiful woman who had not wanted to dance the last dance with death aboard a ship somewhere the previous evening. I don't get much time off from this job, death confided in the child under the tree. Work work work. I am much misunderstood. I actually have a wonderful sense of humor and I get along well with others. I'm a people person, death told the child. Death climbed the front porch steps to make faces behind the black healing woman. Death folded his eyelids back, stuck out his tongue, then pinched his cheeks, forgetting about the scratches. Ow! death said. The black healer woman did not hear death nor see death but to her credit, she shivered when death blew on the back of her neck.

The child followed the black healer woman and his mother into the back bedroom where his brother stank. The black healer woman burned some sage cones and rubbed charcoal on the brother's temples and on the soles of his feet to draw out the fever.

How come you don't work? the black woman said to the child.

He's just a child, the mother said. The mother was stripping the brother's bed around them to boil the sheets on the stove.

When I young, I work, said the black healing woman.

I can make baskets from reeds, the child said.

What do people need reed baskets for when they give wooden ones away for free at the tomato fields, said the woman.

When the brother sat up and shouted Get the monkeys! the black healing woman said to him Your little brother here going to get them monkeys, your little brother going to get them monkeys and put them under baskets, under *wooden* baskets, she said to the child. Won't no *reed* basket hold no monkey, she said, and the brother lay back down.

Here's the rent money, the mother said. I don't want anybody to come in the house while we get your brother's fever down. The child said Yes ma'am. He took out the messenger pouch his brother had sent home in the box with the statue. It was not a purse. It had two long pockets and a waterproof pouch in case you had to swim a river. The child put the rent money in the waterproof pouch because it had two good snaps on it.

When the landlady's son came to collect the rent, death told the child to ask for a receipt.

I want a receipt, the child told the landlady's son.

You want to be evicted? the landlady's son said. You want us to throw your sorry asses out on the highway?

Don't worry, death said, he's afraid he might catch what your brother has. He won't go in the house. Tell him you want a proper receipt, tell him to bring a proper receipt for the rent.

Before the child could say all that, the landlady's son said Give me the money I bet you got in that purse!

It's not a purse! the child said and yanked back on the strap.

All right, I'll be back tomorrow, said the landlady's son.

Death sat on the edge of the porch and lip-read a new fortune cookie. It looked like a word near the end hung him up.

That's a good one, death finally said, and he crunched the cookie in his big white teeth.

The brother's tongue grew fuzzy and his ravings were barking up the bad neighbor's dogs down the road all night.

The black healer woman came out on the porch.

You get me a shoebox of scorpions, what I need, she told the child. Try get me white ones. They stronger than the piddly brown ones. Go on and get me them.

They had scorpions in the woodpile, scorpions in the sandbox, scorpions in the clothespin pouch, scorpions in the cinderblocks where they burned trash, scorpions under the bathroom sink, scorpions in the icebox water tray, and scorpions in the baby crib. They didn't have a baby anymore, so it was all right.

I wouldn't fool with scorpions, death said. Some people are highly allergic. It's a neurotoxin thing in the stinger, death said. Death followed the child around trying to find a shoebox. The child could not find a shoebox. He had an old wooden-style cigar box. The lid was broken.

I wouldn't use that cigar box, it's got no lid, death said. The child said he could see that.

The child took the rent money out of his waterproof pouch and put it in his pocket. He cut a good stick and found three brown scorpions and one white scorpion by lunchtime. He put the scorpions in the messenger pouch and snapped it shut carefully so as not to crush them, and shook the bag down every time before he opened it so he would not get stung. He had never been stung before and had heard it was ten times worse than a wasp, maybe fifty times.

It looks to me like your brother's got a neural infection that may be at the stem of his brain, death said. Of course, that's just a layman's guess.

The child was beginning to tire of death hanging around so much and talking talking talking. Death never seemed to shut up. Down where the bitter brown gulf water foamed dirty, death talked about time zones and the speed of light. Under the big yard tree, he talked about pine cones that broke open their seeds only when they burned. Under the brother's window looking in on the mother and the black healer woman, death said the brown statue of the girl holding the seashell to her ear was pedestrian terra-cotta.

I bet it's valuable, the child said, and death said Yeah, maybe as a boat anchor.

The mother took back the rent money to fetch a real doctor. The landlady's son came by with a friend who smelled like vomit and the friend who smelled like vomit threw a dirt clod that hit the child in the mouth. The landlady's son kicked open the front gate. The child had forgotten he had taken the rent money out of the messenger pouch so he held on to its strap until the landlady's son broke it and said Here's your receipt, and he rabbit-punched the child twice in the ear. The landlady's son and the friend who smelled like vomit roared off in their car with the messenger pouch, taking with them, inside the pouch, the little yellow furled fruit cocktail umbrella, twelve white scorpions, and thirty, maybe even fifty, brown scorpions in the waterproof pocket. Death laughed in the treetops.

Death flocked down beside the child. He said maybe the scorpion cure would have worked and maybe it would have killed the brother outright. It would have depended on if the black healer woman could figure a good way to extract the neurotoxin and put the brother into moderate shock to break the fever. I guess it could work, maybe in a laboratory, death said, and the child, holding his ringing ear, said You just want an easy way to take my brother from me, and death said the child had completely misunderstood him. That was all right, because he was much misunderstood, death began again, and maligned, and the child left death in the front yard making speeches, and to the child's one good ear, it all sounded like wind in the stovepipe.

The doctor hardly thought it worth breaking a car axle to drive down and look at the brother, so he took the rent money for his trouble walking and said to bathe the brother in alcohol and put these sulphate powders in honey tea. The doctor gave the brother a shot and on his way out said the child needed some fish oil but did not give him any.

You find them scorpions for me? the black healer woman whispered after the doctor had gone.

I had a bunch that got away from me, the child told her. She said to get her a new bunch unless he wanted his brother to die. Tonight, she said. The black healing woman had no faith in the shot or the sulphate or the doctor. She said she had seen him swing little newborns by their heels against tree trunks back where the real white trash lived. Go get them scorpions and get them quick, she said.

Death sat on the levee pipe and watched the child weave a reed basket. Death said baskets done well like that could fetch maybe two, three dollars from tourists. Of course, the child would have to learn to weave the popular check-cross design, and not just the standard lanyard double-tuck.

This is for scorpions, the child said. The child said he noticed death had not come around the house when the doctor came, and death laughed and said he liked doctors, that you could make a career following doctors. No, death said he had just had an appointment that had taken a little longer than he had planned for, and he offered the child a fortune cookie.

No thanks, said the child, weaving his basket.

Death read his fortune. Sometimes these things are incomprehensible, he said, and he let the little white paper float away.

That night the brother broke the mother's jaw. Punched her right in her damn monkey teeth, red and chattering at him.

No one knows their time. The brother recuperated and returned to the war, and afterwards, operated a small, profitable import business until his death at age fifty-eight from smoke inhalation. He had been trying to retrieve an old three-legged dog from a warehouse fire.

The man who smelled like vomit died of emphysema at age seventy-two living on the benevolence of the state. The state ridded itself of Bad Bob Cohen at age forty-one with a lethal injection.

It is believed among the black healing woman's family, and among those to whom she administered, that she was commended by God, that God spared her from death entirely, that He lifted her directly into heaven, for one day she simply disappeared.

The mother died seven years after the older brother recuperated. Her jaw did not heal well and her weight dropped to slightly below normal for her height, diet, and hereditary dispensation. The mother's passing away at age forty-eight was generally ascribed to grief, from finding her youngest remaining son at the edge of the hot brown gulf. According to the deputy and to the coroner who drove the station wagon to fetch the body, it appeared that the bottom of the reed basket the child had been carrying had flung itself open somehow, as if whoever had made the basket had folded the reeds backwards, upside down into the spiraling center instead of outward to the edges, and the action and weight of several hundred scorpions inside the basket had broken through the bottom. The child had been stung too many times to count. The neurotoxin, to which the child was highly allergic, had caused his windpipe to close, and when they found him at the edge of the gulf, he had already turned blue, his protruding tongue black and flyspecked. It was as if the child had run down to the gulf while being stung to drink the bitter water and could not drink, could not force down what he thought he felt he could not swallow, and only death had seen him try, death saying to him Run to the water and drink, come on, run with me to the gulf and drink, and the child had taken death's outstretched hand because he was beginning to stumble, and death encouraged him Run with me! and the child ran with death and finally he was no more, for death had taken him.

As for the landlady's son, he is one of many who have long since been forgotten.

––––––––––

Mark Richard grew up in Virginia and Texas. His short stories have appeared in *Esquire, The New Yorker, Harper's, The Paris Review, The Oxford American, The Quarterly, Grand Street, Antaeus, Shenandoah,* and *Equator*. His first collection of short stories, *The Ice at the Bottom of the World*, received the PEN/Ernest Hemingway Award. His novel, *Fishboy*, is "still selling steadily to a growing cult following," according to his publisher. His new collection of stories, *Charity*, was published this year.

*O*n my way to an uncle's funeral the summer before last, I was stranded in the Houston bus station. I waited all afternoon for a bus that would take me across the Sabine River and on into Louisiana.

In the hours I spent in the bus terminal, I saw many things. I saw Mexicans in freshly-mudded, river-waded clothes. I watched a long and sad unloading of poor cripples returning from a miracle cure clinic south of the border. I saw some crackheads try to hustle a mixed-race couple clutching their baby daughter. I watched a hand-holding middle-aged Down's syndrome couple giggle and point at the selections in a nearly empty vending machine.

I watched an ex-con just released from the Texas Department of Corrections in his pressed denim and his unlaced black institutional shoes open his crisp manila envelope and fill out his state-issued travel voucher. And I saw Death. I saw Death come into the bus station and buy himself a ticket. I sat there and wondered where Death was off to. Later on, I wrote this story.

Sara Powers

THE BAKER'S WIFE

(from *Zoetrope*)

Most Friday evenings since they were married they spent on their porch that listed steeply toward the street. They sat in loose-limbed wooden chairs that seemed as if they might at any moment slide off down the steps, drinking cold bottles of beer and letting the fragrant Texas evening rise up around them until it was night. And on one night, this night that concerns us, they told lies, wove them into the net of conversation like tails of seaweed threading themselves through a fisherman's seine.

"Three lies," Louis said—and she thought, God what a face he has: lean and freckled, red sideburns shaved to a point under his cheekbones—"about anything. Just drop them in the conversation."

"That sounds dangerous," she said, half meaning it.

"Tomorrow we'll tell each other what they were." He wore silver rings on his fingers. His hands, long and elegant, were the hands of a musician, the hands of a snake charmer.

The conversation looped and strode; they gave each other presents of the stories that held their past selves like miniature scenery trapped in glass: she told him of her flirtation with exhibitionism, her dance before the window with the blinds half lowered, yellow light blazing out from behind her silhouetted hips, and a silent audience smirking around curtains across the courtyard. He was intrigued and excited by this, but skeptical. Not a very good liar, he thought. And he told her about a little dog he had thrown off a neighbor's third-story balcony when he was six; she was horrified. "They said they'd beat me up if I didn't," he said. "So I picked it up and threw it over the railing." "Poor Louis," she said. "Still, I think I would have been beaten up."

"Not me," said Louis. "I heaved the thing right over."

They had met a year and a half before, at Christmastime; they fell in love. She was a photographer; too pretty for her own liking, she bleached her hair white blonde and wore boys' clothes that hung loosely over her thin frame. He was a pastry chef and a fiddle player; shabbily elegant, he wore a tiny row of sapphire studs in one ear. One night, several days after they had met, they sat in a tapas bar on a dark street of warehouses, drinking wine and ordering the small plates of food from a doleful bartender. They speculated about him.

"Brokenhearted," Louis said. They had a bowl of olives and a plate of sausages and manchego cheese.

The bartender was cherubic, with downturned eyes. "An older woman just left him," she said.

"Look at the way he wipes the bar, so sadly," Louis said. "I feel bad disturbing him."

But they were infatuated, and feeding each other olives, tasting the olives on each other's kisses; each kiss was a small revolution starting in their mouths. Sophie was absentmindedly running her hand up and down his thigh; she took it off to gesture at something.

Louis looked stricken. "Whatever else you do," he said, "don't stop that."

She moved her hand back; his thigh was so thin and hard under her fingers that he seemed almost breakable. She wanted to cradle him. But as he tipped back the squat bottle of Spanish beer and drank, she knew there was something fierce in him too.

"What are you thinking?"

She smiled, still kneading his leg with the heel of her palm. "I don't know if I should say it," she said. "I'm afraid to say."

Looking at her he said, "There is nothing you can't say to me. I want to hear everything." Sophie was looking at him and knew that it was true. Dorothy brought oil to the tin man and he felt that same moment of awful bliss. Louis was asking everything of her and yet only that she be entirely herself. All she could say was "All right." Then she married him.

At the Canadian border, he told her, he and the rest of his band squatted naked in a jail cell for eight hours, bare feet flat against the cold floor, while the Mounties searched the bus for drugs. She said she had her first orgasm with an electric toothbrush. He said they would have beautiful children. She told him about a famous female sculptor who had tried to kiss her, whose breath smelled of celery and garlic, whose unhappiness was like a household pet. They walked down the hill to the corner for more beer. He told her about climbing a stony mountain in Mexico with a blonde and humorless girlfriend, hiking for hours under the hot sun, and how she walked farther and farther away, refusing to talk to him, until at the top she told him she didn't want to see him anymore. Sophie told him he was her muse.

"Sophie," he said. He loved her name, the softness of it like the velvety night.

For a long time, it was like this: taxi drivers asked them if they were on their honeymoon; waitresses turned away from them with sweet tears blossoming in the corners of their eyes; the rain fell around them in sheets, shielding their kisses. Even cats followed them home.

People said, "Let's have a drink," meaning: we want to be close to you because you are radiant and drunk on each other.

They drank that evening and the stories looped outward toward the absurd, the lies were flung recklessly and dangled like shimmering strands of audiotape from the tree branches. They laughed, lost hold of lies in midtelling, caught each other and confessed.

"My uncle," she said, "was a playboy, lost it all in the crash of 'twenty-nine, and drove a bus in Newark for the rest of his life."

"My grandfather," he said, "was a confidence man."

"And you're not?" she asked, smiling at him. "How do I know you don't have three other wives in three other towns?"

"They're getting mad," he said. "I haven't seen any of them in a while."

"Send a card," she suggested. "No need to be rude."

"Maybe I will." He grinned.

She turned toward him and rested her bare foot on his thigh, kneading it with her toes. "I encountered a ghost once."

"Liar," he said.

"Nope. Listen," she said. "It was in Saratoga in this big old country house where I was staying. Things had happened there; I forget what: children drowned, tragedies . . ."

"What did it look like?" he asked.

"I didn't actually see it," she said. "I was too scared. I felt its presence. It picked up my mattress and bent it. Eleven-thirty in the morning. I was napping."

"That's what you get for being so lazy. It was the ghost of sloth coming to get you."

"Whoever it was, it was terrifying."

"So very cosmic," he said.

"Shut up, Louis," she said, going inside to the bathroom.

When she came out she kissed the top of his head, loving the hard shape of his skull beneath his hair.

"So nothing paranormal has ever happened to you?" she asked.

"A weird thing did happen a few weeks ago," he said slowly. "Did I tell you this? Edwina and I had the same dream."

"Exactly the same, or sort of the same?" Pretty Edwina. She felt a brief current of jealousy run through her.

"Actually, it was really eerie. They were almost identical. We were bank robbers—"

"You and Edwina?"

"Yeah. And we got arrested and were out on bail and everybody was crying about it. You were crying. Edwina and I weren't though. We were too far gone. We didn't care."

"I wasn't crying," said Sophie. "In fact, I'm the one who turned you guys in."

"Bitch," said Louis. "I'm going back to the wife in Kansas City." He went into the house and got cold beers from the refrigerator. As he sprung the caps off with the opener, he thought of his wife's face when he'd mentioned Edwina, and wondered if he'd said too much.

When he returned she said, "I punched a drunk in a bar once. Just like this." She demonstrated, a short jab to the mouth. "He wouldn't leave me alone. I told him, 'I'm gonna punch you.' He started on some bull about how he knew karate, and bam! mid-sentence I hit him."

"What'd he do?"

"He put his hand up to his mouth like this, and said, 'Bitch hit me!' Then they threw him out of the bar. I saw him the next week and he bought me a drink."

"Now I know you're lying."

"I swear. Then he started hitting on me again. I thought I was going to have to do it all over again."

Laughter. The moon sat on the treetops like a big yellow hen on her nest. The drunk who lived under their house roared. Soon he would turn his radio up, and the Mexican songs would battle the floorboards, dividing the night with horns.

"Louis," she said. She heard it in the creaking of the floorboards of their crooked little wooden house, in the stretch and moan of the live oak that hovered over the porch. "Louis," the house would say sometimes when she was there alone during the day.

A couple emerged from the shadows of the old tree, wraiths holding hands.

"Pipe down," said the larger half, which turned into their friend Harry. "You two drunks."

The other half was Edwina, little Edwina with her pointed chin and her sundresses, her friendliness and her slight air of calculation, whom Harry had found somewhere in Tennessee and brought back to Austin with him.

"Fast Eddie," said Louis. "Come here."

Edwina let loose of Harry's hand and climbed the stairs, smiling at Louis, and bent and let him kiss her. She turned and kissed Sophie.

"All that laughing was making my bones hurt," she said. "What are you two up to?"

"Lying," said Sophie.

Louis agreed. "A little fibbing."

"So it comes down to that," Harry said. His shadow was immense, draped across the steps and the two in the chairs. "Married and nothing left to say to one another but lies."

"Could be fun," murmured Edwina to Louis. He winked at her.

"Harry," said Sophie. "Come here." He was a big man with broad bony hands and eyes the color of the noonday sky, and he could make music out of any instrument he picked up. She kissed his stubbled cheek.

"Where's the beer?" he asked, cupping one of his big hands over the top of her skull.

"You can have anything you want," she said, at the same time that Louis said, "Settle down, big man," and was on his feet and through the screen door. Edwina followed him in.

Harry glanced briefly at the closing door and sat on the step at her feet.

"So what's new in Sophie's world?" he asked. "How is the graven image business?"

She poked him with her big toe. "Slow. I'm not making enough money yet."

"Give it some time," he said. "You're still new in town. We're still trying to suss out the Yankee."

"I guess so," she said. "But Louis works so hard, and I know he's sick to death of baking, of getting up at the crack of dawn, of picking dough out of his hair at night. The band needs to get some kind of break."

"We all do," said Harry, but they both knew that his situation was different: his grandmother, a leathery West Texas housewife, raised seven kids and spirited spare change into a stock portfolio that she left to her favorite grandson. Harry lived modestly and knew he would never have to work.

Inside the house Edwina studied pictures of Louis and Sophie that were stuck to the refrigerator while he pulled the damp bottles from inside it.

"How old were you in this one?" she asked.

He came around behind her, frowning at the picture. "Oh, twenty-five, I guess."

"Were you wild? Look at you with that crazy hair and those eyes . . ."

He laughed. "Don't bring up my checkered past; you'll get me in trouble with my wife."

"She's jealous of your past?"

"Maybe just worried that I might still have atavistic habits from my former self," he said.

"Where was this taken?"

"I don't know, Eugene, Oregon, or one of those towns . . . on the road somewhere. Back when I had the rock-'n'-roll life full-time."

"You miss it a lot?" she said, turning to face him.

He took a step back and set the beers on the counter to get a better grip on them. "Of course," he said. "I'm so sick of baking. All I want to do is play fiddle."

She was still looking at him with a slender smile, slouched slightly against the refrigerator.

She waited.

He grabbed the bottles up. "Those people are likely to parch to death if we stay in here yakking. Here you go." He handed her a couple of the bottles and loped off through the living room.

Edwina followed, wearing her delicate smile.

Later, as they lay in bed, two heads on one pillow, Louis confessed two but not the third of the lies he had told her.

"So wait," she said. "What was the third one? You told three, right?"

"I don't know," he said. "I mean, I remember that I told three but I can't remember what the last one was."

"What do you mean you don't remember? You have to," she said.

"It's not fair. Otherwise there is going to be this thing about you that I'm going to believe in that's false."

"Well, tell me yours and maybe I'll remember the other one."

"I don't want to tell you mine now," she said. "Anyway, maybe a little mystery is good for a marriage."

"Hold on," he said, laughing now but raising himself up on one elbow in the dark and looking down at her face. Eyes closed, it was a pale oval darkened by a wide slash of mouth, framed against bleached hair, white pillow. "That's not fair. I told you the two lies I remember. You've got to tell me at least two of yours."

"Guess," she said.

"Your first orgasm was not with an electric toothbrush."

"It was," she said. "Eleven years old."

"I don't believe it," he said. "You heard that somewhere." He put his face right down to her cheek. "Remember, the deal was you have to tell the truth now."

"Ha! Don't you get picky about rules, mister." She opened her eyes and grinned, rolling a half turn away from him. "I was a perverse little child."

"Precocious is more like it." He put his arm over her and pulled her around to face him. "I think it's great."

"Water, please," she said, and he handed her the glass from the bedside table. She leaned over him and drank it. His fingers traced the lobe of her breast as she drank. She put the glass back and said, "I can't believe that was a lie about your first love. What was her name . . ?"

"Fatima Nelson," he said, hand over his eyes, laughing, "I can't believe you bought that name."

"That's a terrible thing to lie about," she said, sinking back down. "Your first love—that's a sacred thing. Fatima Nelson, oh my God . . ." They lay side by side giggling. "And she was fat and you were fat . . ?"

The giggling faded and they rolled toward one another, and crooked arms and legs around each other, their breathing slowed and they slept. And they dreamed.

She started awake in the middle of the night; Louis's back was a pale comma curving away from her. He slept with his face in the pillows like a child. It had been a dream that woke her, she realized, about Edwina. Sophie and Louis had been in a dim, narrow bar, and as they stood she had looked back toward the door; through the rectangle of glass she had seen Edwina—the short black braids, the elfin, pointed chin. Edwina had leered at Sophie as their eyes had met through the door, and she had felt evil in the look, as though Edwina was some kind of corrupt spirit assigned to her. Sophie touched Louis's back, for luck or protection—his smooth cool skin her church. As she sank back toward sleep she remembered the rest of the dream: she had risen and flown right at Edwina through the small square window. Although Sophie had been terrified, bluffing as best as she could, she had not turned away, and it was Edwina who did, shrinking to the side with a grimace. Sophie had won. Then she slept again.

At six he woke, pulled back the covers, kissed her stomach, and was gone. Sophie woke up later; the sun was pushing at the back of the blinds and she felt sticky under the comforter. She threw it off her and lay there, absentmindedly running her hand down her body; she felt ripe, she thought, and wondered if her body wanted a baby. Rolling over, she smelled Louis's side of the bed; his scent was there like cloves on the sheet. He had said they would have beautiful children; she pictured them freckled and thin with that large-headed look that skinny children have. She imagined herself loving them and could almost feel it, the ferocity of love that wasn't born yet. Then she remembered the lies, and the one undiscovered lie, the snake hidden somewhere in the tall grass of the night's conversation. She frowned, her legs tangled in the sheets, and forgot about the slim little bodies of her children and thought only about the untruth that lay between her and Louis. What had he lied about? She strained to recall everything they had talked about, but the beers and the hours had stacked up one on the other and trying to grasp any one piece of the conversation was like chasing light. Her secret was that she had only told one lie; the others she had lost control of at the start, her mouth twitching as she tried to lasso a crazy grin, or had considered and discarded knowing she couldn't pull them off. But he didn't need to know that. Not now.

Louis was making *mille-feuilles*. His chef's jacket was buttoned wrong and he had a smudge of flour on his cheekbone, but his hands were nimble and delicate as he rolled dough paper thin. He was trying to recall the third of the lies he had told, was running what he could remember of their conversation over in his head. So easy for him to lie; stories rolled off his tongue as easily as the pastries bloomed lightly under his hands. He didn't want to lie to Sophie; lying belonged to his past, in the sarcophagus of all the past selves he had discarded. But it worried him slightly that he had lied with such nonchalance that he couldn't even remember it; he knew he needed to be vigilant or the habit of lying would creep back up on him.

While Louis worried about deceiving his wife, the dough fluttered from under the rolling pin; thin as leaves, silky as the surface of a still pond, it fluttered and grew across the marble counter.

* * *

She finished developing film, hung the wet and pungent strips from the shower rod, squinting at the images. There was Louis, sitting on the porch steps, hand on fist, head cranked around toward the camera, eyes directly into the lens. Doubt my sincerity, his eyes challenged her. Go ahead. She let go of the film and wandered out onto the porch. The neighbor's yellow Lab limped up the walk and settled its swollen torso against the lower step. Afternoons were quiet on their street; cats lorded over the porches, curtains were drawn, and air conditioners exhaled steadily out of windows. This time of day it seemed that even the angels napped; the steady rhythm of their breathing was the heartbeat of the afternoon. She sat on the steps and let the heat wrap around the back of her neck like a hot fist. The fact was, she knew he had been a liar before she married him. In a worn, old, wooden railroad hotel out in the Hill Country, she lay on his stomach and asked him, "So, what are your faults?"

"My faults," he said. "Well, I used to be quite a fibber. Not any more though. I had to quit it like cigarettes. And, I guess I can be cruel when I'm backed into a corner."

They were quiet a moment, both considering his faults.

"What are yours?"

"Ummm," she said. "I'm mistrustful. I want to be liked too much and it makes me weak. I can be very self-absorbed." She squirmed, uncomfortable with naming her own crimes. What generosity he showed then when he ran his fingers over her ribs, around the flare of her hips, and grabbed her legs just where they swelled into buttock. All the air in her lungs released itself as she pushed her legs into his hands, and talk, of flaws and all else, was forgotten.

Sitting on the porch remembering this, she felt the first tendrils of doubt unfurl in her midsection. Who was to say, after all, that last night was the first night he had lied to her? She thought of his face, open and honest, of the steadiness of his gaze when they talked, and it seemed unlikely that underneath the man she knew there could be another, slicker man who lied; but, she thought, maybe he couldn't help himself. What could he have lied to her about? She searched back over the year for strange moments, moments of doubt or awkwardness that she had let go at the time. There were a few times when he was strangely evasive, when he had the strained voice and aggressive eye contact of a liar. One morning she had startled him on the porch—he had woken earlier and made coffee and collected the mail—reading a letter. When he heard the screen door creak his head snapped up, and as he turned to look at her, his hand creased and folded the letter.

"Hey," she said.

"Morning, doll," he said, and by then he was already lazily seductive, his mouth carving out one of his lapidary smiles. The hand with the letter was low in his lap.

"Who'd we get a letter from?" she asked.

"Just my brother. He wrote me. He's having some girl troubles." He crooked an arm around one of her skinny legs. "I have an idea," he said. "Let's have a breakfast picnic."

He jumped up and was at it full tilt, banging open cupboards and rummaging in the refrigerator, sending her to the corner for fruit while he made crêpes; she put on her shoes and hugged him, but an afterimage of his head jerking up and his hand falling away into his lap burned just below her happiness.

At the time, she had decided that it was nothing. After all, she had thought, he chose me, this beautiful man. Now she wondered.

She stared at a grackle, its feathers an oily green-black, that pecked at the cracks in the walkway. It hopped, cocked its head, and half stretched its wings, and that gesture reminded her of her dream about Edwina. Then, still staring at the bird but no longer seeing it, she remembered Louis's tale about he and Edwina having the same dream. That must be the third lie. What a strange lie, she thought. Why? Then she remembered her own jealousy at hearing the story, and she laughed out loud, scaring the grackle, who danced stiff-legged to a safer distance. Inside the dark house she picked up the phone and dialed the restaurant. It rang and rang

and finally she put the receiver down. She imagined the two of
them laughing about it when he got home, his shirt damp from
the heat, as she poured him a glass of wine, and the relief they
would both feel when there were no secrets between them. She
would tease him about trying to make her jealous, and he would
grab her and slyly slick the wine off her lips with his tongue.

She was giddy with relief, and knew she wouldn't be able to return to the still, stubborn images of her film. She didn't even want
to stay in the house, but outside the afternoon blazed away and
made it nearly impossible to do much else. She walked through
the rooms of the house and settled on doing the dishes. They were
nearly done when the phone rang, and she bounded for it.

"I was thinking," Edwina said, "that on a day like this the only
thing to do is go to Barton Springs. Should I pick you up in a bit?"

"I'll walk over," Sophie said, impetuously.

She headed up the steep short hill their road climbed, passing
crooked little wooden houses bleary with vegetation and bright
splashes of flowers. Porches overflowed with flowerpots, wind
chimes, rocking chairs, porch swings, tricycles, and blinking cats.
Sophie loved the ramshackle and the clutter; it was her home and
it was soothing to walk slowly in the heat up and down the steep
narrow streets. A thread of sweat traced her spine. She walked several more blocks through the neighborhood, and then it began to
change to one of Spanish-style houses with lawns and the occa-
sional small apartment building. She kept walking, cutting across
the elementary-school playing field shaded by the twisted branches
of a live oak, and came out behind a small row of shops. Harry and
Edwina's house was a small, one-story bungalow almost sunk in
vegetation. She leaned her wet brow on the cool wood of the door
—walking anywhere in midday always started out seeming like
such a good idea, and ended with the blood throbbing in her neck
and her body slick with moisture.

She could hear the notes falling as distinct as raindrops from
Harry's mandolin in the cool interior of the house, and then the in-
sectile trilling of the telephone interrupting it, and Harry's heavy

footfall. There was a strange pleasure in being there, just beyond the source of these sounds. Sophie lingered on the porch, in no hurry to puncture her solitude. Maybe it was the echo of the telephone that made her remember, with a surge of mistrust, the morning when she woke to find Louis's side of the bed empty; when she went looking, she saw that he was out on the porch with the telephone. She had stood quietly for a second beside the screen door, but he was talking low and she could only hear the lilt and murmur of his voice, and there was something too soft in it. She turned away because it made her feel uncomfortable to stand there like that, half listening; she knew it wasn't right. Now she held that memory in her hand angrily, like it was the single screw left over after she had reassembled a broken appliance. It made the heat hotter, it broke her spell, and it made her lift her knuckles to the wooden door.

When there was no answer to her knock, she opened the door; the air conditioner was running full blast and Harry was singing softly.

"Sixteen tons and what do you get? Another day older and deeper in debt . . ."

He put down his mandolin when he saw her. "Hey darlin'. She's out in the garden." Edwina worked for an organic greenhouse several days a week and spent the rest tending the garden that erupted lushly from their small backyard.

She put her hand on his shoulder as she walked by. "Keep singing," she said. Harry always made her feel good.

Sophie walked back through the kitchen and the sunporch and paused at the door. The heat of the day cast even the garden in a whitish tinge; she squinted and saw Edwina kneeling beneath a huge straw hat, tying a bean plant to a stake.

"Crazy woman," she called out. "Get out of that sun and let's go to Barton Springs."

"Hey girl," Edwina looked up. "I'm ready."

She wore her hair in short braids that made her look even younger. Louis had once called her "fetching," and the word always

popped up in Sophie's mind when she saw Edwina. She had suspected sometimes that Edwina had a small crush on Louis.

Sophie stepped outside and down the few steps to the backyard, into the sun and heat and the smell of vegetation, the beans
swooning away from their stakes, and the tomato plants heavy
with green globes. The insect life clicked and hummed under the
leaves. Edwina gathered her string and scissors and stood for a moment looking over the garden: queen of her kingdom.

"Something's eating my cucumbers," she said. "I'm going to sit
out here one of these nights with Harry's gun and find out who's
doing it."

"I swear it's not me," said Sophie. "Let's go."

Edwina put on her bathing suit, and they got into her truck.
They turned on the air-conditioning and put the windows down,
letting the hot air roll across their faces, an indulgence they shared
without guilt. Edwina smoked a cigarette and drove too fast; the
sunlight raked the windshield.

"How's Louis?" Edwina asked.

"Baking," said Sophie. "I haven't seen him all day."

"I saw him this morning at the bakery on the corner when I was
driving by. He was wearing overalls and no shirt and sipping a cup
of coffee at one of the outside tables. He looked adorable. Girl, I
sure wouldn't let him walk around like that if I were you, showing
all that skin and his tattoos—some little rock chippy will snatch
him up."

Edwina looked over at Sophie, then back at the road as they
pulled into the Barton Springs parking lot.

Sophie laughed. "I can hear myself yelling, 'You ain't leavin' the
house like that, boy!' "

"You two were having a great time last night. We could hear you
laughing from the top of the hill. You guys always seem like you're
having so much fun together." Edwina smiled. "I'm jealous."

"But you have a great man," said Sophie. "I love Harry."

"I know," Edwina said. "And I love him to death too. But we
don't have fun like that."

"I have to admit I do have more fun with Louis than with any-one else I've ever met," Sophie said. Her good fortune rose in her like a charmed snake.

"Me too," said Edwina, pulling into a parking spot.

They gathered their towels and lotion and crossed the dirt and grass in the slow motion walk peculiar to summer afternoons. It was too hot to speak. They paid their money and found a spot under the live oaks where the sun and shade mottled the grass, high above the long cool rectangle of water.

They sat on the towels and looked down on the bobbing heads, the white ghosts of bodies wavering below the surface, the dogs barking and splashing below the spillway.

"Can I ask you a weird question?" Sophie asked, pulling her sunglasses down over her eyes and fiddling with the cap of the sun-tan lotion.

"The weirder the better," said Edwina, pulling her bathing suit straps down to rub sunblock on her shoulders.

"Have you ever suspected that Harry was lying to you?"

"Nah," Edwina said. "Harry can't lie. He's the worst liar in the world. He knows he can't pull it off, so he's smart enough to stay honest."

"Can you lie?"

"Sure. All good Southern girls can tell a fib or two." She turned and smiled at Sophie. "My mama raised me right," she said. "But the truth is good enough for me."

They sat quietly for a moment looking at the swimmers moving about in the water, as randomly elegant as the dance of ants busily crisscrossing a patch of dirt.

"So you think Louis is lying to you about something?" Edwina settled on her back and pulled her sunglasses down over her eyes.

"I don't think so," said Sophie. She wasn't sure how much to say to Edwina. "But we were playing this lying game last night, and Louis . . . he seemed too good at it."

Edwina thought about it and said, "Well, honey, Louis does have his slippery spots, but I'm sure he's not lying about anything serious."

"Slippery spots?"

"All men have their slippery spots, their little slick patches, their hiding places. Especially men in bands."

"Except Harry," Sophie reminded her.

"Except Harry," Edwina said. She paused. "Sometimes I almost miss it. You know what he's like? One of those streams where you look in and you can see everything on the bottom, the different colored rocks, the fish . . . snails . . ." She laughed and stood up. "Speaking of water, it is too damn hot not to be in it."

Sophie insisted they walk a little farther down the pool to a place where they were allowed to dive. She was addicted to that moment of flight; she loved to feel her body stretched taut between the poles of skull and toes, to slice into the cool, slightly silty water of the springs, and to feel the momentum push her through the water until it released her back to the surface. She felt perfect when she dove. When they pulled themselves out and climbed lazily up the slope to their tree, Edwina said, "Go on now, what is it you think he's lying about?"

Something in Edwina's voice made Sophie hesitate. "Oh, nothing really. That game just pushed me off balance, set my imagination running where it's got no need to go."

"Everything okay between you two?" Her voice was a shade too light.

Sophie looked over at Edwina. She could not see Edwina's eyes behind the glasses.

"They're great," she said. "Can I have that sunblock?"

Edwina surprised her by laughing. "Then girl, you have an overactive imagination. It was a game. Louis loves the fuck out of you." She turned over on her stomach after she said this and rested her cheek on her arm, looking away from Sophie. Her black braids leaked water over her shoulders.

They lay without saying anything for several minutes. The locusts trilled and buzzed, singing in the heat.

Dreams could leave a stain on her day, Sophie knew, and as she remembered the Edwina of her dream grimacing and cringing away from her, she wondered if this accounted for the strange, subtle tensions she felt between them.

She looked over at Edwina's small dark arms and legs, as hairless as a child's, and then she couldn't resist looking at her own pale, thin legs with their scratches and old scars. She lay back down and looked up through the tree at the mosaic of dark branches and blue sky. The color of Harry's eyes, she thought.

After a few minutes she rolled over and scratched her fingernail lightly on Edwina's arm. "Hey."

"What, lady?" murmured Edwina.

"Did you ever—excuse me if this just sounds too weird—dream the same dream as Louis?"

Edwina raised herself up on her elbows and looked first down at her towel and then over at Sophie. "The same dream?"

Then it was a lie, thought Sophie. She doesn't know about it.

"Oh, something stupid. One of the lies Louis told last night. I should have realized . . . he said he had some dream in which you and he were bank robbers and you got caught and everyone was crying and I was crying. But the weird part was that he said you had also had the same dream that same week, and somehow you both discovered it. It's too ridiculous. I don't know how I ever thought it could be true."

"Sophie," said Edwina. "We did." She looked up at Sophie. "We both did have that dream. About two, three weeks ago. It was the weirdest thing."

"Are you sure it was the same?" asked Sophie, more sharply than she meant.

"Yeah. In mine we started out robbing stores, but then it was banks, and we got caught. And I remember you—you were crying."

"How did you guys discover this?" asked Sophie. "Do you two talk about your dreams a lot?"

"Louis came by one day last week to drop off something for Harry, and we had a chat. He told me about his dream, which turned out to be almost exactly like the one I'd had a few days before. I guess he didn't say anything then because . . . well, you know, it was just kind of weird."

She looked up and gave Sophie a little shrug of her shoulders.

"That is very strange," Sophie said slowly.

"I don't think it's that weird," said Edwina, sounding annoyed. "I mean, Louis and I have always sort of thought alike."

No, thought Sophie. Louis and I have always thought alike. She rolled onto her side, facing away from Edwina. She needed to think. If the dream story were true, she thought, then there is still a lie floating around somewhere between last night and today, between her and Louis.

"It wasn't the only time," said Edwina from behind her. "It had happened once before." Sophie rolled back to face her.

"I remember it because it was New Year's Eve. We all had brunch the next day. You and I didn't know each other well at all then. I had dreamed that I kissed Louis, and I probably shouldn't have told him, but I did. I'm honest."

"And?" said Sophie stiffly.

"He had had the same dream, that he kissed me in a club." More softly, she said, "It flipped us both out a little."

"Where was I when this conversation took place?"

"We were in the kitchen."

Try as she would Sophie could not bring details of that hungover meal into focus; she remembered only a vague impression that Edwina was pretty, quiet, and crazy about Harry.

"Soph . . ." said Edwina. "Are you upset about this?"

Sophie rolled onto her back. "It's very strange," she said finally. "I wish . . . that I had been told."

Edwina, floating face down in Barton Springs, those delicate arms spread like a bird's wings across the surface of the water. Edwina waking from sleep with the taste of Louis's dream kiss in her mouth. And the worst, Louis and Edwina, in Sophie's kitchen, gazing at each other in astonishment as they compared dreams.

Sophie was not adept at anger; it only made her feel muddled and heavy; it dulled rather than sharpened her.

"Sophie?"

She turned her head.

"They were only dreams. I don't want . . ." It was Edwina's turn to lose her words. It crossed Sophie's mind that Edwina might be lying.

"I'm like Harry," she interrupted. "I can't lie and I can't tell when other people are."

Edwina ran her fingers down her braids, squeezing out the water. "Well, it takes practice," she said. "Maybe that's all you need. You could tell lies if you wanted, just start with a few small ones. See how it feels."

"More lies are not what's needed," said Sophie.

"Who knows? It might make you feel better just knowing you could if you wanted to," said Edwina. "It would make you feel less vulnerable. Equalize the balance of power."

The balance of power, Sophie thought. Cold War. Mutually assured destruction. She was suddenly very, very tired, and she willed Edwina to shut up.

Louis was mixing batter in a bowl big enough to sit in. He watched the beaters swivel around each other in their herky-jerky dance and picked a dried crust of batter off his wedding ring and shut off the mixer. He had stopped trying to remember the lie he had told. It didn't really matter. It was an innocent tale, a fiction meant to entertain like his other concoctions: his pastries mounded with sweet fruit, his keening, soaring fiddle music. But in combing through his conscience, he hit a snag. At first he had ignored it, instead he had begun constructing a new dessert that had been taking shape in his imagination. There were elements in it which still puzzled him, and as he labored the kitchen grew hectic around him: he pulled pans from the oven, reduced sauces on the stove, dissolved gelatin and greased molds on the counter. This chaos was his most comfortable refuge from his own conscience, but when his cakes were cooling, and his poached apples sliced and piled, he sat on his stool and treated himself, as he liked to in the aftermath of a frenzy of work, to an image of his wife, lovely and undressed. In today's version she was on the couch, reading, her hair caught up in a clip. When he gave himself this small present, though, the other image, the one that he had snagged on, floated back.

She was at rehearsal and she was at the gigs and she would stand back against the wall of the club and he thought sometimes, but couldn't quite tell, that she was staring at him. She was small and dark and somehow incredibly sexy to him, with her pointed chin and her childlike limbs. One night when he came down from the stage, sweat along his hairline, and his shirt damp with the effort of making music, she walked up and handed him a cold beer. "Thanks, Edwina," he said. Of course he knew her. She was Harry's.

He didn't kiss her then. It was New Year's Eve, when Sophie was waiting for him to arrive at a friend's party after his gig, and he was drunk on all the drinks that had been sent to the band, and they were in a narrow hallway outside the bathrooms. Harry was in New Orleans, recording with a band Louis had wanted to play with. Her mouth was sour with liquor and her tongue was short and hard; it moved insistently in his mouth. He was un-expectedly aroused by this, but he had placed his hands on her shoulders and shaken his head, and after that kiss he avoided being alone with her. He desperately did not want to be unfaith-ful. Sophie had come into his life like a force of nature; boyish and sharp-minded, she had saved him. Then Edwina had sent the letter. It was the most erotic letter he had ever received. He read and reread it; finally he burned it in the kitchen sink one afternoon.

"Look," he said the next time he saw her, on the porch of her house when he came to pick up Harry's equipment. "You are in-credibly sexy and . . ." He looked out at the van and at Harry's broad back and his straw-colored hair. "And I'm very flattered by your interest, but I'm married and I love my wife and I'm faithful and your boyfriend is one of my oldest friends." There it had ended. Still, it disturbed him that he kept it from Sophie. It was not how he had envisioned his marriage.

The wall phone rang and he wiped his hand on his sleeve and picked it up.

"Raoul's."

"I'd like to speak to Louis please," said the voice, which he recognized.

"Randy," he said. "This is Louis. What's going on?"

"I got some good news for you, my friend."

"What would that be? I've got cakes baking here."

"Martin wants you to go on tour with him this summer. West Coast, East Coast, Midwest, South, Canada. Two months."

Louis looked at the cake pans in his hands and knew that this meant the end of them. No more getting up at six. No more dough under his fingernails. No more day job. Just music and money enough to live.

"Louis?"

"Yeah, that's great. That's fantastic. When do we start rehearsing, and when do we go?"

"I'll call you in a few days with the details when we've worked them out. I just wanted to let you know. I figured you'd be excited."

"More than that man," Louis said. "You just made my year."

After they hung up, Louis filled the cake pans again and slid them in the oven and sat back on his stool. His shoulders hunched his lanky form into a crescent. A finger to his lips, he stared at the stained apron draping his lap as if his new good fortune were gathered there. I ought to call Sophie, he thought, and then, all at once, he remembered the lie he had told. He laughed out loud on his stool to remember it. He laughed to think of his sweet and brittle wife believing him when he said that he shared a dream of robbing banks with dark little Edwina. Passing by the kitchen window, a neighborhood child saw the crazy baker laughing alone among his sugars and his pans.

She stood at the door of their bedroom, heart beating like a bird's in her chest, when she should have been printing: at the foot of the bed were his crumpled jeans and yesterday's T-shirt; a glass

with an inch of water stood on the bedside table. She picked up
the clothes in her arms and instinctively lowered her face to them,
started toward the laundry hamper and then stopped, turned and
lay the clothes on the bed as if they were waiting for a wearer.
Louis's clothing, his collapsed hollow image, waited as she slid open
the drawer of his dresser. What was she looking for? Her fingers
brushed the surface of his faded fragrant shirts, she lifted the edge
of one; a single narrow finger dug to the bottom. She had been
thinking of petal-thin sheets of writing paper pulled from en-
velopes, of unfamiliar script, of nothing at all, until it drove her to
this. Yet when her nail scratched the wood bottom of the drawer
she pulled it away as if it were burned. She slammed the drawer
and left the room, pausing to glance at the clothes on the bed, and
with a quick motion she scrambled them into a pile. This was not
the person she wanted to become.

I will wait until he gets home and talk to him, she thought. She
would tell him how that funny episode, that drunken storytell-
ing evening, had metastasized into this doubt and ugliness. He
would reassure her that he was the person she thought he was;
she would lay her worries down like a baby to a nap. That was all
she wanted. She thought for a while; she rested her sleek flaxen
head on her knees. But she could not rest and, wandering back to
their bedroom, she lay down next to the clothes. She pulled them
to her and then pushed them away, seeing too clearly Louis leaning against their kitchen wall, Edwina gazing up at him, the kiss
hanging, dreamed and considered, in the air between them while
Sophie drank her coffee with Harry in the dining room. A half
hour later, leaving the pillows clenched like fossils of her anger and
tear marks on the sheets, she got up off the bed and paced the
creased wood floors, barked a rough exclamation of anger once at
the ceiling, and decided what she would do.

Louis was icing his cakes when the phone rang again.
"Hey mister," Sophie said when he picked it up.
"My girl," he said.

"You coming home soon?"

"I'm almost done with my cakes. But then I've got rehearsal."

"I'll be asleep when you come in," she said. "So I'm going to tell you now."

"What's that?" he asked distractedly, thinking about how he would tell his good news.

"Louis," Sophie said, and her hand was trembling on the receiver. "We're going to have a baby. I'm pregnant."

Silence. Nothing. Nothing went through his head. He closed his eyes and opened them and tried to process this. A baby.

"Oh my God, Sophie." And then, "Oh my love."

"Just think about it," she said. "Tonight while you're rehearsing. Imagine it. And it will be real to you by the time you come home and put your hand on my stomach."

Her hands shook for a few minutes after she put down the phone. She had thought she might practice a little first. Start small: tell him that she spent the day getting drunk with her friend Isabelle, or that she forgave him for forgetting his third lie, or that an old boyfriend had called her. She had meant to tease the game out a little longer, to find her way back to solid ground by dropping little fibs like a trail of bread crumbs. But the physical laws that govern the actions of the heart are both capricious and absolute, and they demanded from her the lie she told. She reassured herself as she stood in the living room with the late afternoon sun spilling over her shoes. There would be time later on to let him know she could lie as well as he could. They would be sitting on the porch, the beer bottles sweating slightly, and she would say . . .

He hung up the phone and leaned his head against his arms on the wall. A kind of airlessness enveloped him. Oh, Sophie, he thought. He imagined her tender belly. He pictured her breasts getting fuller. He turned his back to the wall and slid down it. His arms on his knees, his head on his arms, he sat for a long time. Every now and then he could be heard to say his wife's name.

She opened a bottle of wine and had a glass, lying on her back on the couch. It tasted faintly of bananas. She had another glass. The orange hour came—it was her favorite hour—and it went, and still she lay on the couch letting the shadows form and reform around her. The drunk who lived below them turned on his music, and it came up through the floorboards and moved past her into the air above. Once she said into the room, "I am a liar," testing it. She thought it sounded pretty good.

If you had seen him play that night you would have recognized, carved in the tautness of his facial muscles, a great strained tenderness. He excused himself from the rehearsal once and made a phone call. Above the laughter, and the tuning of guitar strings, you might have caught fragments of what he said, "I'm sorry . . . bad timing . . . very much wanted to do it but it's impossible. . . ." Returning from his phone call he took the offered beer and hoisted it. "Cheers," he said to his bandmates.

The cab of his truck was dark as he drove home, and his lights swept the darkened city. Worried about what he might say or do, he spoke out loud. "She doesn't need to know," he said.

She is dreaming when the bedroom door opens, and he comes in, his shirt and shoes off already. In her dream a large bird looms over her, as he kneels next to the bed. He pulls back the sheet and puts one long-fingered hand on her abdomen. His ring shines in the moonlight coming through the window. She senses him there and wakes just slightly, knowing there is something she has to tell him. She thinks she says, "I was just lying. Getting you back." Perhaps she hears herself say it in her dream, but all he sees is her lips twist a little in sleep, parting slightly with a small, sticky sound. A little sigh escapes.

When he takes off his jeans and gets into bed, she rolls over and pulls him close. He puts his hand between her thighs. He buries his face in her neck. A little while later, if she weren't so sleepy, perhaps she would have recognized the slight fizzing, the tiny burst of activity deep within her. Perhaps she would have known that they were making a baby.

———————

Sara Powers grew up in New England. She is a graduate of Bard College and received her MFA from Columbia University, where she was a Graduate Writing Fellow. Her stories have been published in *Story, Zoetrope, VLS*; in translation in French *Elle*; and in the anthology *High Infidelity*.

"*The Baker's Wife*" was the first story commissioned by Francis Ford Coppola's literary magazine, Zoetrope, last year. None of us—Coppola, editor Adrienne Brodeur, nor I—knew whether this undertaking would work at all. My guidelines were simple—to write a "happy love story that contained some wit and wisdom," with four characters. Francis had also vaguely discussed the idea that two of the characters might share this same dream. With no more direction than this I was left blissfully alone and free to create my own mess.

I had for some time wanted to write about a reformed liar, and the first scene, in which two lovers tell each other lies for fun, had existed in my head for a while. I began with that, and the rest of the story's twists and turns were born from the natural contortions of trying to incorporate the elements of the commission in some kind of organic way. It was certainly the oddest process of composition I've ever experienced, but ultimately one of the richest.

Frederick Barthelme

THE LESSON

(from *The Southern Review*)

Gil and Harold worked together at the Jitney Jungle grocery store in north Biloxi—that's where they met. Gil was from Tarzana. His family had moved to Mississippi when he was in his early teens. His father did something for NASA, so they moved to Picayune, just outside the NASA complex. Later, Gil had gone two years to the George Tyler Community College in Belhaven, and then, when the casinos came in on the coast, he had moved down to Biloxi.

Harold was a local boy—gangly, tall, awkward, slow—born and reared on the Mississippi Gulf Coast, mostly by his mother after his father left when Harold was five. His mother had worked for the county court as a stenographer. After high school, he'd gone straight to work for Colonel Sanders, and from there to the Jitney Jungle.

Gil and Harold shared a distaste for the manager, Clovis Heimsath, who was from Alabama, and who seemed to enjoy giving them more sloppy work than they could handle.

They were stocking and fronting canned vegetables. "I feel like we ought to handle old Clovis," Harold said, wagging a can of beets at Gil. "We ought to can him; what do you think?"

"That's a big amen," Gil said.

"We're going to need a sealer," Harold said, giggling. "We're going to need a butcher's saw."

"Use the one in back," Gil said.

"I seen this one on television," Harold said. "They cut off parts whole. Like hands and feet and legs and arms. We're going to need mighty big cans to put his arms in."

"We'll cut 'em up and run them through the grinder, have us some ground Clovis. We can design some labels in that computer system of his."

"We ought to do Margie, too," Harold said.

Margie was the head checker and Clovis's favorite—a bit of a looker. Her uniform was always cleaner than anybody else's, and she looked sexy in it. She always had that top button open, and the skirt was real smooth over her backside.

"No, maybe not Margie," Gil said.

"You got the burns for Margie," Harold said. "That's what it is."

About then Clovis and Margie turned onto the aisle. Clovis touched Margie's arm and stopped her. They were ten feet from Gil and Harold.

Clovis said, "Now ain't that pretty? I like to watch a man work."

Margie smiled and waved hello to Gil and Harold.

Clovis put one hand against a shelf, disturbing the corned beef hash. "Look at them skittering around up there," he said. "You ever see two gerbils in a cage—how they go round and round?"

"Hey, Clovis," Margie said. She gave him a play slap on the shoulder.

"Yes sir, boss," Gil said. "Whatever you say, we're after it. We're doing our job here. We're smoking these cans."

"I've been thinking about getting them one of those wheels," Clovis said. "Let them run around on that for a while." He put his arm around Margie's waist, around the white plastic belt that cinched her pale pink uniform shirtwaist, and guided her between Gil and Harold.

When they got next to the Libby's at the end of the aisle, Clovis let his hand slip down over her butt. He didn't even turn around to see if Gil and Harold were watching—he was that sure.

When they'd gone, Harold said, "He's going to do her, right now."

"No," Gil said. "I don't think so."

"He's going to do her," Harold said. "He's taking her back to Meat. He's going to take her apart."

"She looked kind of unhappy," Gil said.

"You got to pay the price to be head checker," Harold said.

They did more cans until Harold ran out of the small white round potatoes. "I'm going to the back," he said.

"What do you mean?" Gil said.

"I need more potatoes," Harold said. He dusted his hands on the seat of his pants.

"Sure," Gil said. "Everybody knows."

"If I happen to see something while I'm hunting potatoes," Harold said, "well, be that as it may. That's just an accident."

"Get caught and we're slimed," Gil said. "I need the job."

"I ain't getting caught. I ain't doing nothing," Harold said.

"Maybe I ought to come," Gil said. "Keep you honest. Keep you clean."

Harold did an awkward dance toward the back and started singing the Mr. Clean song, but he had trouble remembering details, so he just repeated the "Mr. Clean, Mr. Clean, Mr. Clean" refrain and did the big fairylike sweep down the aisle.

"Shit," Gil said, getting off the overturned red plastic milk crate he'd been sitting on. He liked the grocery store, liked the order of things, the variety, the people who came and went—he thought it was all pretty. He liked the job and the miniature apartment he had on Crouch Street and the new TV he bought at Cowboy Maloney's Electric City, out on Pass Road. He liked nearly everything about his life, and as he watched this six-foot-five beanpole dance toward the stockroom, he began to fear that his whole life was about to change.

Gil found Harold in the narrow, dark-paneled hall leading to Clovis's office, doubled over and peeking through the hole where the second door lock had been. Without turning, Harold waved at Gil, telling him to stay quiet, stay quiet.

"What're they doing?" Gil whispered.

Harold flattened his palm over the hole and turned. "This is *exactly* like that *Red Shoes Diary* show," he said. "He's wonking her right here. She loves it."

"Lemme look," Gil said.

"No, you don't want to take no look," Harold said. "You're too busy. Get out of here. Go rack them cans."

"I'm taking a look," Gil said. He put a hand on Harold's shoulder, gave a little tug, but Harold was surprisingly strong and didn't budge.

"Get on out of here," he whispered to Gil. "You're making too much noise." He bent to the hole again, and soon he was making little grunting sounds as if in time with what he was seeing. Gil leaned against the paneling and slid down the wall.

"Come on, Harold," he said. "Fair's fair."

"My ass," Harold. "You got a dollar?"

"You're going to charge me for a look?" Gil said.

"Get that dollar out here," Harold said, grinning. He went back to the door lock and pressed his face against it. "Oh, baby," he said. Oh baby, oh baby, oh baby."

"Shit," Gil said. He went into his wallet and got out a couple of bills. The compressor on the big freezer compartment just the other side of Clovis's office kicked on, and everything in the place started to rattle and hum.

"They're going round the world," Harold said.

Gil grabbed Harold's shoulder and shoved a dollar into one of his hands, tried to push him aside, but Harold wasn't giving up this part.

"Scoot, boy. Get away."

"C'mon. I gave you a dollar," Gil said.

"Price's going up," Harold whispered. "Whooee. You go, girl. Uh-huh."

Gil yanked at Harold but couldn't get him to move, and in a few seconds more Harold gave up the hole, leaned back against the wall, and shivered all over. "Holy Jesus," he said.

Gil jumped forward, bumped his head into the doorjamb, tried to center his eye over the old keyhole. All he saw was Clovis standing by his desk with his shirt on but no pants. He had a lot of hair on his legs.

"Where's she?" Gil said.

"Probably the head," Harold said. "It's over left."

Gil kept his eye at the hole, twisting left and right, trying to see more, trying to find Margie. "I don't see her," he said.

"She's in there," Harold said. "Hang on a minute. She'll be out. Maybe they'll go again. Gimme another dollar."

"I ain't giving you squat," Gil said. "They gone. They ain't going to do nothing more. I'm just picking slag here."

"Boy, she is fine," Harold said. He was rubbing his eyes with his thumbs. "Mmm. Hardworking woman."

"Don't start up, OK? I ain't seen nothing. You're just giving me nothing."

"Keep your eyes on it," Harold said. "She's bound to come out."

Clovis pulled up his trousers and tucked in his shirttail while peering out the head-high glass that let him watch the store from his office.

"We better get going," Harold said.

"I ain't going anywhere till I see her," Gil said. "They can walk right out this door, and I'll be standing here telling them hello."

"They're coming," Harold said.

"I don't care," Gil said. He kept his face pressed to the door.

Clovis's office was a mess. It was a crummy storeroom with a steel desk and piles of paper around. There were stacks of flats of canned foods, and little eight-by-twelve plaques on the wall. Clovis stood tall in that room. As Clovis straightened his clothes, peeped into the store through the mirrored glass, Gil thought that Clovis didn't have a bad deal at all: like everybody, he got paid for getting in out of the rain, only he got paid more, and got special privileges like Margie, and got to make fun of stock boys like Gil and Harold. As Gil watched, the idea of cutting Clovis into little parts suddenly began to seem more appealing. He imagined draping Clovis over the butcher's saw and shoving him through so that his leg buzzed off. He heard the sound of the saw ripping through his skin and hitting bone. He pictured the blood showering out, jetting everywhere. He thought about running an arm through that bandsaw, just like a two-by-four, zipping off a hand. Maybe he would throw the hand at Harold, something like that. But Harold wouldn't be paying attention, he'd be over in the corner humping Margie, who'd be squealing.

"What's happening?" Harold said. "Let's go."

"She ain't come out yet," Gil said.

"Why don't you ask her about it later," Harold said. "We're going to get our ass caught if you keep standing in that door like that."

"I wouldn't mind sawing him," Gil said. "But not her. I mean, I want to *do* her, but I don't want to saw her up after."

"You're crazy," Harold said. "We ain't sawing anybody."

Gil turned away from the hole, looked at Harold, who was sitting on the floor, his immensely long legs jacked up in front of him. "I know that," Gil said. "But you're the big talker. You wanted to put 'em in cans."

"I'm gone," Harold said. He struggled to his feet and limped down the hall. Gil pressed his eye to the hole one more time, saw Margie come up to Clovis's desk, straightening her uniform. When she headed for the door, he beat it down the hall, then cut left and went around to the refrigerator room. He broke open a carton of ice cream sandwiches, peeled and ate one while he waited for Clovis and Margie to clear.

Gil and Harold and Margie had lunch together at the McDonald's by the gas station on the corner of the shopping center. They sat in a booth by the window watching cars go by. Margie was as happy as could be. She waved a french fry at Gil and said, "I hear you boys were watching."

"We were," Gil said. "Well, he was. I was more or less bystanding."

"I seen it all," Harold said.

"You mean you didn't get to see?" Margie said to Gil.

"Saw you straightening the uniform," Gil said.

"That's not too much," she said.

"I thought it was pretty good," Gil said.

"You're a sweetie," she said. "Natural born."

"I got two dollars out of him," Harold said.

"To tell you the truth," Gil said, "I saw more than I wanted. You and Clovis, I don't know. I'm troubled by it. I wish you wouldn't do it anymore."

"What is this? A declaration of love?" Margie said.

"Hey, boy," Harold said. He looked like a giant basketball player in a yellow kid's booth there in the McDonald's.

Gil said, "I just think it's unsightly, you know? It's kind of beneath you."

Margie smiled real prettily, powerfully. Like a woman will. "Well it *is* a declaration of love," she said. "What do you know."

Gil knew she was right, and was proud of himself for saying what he had. There were thunderstorms all that afternoon, and everyone who came into the store was sopping wet. Margie seemed perky behind her register, chatting and laughing with the customers as she pinged bar codes over the reader. Gil was all around the store, working the shelves, the stock, mopping the back. Whenever he could, he went and sacked for Margie, just to be close to her. Clovis was gone most of the afternoon but came back around five and even manned a register. They got the five-to-six rush, then things started slacking off, and by seven the place was near dead.

A little after seven, Gil came to the front after resetting the bananas, apples, and oranges in produce. Harold was over there watering things down. Gil caught Clovis and Margie chatting by her register. Clovis had his back to Gil, and as Gil came up he heard Clovis say, "Let's take a little trip, what do you say?"

"I'm tired, Clo," Margie said. "It'll keep."

He jangled his keys. "I don't know. I think the Boss is ready to go."

She patted his shoulder and smiled. "Give him a chill," she said, then she waved. "Howdy, Gil."

Clovis turned, surprised that Gil was so close. "What are you doing here, kid? You finished in produce?"

"Harold's handling it," Gil said.

"You mop sixteen and seventeen?" Clovis said.

"Sure did," Gil said.

"The new milk out?" Clovis said.

"Yes sir," Gil said.

"Why don't you go out front and round up the baskets then," Clovis said. "Margie and I have a little business." Margie made a face.

"It doesn't look like it to me," Gil said.

"What?" Clovis said.

"Let it go, Clovis," Margie said.

"Sure, fine," Clovis said. He turned back to Gil. "Get the baskets, will you? Everything's fine."

"Why don't you get the baskets?" Gil said.

"Hey, listen, hit your time card on the way out," Clovis said. "Have I got your address up there? Thanks for everything."

"Oh, come on, Clovis," Margie said. "Leave him alone. He probably needs the job."

"If he needs the job, then he shouldn't be mouthing off to the boss," Clovis said. "You need the job, Gil?"

"Not bad enough," Gil said.

Margie pulled Clovis down to her and whispered something in his ear. It seemed to go on for a long time. When Clovis stood up and turned around, he was smiling. "I get it," he said. "OK, fine. If you don't want to do the baskets, fine. Ask Harold to go get the baskets, will you?"

Gil grabbed the microphone and switched on the PA at the register. "Harold, come to the front. Harold, to the front." He looked up at the white painted corrugated metal and bar joists and air-conditioning ducts. Sometimes a bird or two lived up there. It was always a mystery to Gil how they could get in. When customers complained, Gil and Harold had to chase the birds out. Once Clovis brought a BB rifle, and they had taken turns shooting at a bird until they popped the glass on a case in Meat. Then they tried herding it out, propping the doors open and running through the store with brooms, throwing things where the bird was sitting on one of the joists. Gil was still looking at the ceiling when Clovis put an arm around his shoulders and started walking him toward the rear of the store.

"You know, Gil," Clovis said, "nobody's getting hurt here. You shouldn't get upset just because I have a little bit of good fortune. See, you've got your whole life out in front of you. Anything can happen to you, but I'm past forty. I've got a college degree, and now I'm paying for a couple of kids that don't like me very much, and I can't sleep. At three o'clock this morning I was up watching *Lingerie Dreams II* on Pay-Per-View. And I'm a churchgoing man, so that made me feel bad, just like other things do. But we do things anyway, you know what I'm saying? Don't know why, don't seem to have much choice. You look at it one way, and I'm taking advantage of my high position here at the store. Look at it another way, I'm an old guy being treated kindly."

"That's a Continental attitude," Gil said. "I've seen that in the movies."

"Well, yeah," Clovis said. "Maybe it is. But I tell you what, I'll try to keep it down in the future. How's that?"

"I think we'd all appreciate it," Gil said. He noticed how stiffly he was walking.

Clovis pulled away, patted Gil's shoulder, and turned to go into his office. Gil stopped in the middle of the aisle in front of the packaged meats, idly straightening some ribeyes and some fillets, some strip steaks. Later on, when he went home, he would wonder what had happened exactly. He wouldn't be able to put his finger on it, but he would think he had either learned a lesson or missed a step, and not knowing which it was would haunt him for a very long time.

Frederick Barthelme grew up in Texas and lives in Mississippi. His fiction has appeared in *Esquire, The New Yorker, GQ, Ploughshares, North American Review, TriQuarterly,* and elsewhere. His most recent novel is *Bob the Gambler,* published in 1997 and scheduled for paperback publication in 1998. Also in print is his novel *Painted Desert.* Several of his earlier book-length works, including *Second Marriage, Two Against One,* and the collections *Moon Deluxe* and *Chroma,* were recently reprinted in new paperback editions. He has won numerous awards, including a National Endowment for the Arts Fellowship. He directs the Center for Writers at the University of Southern Mississippi, where he also edits the *Mississippi Review.*

"The Lesson" baldly echoes the great Updike story that's in every freshman English anthology ever published. I wanted it nasty and brutish and grotesque and smelly, which is the way things are these days, or at least that's how they seemed to me at the moment of writing this story. Since then my position has moderated somewhat, but I'm still fond of the story and its nastiness, and especially the charming twist near the end where folks do things more like they do in life and less like they do in literature.

Later I did a second version of the story, rather thoroughly different, which appeared as a chapter in the novel Bob the Gambler. *I changed the main character to a forty-year-old, changed a good deal of the "business" of the story, added a few bits and pieces, altered the overall attitude to fit the novel, and concluded with a less ambiguous turn. It's surprising how much utility there is in the framework, and how different the stories are, given their basic similarities.*

Padgett Powell

ALIENS OF AFFECTION

(from *The Paris Review*)

All along the watchtower—which he had never been on before and now that he was on it could not imagine what it
was, or what it looked like, or what he looked like on the watchtower, other than the way he usually looked—Mr. Albemarle patrolled. At each end of his walk, or watch, or beat—he had no idea
what you called the path he trod until the fog suggested he turn
back and trod until the fog at the other end suggested he turn back
again—Mr. Albemarle crisply about-faced, having seen and heard
nothing. He was on the top of a wall, as near as he could tell, which
was one of several walls, as near as he could tell, constituting a garrison, or fort, or prison, or, as near as he could tell, someone's cor-
porate headquarters. Where or how the term *watchtower* had
obtained and why, he did not know. He was not on a tower, and
if he watched anything it was that he not step off the wall into the
cool gauzy air and fall he had no idea how far down onto he had
no idea what. If he was on a watchtower, he could only surmise
there was a moat, ideally with something dangerous in it, below.
But he had no actual vision of anything, and no idea why he was
on the watchtower, or whatever it was, no idea why he was walking it and no idea what he was watching for. He had an idea only
about why the phrase *all along the watchtower* kept playing in his
head: he'd heard it on the radio.

What he seemed to be doing, more than watching or towering or guarding, was modeling. He kept seeing himself stroll and turn in the fog on the wall as if he were on a runway, and he had multiple angled views of himself as if he were turning around before the tripartite mirror in a clothing store. There he was: some kind of guard (for what?) showing, mostly to himself, some clothes that looked strange on him, or not, that he would buy, or not, and have put in a bag, or not; he might wear them out of the store with his old clothes in a bag. That moment had given him a good feeling as a young man—wearing, as it were, virgin clothes fresh from the rack to the street, his old sodden worn duds in a lowly sack at his side. There were no pleasures, large or small, in his life now. He had mismanaged his affections.

All along the watchtower, then, in the fog, he watched, he supposed, for affection. That was the enemy. It was in the belly of a beautiful gift, companionship, which gift was always good to receive until this monster of happiness began to pour out of it and run amok and make him so happy that he betrayed it. Nothing so sweet as true affection could be trusted. True affection is too good to be true. It contains, perforce, disaffection. He walked his wall, all along the watchtower. The fog was lustrous and rising and a comfort. Mr. Albemarle pronounced, orated really, as though he were Hamlet, or some other rarefied speaker, which he was not, the following speech into the fog, aware that loud disputations of this sort surely violated the prescribed duties, whatever they were, of those who perambulate the watchtower: "My specialty is the mismanagement of affections. A cowboy of the heart, I head 'em up and move 'em out: lowing, bellowing, grunting, snorting emotions of slow stupid tenderness driven in mad droves to their end. All you need for this, in the way of equipment, is a good strong horse between your legs. I am a cowboy, or as they say in Sweden, a cawboy. Caw."

Some sodiers showed up. "Hey! Cawboy!" they said, or one of them said. It was a sudden foggy profusion of boots and nylon webbing and weapon noise, all halt-who-goes-there, etc. Mr. Albemarle defended himself against soldiers by calling them, in his mind, sodiers. He defended himself against not ever having been one and the possible indictment of manhood that might constitute, and he defended himself against their potential menace now—as they halted him when he should have been halting them by the terms of his not clearly understood position all along the watchtower—by calling them, in his mind, sodiers. The sodiers said, "Hey, cawboy, you got any cigarettes?"

Mr. Albemarle did and shared them all around and they were immediate fast friends, he and the sodiers.

"You sodiers are okay fine," he boldly said to them.

"We know it," they said, lifting their heavy steel helmets to reveal beautiful multicolored denim welder's caps on backwards on each of their heads. They all smiled, each revealing one missing central incisor, right or left. There were nine sodiers and Mr. Albemarle did not have time to get a count, how many right, how many left incisors missing. He had once considered dentistry as a sop to his mother's hopes for him. A dentist talked him out of it. "I clean *black gunk* out of people's mouths all day, son." That did it. The same dentist, it occurred to him now, had earlier talked him out of being a sodier. "All you do is say, 'You three guys go behind that truck and shoot the enemy.' What's there to learn in that?"

This was a sufficiently strong argument, with the black gunk looming as well, to talk young Mr. Albemarle out of enlisting in ROTC and getting educational benefits to allow him to go to dental school. The final straw was the dentist's asking him what he, the dentist, might do about his sagging breasts. His years of cleaning black gunk, slumped over patients on a short stool on wheels, had not maintained a firm tone in the dentist's pectoral muscles, and they indeed drooped, reminiscent of a budding girl's breasts. Mr. Albemarle, who was then eighteen and in fine shape himself and not called yet Mr. Albemarle, told the dentist to lift weights, but to his knowledge the dentist never took his advice.

"You sodiers have good shit, it looks," Mr. Albemarle said.

"We have very good shit," they said. They each searched themselves and gave to Mr. Albemarle a piece of gear. He received from them, all of them standing all along the watchtower and blowing exhales of white smoke into the white fog, a collapsing titanium mess cup with Teflon coating on it that was very sexy to the touch, a boot knife that was too sharp to put in your boot, an OD green tube of sunblock, a jungle hammock, with roof and mosquito netting, a pair of very fine, heavy socks (clean), a box of 9 mm shells, an athletic supporter, a flak vest, and a jammed M16 rifle that the sodiers thought was easily fixable but for the life of all of them they could not fathom how.

Mr. Albemarle put on and strapped on all of his new gear and passed around more cigarettes in a truly warm spirit. "Do you sodiers," he asked, "know anything about all-along-the-watchtowering?"

"What do you mean?" they asked.

"Like, what I'm supposed to do."

The sodiers looked at Mr. Albemarle and briefly at each other. "You *doing* it, dude," one of them said, and the others agreed.

"All right, I can accept that," Mr. Albemarle said. "But there is a certain want of certainty regarding just *what* it is I'm doing."

"Well put," a sodier said.

"We are in a not dissimilar position ourselves," said another, to general nodding all along the watchtower.

"We worry it not," a third said.

"A constituent of the orders—"

"To not know—"

"Precisely what we are about."

"So we just, as men with balls and ordnance must, go about the business at hand, whatever it is."

"And we suggest you do too."

This made fine sense to Mr. Albemarle. "One more question of you fine fellows, then," he said. "Down there—" he pointed down and over the edge of the wall—"any idea what's down there?"

"Moat," a sodier said, "with something dangerous in it."

"That's what I thought," Mr. Albemarle said. "Any idea what?"

"Crocodiles."

"I think badly deteriorated scrap metal, like thousands of bicycles, cut you to ribbons."

"Get tetanus before you hit the water."

"Definitely."

"Get a booster, dude, you plan on swimming in that moat."

"I don't *plan* on swimming in that moat," Mr. Albemarle said. At this the sodiers laughed solidly and loudly, approving of Mr. Albemarle's prudence.

They all shook hands, and Mr. Albemarle thanked them for the gifts, and they him for the smokes, and the sodiers decamped. Mr. Albemarle was feeling good. It had been a fine rendezvous all along the watchtower, and as he resumed his pointless patrol, he patted and slapped all of his fine new gear, more ready now than ever before for whatever it was he was ready for.

"I prefer the cloudy day to the sunny day," he announced toward the moat, trying to detect from any echo if it were crocodiles or bicycles down there, or anything at all. No sound came back.

Some aliens showed up. This was clear, immediately, to Mr. Albemarle. That they were aliens made sudden eminent sense of his theretofore murky task. He had been all along the watchtower watching for aliens. No one could have specified this without appearing to be crazy. Mr. Albemarle understood everything, or nearly everything, now.

The aliens were very forthcoming. They looked perfectly alien, no bones about it. All gooshy and weird, etc. They made calming hand gestures, inducing Mr. Albemarle not to raise his jammed M16 in their direction. They slid up to him as if on dollies and said, "We are aliens. We are aliens of affection."

"What?"

"We are the secret agents, as it were, in cases of alienation of affection."

Mr. Albemarle said, "You mean, when a man finds his wife

naked on another man's sailboat and he sues the yachtsman for alienation of affection—"

"Yes. We are in attendance."

"We are on that boat, usually," said another alien of affection.

The first alien slapped this second alien upside the head with a flipper-like arm. "We are *always* on that boat."

Mr. Albemarle offered the aliens of affection cigarettes and looked at them closely. In terms of gear, they were without. In terms of clothes, they were without, yet you would not, Mr. Albemarle considered, be inclined to regard them as naked. The slapped alien appeared ready to accept a cigarette until he received a stern look from the first alien and put his arms, or flippers, approximately where his pants pockets would have been had he had on any pants. Mr. Albemarle reflected upon—actually the thought was exceedingly brief, but trenchant—the apparent absence of genitalia on these aliens of affection. To his mind, affection and genitalia were closely bound up. The notion of secret agents of affection without genitals struck him as either ironic in the extreme or extremely fitting. He looked closely at the slapped alien, up and down, to see if there were misplaced genitals, if that would be the correct term. He saw none.

"What do aliens of affection do?" he asked, aware only after he did so that he might be forward in his asking.

"We alienate affection," the first alien said.

"There's Cupid and there's us," the second said. Mr. Albemarle expected him to receive another slap for this remark, which struck him as impertinent, or low in tone, but there was no objection shown by any of the other aliens. There were nine of them, as there had been nine sodiers. Mr. Albemarle was unable to detect the status of missing incisors because he could not determine, watching them speak, if they had teeth at all, or, really, mouths. They were weird, as he supposed was fitting. They were so weird that they weren't weird, because aliens are supposed to be weird, and they *were* weird so they *weren't* weird. He liked them, rather, but he was not as fond of them as he had been of the sodiers. They did not give him any gear, but beyond that they did not give him any comfort. Why should they? he thought. He had mismanaged his affections, and now it appeared feasible these guys might have had something to do with it. Every time he had broken a heart, or had his broken, maybe one of these gremlins had been there aiding and abetting, helping him fuck up. Perhaps this was the enemy. Perhaps these thalidomide-looking wizened things were why he was walking all along the watchtower in an ill-defined mission, preferring cloudy days to sunny.

"Let's take a reading on Loverboy here," the first alien said, and very quickly the slapped alien was very close to Mr. Albemarle. He had in the popular expression invaded Mr. Albemarle's air space, as had once a homosexual photographer who stood inches from him with wet lips and gleaming eyes and asked, "Do I make you nervous?" Nervous, Mr. Albemarle of course said, "No." Another time his air space had been invaded by a turkey in a barnyard, a big cock turkey or whatever you called the male, which could in raising its feathers expand itself about 300 percent and make you pee in your pants if you were, as Mr. Albemarle was, disposed to be frightened of all things in a barnyard. Mr. Albemarle was not similarly afraid of a wild animal, but all things in a barnyard had been husbanded there by a human malfeasant who wore wellies and had relations with the things in the barnyard, which consequently would bite you or kick you or step on you when they could. The slapped alien stood next to Mr. Albemarle with a gleam in his eye and had a lip-smacking expression, if a lip-smacking expression can be had by a party without, apparently, any lips. As he had with the photographer and the turkey, Mr. Albemarle held his ground, standing erect and turning ever so slightly askance to the alien so there would not be a clean, open shot to his private parts if it came to that.

It came to that. No sooner had he thought of that turkey the size of a tumbleweed in its waist-high dirty feathers gazing with its evil scaly wattled head at his crotch than the alien of affection touched him there very lightly and very quickly with a flipper. "Hey!" Mr. Albemarle said.

"Just a reading, old man," said the alien. "No fun intended."

"What's a reading?"

"We read your affinity for affection," the first alien said to Mr. Albemarle. Of the second alien he asked, "What's he look like?"

"Twisted."

Mr. Albemarle adjusted himself subtly in his pants and turned a little more askance from the alien who had touched him. "What do you mean, *twisted*?"

"The worm of your passion," the first alien said, "is twisted."

"Well, it straightens out," Mr. Albemarle said.

"No," the alien said. "*You* straighten out, sir, as Johnny Carson once elicited from Mrs. Arnold Palmer that she straightens out Mr. Arnold Palmer's putter by kissing his balls. *You* straighten out, sir, but the worm of your passion is twisted."

"Your desire, in other words," the second alien said, now a respectful distance from him, "is not clean and open but dirty and veiled. Something untoward happened to you at a delicate moment in the opening of the petals of your heart—"

"Shut up," the first alien said. "Excuse him," he said to Mr. Albemarle. "He tends to make jokes when he should not. We are safer in not speaking of flowers. We are safer in speaking of worms. And the worm of your passion is twisted, bent, kinked, and not, as it should be, straight, straight, and straight."

"Is this bad?"

"It is bad, yes, but you are not alone. Only one person on earth we've checked out is straight. That's Pat Boone."

"Everybody else is . . . twisted?"

"More or less. You are more than less."

The second alien, who had taken the actual reading, said, "Lucky you're alive, man. It's like a Grand Prix course down there."

"What he means, sir," the first alien said, "is that before the engine of your desire crosses the finish line it must negotiate a tortuous course and use the transmission to preserve the brakes and discard and remount many new tires and—"

"Hey!" It was the second alien waving them over to the edge of the wall. There all the other aliens were, peering down.

"Can you guys see down there?" Mr. Albemarle asked. "Take a reading?"

The aliens of affection were whistling to themselves in amazement. "Never seen the like of it." "That is *bizarre.*" "Takes the effing cake."

"What is it?"

"Nothing, man," one of them said.

"Nothing? Don't *nothing, man* me, sir. I patrol the watchtower and have every right to know what is down there."

The aliens went on marveling at whatever it was they could see or detect in the moat, if it was a moat. Mr. Albemarle looked in appeal to the first, apparently chief, alien, who pulled him aside.

"We've encountered the odd thing of the heart in our job," he told Mr. Albemarle.

"What's down there?" Mr. Albemarle observed the alien in apparent consideration of whether, and how, to tell him.

"I'm in *charge* here," Mr. Albemarle said. "Need to know." He'd always liked that phrase: we'll keep you on a need-to-know basis, so when they torture you, you will only be on a need-to-be-beat basis for so long.

"Broken hearts," the alien said.

"Sir?"

"About four million broken hearts down there, scrap hearts, badly deteriorated, cut you to ribbons before you hit the water."

"Not crocodiles or bicycles?"

At this the alien started laughing. The other aliens came over to see what was funny.

"What?" they said. The alien laughed even harder and refused to tell. They began goosing him with their flippers, trying to tickle it out of him, Mr. Albemarle supposed. Mr. Albemarle became embarrassed. He had said something, it was clear, ridiculous. But a moment ago, crocodiles on the one hand and bicycles on the other had made sense.

"I said crocodiles or bicycles," Mr. Albemarle told them. "I thought it was crocodiles down there, and some sodiers thought it was old bicycles."

The group of aliens politely tried to contain its mirth. The slapped alien generously came up to Mr. Albemarle and comforted him. "Understandable, man. No way you could know. We've never heard of it ourselves."

"I don't even know what I'm *doing* out here, all along the watchtower," Mr. Albemarle said. "Let alone what's in a goddamn moat I can't even see."

"Well, buddy," said the slapped alien, to whom Mr. Albemarle felt the most affinity (and he hoped it wasn't because this alien had touched lightly and quickly his crotch), "you know what you are doing now. You are watching over a giant spoilbank of broken hearts."

"My God. Still, what do I *do*?"

"Not sure on that. We break them. We are not concerned with their repair or storage. It would appear that these hearts here have been, in Navy parlance, mothballed. It appears you are simply to *watch* them."

"Watch all the broken hearts, all along the watchtower."

"Yes."

"In the world."

"Yes."

"And mine—it's broken too?"

"The worm of your passion is twisted, sir. Your heart is up here on the watchtower, not altogether broken. We have no orders to break hearts. We merely alienate affection. The broken heart is, you might say, collateral damage."

"I have mismanaged my affections."

"That you have, sir. In spades. We have no orders to further alienate your affections. The reading we took of you was casual, informational only, whimsical."

"The worm of my passion is twisted?"

"Twisted badly, sir. But the worm is alive."

"Is that good?"

"Depends, sir, on your outlook. Are you an absolutist or a relativist, ideal or practical in your worldly posture?"

"I am a muddle of—"

"Muddlers, sir, do not go unpunished. The moat is filled with muddlers."

At this Mr. Albemarle peered over the edge of the wall, frightened and yet oddly buoyed up by this talk. He was a twisted muddler but not (yet) down there on the spoilbank of the broken. It gave him a sudden hankering to have his hair cut in a barbershop where they'd put sweet-smelling talc and tonic on his shaved neck and let him chew Juicy Fruit in the chair. He could chew fresh Juicy Fruit after the haircut walking down the street in the sun with his perfumed head gleaming in the sun. He could find a girlfriend and try it again.

"Hey!" he said to the aliens. "If you guys . . . I mean, do you guys have any plans for me? Am I on the list?"

"No. You're singing the blues already, sir."

"Okay."

In a flurry of salutes and waves—Mr. Albemarle did not want to shake hands with the flippers, and the aliens did not actually offer them—the aliens were gone.

When the sodiers and aliens had left him alone, patrolling all along the watchtower better informed of his mission and better equipped for it, Mr. Albemarle felt momentarily better. He had that new-haircut sweet air about him and felt he was wearing new clothes, and he stepped lightly and lively all along the watchtower.

But soon the drug put in him by the sodiers and the aliens wore off. The gear began to seem a rather *Sodier of Fortune* aggregation of pot metal and fish dye and it was clanky and in the way. He discarded it in a neat pile.

What the aliens had given him was worse: the worm of his passion was twisted. This news, coupled with the revelations about the moat of hearts and about their having no call to further alienate his own affections, had calmed Mr. Albemarle when the penguinesque aliens of affection had been present. But now that they were gone he was nervous. It was like, he supposed, turning yourself in to the doctor during illness; you were still sick as a dog, but the mere presence of a man in charge of that in a lab coat and in an ethyl-alcohol atmosphere suggested your troubles would soon be over.

Now Mr. Albemarle realized the aliens had given him no such assurance. They had said in fact he was too alienated in his affections already for them to bother with alienating them further, which was not unlike being deemed terminal by the good doctor.

At first the aliens' pronouncing "The worm of your passion is twisted" had had an oddly calming, if not outright narcotic, effect on Mr. Albemarle. *That explains everything!* was what he had thought. Now he thought it explained nothing, and where it had calmed him it frightened him. "The worm of my passion is twisted," he said to himself, and aloud over the moat, and all along the watchtower, feeling worse and worse and worse. "The worm of my passion is twisted."

Mr. Albemarle then had a vision of his genitals twisted into knots. This was oddly comforting, also. It did not bother him. He chuckled, in fact, at the idea, and he recalled a woman once at a cocktail party declaiming to people whom she thought interested but who were not, "My husband's genitals are like knotted rope." Everyone had left her and gone over to talk with her husband in sympathetic moods.

Mr. Albemarle knew that the aliens meant something deeper and worse, as they had told him, and that they were right. His passion was bent and his desire was dirty and veiled. He knew men whose passion was straightforward and whose desire was clean and open and who were not Pat Boone. They were true cowboys of the heart. They saw what they wanted (and knew it), they asked for it, and when they got it they sang praise around the campfire in a clear voice and got up early and made coffee for it and kissed it and hit the trail, the happy trail, until nightfall and bedfall and bliss. These cowboys had cowgirls: open-eyed girls in red skirts who danced with you if you asked and kissed you back if you waited long enough to kiss them first. And a true cowboy knew how to wait, and he knew whom to kiss in the first place.

Mr. Albemarle did not know whom to kiss because he wanted to kiss no one, really, and when he got tired of that he wanted to kiss everyone. At that point, waiting seemed contraindicated. Waiting for what? For *everyone* to say yes? It was ridiculous. He had the image of a real cowboy of the heart, his passion straight and clean and open, sitting a bull in the chute, packing his hand in the harness very carefully and taking a long time while the bull snorted and farted and stomped and fumed and flared, giving the word when he was ready, and in a happy breeze of preparedness blasting into danger and waving for balance astride it for a regulation period and vaulting into the air and landing on two feet and walking proudly across the sand to receive his score, with which, good or bad, he would be content.

By contrast, Mr. Albemarle would not deign get on the bull until the last minute, and then would disdainfully sit sidesaddle on it and it would erupt and the rest would be an ignominious confusion of injuries and clowns coming to his rescue. That is what "the worm of your passion is twisted" meant. It meant not a ride and a score but injury and clowns holding your hand.

Mr. Albemarle walked all along the watchtower, whistling gloomily and studying the clouds. He imagined the hearts in the moat—the aliens had said a spoilbank of hearts—in great cumulus piles, great billowy stacks of puffy, shifting, vaporous grief, under the still water.

He cupped his mouth and in a low, smooth, strong voice intoned to the moat:

"Cawboy to moat, cawboy to spoils of love—

"What am I going to do with myself, now that I know it to be useless? I am tenebrous, or tenebrious if you prefer, it's all the same. When the big bulldog get in trouble, puppy-dog britches will fit him fine."

The water, or whatever was actually down there, remained still.

On his next morning's patrol, which he went about naked, having liked the sensation of discarding all the sodiers' gear and not seeing the logical end to discarding things, he met a woman on the wall. This is the way it is in life, he reflected; when you go naked, for once, you run into somebody you might prefer not see you naked. There was a woman not fifty yards ahead and Mr. Albemarle at least had the gumption to keep going, not to run. His nakedness if anything emboldened his step, martialized it a bit, so that by the time he actually came up to her he was in a subdued goose step and was looking perfectly natural about it.

"Hey, *cawboy*," she said with a leer. "I been hearing you sing the blues up here all the livelong day." This testiness was coming out of an otherwise happy, innocent-looking woman reminiscent of Dale Evans. She had on the red skirt that Mr. Albemarle had pictured when he was taking inventory regarding straight desire and twisted desire. The red skirt flared out wide and short and had a modest but sexy fringe on it. It allowed you to see where the leg of the wearer began to be the butt of the wearer, and it gave the onlooker pause and a kind of stillborn gulp.

He was looking at this Dale Evans in her skirt saying this contradictory Mae West stuff to him, naked and in the arrested gulp and not now looking at the skirt or the legs or the legs grading into the butt, actually there was nothing gradual about it—

"Cawboy," Dale Mae was saying, "I want you to sing me some o' them blues."

"I don't sing," Mr. Albemarle said.

"Yesterday you sang:

'When the big bulldog in trouble, Puppy-dog britches fit him fine.' You sang this in a clear campfire voice that lulled the cows and woke me up. I been sleepin' a long long long long long long time."

"That sounds like a long time," Mr. Albemarle said, stupidly, desperately trying to calculate how she heard him, where she was or had been to hear him singing to the moat. *In the moat?*

"Are you from the spoilbank of broken hearts?"

"The what?"

"The moat?"

"The what?"

"Is your heart broken?"

Dale Mae looked at him as if she had noticed for the first time he was naked, or as if he had lost his mind, which was, he considered, the same look. "Why don't you get dressed so we can dance," Dale Mae said. "Put on some of that Soldier of Fortune shit in a pile over there."

"*Sodier* of Fortune," Mr. Albemarle corrected, liking her. He fairly skipped over to the military paraphernalia and slapped on a quantity of it and stood almost breathless before Dale Mae in her flared red skirt and delicious fringe, ready to dance, or whatever.

"I warn you," he said. "I put you on notice right now. I have . . . the worm of my passion is twisted."

"It better be," Dale Mae said.

"By all assurances, it is *badly* twisted."

"When the big bulldog get in trouble, he should turn on some music and dance," Dale Mae said. "Take this bitch in hand, sir, and fret not your twisted passion."

"Yes, ma'am."

Mr. Albemarle did as he was told. All along the watchtower, they danced. It was a stepless but not beatless dance, hip to hip, pocket to bone, thrust to hollow. Gradually Dale Mae swatted away the annoying military hardware and left Mr. Albemarle as elegant as Fred Astaire, and gradually she herself softened and melted and fairly oozed into his arms, and they made in their heads plans to remain together and untwist Mr. Albemarle's passion and to do to Dale Mae's passion whatever in the way of no harm could yet be done to it. Dale Mae had a beauty mark on her cheek, which Mr. Albemarle admired until he touched it and it came off on his finger and appeared to be a piece of insect and he flicked it over the wall and thought no more of it and admired without impediment the dreamy, relaxed face of Dale Mae who had come to him unbidden and unhesitant and unheeding of certain dangers. This gave him a good feeling and made his puppy-dog britches fit him a little less fine. He was bulldog big enough already to kiss this cowgirl on the neck.

"Sugar," Dale Mae said, "it's the hardest thing to remember. All I can be is me, and all you can be is you."

"What's that mean?"

"I have no idea. Sing me some of them blues."

Mr. Albemarle sang:

"What I like about roses I like a lot—
I like a smell, a thorn, that jungle rot.
I like a red, a yeller, a vulvate pink.
And a king bee going down the drink."

Mr. Albemarle and Dale Mae got themselves some coffee and got naked and got squared away for some intimate quality time together in a small bungalow he'd found in the fog, which intimate quality time Mr. Albemarle kicked off by announcing to Dale Mae, sitting cross-legged on the bed with her coffee steaming her breasts and looking to Mr. Albemarle some deliciously beautiful, perfectly joined in her parts and the parts appearing to be cream and vanilla and cinnamon and cherry and chocolate, and some of her looked like bread, also, smooth tender bread like host wafers—he tore himself away and said, "I warn you, I'm a bad piece of work, emotionally."

"Well bully for you," Dale Mae said. "Do you know what to do *with me*?"

"I believe I do," Mr. Albemarle said, gently placing a knee on the bed and taking Dale Mae's coffee and setting it safely on a night table so she did not get burned in the clapping straits of his desire. He clapped onto her like an honest man. She returned everything he gave her by time and a half. It knocked him silly and made him pat his own butt, looking for his wallet, when it was over. He did this when he wasn't sure who he was. In the willing arms of an agreeable woman possessed of reason and courage, Mr. Albemarle had to doubt it could really be him she was holding and he wanted invariably at these moments to see his wallet.

"Relax, you piece of work," Dale Mae said.

"Okay."

He did. It was diffficult, to do that. Relaxing was hard, and dangerous, he did not trust it. That was why you had drunks. They had the most difficulty relaxing. They wanted it most, feared it most, claimed it most, almost never managed it.

"I will break your heart," he said to Dale Mae, breathing hard on her breast, a sugary warm air coming from it as if it were a lobe of a radiator.

"Hmmm?" Dale Mae asked. "You go right ahead."

"Go ahead?"

"Why not? Break break break."

Some day, maybe today, he was going to do a woman right. Dale Mae's breast was next to his eye and looked like a cake with one of those high-speed-photo milk-drop crowns on it. He had a tear in his eye and was hungry for cake. It was *thanklessness* that plagued and dogged hard the heels of affection. Affection was that which, and the only thing on earth which, you should be eternally thankful for.

When Mr. Albemarle got up from these his exertions upon Dale Mae the warm giving stranger, he felt fresh and sweet as a large piece of peppermint candy. He told Dale Mae this and she told him he'd better take a shower, then, and get over it. He kissed her and she kissed back and he took the shower and she was still there when he got out. Her heart hadn't been broken yet. It was progress. There was hope.

"It's not easy," Mr. Albemarle said later when they were strolling all along the watchtower hand in hand and in love, "to work this particular bit of magic."

"What particular bit of magic?" Dale Mae asked.

"Marriage."

"Indeed," Dale Mae said, noticing a piece of shale on the walk and throwing it over the edge. Mr. Albemarle waited to hear it land, curious he had never tried a sounding in the mysterious moat before. He was still keening his ear when Dale Mae said, "*This* particular bit of magic? You deem us *married*?"

"In a figure of—"

"In a figure of nothing. Not speech, not nothing."

"*Okay.* Sheesh! What's up your reconnaissance butt?"

"My what?"

"*Nothing.*"

He held her hand, petulantly but not unhappily. Marriage *was* a tricky bit of magic. Holding hands was a tricky bit of magic. She needn't be so hyper. There were—it occurred to him, now having been posted to the old verity that he was, whether holding hands or married or not, finally alone, always—there were people who had in their minds something called "a true marriage," as opposed, Mr. Albemarle supposed, to a *pro forma* marriage. He had no idea what this true marriage purported to be. He was not speaking of it when he constructed his pithy impertinence about magic and a marriage being made to work. He meant the false kind. It was a tricky bit of magic to *stay together,* was what he meant.

"I meant, it's a tricky bit of magic to *stay together*," he now said to Dale Mae, who squeezed his hand and patted their held hands with her free one as if to say, "You'll be all right." This little gesture proved his point: it was condescending enough that he wanted to take his hand back.

But she was, of course, right. Magic or not, tricky or not, it would bear no comment, it needed no more pressure upon it, the gratuitous happy union, than was naturally on it, the meeting and clinging together of two naturally repellent, irregular surfaces. They clung together out of desire but were aided, in his view, in their sticking together by a sap of hurt. This glue oozed from them despite themselves. For all Dale Mae's tough rightness, she was holding hands too. She was very tough and very soft. She was nougat.

"You're a nougat," Mr. Albemarle said to her, announcing it at large all along the watchtower. Emboldened, he then said, a little less broadly, a little more conspiratorially, "True marriage schmoo schmarriage."

"What?"

"Schmoo schmarriage," he repeated.

Dale Mae thumped him on the nose and held him by the back of the neck with one hand and at the small of the back with the other and pulled hard with both hands, scaring him with her strength.

All along the watchtower, it was quiet. "I think songbirds are overrated," Mr. Albemarle offered. "Really inflated. Not nowhere *near* what they're cracked up to be."

Mr. Albemarle got them two buckets of range balls from a vending machine he'd never seen all along the watchtower before. As much as he had patrolled it, this caused him wonder. The machine itself was a wonder: a plastic fluorescent box dispensing not junk food or soda water but golf balls. What would come out of a vending machine next? Shoes? Pets? Beside the machine, incongruously to his mind, was a barrel full of clubs, for free use in ridding yourself of your buckets of balls. Mr. Albemarle got them each a driver, and he and Dale Mae slapped and topped and scuffed and hooked and sliced and shanked and chillied the balls into the moat of spoiled affection. Mr. Albemarle had the feeling that each ball contained a message of some sort to the brokenhearted from the not yet broken. They were like fortune cookies except that they were more like misfortune cookies. He could not imagine what one of these misfortunes might actually have said, and when he inspected a ball it read only *Pro-staff* or *Titleist 4* or *The Golden Bear.* Yet he felt that each ball, whether it soared over or squibbed immediately down into the moat, carried a secret meaning from the players all along the watchtower to the wrecked players beneath it.

They had a good time. Each ball was a small celebration of their gratuitous, so far successful affection above the moat of moping:

each ball said, "Here, you sad sacks, *here*." They were probably, in their hand-holding glee and innocent kissing mirth, only minutes away from hurling themselves like badly hit balls themselves down into their broken brethren, but for the moment they felt fine and superior, lucky and happy, the way a new couple is supposed to feel.

Mr. Albemarle addressed each ball with a little wiggle of his butt and hands, a steadying sigh, *arm straight, head down, slow uptake, pause, how long will it be before she and I are back to normal, at each other instead of on,* whap! ball going God knows where, anywhere but straight. Mr. Albemarle could somehow induce a golf ball to wind up *behind* him. Dale Mae, in her red, fringed skirt, the fringes snapping like tiny whips when she cracked a ball into the ozone of ruined love before them, did better: her balls went forward.

That's how it is with women, Mr. Albemarle thought. They want forward, they get forward. Not so with me, which is where all the bluster obtains. *Talk* forward if you achieve backward. Bluster and cheer, the man's ticket to the prom. Bluster and cheer take reason and balls to the dance of life, and it goes reasonably well as long as the corsage is fresh. Then reason divorces cheer, and balls beat bluster, and the long diurnal haul to mildew of the heart is on. Mr. Albemarle teed up an X-out and hit it, smiling, best he could.

When they got back from the range, such as it was—the glowing ball dispenser, the ball baskets like Amazon brassieres, the clubs on the honor system—they prepared to frolic naked. Mr. Albemarle dropped his wallet on a chair beside the bed and out the corner of his eyes saw the wallet move. "Look," Dale Mae said, "there's a lizard."

There was a lizard coming out of Mr. Albemarle's wallet. It was nearly the color of the dollar bills from which it emerged, its head made quick birdlike assessments of the situation, and it ran.

"What *was* that?" Mr. Albemarle asked.

"That was Elvis," Dale Mae said, "in a green one-dollar cape. *Get in the bed.*"

Mr. Albemarle did as he was told.

There is much to be said for doing as one is told. Mr. Albemarle had come to see life as a parabola of sorts plotted over time against doing and not doing as one is told. Roughly, infancy and maturity were close to a baseline of obeying what others expected of you, and puberty and its aftermath, which was a variable period, took you on the upward part of the bell-like curve away from the baseline of doing what you were told. You soared on a roller-coaster hump of doing *not* what you were told and it felt good but finally your stomach got a bit light and uneasy and you started, through natural forces and not reluctantly, to come back down toward agreeability. Having ridden around with your hands off the bar and screaming, you were now willing—it was even exhilarating—to do precisely as you were told. It was fun in fact to subvert the voice telling you what to do a little by being instantly agreeable, by even anticipating instructions. This was pulling the wool on the bourgeois.

This was one reason Mr. Albemarle did not object to his current job, walking all along the watchtower. He yet had no good idea what he was doing, despite the large assurances and hints supplied him by the aliens of affection, but he found doing it agreeable because he had apparently been, however mysteriously, told to do it. So he did it. Living well was not the best revenge; doing exactly what you are told is the best revenge. The blame or fault in your doing it, if any obtains, rests upon those telling you what to do. The masses of folk going over cliffs in the name of this or that religion were onto the beauty of this revenge, but Mr. Albemarle liked the less obvious vengeance of obeying the smallest whim, the fine print of commandments that were issuing like radio signals from everyone and everything around him, from the very fabric of civilized life. From utter strangers on the street, to foreign governments, everyone had ideas about what you were supposed to do. Your job, as baseline parabola wire walker, was to divine their (sometimes tacit) wishes and appear to obey them. This is what civilized human life boiled down to.

Animals, Mr. Albemarle had noticed, and it was not surprising, were immune. They could not hear the radio. They heard only their "instincts," which excused all their nasty behavior. Periodically an animal would be trained—i.e., forced to listen to the radio. Animal trainers were, ironically, those most wont on earth to speak of human freedom, iconoclasm, nonconformity as *summae bonae.* And they were, appropriately, dirtier than most people, unruly, outspoken in hard-to-follow ways, united beyond these traits in their insistence that tuning in a horse or a bear or a dog to hear the radio of doing what it was told somehow increased *its* freedom. These notions gave Mr. Albemarle the idea of opening an obedience school for dogs all along the watchtower. He would train all the dogs all along the watchtower to leap into the moat and become brokenhearted-man's best friend. He liked this idea very much. Training a dog to leap into space would be a test, probably, but it would be imminently possible if you weren't softheaded. The larger problem with the idea was that he hadn't seen a dog in all his days all along the watchtower.

When Dale Mae woke up, looking ravishing, he said to her, "Do you think we need a dog?" She said, "I don't think we *need* a dog."

That was that.

"I'm like one of those Iroquois steel workers," Mr. Albemarle said. "I just naturally put one foot down in front of the other, straight, without looking down, all along the watchtower whether there are dogs on it or not and all along the parabola of doing what I'm told. I can walk that line as steady as Ricky Wallenda on a wire, but no leapfrog."

"No leapfrog?"

"No leapfrog. Ricky Wallenda quit leapfrog. He fell doing leapfrog."

"I see."

"Just do what you're told, but no leapfrog."

"I see."

The amazing thing about Dale Mae, about any tough woman who could still smile after enduring her own time on the parabola of doing and not doing as she was told, was that she *did* see. They could see right through a fog of nonsense to the rock or reef behind it. They'd abandoned radar in favor of a finger in the wind. This is why men liked them and were driven crazy by them. Men were content with a finger in the wind only when they were defeated or tired. Women used a finger in the wind cinching victory first thing in the morning. Without women, men would be giant raw quivering analytical anuses. Mr. Albemarle was comforted by this summation he had formulated and went to sleep on Dale Mae's bosom.

Mr. Albemarle found a writing desk all along the watchtower and stationery inside it, so he sat down to write a letter. "Take a letter," he said to himself and by way of sexual harassment palmed his own butt and sat down.

Dear [blank; he couldn't determine whom to write],
    I know you think ill of me. That is because I am weak and mean. But keep in mind that . . . [here he faltered] . . . that . . . [he could think of nothing now in his behalf, in his defense, to say to the person or persons whom he could not think of either] . . .
                                                                Love,
                                                                Troy

Troy was not his name, nor did he want to assume it. He looked the letter over and liked it. It summed up his position nicely. It was all you could say if the worm of your passion was twisted, your affections were all mismanaged and *always would be.* "Keep in mind that . . . that . . ." that nothing. *Love, Troy.* Did he mean the city, the myth of epic war over an impossibly beautiful woman? Who cared.
    He decided to make a thousand copies of the letter and somehow devise a mailing list that would be appropriate and have mailing labels applied by a machine so the entire affair would not be labor-intensive and he wouldn't have to lick a thousand stamps and write addresses and harass himself further. The sexual harassment of one's own self was the most insidious form of sexual harassment and there was to his knowledge no legal protection against it.

That want seemed a huge oversight on the part of the stewards of modern civilized life who had turned life into injury and redress, loss and litigation. The final moment in it all would be every citizen suing himself or herself for damages resulting from his or her own excesses and negligences with respect to himself or herself and his or her personal aggrandizement or lack thereof. The vista of the denizens of the modern world suing themselves into bankruptcy gave hope where there had not been any. This was a beautiful prospect to Mr. Albemarle, patrolling all along the watchtower—a kind of global legal self-immolation that would leave a few survivors who bore no one else and themselves no ill will. He suddenly felt, in possession of this vision, that he might be a prophet of some sort: the elect, here all along the watchtower not to guard a moat of the brokenhearted but to witness a Trojan War of tortes. He was going to observe World War III, which was going to be a global litigious meltdown, from a safe purchase on his lawless wall.

Mr. Albemarle left the letter on top of the writing desk with instructions for its copying and mailing to one thousand appropriate parties, TBA. He had no idea whom the instructions were for, but if someone came along and assumed the duty it would be better than if someone didn't. Leaving the desk he noticed a phone booth he had never seen before and stepped in it and dialed a number.

"Hello?"

"Hello. Good, it's you."

"Who is this?"

"Troy Albemarle."

"Who?"

"I don't know. I just wanted to tell you that I'm lonely."

"You have the wrong number."

"No, I don't."

"You don't? You don't know me and I don't know you."

"You're a *woman*," Mr. Albemarle said, with more force than he intended, "and I just wanted to tell you that I'm lonely."

"Look, mister. That's what you tell your *own* woman, not a stranger."

"Look, yourself. If I tell my *own* woman I'm lonely, she'll think me silly."

"Maybe you are."

"Maybe I am. I don't dispute it. But to accede that one is silly is not to deny that one is lonely."

"It probably accounts for it."

"It *probably does!*" Mr. Albemarle all but shouted, slamming the phone into its chrome, spring-loaded cradle, fully satisfied.

When he saw Dale Mae, approaching with a shotgun, he thought to test the wisdom of the conversation with the strange woman, with whom he was in love.

"Dale Mae, I'm lonely."

"Don't be silly," Dale Mae said.

"Yes!"

"What's the matter with you?"

"Nothing."

"Do you want to shoot some skeet?"

"Of course I want to shoot some skeet."

"Well, come on. There's a skeet range down the way."

"I never saw a *skeet range* all along the watchtower," Mr. Albemarle said. "A *lot* of things, actually, are—"

"Come on, lonely heart. My daddy taught me one thing and I'm going to show you what it is."

"Do, do, do," Mr. Albemarle said, taking a look around for the presence of witnesses to this exchange. There were none that he could see, which, he knew, meant not much. *Nothing apparent* meant more, in these days, than *something obvious*. He was getting used to that. It took some doing, but he was doing it.

The skeet range was of the nothing-apparent type. Dale Mae stopped walking, put two shells in her gun and crisply closed it, looking dreamy-eyed at Mr. Albemarle and patting the gun and saying of it "Parker" in the lowest, sexiest voice he'd ever heard, and then her eyes cleared and she turned to face the void beyond the wall, said "Pull," and blew to infinitely small pieces a thing which seemed to fly from the front face of the wall. It looked like a 45 rpm record before she hit it; Mr. Albemarle concluded it had been a clay skeet after she hit it. She kept saying "Pull" and blasting that which flew, left right high low, to bits, and she took a long, lusty snort of the thick cordite smell in the air and scuffed some of the wadding from her shells off the wall and said, "Mone get me some iced tea and fried chicken when I get through shooting, and then kiss you to death," and resumed firing, shooting backwards and between her legs and one-handed from the hip, like a gunslinger with a three-foot-long pistol, *missing nothing,* and Mr. Albemarle started talking, uncontrollably, agreeably:

"In the first grade had a teach name Mrs. Campbell that was the end of sweetness for me in the, ah, official realm. Next year ozone, I mean second grade in orange groves, etc. Mother had water break and taxi to hospital, golf-course father, had swimming lessons chlorine nose. A siege of masturbation ensued. Declined professional life—had *choice,* too. Somehow at juncture early in life where you elect to watch birds or not I deigned not. *Fuck birds.* This is sad. I am holy in my disregard of the holy. Sitting upright in a Studebaker or some other classically lined failure is the attitude in which I see myself for a final portrait in the yearbook of life. Depth charges *look* like fifty-five-gallon drums but I suspect they are really not that innocent-looking up close. Reservations at hotels and restaurants and airlines are for—" he stopped and snorted lustily the cordite himself and realized he had been aping Dale Mae's shooting in mime. He looked like a fool. She kept shooting. She was a one-person firefight. She would fill the moat with clay shards and wads.

"I want the certainty of uncertainty. I declare nothing to customs, ever. Transgressions of a social and moral sort interest me: philosophically I mean. They assume—I mean those *who* assume to know a transgression—that the points A and B for the gression to trans are known. I've had trouble, since the ozone of second grade and the chlorine and my mother holding herself, having peed in her pants and cursing my father, and since the large beautiful hognose snake I was too scared of to pick up in the orange grove so went home to get a jar to invite him to crawl into, which took about a half hour and, well, the snake didn't wait around, I've had trouble knowing point A and point B in order to correctly perceive, or conceive, transgression."

"Let's go get some chicken," Dale Mae said.

"That sounds delicious. That sounds good. That sounds not urbane but divine anyway—"

"Shut up, baby. I can't kiss you, you go off your rocker."

"You shoot that gun I shoot my mouth, is all. I—"

There was, not improbably, tea and fried chicken in a handsome woven basket, and a red-checkered tablecloth for them to have the picnic on, all along the watchtower.

Selling hot, melted ice cream from a rolling cart, like soup, or to put on pastries, or something, he supposed, Mr. Albemarle pushed an umbrellaed cart all along the watchtower. It had four rather small wheels instead of the more conventional two large wheels used by food vendors, and they flibbered and squalled, drawing his attention away from trying to figure whose idea it was to try to sell hot ice cream to pondering how much of life, finally, was pushing things around on wheels. The sick were flibbering and squalling down halls of disinfectant, the healthy down freeways of octane, dessert in a good restaurant flibbered and squalled up to you in a cart much like his—if the human race had gone as mad for fire as it had for the wheel, the earth would be a black cinder. Instead it was a scarred, runover thing, tracks all over it, resembling in the long view one of those world's largest balls of twine, in this case one as large *as* the world.

Dale Mae was down the way and Mr. Albemarle moved along the way. Who was going to buy hot ice cream? Who, all along the watchtower, was going to buy anything? There *was* no one all along the watchtower, so far, except the sodiers, the aliens of affection, and now Dale Mae. Mr. Albemarle looked around to see

if perchance anyone was watching and pushed the cart of bub-
bling ice cream—it smelled cloyingly sweet—over the edge of the
watchtower into the moat, brushing his hands together briskly as
if he'd handily completed a nasty task. He whistled a happy tune,
one that appeared to be random notes, and sauntered all along the
watchtower.

Mr. Albemarle stopped his whistling and sauntering in midblow
and midstep. He had an old-fashioned crisis. He was suddenly
transfixed by one of the old human antiverities: he had *no idea
what he was doing, or was supposed to do.* Pal with sodiers, let aliens
of affection feel you up, romp with a Dale Mae, push boiling ice
cream into a moat—these things you did in life because they came
along. You did them. You even did them well, if you cared to—
Dale Mae said the worm of his passion was *exquisitely* twisted. But
so what? What of it? What *then?* What *now?* What *point?*

He stood there feeling slump-shouldered and low. He had a vision of a different kind of life. There were men who, say, ran car
dealerships and bought acreage and had their friends out to shoot
quail and they all drank out of these Old-Fashioned glasses with
pheasants painted on them, painted "by hand" it said in the expensive mail-order catalogue the car-dealer quail-shooter's wife ordered the glasses out of. The wife and the other wives were in the
kitchen discussing what the wives of car dealers and bankers and
brokers discuss. They were wearing pleated Bermuda shorts and
none of them was too fat. The men were content with them, even
loved them, and did not have affairs too much. The men laughed
easily among themselves at things that were not too funny. Mr.
Albemarle was outside this, all of this.

He knew that were he inside it, the point-of-life problem might
not be resolved, but he knew it would not, if he were drinking
Wild Turkey and talking Republican politics, come up. From his
vantage and distance, quail glasses and okaying the deficit might
well be *exactly* the point of life, he could not tell. But he was certain that he—all along the watchtower with (accidentally) a woman
who could (incidentally) shoot the quail but who would (cer-

tainly) shoot the quail glasses also—was never going to get the point. He was, he realized, standing there looking at the ball. He did not see that it helped anything. If you paused to look at the ball you were going to be tackled for no gain, or for a loss; whereas if you just at least *ran,* you stood a chance of gaining yardage. That you had no idea what a yard meant was no argument to lose yardage, or was it? How had he gotten to walking all along the watchtower? Was it not a losing of yardage? Was being on the watchtower with a woman who could probably shoot the painted quail off a glass without breaking the glass not somehow the negative image of life on the plantation, where the plantation had nothing planted on it but feed for the birds who would be painted on the glasses lovingly held and admired as symbols of the good life? At this cerebration Mr. Albemarle was forced to sit down and say, "Whew!" He'd had, he thought, some kind of epiphany. "Whew!" he said again. It helped.

"What's wrong with you?" Dale Mae said, scaring him. He'd not heard her come up. He wondered if the watchtower were getting softer, or something.

"Nothing," he said. "If I threw a hand-painted quail glass in the air, could you shoot the paint off it without breaking the glass?"

"Do it all the time," Dale Mae said. "Problem is catching the glass. That's hard. Usually you get you a party of car dealers and brokers to shag 'em. Out there in their Filson pants and Barbour coats, pumping hell-for-leather through the gorse, flushing actual quail. There are ironies."

Mr. Albemarle looked at her hard. Either she was demonic and had possessed his brain, or something else of a weird and too intimate nature was going on.

"Where are the wives?" he asked.

"What wives?"

"To the glass catchers."

"In the kitchen with Dinah strummin' on the old banjo."

"Thought so."

"Let's get us some ice cream."

"Can't."

"Why not?"

"I rolled the cart into the moat."

"You *what*?"

"Well, it was *boiled* ice cream. Did you want *boiled* ice cream?"

"No. I want hard cold ice cream."

"Me too."

Like that, they were together, hand in hand, strolling all along the watchtower looking for ice cream proper, Mr. Albemarle's epiphany behind him.

They walked by the writing desk where Mr. Albemarle had left instructions for the phantom secretary to mail his one thousand letters it seemed just seconds before, and the desk was covered in vines. He remarked on it to Dale Mae.

"Heart mildew," Dale Mae said.

"What's that?"

"It's what grows on sites of affection. If you'd left that desk alone, or left a real letter on it that was to be mailed to one thousand people for whom you never had or expected to have affection, there'd be no vine on it. Your letter, lame-o one that it is, brings on the jungle. Am I on that mailing list?"

"Not yet. I only have the brokenhearted on that list."

"A thousand?"

"Well, I rounded up."

"As well you might. As well might we all. It is a proposition of such close tolerances, at least before the parts are worn out from friction, that pairing a thousand bolts to a thousand nuts does not seem excessive. Consider thread count, mismatched metals—"

"Dale Mae, could we talk about something else?"

"Sure, baby. What?"

"I once threw away a Craftsman circular saw when all that was wrong with it was a broken tooth on a drive gear. This, the whole-thing throwing away, was a waste. I regret it. That whole saw—motor, blade, and all—in a plastic garbage bag, now in a landfill,

I guess, with its bad gear nearby somewhere in the great non-composting amalgam of jetsam, if you have jetsam on land, or flotsam, I don't know the difference, but anyway it, the saw, in its exploded view (I did not reassemble it) is packed into some clayey sand with whatever else I threw away with it and whatever else other people threw away that day and there are seagulls flying overhead so maybe it's fair to call the saw flotsam, or jetsam, where you have gulls you have salvage, just as where you have smoke you have fire."

"Is that it?" Dale Mae asked.

"No. That is the tip of the lettuce. I once took four baby cardinals from their nest in a relocation program of my own devising. They, the hairless little blue pterodactyls, were to be moved to a 'safer' place, God knows where. For this transport they were placed on a wooden paddle of the sort you are to strike a rubber ball with repeatedly as it returns to the paddle via an elastic band. I have blocked the name of the toy."

"Fly Back," Dale Mae said.

"The birds," Mr. Albemarle said, "peeping and squalling, were red-skinned and blue-blooded underneath the fine cactusey down on them, giving them a purple scrotal texture until they fell off into an ant bed. The kind of squirming they did, which made me unable (afraid) to cup them on the paddle, did not look radically different from the kind of writhing they did once they fell off and the ants were on them, but it was. They writhed to death, the baby cardinals, right there at my feet, at the foot of the tree in which their erstwhile happy safe home sat empty but for the hysterical parents flitting in and out. Right there at my feet, except I slunk my feet off somewhere to contemplate what went wrong, how the little bastards should have known better than to *scare me* like that."

"Is that it?"

"No. Another time I sold a puppy to the right people and bought it back and sold it to the wrong people, who got it stolen. The right people I *thought* the wrong people were kids in a garage band who wanted the dog to protect their equipment. When I got there to buy back the puppy, it was on the knee of one of the boys, watching cartoons with them. *I took the dog back.* Then I resold it to a family man who had children not yet rock 'n' roll age. He managed to let the dog be stolen, which the rock 'n' roll boys would never have done. And what would protect the boys' amps and drums and guitars now? My point is that my entire life is probably just a series of this kind of blind self-serving fuckup. *Everything* is cardinal-nest robbing and taking puppies from watching cartoons with their devoted new masters. *Every breath is dumb.* Even if you are on to this, you have no way of proving it. But the principle of reasonable doubt obtains. There is reasonable doubt that I have done one sensible thing in my life."

"Is that it?"

"That's it."

"You need to chill."

"To what?"

"Chill."

"Are you black?"

"Do I look black?"

"My point is, let them have their baby cardinals. Don't put them on your paddle," Mr. Albemarle said.

"Oh, brother."

"Are we having a fight?"

"No, babe. We are going to bed. You're a case."

"Well, bully for me."

Dale Mae smelled of gun oil, and Mr. Albemarle kissed her recoil shoulder, imagining it slightly empurpled from her shooting, but it was not. Her shoulder was pale and strong. She cleared his head of broken saws and wheeling gulls and writhing blue baby birds and misplaced dogs.

He put all of what was left of his desire, dumb or twisted or not, on top of and in this Dale Mae, and went through the motions, which is to say, vulgarly, made *the* motion, the curious in-out yes-no which all primates figure out or they die out, and it was a more or less standard bed-roll except that not only did Mr. Albemarle's astral body levitate above them but *two* astral bodies levitated above them, and impersonally looked at him doing this personal thing. This always happened with his one astral body, but with these his two astral bodies the impersonal viewing of his doing the personal thing, yessing noing yessing, was in stereo, as if he were a card in the trombone slide of a stereopticon.

As happens in that moment when the illusion of three dimensions obtains, Mr. Albemarle felt himself deepening, receding, *going in*. He lost himself in the picture a bit, or altogether, and lost himself in the personal thing, in the vulgar, in the sublime, in Dale Mae, in a hallowed and haunted way that 3-D pictures viewed this way can be hallowed and haunted, more rich-seeming than the flat life that their two separate views depict. He left his common dimensions. He got into it.

His mind decamped. He thought he saw the sodiers for a moment on his left, the aliens to his right, in tiered banks and waving at him as if he were on a float in a parade. He looked at Dale Mae but did not see her clearly—more precisely, he saw clearly *into her pores* if he saw clearly anything at all. The watchtower *was* getting softer, he thought, absurdly. The brick was turning to mush, his mind was turning to mush, he did not much mind. Had he been in the tiers of parade watchers waving, he would happily have waved at himself going by, or rather down, the street, or the tunnel, down whatever, wherever he was going, happily, down. He had waited a long time for once-was-lost-now-am-found, and he had no reservations about its general oddness or peculiar particulars. Dale Mae herself was already behind him, a warm soft old way of being. He was a new man, even if that meant, as it seemed to, not being exactly a man. That—exactness—was exactly what was being lost. It was being lost with an inexact agreeableness that felt at once intellectually irresponsible and shrewd. Mr. Albemarle was gone.

Padgett Powell's first novel, *Edisto* (1984), was nominated for the National Book Award. He has since written four more books of fiction: *A Woman Named Drown*, *Typical*, *Edisto Revisited*, and *Aliens of Affection*. He teaches at the University of Florida.

"Aliens of Affection" had its birth, I suppose, when I learned from reading the late Albert Goldman's very funny Esquire *piece about Charleston, South Carolina, in about 1979, that a man who found his wife naked on another man's sailboat sued that man for something called alienation of affection. Or let's say that is one moment of its generation.*

Another, larger, longer moment is the sad discovery that I would not be a rock star and would have to be a writer instead if I was to get any satisfaction. Dylan and then Jimi Hendrix could do "All Along the Watchtower," where was mine? I tried in 1988 and could only write the phrase itself. Then I got more witless with age, and lonelier, and it got easy to write about being witless and lonely, and I whipped out my Compaq Stratocaster and done one.

Michael Gills

WHERE WORDS GO

(from *Quarterly West*)

I'm a word man, can start anywhere. Monday. Three o'clock
sun shreds the unspeakable trees. Outside, where snow humps
in patches, men who grew up loving angry women walk heavy
under the chain-link sheen. My students today, nine, they circle the
cinder-block room. I make ten. Three sex crimes steer clear, look
at their feet, know stories but are Jesus freaks now and won't tell.
The thieves stare at these, see open game. I've been warned. One,
Celestino Gaza, vehicular homicide, carves his dry forearm with a
thick ridged thumbnail, he's ex-marine, is carving a penis, a flower,
himself. To him, I'm nobody he wants around. I wish for ripe gold
light, slant through blackjack oak in Arkansas autumn, persim-
mon chilled sweet in frosty air, blacksnake sliced into alfalfa bales
fallen in elysian pastures, I tell them, my inmate writers, about my
brother, Jimmy.

"He was a stutterer," I say. "Have I told you this?"

Ray, bright-eyed molester, has me nailed, stiffens for the lie of
how we all overcome handicaps. Dark Tino bench-presses 305, a
guard watches him through the door window. The wall clock ticks.
Pencils and paper are holy.

"Why I'm telling you this is because you've got to figure out
your hot spots. You got to know what *means* something to you.
Anyone played poker with toothpicks?" The air we breathe seems

breathed already, fake air, airplane air. The god with the big stick has walked out, but you can still smell him.

They nod. We talk poker. Five card, seven card, Mexican Sweat, the jack with one eye. All decks are marked here, stacked time. "But why won't toothpicks work?"

"Ain't no bet." Ray's voice sounds nothing at all of cigarettes, of urgency whispered under low lights.

"That's the truth. What's on the line?"

Sometimes you can *see* them go home in their heads. Tino's arm leaks a tiny thread of blood. He makes letters, a cross. The still room has a feel, a velocity.

"Jimmy stuttered. He was eighteen. That makes me twenty-four. The year I cured him."

All my life I've heard about here, a man with a tattoo on his ass —*abandon all hope ye who enter here.*

"It's August. Arkansas. I'm from Arkansas. We drive up Cut Hill, a mile top to bottom. The highest place we can find. And there's a God sign on top that says *Prepare to Meet God,* and Jimmy and I piss there. We've brought beer, a case or something. Bud. It's not the first time. Alcohol is forbidden in my family. It made my old man crazy if he knew we boozed. He's recovering. Recovering whores, pious bitches."

Ray winces, a reformed whore, sodomy, buggery, love misguided.

"Jimmy's driving because I've lost my license. DWI Number five. Felony. It's dark and we're out in the county, that country-ass smell when dew hits the bitter weed. Someone has thrown a gutted gar on the side of the road. We can smell it, but don't care. We drink and don't talk, under a sky where Jupiter's just come out. My brother and me."

"Can I say something?" A thief whose name I can't put my finger on raises his hand.

The rule is that we don't raise hands. I believe in interruption; my religion.

"No." My session is after lunch, kill time. "Jimmy cut a hole in his and shotgunned it. Two, three, we'd drink like that. You know what I mean?"

A long time without liquor, they almost smile. The guard in the ugly window hates it when you smile. His stick is so beat up it seems real. What ta fuck you grinning at? he'll ask you.

"Jimmy starts his car. We're high by now. He guns it, keeps the lights off. And we drive down Cut Mountain full throttle in the dark. We don't talk about it. And we don't turn the radio on. It's my idea so I make the rules. No talking allowed on the way down. Piss your pants, fine, but no talk. And when we get to the bottom, I don't know why, I couldn't tell you with a gun to my head, doesn't matter, because he could talk then, open up and let fly, read roadsigns, anything. He didn't miss a lick. We'd go out, dance with Air Force women. Jimmy quit stuttering. It worked."

Tino says, "Big shit." All men wish to seem dangerous. If you can't inspire love, fear.

"My daddy set me on fire oncet." Ray pulls up the front of his blue issue, exquisite welts pinken into strands across his skinny, sunk-in chest. "Guess that qualifies as a hot spot. Lay money again that."

It's Wednesday, we meet three days a week when they let us. Six of us today, we're losing weight. Tino to my left this time, never sits the same spot twice. Our guard's chewing on a ham biscuit, his jaws saw just outside the door window.

"Shoot," I say.

"Some of it's a lie. You said that's okay."

We are allotted half-hour slots for our workshop sessions. Today, it's me, Tino, Ray, a small-time called Two Chicken and another fellow I have trouble placing because he neither talks nor moves. God makes six. "That's what we're here for. To lie."

"The winter my old man burned our clothes on a fireplace grate. Just like that. Come home and instead of being dog-ass drunk he's straight sober. Our electricity was shut off that January so we had a fire going in the fireplace and had burned a quarter mile of wood-fence all the way to the curve in the road where the swaybacked horse was buried. Come walking in. Just walk on into the living room."

Ray's eyes go aflutter; he's a believer gone home. Nobody in here says *bighouse*.

"Right past my mother and duddn't say a word, not to me, not to my sister, not to the goddamn dog, not to nobody. Nothing, not even a funny look in his eyes. He was just home, hungry probably. And then he comes walking right back in with an armload of mama's clothes from her closet, drops them on the fire. My mother asked him why he was burning her clothes on the woodfire. He said, 'Pray,' and went back for some of mine. 'Happy birthday,' he'd say, or 'Merry goddamn Christmas' and let fly with a can of lighter fluid. Our dog was biting a hole through the back door, gnawing nails, bolt plate, her name was Suzie. She wanted out. My mother's chiffon robe, and the yellow ducks on my brother's pajamas, and my cowbow shirt, some handkerchiefs, the heel kept falling off one of his boots. He was crazy for that fire, glowing like that. Behind me, my mother said I had to go start the car, point it toward the highway. But before I did it he squirted me and I still don't know why he dit tat, he'd never done at before so why'd . . ."

"You said the fire was already burning." The nameless sex offender, Ray's kin, coming at someone's sister from behind, six-inch blade honed for an hour by the clock until it shaves hair. Jesus forgives, my ass. "Why's he need lighter fluid if the fire's burning?"

"Shut up. He dit it then. I burnt good. Bright sparks, moments of light, I saw it snowing up out the chimney while she ran out the front door saying for me to drive that car and I did. My first time behind the wheel spewing gravel and smell of my skin where the lighter fluid had caught. Look, goddamit. Here. I could smell myself in my own nose. What do you think? What do you think? You tell me what you think it smells like, your own skin in your nose. Out on the highway I rolled my window down. 'Son of a bitch, son of a bitch,' I screamed it in the air and I remember because the air felt good and saying 'son of a bitch' felt good. My mama kept saying, 'Don't. Just drive,' she said."

"What'd it smell like?" Tino.

"Ain't none of it true. It's a goddamn lie." Ray is the shortest man in the room, five two or something. His eyes blink.

"What's at got to do with why you're here. What you did?" Tino's voice reminds me of someone I heard talking from a pulpit once, it livens the air, has a grain to it. Even though I've never heard a smart word come out of his mouth. "Maybe we set you on fire again it'll fix you."

"It ain't got nothin, Gaza, to do with nothin."

The guard—is his name Wellar?—pushes the door open, we're out of time. I say, "Go and do likewise."

Friday morning is Visiting so everyone's all screwed up by the time we meet. Have I told you it's winter, that the light out here is different, that I've left a lot of places behind and it always takes so long to leave? Tino chooses a metal chair dead in front of me today; his eyes are brown for what it's worth. Maybe being an ex-marine latino postal worker is tough, maybe we should grieve our own cowardice, our failed nerve. We both know he'll talk today.

Instructors who work at prisons must first pass tests: the silence between me and Tino gets louder every day, the cells in my body anger, no, rage him, I can feel it happen, proton by proton. I am not a nonstrategic person. "Tino," I say. "Is there anything going on in the world I need to know about today?"

Ray's still pissed about Tino saying we should set him on fire again. His sideways chair breaks our circle, a face that speaks weary glower, hair and twitch. He won't tell us what it smelled like. When he was on fire.

They ask you how you react to danger; are you or have you ever been a felon, or a homosexual, or a multiple gun owner. Are you wanted? Are you the victim of abuse? Do you ordinarily feel angry for no reason? Are you an alcoholic or a drug addict or have you ever been any of these? Have you or are any members of your family been in a *facility* of any kind? Are you bothered by long periods of silence. Are you an alien?

Tino. Invisible now, the carved name, the penis, the flower. I say, "I guess nothing in the world."

I've decided to tell another story: one aimed at, rather than understanding one's hot spots, unearthing the power of words, where they go, how they are living and dead, at once freemen and slave. They cost no money, can go through doors. Shit like that. Tino beats me to the punch.

"I'm not what you say," he says.

Today, we are down to four: myself, Tino, Ray, and the nameless molester, or is he a thief? Doesn't matter. Out in the world, he could be standing at a flea market and his name would be George something and what would it matter? Who'd care? People are everywhere.

"Say?" Not only are his eyes brown, they have yellow in them, shiny flecks.

"That story about your brother. You turned him into a stutterer. Why?"

It is not a question whose answer rockets through my head.

The testers ask you your philosophy of criminal punishment, how you would explain incarceration to someone to whom the concept did not exist.

"Why is so much at stake in that? What's the bet in telling us about your brother stuttering. Or drinking beer. Driving a car down a hill? Air Force women? What are you about?"

"You killed someone, Tino. Put them in a grave. What are you about?" I've been warned.

Tino has good posture, rare. His skin is the color of unbleached olives. "Not talking about me," he says. "We're talking about you."

Ray and the nameless man pass a hand signal. If moments actually verge between one instant and the next, that's what I sense, energy becoming. I say, "Tell me a story, Tino."

He says, "You."

Jimmy, out of my mouth. "That's where they found him," I say. "The bottom of that hill. Where I used to take him. He went through glass. I found his brains on a tree stump. My cure."

Tino yawns. "You ain't got no monopoly on car wrecks. And the world don't owe you no pat on the back. Got me?"

The door is opening inward. The guard's stick clack thuds on hardwood.

Ray says, "It smelled like me. It must have *been* me."

The man whose name I don't know pats the slender pad inside the shoulder of the black coat I'm wearing and walks out, followed by Ray. Tino's last. On his way, he drops a paper wad, tight balled, onto my lap. Alone in the cinder-block room, I undo it, and see. I can leave anytime now, drive on out, hit a bar, whatever. I can go home any time I want.

Michael Gills grew up in Arkansas and now lives with his wife, Jill, and new daughter, Lyra, in Salt Lake City, where he teaches. He was a Randall Jarrell Fellow in the University of North Carolina at Greensboro's MFA program, and recently received his PhD in creative writing from the University of Utah. His stories have appeared in *The Greensboro Review, The Gettysburg Review, Quarterly West, Boulevard,* and elsewhere. He is at work on a novel.

In the first minutes of my workshop, before I take roll or write my name on the board or field questions, I offer my students an outright challenge—to write as if they have everything to lose. This is my way of dodging the prissy, university-infected fiction now so prevalent. My student writers will recognize parts of "Where Words Go" as that opening spiel, a two-minute, half-lied account of how my brother, Steve, got killed in a car wreck. Francois Camoin, on hearing me tell it, suggested that I write it down as the first story in Why I Lie, *my first book of stories. I set the piece in a prison, wrote it outright in two days, and immediately started winning things.*

Once on opening day of spring semester, I made it half through this "write from the heart" speech when eyes started twitching, mouths opening and shutting, and a general look of nausea came over the whole room. Way in back, a skinny boy stuck up his hand.

"This is an anthropology class," he said. "You in the right place?"

IN THE LITTLE HUNKY RIVER

(from *The Chattahoochee Review*)

In the summer of 1968 when she turned fifteen, she made up her mind to get the canoe out of the storehouse and put it in the river, the way her parents had done when she was twelve. When they tipped over in it and fell out and drowned.

The only thing was, she couldn't do it alone. She needed strong arms to get the canoe off the wall and into the water. She needed a boyfriend, but she had no prospects. She'd had no prospects in the winter either.

"What's the matter with me?" she asked BoPeep.

"Less see," Peep said. Peep was nearly eighty, but she did not wear glasses. She did not drag her feet the way old people did, and she still ran the house and cooked the meals.

"You bossy, that's one thing."

"Not around boys."

"You bossy just breathing."

She was Anna Catherine on her birth certificate, but after her parents died she began calling herself Page. "Page Gage," she said to Aunt Florrie. Only one letter is different. And also, it rhymes."

Aunt Florrie said: "It rhymes, dear, but it isn't musical."

It didn't have to be musical, Uncle Oliver said.

Oliver, her guardian, was refreshed by the idea of choosing a new name. For himself he thought of Madison, or possibly Pierce. Pierce Gage would have no trouble shaping up a lumberyard about to go under.

"What else?" said Page. "Besides being bossy?"

Peep considered. "You taller, that's two things. And you makes all A's."

"Grades count?" Page flounced off, but she came back later when Peep was washing grit off the mustard greens. "I really need a boyfriend. Can't you help me?"

"What I gonna do? Go call one up?" Peep dried her black arms and sat down in the rocker that was put in the kitchen for her to take naps in.

Page sat on a footstool her grandmother had made: seven quart-sized cans upholstered in padded chintz and sewn in a circle. "If I had a boyfriend I could take down the canoe and put it in the river."

The Little Hunky. A minor branch that flowed below the bluff the house sat on. She and the boy would float along until something (what?) upset the boat and they both fell out. Not to drown. Simply to discover how her parents had drowned when T.G. was a swimmer and should have saved himself and Janet, too, but somehow didn't, and left Anna Catherine to grow up an orphan in Oliver's house.

"But I can't ask a boy I don't even know who doesn't know me. Can I?" asked Page. "Do you think I could?"

"Uh-huh," said Peep, already dozing.

The day of the drowning Anna Catherine had watched T.G. and Janet with the canoe over their heads, crossing the lawn, disappearing. Oliver, watching too, gave her a quarter and she walked to town and drank a soda. When she came walking back, Peep took her in the kitchen and she found out then that her parents were dead. It was like a story in a book. It was like the carnival moving on and leaving their ferris wheel in Whitman's pasture. As if they didn't need it. As if they could have a carnival without it.

* * *

"So you think," said Page, "that I could just go out and sit in the swing and the first boy to come along, any old boy—" On any afternoon? Maybe even today? Except it was Saturday and Oliver was at home. On a regular day no one would notice her hailing a boy from the front porch. Peep lay on her bed in the afternoon, and Florrie stayed upstairs and wrote in her room.

Florrie, Oliver's wife, was a celebrated poet in Garrison County and known all over for unsolicited recitations at social gatherings. Poems, of course, and lines from stories she started writing but never finished. *Angelique rose before the day was ready to be looked at, while it was yet slouching along in its black overcoat, its hat pulled down over the stars.* On other occasions she quoted scripture. Once at a bridal shower: "To whom will you flee for help? And where will you leave your glory?"

She did it, Oliver said, when conversations got boring.

"She do it," Peep said, "to get the floor."

Peep spoke without restraint about the Gage family.

Oliver's father, Anderson Gage, gave BoPeep her name when he was four years old. When he died, he left her the house her family had always lived in and a sum of money to use as she pleased.

"He put it in his will," Peep told Page. "An put in why. A person name a person be like savin their life. After that, he gotta take care of em long as they live."

That summer that Anna Catherine became Page she spent most of her days with Peep in the kitchen. "Was it very much money my grandfather left you?"

"Be more now than when it was give me, in spite of all the kinfolks I'm doling it out to."

Page ate a brown fig. "Do any of your folks live in Garrison County?" (She hoped to be around when the doling was done.)

Peep, however, had run them all off.

"Always hounding me for nickels and dimes. I told em though, if they got their tails in a crack they could drop me a postcard, and if it wasn't their fault I'd send em a money order."

"What do they do if it is their fault?"

"If that ever happens, I'll let you know."

Peep told Page that Miz Florrie wrote poems because she couldn't write checks. "She a tenant farmer's daughter and they didn't learn her how."

"That's not the truth, is it?"

"She was ten years old before she had any shoes. And goin on twelve before she rode in a car."

"But you like her, don't you?"

"I likes Miz Florrie. Likes her up in her room doin her writing. Likes her a-plenty when she going out the door."

Peep told Page that when Oliver was young he lost a new Ford car trying to go up Pike's Peak in the middle of winter. "Don't nobody do that but jackrabbits and crows." In the spring he went back to dig it out, but there wasn't a sign of it, up or down.

She said Oliver coming home on a dark night from a bachelor party ran over an alligator and thought for three days he had killed a man. He might have carried that burden to his grave except for a newspaper reporter who came along later and took a picture. GIANT GATOR FLATTENED ON FRIDAY.

"Why didn't Uncle Oliver go to the police?"

"The po-lice!" laughed Peep. "Who what's drunk is gonna do that?"

"Uncle Oliver was drunk? Does he get drunk often?"

"Far as I know, he ain't drank since."

Page ate another fig. "My father drank. Did you like my father the way you like Oliver?"

"Don't like nobody the way I like Oliver. He my baby."

"He's not really your baby."

"I got him borned. I slapped the breath in him when he come out blue. Now he watch over me like his papa did. Ever morning fore day he come an knock on my door. 'You in there, Peep?' And I says back, 'Where else would I be?' But if I don't answer I know I can count on him. He gonna put my teeth in and straighten me up fore he call anybody to tell em I'm dead."

BoPeep in her chair opened her eyes. "Turn on the fire under the greens."

Page said, "I can't right now. I'm thinking about something."

"Think about greens. Put em on low and wake me up in time to make the cornbread."

Anna Catherine wore a child's dress to her parents' funeral, one Janet had made, too short and too tight for a twelve-year-old, but Page wanted it on her, wanted to wrap herself in it and cover her head if she possibly could.

At the cemetery she held Oliver's hand and stood next to the statue of Grandfather Gage. When he was seventy-one he commissioned his own monument, a large granite chair with a figure of himself sitting in it. Big stone fingers, stone fingernails. Two marble eyes stared down at Anna Catherine, who knew how to swim, but when her parents were drowning she was down in the town ordering a soda, choosing a straw from the tall glass canister the straws leaned out of when she lifted the lid. She was stopping at the feed store to weigh herself, and swinging the hanging fern pots at the Garrison Hotel.

She wept so loudly Oliver took her to the car and sat with her there until the service was over.

At the house afterward friends ate sandwiches and speculated.

"Janet stood up suddenly before the canoe went over."

"Bob Gordon saw her from his house across the river."

"A bee might have stung her."

"Or stung T.G. and she stood up to swat it."

"It was Fate pure and simple."

"It was predestination."

Anna Catherine sat on the stairs. As soon as she was older she would go down in the river and see what was there. Seaweed, she thought. And water snakes, tangling her parents' arms, wrapping around them. It might be necessary to take a knife.

When everyone had gone, Florrie stood in the dining room, in tears again. "Oliver, do you see? Do you see what has happened to

our great and wonderful family?" Years before when she married
into it, seventeen members were living on the same street. "They
have all gone from us. They have lain down in darkness and left us
alone on this withering plain."

Peep spoke from the kitchen. "You still got cousins living in
Atlanta."

"They are not Gage cousins! All of the Gages have departed
from this earth except we four. We are the remnant."

"Don't count me. I ain't a Gage."

Florrie lifted her voice. "You are a Gage in spirit! You've been in
this family longer than any of us."

"The cat by the fire don't eat at the table."

"You are welcome, BoPeep, to eat at our table at any time. As
you already know. And if you don't, you should be ashamed."

"Miz Florrie," Peep said and went back to the dishes stacked on
her drainboard.

Florrie crossed the room and kissed Anna Catherine. She recited
a long passage about the waters of Babylon and the hanging of
hearts on willow trees, and then she went upstairs to change into her
writing clothes, an assemblage of scarves she wore over pajamas.

Oliver said, "She won't come down again until tomorrow."

"So us," said Peep, "got to git ourselves together. Anybody want
coffee?"

Anna Catherine said yes, she'd have a cup.

Oliver brooded over scattered plates and crumpled napkins.
"I'm going back to the cemetery and see if the graves are covered
over and the flowers put on. Anna Catherine, honey, do you want
to go?"

"She havin her coffee!" Peep said.

So he rode off alone down the boulevard and into the trees.

It was a bad idea, his father always said, to plant trees in a cemetery, especially oaks, with their roots going everywhere, burying
themselves and crowding out people.

It was a lumberman's view Oliver didn't share, like so many
things about the lumber business, but it was too late now to walk

away. He was the whole cheese now. He was Gage & Sons all by himself.

He fixed his attention on his Oldsmobile. Princess Pat, he called it, for no other reason except pure love for its faithful service. When he bought the Olds his mother was still alive, and his dear sisters too. Also Aunt Jessie Fields under those cedars and others he rolled by who had passed away while his odometer was turning.

At the two fresh mounds he halted the car and sat looking at the graves blanketed with flowers: white narcissus blooms and other yard blossoms friends had brought over in the morning wrapped in green tissue paper and laid on the porch, an old custom he hoped never died.

People died. His father, his mother. Amelia and Mary. Now T.G. and Janet. Gone, as Florrie said, from this withering plain, leaving him to be last, the last Gage male, with no hope in hell of producing another one.

He meditated on that sorry fact until he found himself wondering what Peep would serve for supper. More funeral food? Or grits and eggs?

The sun going down lit his father's monument. Without thinking about it, he crossed the lot and climbed up and sat in his father's lap.

The stone came from Italy. His father had gone there and chosen it himself. He was there six weeks, posing for the sculptor.

A prosperous man, Oliver thought. "And I," he said aloud, "can't afford a hammer."

He laid his head against his father's chest and began speaking about the state of their business. Of Gage & Sons. "Down now to Son. *Run*-down. Inventory down. Workforce down."

He gazed at leaning tombstones pocked with lichen, and artificial poinsettias six months old.

"T.G.," he said. "T.G. was taking money."

He half expected the stone chair to crack. He wished it would, wished it would throw him down the hill and into the river where he could lie, unaccountable, on its slimy bottom until he was scooped up and put in his grave.

"The first I knew was last Wednesday morning. T.G. broke down over a big stack of bills, and I saw the whole picture, saw it all at once: the gambling and the drinking. He wasn't spending Janet's money like I thought he was. The Yard's money was buying those cars and fancying up his house. Gage & Sons was tumbling down. And what was I doing? I was walking around, joking with customers, and not even noticing how few there were."

A mockingbird sang, running through a repertoire of ten or twelve birds and a barking dog. A setter, thought Oliver. Old man Jenning's. It never shut up.

"T.G. promised to pay it all back. He'd get a loan from Janet's father against her inheritance. Of course, first, Janet had to agree. I don't know if she did. That was Friday. They drowned on Saturday."

Foolish, the evening buzzed. *Foolish, foolish,* as he himself had been numbers of times in his silly life, imagining himself wise, picturing himself as somebody to envy.

Oliver closed his eyes, letting exhaustion take him down the hill, into the water where what happened had happened. Whatever it was.

When he woke again, night had come on. A man Peep had sent was tugging on his foot, calling out fearfully, "You awright?"

Page said at the table after cornbread and greens, "What is everybody doing this afternoon?"

Peep announced that after cleaning up the dishes she was going to her house (a smaller one back of the big one) and have a lay-down until half past three. Or if she felt like it, half past four.

Florrie said dreamily she'd be going upstairs to work on her piece, a rhyming saga about the Gage family and the Karankawa Indians (a cannibal tribe which, according to her research, had eaten a Gage).

Oliver's intention was to put up a ladder and start painting the house.

"What a ridiculous idea," Florrie said.

"You too old," Peep said. "If you come crashin down, we'll have to shovel you up."

"Forty-six is old? Men my age are running three-legged races."

"Exactly," said Florrie. "Do something entertaining on your afternoon off."

Page laughed. "He'll need another leg. Are there volunteers?"

"Seriously, sweetheart," Florrie said. "You had a man from the Yard come and do the scraping."

"At great expense. And now he's through."

Florrie heard his regret. "The way to handle that is to have him come back."

"Florrie dear, that's the way I would have handled it if we still had money."

He saw her startled look. "Have we run out of money?"

He had pledged to Florrie when he took her from the cotton fields that she would never have to worry about anything again. As far as he knew she never had. He told his troubles to Peep and told Florrie nothing. Protecting her, he called it when Peep disapproved. But now all at once—no, not all at once, just since noon when he propped that damned ladder against the house—a rebellion had started, a powerful urge to unburden himself, to open the cage and let the tigers run out.

Page should know her father was a thief. Florrie ought to be told how her bungling husband was running the family business with a blindfold on. . . .

"Are we," Florrie repeated, "out of money?"

"Not entirely. We're not in the poorhouse. We. Uh. We just have to be careful because business is bad."

"We have to Cut Corners," Page put in.

Florrie looked around the table. "Haven't we been doing that for years and years?"

"*We* has," said Peep, and went out to the kitchen.

Florrie had not applied herself to Cutting Corners because in her view she spent no money. She did not buy groceries; Peep did that. She did not drive the car so she bought no gas; and she rarely bought clothes, preferring to costume herself in the elegant antiquities she found in the attic.

She turned again to Oliver. "Shouldn't we by now be making a recovery?"

"Recoveries take time."

"Oliver," she said, "what happened to the money?"

His head swam as if he were already tilted against the second story. "It's too complicated to get into now."

"But Uncle Oliver," said Page, "what did happen to it? Didn't my father have money?"

"And your father, Oliver. All of the Gages have always had money."

Peep boomed from the kitchen, "Money come—and it go!"

"Like a tide," said Oliver, barely audible. The tide right now was pretty far out, but there were indications things might get better. For the last three years he had hung on by his toenails, shuffling small payments among his creditors and trading on the Gage name until he had worn it so thin he felt naked behind it. Then a piece of luck: a buyer came along for T.G.'s house and paid straight-out cash. A few weeks later Oliver gained another inch by selling Janet's car and her custom-made furniture for way more than he figured they were worth. Risking those profits (plowed back into the business in Anna Catherine's name) he had bid on a clothing store and a small addition to the elementary school. To his surprise, both contracts went to Gage & Sons, inspiring one of his old carpenters to come back to work. Luck bred luck, or so it seemed. Or so he *hoped,* with the ladder waiting for him.

He pushed back from the table and said with false heartiness, "Time to paint."

"Oliver," said Florrie, "you hate heights."

"I used to hate heights. I'm over it now."

She rose beside him and kissed his cheek. "'May the Lord your God hold your right hand.'"

"Thank you, Florrie."

"And I," she said, "will hold the ladder."

"Florrie, no—You go on upstairs and work on your Indians."

"I think I will enjoy painting the house."

Peep gave a little moan. "You hear that, Lord? If she gonna help, I gotta help too. She gonna want ice water ever five minutes."

Page said, "I wish I could help," thinking of the Little Hunky, of going down in it where the water snakes were. But it was the right thing to do, a high-minded thing Grandfather Gage was bound to approve of. And she had prayed for a helper this afternoon. He might be on his way. "I'll be out on the porch. Reading a book. For school," she said.

"School done out," Peep reminded.

"It's a summer project, which I mentioned to you, but you must have been asleep. Uncle Oliver," Page called, "be careful on the ladder."

Oliver was careful, but he fell to the ground about a quarter to three.

He fell at the same instant that Fate (or possibly predestination) brought a white black man into Garrison on a bus.

He was the boy Page had prayed for, although he was older, a man of twenty-one in a suit and tie. But he looked like a boy. He was nervous as a boy. He asked for directions and started on foot toward the boulevard.

Page was not reading her book when he arrived. She was pedaling her bicycle back from the hospital. When she saw a stranger standing on the porch, she was too full of everything to connect his appearance with the prayers she had prayed. It was the coat, she thought later, and the suitcase he carried.

She threw down her bike and rushed up to him. "If you're looking for the people that live in this house, they're all at the hospital. I've been there, too, but I've come home to call the Yard to send a car after them. And also," she panted, "to see if Peep left the burner burning under the coffeepot."

The young man said, "Miss BoPeep Bailey? Is she in the hospital?"

"She's at, not in. But this is not her house. Her house is around back."

"Where it should be, of course," the young man said, but he said it politely. He had a golden tan as if under his skin candles were burning.

Page looked at his suitcase. "Are you selling insurance?"

He said he was not. "Is Miss Bailey ill?"

"Are you from the North?"

From Chicago, he said.

"I thought you must be. Down here we say 'sick.' I'm Page," she said. "Page Gage."

He was Jarel McDonald.

"Are you Scotch?" she asked.

"Half scotch and half soda."

Page giggled. "Is that a joke?"

"To some people it is. About Miss Bailey—"

"Peep, we call her. Peep is fine. She's just upset. We were all upset because we thought Uncle Oliver was dead, and then when he wasn't, that all his bones were broken. And Aunt Florrie fainted in the ambulance." She stared at the man standing before her. "Why, you're the one!"

Jarel stared back.

"The one who's come to help me! And it couldn't be better—everyone's gone!" In the next ten minutes she could have him in the water! "Listen—" She trembled. "While you're waiting for Peep would you do me a favor?"

He said he wouldn't wait. He was going to the hospital.

"Oh, don't do that! By the time you're there, they'll be here!" She took hold of his sleeve and began herding him around the side of the house.

"Just give me a minute to run in and make a call and see about the burner. Then I'll bring you iced tea and show you the storehouse where I have my canoe."

He halted, amazed. "What's all this paint?" White paint everywhere. On the grass. On the lawn chairs. On a sleeping cat.

"That's what they were doing. Painting the house."

"Not Miss Bailey!"

"Oh no, not Peep." Page told him quickly how the accident happened, how the neighbor's cat (that cat right there) got between Peep's feet when she was bringing out ice water and how Peep threw the water on Aunt Florrie's back, causing her to jiggle the ladder Uncle Oliver was climbing with a fresh can of paint. "Luckily," she said, "he landed on peat moss in the flower bed. It only knocked his breath out. But they're doing X rays. Just to be sure."

Jarel McDonald (Gerald, Page called him even after he corrected her) was glad to have the iced tea and wanted time to drink it. He needed to get himself ready to meet for the first time his Greataunt Peep—his benefactress, he would address her—without whom (without which?) he could not have gone to college or bought a new suit or a bus ticket to Houston, Texas. Without whom, without which, he wouldn't be anything.

But this girl, Page, was like ants were biting her, wanting to show him a storehouse and a canoe she had in it, and then wanting him to get it down, which he did balk at because this was the South and slippery ground he was standing on: this young girl in a white neighborhood with nobody around while he was fooling with a boat that didn't belong to him.

"You want me to carry it down to the river?"

"The Little Hunky. I want us to carry it."

"I think you better wait until your uncle gets back."

"But that's why I want to, don't you see?" She had thought of this, putting ice in his glass. "He and I were going canoeing and now he'll be stiff from falling off the ladder and will still want to go, but he won't be able to carry it down."

Well, all right. He guessed he would. He'd take it to the water, but then he was leaving. (He could call Aunt Peep from the bus station and then get out of here before something happened, which he felt up his spine was just about to.)

"If you leave," said Page, "you'll disappoint Miss Bailey."

"She isn't expecting me."

He is selling insurance, Page thought. But it didn't matter why he was there when he was so close to doing what she wanted him to do. On the bank, in fact, of the Little Hunky. Not a beautiful river, but a fast-flowing river this time of year. On a rise, Page noticed, with logs going down it. A scary river that made her remember she might need a weapon.

"Do you have a knife?"

"A knife!" he said.

"Never mind." She tried to swallow, but had no saliva. "My uncle and I, we really have fun out on the river."

Jarel looked at a limb swirling by. "You're taking a chance, riding in a canoe in this kind of water."

"You float in a canoe," Page said. "And it's lovely, just lovely." She turned up her face. "Why don't we try it?"

"Why don't we try jumping off a building?"

"You can swim, can't you?"

Jarel scowled. "Listen girl, you better ask yourself can *you* swim, going fifty miles an hour to the Gulf of Mexico!"

Page laughed. She liked him this way. Loosened up. Sounding more like a boy than the college graduate he claimed to be, up at the storehouse when he laid his coat on his suitcase and took five minutes to smooth the wrinkles out.

"Come on!" she begged, barely able to breathe with the thrill and the scare of it, all so near. In a minute it could happen.

But he was walking off, leaving, like he said. Before it was done!

"Wait!" she cried. "You have to go with me!"

"I brought the boat down. That's all I'm doing."

"But you're supposed to go! That's why you're here."

He turned around. "I'm here," he said, "to visit a relative."

"You can do that too. You can do it later."

"If you want to go so bad, go by yourself!"

"You think I won't?"

"You're nuts if you do."

"I'm going," she said. "I'm going in this water whether you do or don't." And right in front of him she stepped off the pier.

"Girl!" he cried. "Girl, what are you doing!" He ran to the spot where she had been standing.

She didn't come up.

"Are you drowning down there?"

No bubbles came up.

He jumped in after her.

He had never in his life swum in a river. He was upside down. He was twisted around. *And God Almighty, where was the girl?*

She struck him in the face with arms like oars. She was stuck in the mud, hair streaming from her head in a perfect right angle, hands clutching his ears, grabbing for his shoulders and the cords of his neck.

She was drowning *him!* In a stinking river. In the goddam South!

His anger saved them. Anger and terror and his young man's strength that kept calling up power from the soles of his feet, generating power in his heart and his brain until he was able to do what he had to do: catch hold of the pier-footings under the water and haul himself out, dragging with him an insane girl with a dead-man's grip on his Adam's apple.

They collapsed on the pier while the Little Hunky River ran out of their clothes.

Jarel lit in at once on Page Gage. "You ruined my suit. My brand-new suit!"

She was full of water. Of the memory of water. "Your coat's not ruined."

"I caint go around just wearing a coat!"

"I'm sorry," she said and began to cry.

He was half crying too. "I'd like to wring your neck instead of these trouser legs. Jumpin in that flood! If the mud hadn't caught you, you'd be in Corpus Christi!"

"You're a wonderful swimmer."

"I didn't swim a stroke! You caint swim doodley in that kind of water." He poured half a cupful out of his shoes. "You caint canoe either. You told a big lie saying you and your uncle were takin that boat out. What you were planning was to have a little fun drowning a black boy."

Page raised her head. "Black boy?" She sat up and looked at him. "Are you delirious?"

"You figured nobody would know if the body floated off, if the jellyfish ate it."

"I was trying to find out how my parents drowned!"

Jarel pulled on his shoes. "Girl, you're the limit."

"They did drown! They drowned right here three years ago. Don't you believe me?"

"I believe you're lyin. And if you'd lie about that, you'd lie about anything." He sat straight up. "You'd lie about me." He was cold all at once, colder than he'd been at the bottom of the river. Shivering even, with a vision of bloodhounds licking at his heels. Of newspaper headlines: SWIMMING WITH A WHITE GIRL. ATTEMPTED DROWNING OF WHITE GIRL!

He leaped to his feet, semi-hysterical, and ran toward the bluff. "Aunt Peep gonna come and find me in jail!"

Page ran after him. "Who? Aunt Peep? Peep is your aunt?"

He paused to grab up the wallet he had tossed out to dry. "She spent all that money sendin me to college, now I'm goin to the pen!"

"Are you really black?"

"Hell yes, I'm black!"

"You're as white as I am."

"Who's gonna care when they're hangin me?"

"We don't hang people in Garrison County!"

"Since when?"

"Since Civil Rights! You're so smart, surely you've heard of Civil Rights."

"Surely you've heard of Selma, Alabama!"

"Well, you don't have to worry. You saved my life."

"Listen," he said, "I was savin myself. You got saved cuz you was hangin on!"

"You've sure quit sounding like you came from Chicago."

"It don't matter where I come from—it's where I'm going!" He pushed past her. "Down to that bus station and out of here!"

"Are you going down the street in those muddy pants?"

He stopped again and looked at himself.

"If you have another pair, I'll take those to the cleaners."

"How's any cleaners gonna help me now?"

"Gerald—"

"Jarel!"

"It's too late anyway. Look up yonder."

He looked toward the bluff. Three persons were looking at him.

"Peep and Aunt Florrie," Page said. "And that's Uncle Oliver all stooped over." Page waved her arms. "Don't come down. We're coming up!"

"I'm not coming up!"

"Where are you going, Gerald? Back in the river?"

Jarel stayed overnight and ate supper at the table with Page, Oliver, and Florrie and supposedly Peep, but she never sat at her place. She went to and fro, kitchen to dining room and back again.

Florrie's voice fluttered over them with snippets from poems mixed with subdued little silences when she pictured Oliver lying lifeless in the flower bed.

Page was required to tell once more what crazy notion made her jump in the river. When she got to the reason, they cried again—all except Jarel—as they had on the lawn when they heard it the first time.

Jarel was the centerpiece, the golden hero with a college degree. They couldn't stop looking at him: a black man; yet not a black man, strange even to Peep since all his life his mother, Odessa, had sent her aunt pictures of a black boy growing up (a neighborhood boy), the reason being (Jarel said in his best Chicago diction) that nobody was sure Aunt Peep would spend money educating a white boy.

Then he was embarrassed and Florrie said, "But of course she would have."

"She might not would have," Peep announced, bringing in bread pudding with currant jelly to spread on top. "Might would have thought a boy as white as Jarel could look after himself."

A mauve color came up Jarel's neck. "I always had jobs." He had calmed down some, but he still had the shakes.

Florrie said soothingly, "And now you have a new job in Houston, Texas, with an important firm."

Page asked across the table, "What will you wear since your suit is ruined?"

"That suit'll be fine," Peep said. She had spent sixty years cleaning white linen suits. "Muddy spots take to milk like kittens."

Oliver was asked if his back was hurting when he said after dessert he was going to bed.

Page said, "You were all bent over up on the bluff."

Oliver winked at Jarel. "I was bent over the evidence of a thief on my property. Nice white coat and a good-looking suitcase."

"I'm sorry, sir, you found your storehouse open—" Jarel glared at Page.

"—and your canoe missing."

Oliver shook his hand. "You saved my niece. That's all that matters."

He went up then, taking Florrie with him. Peep and Jarel went in the kitchen and shut the door. Left by herself, Page sat on the bluff and watched the Little Hunky with moonlight on it.

In the morning Page said to Jarel while Peep was at her house putting on her hat for the ride to the bus station, "It was nice of you yesterday to pull me out of the river."

"It was the farthest thing from nice I ever did."

"I think I might marry you."

"Girl!" he said. "You are truly crazy!"

"Anna Catherine is my name if you'd like to write me."

"I would not like to write you! Or ever see you again!"

"Oh, but you will. You saved my life, so you have to look after me until I die."

He backed, wall-eyed, into the china closet.

"Grandfather Gage left Peep an inheritance because naming her was the same thing as saving her life. She had a claim on him. He put it in his will. If you have a will, you could put it in yours."

"You listen to me!"

"Gerald," she said, "will we have black children?"

The bus came early, which it never had, but even before it came into view Jarel said his good-byes and went to stand at the station door, bag in hand.

"Facing east," said Oliver, "toward his first big job."

"In the Exprason Building," Peep said.

"Esperson," said Oliver, watching regretfully as Jarel boarded. "I wish I could have kept him to work at the Yard." Jarel's accounting degree hung on Peep's wall in a nice gold frame he pulled out of his suitcase before supper. "He's a smart young man."

"Kinda jittery though," Peep brooded.

"A lot happened to him when he stopped off in Garrison. And naturally he's skittish about living in the South. But he'll be all right. Everybody starting out has to worry about something."

"And some does that ain't startin out."

"Does the last word always have to be yours?"

Peep waved at the bus. "There he go." She turned to Oliver. "You jittery too."

Oliver sighed. "Last night I had a long talk with Florrie. I told her everything. About T.G. About the trouble at the Yard."

"You musta jarred something loose when you fell off the ladder."

"Anna Catherine jarred me, almost drowning herself. Imagine that child, carrying around such an idea." He cleared his throat. "And Florrie too. Florrie had a surprise."

"Uh-oh. She got a lover in a closet?"

"Florrie confessed that when we were first married her biggest dream was to work at the Yard. To work at my side."

"I said she had starch! It just needed sprinkling."

"She never wanted to be a poet, trailing around in pajamas and scarves."

"She like it pretty good now."

"She's made the most of it, but back at the start what she really wanted was a job at the lumberyard. When she saw I'd be against having her work, she turned literary to distinguish herself in some kind of way from the ladies giving teas and going to club meetings."

"Miz Florrie," said Peep. "Keep her out of my kitchen."

"She wants to work at the Yard now and help me out of this fix."

"We saw yesterday what a help she can be."

"I appreciate it," Oliver said, "but her poet job has taken over now. And it wouldn't do to let the county down."

"She going along with that?"

"Said she would, but she's worried about the money."

"You aint, a-course. You got plenty money."

Oliver started the car. "I see where you're heading and we're not going there."

She attempted regularly to give him her inheritance. "What do I need money for?"

"To support your relatives." Oliver backed into the street. "Look at what you were able to do for Jarel."

"And for all those cousins I bailed out of jail. Been a pity, wouldn't it, if they'd had to straighten up and take care of theirselves."

"There is no way, Peep, I will ever risk losing what my father left you. Now tell me what you need at the grocery store."

"I don't buy groceries on the Lord's Day." She set her hat straight. "Drive around town. Less look at houses. How you like that yeller one over there?"

"I don't like it. Houses ought to be white."

"Uh-huh. Like only white folks is the ones can have money and everbody else got to borry from them."

"Oh, I see. Now I'd be borrowing."

"You was always borrowing. I took that for granite."

"And if I couldn't pay you back?"

"I wouldn't die till you did."

Oliver said crossly, "Stop meddling, Peep! I'll get my house painted in my own time."

"No way Miz Florrie ever gonna let you up a ladder again. And what about the upstairs gutters fallin off? And the boards in the hall that are 'bout to go through?"

Oliver stopped Princess Pat at a green light. "I know you love me. I know you would do anything to help me out, but I cannot take your money, borrowed or not. It goes against everything I ever knew about anything."

"Better move on," Peep said placidly, "or old man Thompson gonna honk you on."

Further down the street she commented mildly, "Start out small."

"Peep, dammit!"

"Borry just enough to shape up the house. Then borry a little more to fix up the Yard. Nobody got to know except you and me."

"I am goddammed tired of keeping secrets!"

"Then put it in the paper." She grinned widely. "Wouldn't be no worse than 'Gator Flattened on Friday.'"

"I will not take your money."

"You and your pride gonna wait five years to git your house painted white?"

"Maybe ten."

"Well, me and my pride is painting mine black. Maybe tomorrow." She reached for the armrest. "You gonna wreck your car if you don't watch out."

"Whoever heard of a house painted *black*?"

"In two or three days, everbody livin in Garrison County."

"I won't stand for it, Peep. I won't allow it."

"Didn't figure you would." She sighed with contentment. "Whenever it suits you, we'll draw up the papers."

Page came into the kitchen at a quarter to five. "Is it still Sunday?"

"You'd know," Peep said, "if you had to fix supper and you was still tired from fixin dinner."

"I'll cook. I'll have biscuits and eggs."

Peep sat in her rocker. "Go on and do it."

"Would you really let me?"

"I'm thinkin about it."

Page sat on her stool. "I'm Anna Catherine again."

"You always was."

"I mean I'm through with being Page. I was hiding then."

"Is that a fact?"

Anna Catherine put her head in BoPeep's lap. "Did you know all along? Did everyone know?"

"More or less. Reach me my piller."

"Don't go to sleep—I want to tell you something."

"Is the burner still goin under the coffeepot?"

Anna Catherine turned it off. "I think I've caught on to the boyfriend business. You scare them, that's all. Men are very attracted to frightening situations."

"Like rats to traps?"

"Traps are too final. This is more like bait."

"You been baiting some boy?"

"Your nephew," Anna Catherine said, watching her closely. "I scared him at the river, and I scared him really bad in the dining room."

Peep rocked. "Didn't seem to me he was too took with you."

"He was, though, and he'll be back. In just a few weeks, when he gets his first check and has a little money to take me out."

"The one you be scaring with this kind of talk is your Uncle Oliver. Jarel look white, but he black as can be."

"I don't care about that."

"There's folks that does. And one other thing."

Peep gazed at the ceiling. "He bout to git married."

"He is not, Peep!"

"Sure is. She Japanese."

"You're making this up."

"She a little bitty thing. A tap dancer."

Anna Catherine went to the window and looked out. "I knew

you wouldn't like it. And now you're lying to me. You lie to me a lot, and when I get older I'm going to hold it against you."

"You cryin?"

"I'm looking at the daylilies!"

"There's boys around here heard about you jumpin in the river and they's so scared they caint do nothin but hunt for your number in the telephone book."

Anna Catherine faced Peep. "That's another lie."

"I knew one of ems name. Let me think."

"Russ? Was it Russ?"

"Russ. That's it."

———————

Annette Sanford lives in Ganado, Texas, where she taught high school English for twenty-five years and began her writing career, which has spanned thirty years. *Lasting Attachments,* her short story collection, won the 1989 Southwestern Booksellers Association Literary Award. Currently, she is completing a second collection.

I had been working a long time on another story that I thought was almost finished. Then it died one afternoon, lay down in its tracks and would go no further.

When such a thing happens, there's usually a long bad patch, days or weeks of tentative beginnings before a new story starts.

This time, however, one was waiting in the wings, stomping around back there, ready to get going. Before I could clear my desk I had to stop and type the words In the Little Hunky River.

The Little Hunky River? Where did that come from?

Page Gage started talking—and BoPeep in the kitchen. Oliver entered and brought Florrie with him. A white black man got off a bus. It took 170 hours to sort out all they told me.

Where they got it, I don't know.

Jennifer Moses

GIRLS LIKE YOU

(from *Ontario Review*)

This your second baby? New White Lady say. She make a
pursed-up face like she taste something bad. Pink lipstick
lips all squished together like some worm. It say on your transcript
that this your second baby.

Yeah white ho', what of it? Onlies I don't say that. Don't say
nothin. They hates that, when you don't say nothin. It say fuck-all
on my transcript. Ain't no transcript say I got no baby. First White
Lady gone tell her. First White Lady even uglier than new White
Lady: teeth all yellowish, dent down her forehead like she hit with
a truck, big butt and no tits. Titless Wonder I called her.

Full name?

But I just gives her more nothin. Say on my transcript full name.

Okay, Retha, she say. You want to play dumb, play dumb. Your
life.

Fuck right 'bout that, bitch.

Only I got a piece of paper here from the School Board say it my
job to educate you while you pregnant. Would you like to see it?

All I like to see is *Oprah*. On any minute. Momma and Jancine
(that my baby girl) sitting in the front room right now warmin' up
to watch. Peoples gets on say the stupidest thing. And old Oprah
sleek and fat like a hog and rich too, but still no man wants her. I
like to know why? Maybe she secretly like the womens? Still, I like

to get on the Oprah show, say: Where I come froms, the momma do it in fronts of the childruns, see? Dat way we knows how to give good pussy. See old Oprah's mouth drop open. Hear her talkin' all that feelings shit.

That a good one.

New White Lady snort, wrinkle up her nose. Say: Says on your transcript you in the seventh.

Read real good, don't you?

Say on your transcript you fifteen years old. How come you still in the seventh?

You know everything, bitch, so you tell me. Only again I don't say that. I don't say nothin. Let her guess.

Okay, she say after a little bit more time pass. Now I can hear the TV real good: the Oprah song has come on, and the clapping from the audience. Shit! So hot in this kitchen, feel like I stuck in somebody's bad breath. New White Lady sweating, too. Only she actin' like she *pretending* she ain't sweating. Like it beneath her.

Whole lot of no talkin going on here. Sure wish I had a Coke and a slice.

You think you the first pregnant teenager I ever taught? New White Lady finally say. (You leave 'em be long enough, they always start blubbering.) You think you so tough? You think at fifteen you seen everything?

Ooh my, but she worked up now. Face red. Forehead shiny. Ugly old gray-yellow hair frizzing. Probably dried up inside, that why she so mean. No juice left. That what happens when you git old.

Fine, Retha, we'll just sit here for an hour while you think about it. Then tomorrow I want a paper on the subject.

That when I git mad. Bad enough bein' bossed at school from that snot-nosed Liver Lips (real name Ms. Milton). Bad enough sit-tin' through Algebra with that fat-assed Ms. Gireaux (I calls her Miss Girdle). But this my kitchen; this my house; this my baby.

You got a booger hangin out, I finally say.

What?

A big gooby one. Hangin out your nose.

New White Lady swipe at her nose with the back of her hand, then reach down to her pocketbook, lookin' for a tissue. Then she wipe her nose, real careful like. Tissue all wadded up, like it used before. Some of these people, their hygienic care ain't too good.

I big so no ones mess with me too much, not anymore. Didn't no one at school knows I had a baby growin' insides me. Just kept puttin' on them big old shirts, and no one can tells the difference. I knew, though. Your monthlies stop, mean something going down. (Not like Jancine, that my baby girl. When I pregnant with Jancine, I too little to know anything. How I know I pregnant? Now I experienced.) Ain't no one at school gonna mess with me nohows. Then one days it so hot and in the middle of Social Studies class teacher droning on and on, she won't never shut up, that Liver Lips, and then she looks right at me and she say: Miss LaMonte? Are you with us today?

No, I am a clone of Miss LaMonte, you blind?

Class crack up at that one. But Liver Lips, she just go on.

Perhaps then you can tell us where Miss LaMonte went? Perhaps she's on Mars?

She a Martian, yeah. She come down zap your butt.

(No liver-lipped Ms. Milton gonna get the best of me. She think she better than the rest us niggers. Talkin' all the times about when she was All-Honors at Southern. Right down the road, she always saying. Historical black school, she say. Who care?)

Do you have your book today, Miss LaMonte? Or did you perhaps leave it on Mars?

(All those little kids lookin' at me. Cause I kind of a hero to them, being so much bigger. Liver Lips with her tight-wrapped hair put me in mind of aluminum foil. I could take her down in ten seconds flat.)

Book here, I say.

Perhaps, then, you could tell us what system of government we have here in the United States of America?

Fuck the United States of America. This ain't no United States of America. This here Baton Rouge. Woman think I can't read a map.

So I says: the answer is—and then I say the first thing that comes to mind—Ain't nobody, ain't *nobody,* can beat our low low everyday prices!

Oooh. Kids falling out laughin'. Liver Lips face turnin' Coca-Cola colored, looking like she about to start blubbering.

But then I gets to feelin' woozy-like, like my head fill with bubbles, then my throat fill up too, then I hot down the back of my neck and nex' thing I know I wakin' up all them boogery pimple-face kids lookin' down at me and Liver Lips herself holdin' up my head.

Takes me down to school nurse. School nurse dumb as they come. School nurse takes my temperature, like I got fever. Makes me breathe in and out. Ask me all kind of dumb-butted questions: have breakfast? What you eat? (I eat four Chips Ahoy.) Stupid cow finally says, You pregnant again girl? Two days later I out of school again, back in the Special Program for Girls Like You.

First White Lady was always asking stupid questions. Where you from? she say. Dumb bitch. Where I from? Ain't she sitting in my house? North Twelve Street, Baton Rouge, Louisiana. No, she say, I mean, where your *people* from? What part of the country? What part Africa?

What I want to know about Africa? Africa where they got all thems voo-doo peoples dying of AIDS, not just the homos and whores but the women and children too. Africa where they got all that dying, and I mean every day. She think I stupid? She think I don't know my World Events?

What part of the South? Did your ancestors work the plantations? It's your history, it might be interesting to find out.

Yo Momma. Where great-great-great-great-grandmammy born? She come over on the *Mayflower?* So I just looked at First White Lady like she some ghost all covered with slobbery-spit.

(First White Lady kept wanting to know who Jancine daddy is.

But I never would tell. She kept shaking her head. Only twelve years old, she say. That a tragedy.)

Truth is, I didn't really knows I got a baby inside me first time it happen, with Jancine, until Miss Caesar who live next door ask me. Then she tell my momma. Then the shit really hit the fan.

Who the daddy? First White Lady say. Then she nag me to go see some Jew lady social worker she know.

How this happen? Tell me, she say.

Momma said she be right back, but she didn't come right back. She gone all day. She missed *Oprah,* missed *Price Is Right,* missed *Fresh Prince*. Me and Oline (that my sister) went and got us some Super Fry chicken for dinner, ate it right there. Momma gone when we get back to the house. Her boyfriend there, waitin' on her. Watching TV. Man send Oline out to get mo' chickens. That when he do it to me.

Man put his ding-dong in you, white slime squirt out, you can get pregnant, everybody know that. I always big girl, even at twelve I got big titties, almost as big as Momma's, and big hips, so I not sure what is what, monthlies or no monthlies. What you doing to me? But man say hush gal this ain't nothin to worry 'bout. Man say: quiet little bitch, I ain't gonna hurt you none, I your friend. I love you, why I want hurt you? Man smelled bad, too, like something rotten. Like rotten fruit. Then man say: yo momma like it like this. Man say: apple don't fall far from the tree. Man say: you a woman now.

Momma real mad when Principal call her that first time. What you done do girl? You shame me? Face turning all kinds of purple. Me and her, we gotta sit in those real slimy chairs they got in Principal's office, back of our legs sticking to the cushion, while Principal tell Momma about the Special Program for Girls Like You.

Say: School Board increase Special Needs Funding. Say: School Board sending Special-Train teachers right to your Place of Residence.

Later Momma and the man yellin' then *pop,* Momma down. Man gone. Momma rubbing her cheek and crying over that man like he some superhero. Ugly man with sour smell, color of egg-plant. I only twenny-eight years old don't I have no right 'round here? Ain't I got a right to have me a life? She in her bed, cryin' all night 'cause that rotten-fruit smellin' nigger gone and me and Oline have to say hush now, Momma, it get better. (Oline bring her two pieces ice in a towel for her cheek and a bottle of Budweiser.)

Cryin' and yellin' that she didn't raise no girl to be no ho'. Then Miss Caesar who live next door come runnin' over say: You blind? Everyone know that man no good.

And *that* how I get Jancine.

I almosts feels sorry for New White Lady. She try, I say that for her. Drives up every day three o'clock sharp in that Chevrolet mini-van, color of a blue popsicle. She got her windows rolled up, her doors locked. Air-conditioning going full blast. Looks right and left. Then walks right up to the front porch, calls through the screen. Retha? Retha? It me. Mrs. Warton. (I call her Mrs. Wart. Oline calls her Mrs. Fart.)

Baby kicking? she say.

Drinking nuff milk? Eating right? Sleeping?

She put the ends of her thumbs together and the rest of her fingers go straight up and she say B go this way and D go this way just like a bed. Her hands suppose to be the bed. The silent E make the vowel say it name, she say. What she think I am, two year old?

She say she got a daughter jus' my age and two sons too. Name Elizabeth and Joe Jr. and Chuck, like upchuck. She say Elizabeth want to be a nurse when she grow up. What you wan' be, she say? You smart, she say. You smarter than you think.

Every day she come I think she ain't gon come no more. She come all the ways from Bocage or the Country Club Louisiana or some fancy do-daw place with swimming pools in every backyard barbecue pits family room with giant color remote control TV and them built-in bars and wall-to-wall carpeting so soft you feel like yo' feet are melting so what she know about me? One day I gon git myself a Cadillac or a Lincoln Town Car and I jus' gon cruise on by old Mrs. Wart's house and say hello.

Last time when I pregnant with Jancine my tits got real big but they didn't droop none. Now they big and droopy-like. Couple mean kids callin' me Great Fruit but I come back on 'em kick 'em in the nuts they don't call me no Great Fruit no more. What them little kids with their little doinkers hanging between their legs know 'bout no sex? Girls getting all worked up about doin' the thang-thing but ain't no great thing once you does it. First it hurt then maybe you git to liking it some but then it all over jes like that anyways, and you panties wet all day long just from the slime going drip drip drip out your pussy. Boys wanting it bad and if you hangin' with the main man you gots to do what he say and my man say, What you 'fraid of Retha, ain't you my woman? You no baby no more you fourteen years old, and he feeling me all over, feeling my titties and my butt and his hand up my pants and I caint barely see *Family Matters* but it a dumb one anyways I seen it before. We gets to doin' it, know what I say? His name Scooter. His real name somethin' else but everyone call him Scooter. I seen him around. All the girls knows him. Then one day he come up to me he say: Who you? Looking me over all slow. I say: I Janet Jackson, want my autograph? Soon we laughing. Then we doin' it. At school people sure enough looks up to me 'cause I hanging with the man got the stuff. Got him the look. Got him the CDs. Got him the car. We all over in that car and he good-looking too. Don't smell like no rotten-fruit man. Don't smell like no dead thing. Scooter got a fine, clean, fresh smell, cause he clean all over. Clean inside and out. Shower three time a day. Wash that car till it shine. Yes ma'am and no ma'am to his Maw Maw who he live with. The lady work cleaning in the Hilton. Don't take no drugs either. Don't smoke no smokes. New pair sneakers every other week he say he don't like things old and scuffed-up none. He sweet to Jancine too. He take her and me drivin' up the river past all them stinking refineries past all them sugarcane fields and the paper plant rotten egg smell coming out of it and he jus' laughin'. Say he ain't gonna work no paper plant. Say he ain't gonna be no garbage man or no janitor or gardener. Say he goin' places, and he is.

I feel like some somebody now. I sure does.

Come home Momma sucking on that can of Budweiser. Oline goin' up and down the street on that fancy new bicycle with the Pocahontas wheels, her little-girl-butt tight and high in the air. Gotta keep an eye on Momma now when she in these mean mood sucking on Budweiser and no man about she say she off men for good! She and Miss Caesar from next door talking late at night and Miss Caesar shaking her old head (she so old nothin' left but bone) saying You give yourselves a while, honey, you ain't the first woman gonna make it by herself. But Momma gettin' meaner and meaner one day she throws all my new clothes that Scooter done buys me out the closet calling me ho' this and ho' that. Another day Jancine and I in bed sleeping she start whapping me with the back of her hairbrush. Why she go do that for? I sock her, she crumple down. I in deep shit now but what she got go bust my butt with her hairbrush? So I say good-bye I don't need you gonna go where I wanted. But over North Street Maw Maw says No teenage slut staying 'round here with no crying baby. So now I got no place to go but Scooter say it okay, you come back when the old lady go to work. She work late shift. And that just what I did. And that very night we do it in her bed and he just laugh and laugh.

That was the happy time.

New White Lady got some of the dog-ugliest clothes I ever seen. Shoes like them nurses wear, rubber wavy soles. Glasses make her look like a frog. Hair like a dirty gray mop. And them legs: ugly blue veins stickin' out of them. She don't even notice. She tell me she got a degree in Education and another in Social Work. Like she some kind of genius.

You can trust me, Retha, she say. I just give her the look. She don't even blink.

You wants to go back to school, you got to keep plugging away, she say. Give me a book. Book 'bout nigger talking to God. Turn into lesbo at end and make these clothes. Lady nigger wrote it, her picture on the back. I hates that book, I tell New White Lady. Book called *Color Purple*. What Color Purple? Ain't bout no *purple*. What kind of dumb-ass title. Should be called: *Nigger Git Fucked By Step-Daddy Turn Dyke*.

How it make you *feel*? she say. Just like on Oprah. Wants to know my feelings.

Make me good and angry. Make me want to throw that there book into the toilet. Nigger lady wrote it, but wouldn't never happen that way. Girl never would git rich makin' no clothes, doing the thang-thang with women, rubbin' their pussies together, make me sick.

She give me another book. This one call *Bluest Eye*. She say, What you think? I don't tell her it make me cry.

When Jancine come thought I on fire. Hurt like I never done hurt before. Hot pain in my spine. Water rushin' between my legs. Who the daddy who the daddy? Nurse want to know. But I tells, then what? Then Momma come kill me for sure. Who the daddy? This chile ain't old enough for no baby, she barely out of diapers. Twelve years old, ain't that a damn shame. Where her momma? (It Oline call 911 'cause Momma cold out on the bed). Hospital nice, though. Where they put me after Jancine got born, prettiest room I ever saw, with pink curtains and flowery wallpaper. Could have stayed there forever. Chocolate and vanilla ice cream. All I got to do is ring a button on my bed nurse come give me Coke. But they make me leave. Then Jancine she up screaming all night, and me bleeding out my privates, and Momma saying she too young to be nobody's grandmother. It gonna hurt again, I guess. Time coming. I try not to think about it too much, all that hot pain.

But the thing hurt most of all was when Scooter, he start takin' up with this bitch calls herself Raven. Cow mo' like it. One them girl-cows always mooing after him. Tell me I a slut and a whore. Then I kicked out of school and no ones talks to me no more. I in the Program for Girls Like You. Then those neighborhood boys whispering: Great Fruit. But I fix them. At home, Momma doing nothing but sucking on that beer bottle, gittin' fat. Oline growing her own pair titties. Jancine crying. New White Lady giving me books to read, but I don't tell nobody about them, they mine. New White Lady be gone soon, too. I almost glad when Scooter done git hisself killed.

———————

Jennifer Moses lives in Baton Rouge with her husband and three small children. Her short stories have been published in *Story, Michigan Quarterly Review, Press, The Gettysburg Review, Commentary, ACM,* and others. Her first book, a work of nonfiction entitled *Food and Whine,* is forthcoming in 1999. She also writes regularly for *The Washington Post.*

"*G*irls Like You" was the first story I wrote about Retha's family. At the risk of sounding pretentious, I was seized by Retha and her plight, so much so that I couldn't stop writing about her. Some months after I wrote "Girls Like You," I realized that I was in fact writing a novel. I'm now living with Retha's entire extended family.

Stephen Dixon

THE POET

(from *TriQuarterly*)

It's snowing, he's in Washington, D.C., carrying his radio
news equipment back to the office (heavy tape recorder, mike
and mike stands, tapes, extension cords, briefcase of books, news-
papers, magazines); gave up on finding a cab; snow slashing his
face to where he can barely see two feet in front of him, must be
eight to ten inches on the ground already, twenty inches or more
are predicted. Snow started this morning when he was taking the
trolley to work, let up, his boss told him to go to the Capitol, which
was his regular beat, and get a few stories and interviews and about
ten choice minutes apiece from some hearings going on, then from
the office window of a congressman he was interviewing he saw
the snow coming down blizzard-like. "Jesus," he said and the congressman said "What's up?" and turned around and said "Holy
smokes; well, worse comes to worse, if I can't get to my apartment
across town I'll spend the night here on the couch." He called his
editor, it's around 3 P.M. now, and Herb said to hustle right back,
government's been shut down, "You might as well get here before
you can't get here, as we're short of air material so can use whatever you got so far." Called cabs, waited for cabs he called, went
into the street and tried hailing the few passing cabs, for they're allowed to pick up four different fares at four different spots; nothing. So he'll walk, he thought, slowly make his way back till he

153

finds a cab or bus going his way. It's about a mile to the office on K Street from where he is now. Or even farther—two miles—for these streets are so long. No bus, and when he stuck out his thumb several times, no cab or car stopped. Well, who can blame them, for nobody wants a sopping-wet rider or stranger in his car and all his sopping-wet gear. Walked about a half-hour in the snow, only has rubbers on, "trudged," he means, instead of "walked," feet are frozen, hands will be next, pants soaked to the knees, doesn't see how he can make it to the office with all this equipment—it must weigh sixty pounds altogether and is cumbersome to carry. He might have to go in someplace, a government office building if one's still open or a museum, and plead with someone there to store his stuff till tomorrow. Should have left it in the House radio/TV gallery while he had the chance, then walked to the office with just the tapes to be edited and aired, and he might have got a hitch without all the gear, when a car pulls up, driver leans over the front seat, rolls down the window, and says "Need a lift? I'm heading toward Georgetown, I hope I can get there before I have to abandon this car, but you seem stuck." It's the Poetry Consultant to the Library of Congress, did an interview with him a few months ago; same outfit and tobacco smell: tweed jacket and button-down shirt, bow tie, pipe back in his mouth, smoke coming out of the bowl. "Gosh, you bet, but I'm awfully wet and I've got all this stuff with me," and the poet says "So what, this rattle-trap's seen much worse," and puts his blinkers on, jumps out of the car and helps him stick the equipment into the backseat, they both get in and the poet says "Where to?" and he tells him and the poet says "That on the way to Georgetown? I still haven't got my bearings of this town," and he says "It's sort of, with a slight diversion, but I wouldn't want you going out of your way—you've been too kind as it is," and the poet says "Ah, listen, you help a guy in need, you earn a few extra coins to use in the slot machines in heaven, so why not? If it's at all feasible, I'll take you to your door, and if we get stuck in a drift, you'll help push me out. You must have a ton of belongings back there—what do you *do*? A *TV* repairman?" and he says "Radio, a newsman, you don't recognize me, sir?" and the poet says "Why, you famous? Someone I should be listening to to know who's who in town?" and he says "Me? Just starting out, but a small news service so I get to cover just about everything. I interviewed you when you took up your position. Your first news conference. I mean, you gave one, right after you got to Washington, also read a poem for the TV news cameras, and then I asked you for a more personal interview and you granted me one in your office." "No kidding. I did that? Did I say anything intelligent? But I must be a nice guy, seems like, but a forgetful one. Maybe it's your hat and your snowy eyebrows," and Gould takes off his hat and rubs his eyebrows and the poet says "You want to shake the chapeau over the backseat?" and he does and the poet says "And the snow on your shoulders and hair—you'll catch a cold," and he says "Sorry, should've brushed myself off before I got in here," and the poet says "Don't worry, nothing'll hurt this heap and these are intemperate times where just survival is in order," and looks at Gould and says "You look a little familiar. What'd we talk about? Did I dispense my usual nonsense, for I tend to freeze up before you electronic news guys when you jut your paraphernalia in my mug," and he says "No, you were fine, my boss said. He was afraid, in his terms, I'd get a supercilious literary stiff, since I was the one who suggested my going to your press conference, your building being so close to the Capitol, which I normally work out of. But you know—about your job, what you'll do in it for the year you're here or two years if you feel like staying on. What poetry means in America—there never was a time it commandeered, you said, anything close to center stage in the States. And how you plan to make it more a part of the mainstream—your primary goal," and the poet says "I propounded the possibility of that? What an idiot! And of course I gave no ways how I'd go about it. Listen, poetry will always be for a small devoted clientele, and nobody in government's interested in it in the slightest. My position's a sham— no one consults me and I can't find anyone to consult—and it took a coupla months to learn that. But I am getting plenty of writing done—teaching's much tougher and more time-consuming—and meeting a few nice people, though no one who's read a stitch of my work or knew me from Adam till I arrived here, and I know they think anyone calling himself a poet's a joke, except Sandburg and Frost, because they were homespun and made it pay. Next time disregard any poet who takes on a government sinecure, even with the word poetry in it, or holds a press conference, at least during the first two months of his job." The drive's slow, poet's funny, garrulous, and lively, slaps his knee, relights his pipe several times, offers him a candy, and when he refuses, a mint and then a stick of gum, drops him off in front of his office building, Gould shakes his hand and says "I can't thank you enough, sir. I would've frozen out there if you hadn't showed." The poet says "Drop in on me if you like—when I'm there, door's always open. I can use the company—all the officials and librarians in the building stay away from me as if I've the plague. I won't have anything to say into your machine, but we can have a coffee and chat." He tells his boss what happened—"I meet him in a blizzard and he turns out to be the nicest guy on earth." "Did you get another interview with him? Would have been a good bit; Washington conked out by its worst storm in twenty years but it doesn't stop the muse." "Oh come on; the guy helped me out of a terrific spot." "You could have put the recorder on the floor, held the mike up to him while he drove. He would have loved it, maybe composed a sonnet about the storm, on the spot. Poets die for such attention, and like I told you on the phone, with the Hill probably shut down the next two days, we'll need more tape than you ever could have brought in," and for the first time since he got the job he thinks he has to get out of this profession.

Now he hears the poet's in a nursing home and most likely will never come out. He's past ninety, has been sick and so disoriented that he hasn't been able to come to his Maine summer cottage for two years. Gould met him once up here; no, twice. First time at a reception after a poetry reading ten years ago. Was sitting next to him and said "Excuse me, sir, you no doubt wouldn't remember

me, but around twenty-five years ago you did something for me
I was always thankful for and could never forget," and the poet said
"I did? We're acquainted? Here, at the colony, or at my university?" and he said "No, this is the first time I've seen you since the
incident. You were the Poetry Consultant then—this took place in
D.C.—and I was a radio news reporter, and one of the worst bliz-
zards to ever hit the city was going on and I had all this radio
equipment to carry back to my office. I couldn't get a cab so I
thought I'd shlep the stuff rather than leave it in the Capitol building, which is where I worked from. Nothing was transistorized
then, everything was still tubes and complicated circuitry, or at
least my tape recorder. That's right, some radio newsmen had started
to use these hand-held ones, but my outfit stayed with the enormous Wollensaks because they said the sound quality was better.
I'm just trying to show how heavy my equipment was—metal mi-
crophones and mike stands—and so how grateful I was to you
for giving me a lift," and the poet said "How'd I do this again?"
and he said "You stopped me on the street in the middle of a blinding blizzard—you were in your car and must have seen me strug-
gling in the snow. I'm not getting this out right, but without
knowing who I was and that I'd even interviewed you in your office a few months earlier when you started your position, you offered me a ride back to my office. You even jumped out of the car
and helped me with my equipment. It was—I don't mean to em-
barrass you with this but—one of the most magnanimous kind-
nesses ever done to me, for you were risking your life almost. Oh,
that's going too far, though the streets had to be very slippery and
big drifts were piling up fast. I know, for I was trying to wade
through them, without too much luck, and I don't even know if
you made it back to your Georgetown residence after you dropped
me off," and the poet said "Where'd all this happen again?" and he
said "Washington—when you were the Poetry Consultant; your
first year. Winter, during this record-breaking snowstorm, and you
were probably driving home from the Library of Congress, told
like everyone else to get the heck home while you still had the

chance. They closed—the government did—all their offices early because of the storm, Congress included. But who actually does give the order for the government to close up? I just thought of that. Probably no one person or office but each branch, given the separation of branches and such, or even each department gives orders for its own closing, wouldn't that seem right?" and the poet said "Don't know," and stood up and said "Lucy, listen to this. This nice young man here. I stopped for him in a blizzard when I was the Consultant in Poetry in Washington and gave him a lift," and he said "Consultant in Poetry? That was the official title? Now it's Poet Laureate, but—" and she said from across the room "When did all this occur?" and the poet said "I just told you; in D.C., Washington, the capital, when I was the C.P. to the Library of Congress, or should I say 'the C.P. to the L.C. in D.C.,' though no one called the Library that. The institution, you remember, which typically came with all the honors and regard money couldn't buy, but scant remuneration. I don't recall the episode myself, not even the blizzard, but this nice young man here seems to recollect it perfectly. I pulled over for him during a raging snowstorm, it seems like. Act of kindness, he calls it, because he had a bevy of heavy radio equipment for his news work, and I took pity on him, I suppose, when I saw him trekking through hills of snow. I did that. Do you recall my ever telling you of it?" and she said, people she was sitting with looking at him too, "That was around thirty years ago?" and the poet looked at Gould and he nodded and the poet said "I believe so," and she said "No, but it would be like you to do that. That's how you were. But at this moment, for me, though I remember the consultancy well, it's as if this is the first I've heard of the incident, which would also be like you—not so much not to remember but not to tell me of the good deeds you did then. But I could have forgotten," and the poet said "It was sort of nice of me to do it, wasn't it?—something I couldn't afford to do today because of my age. And I don't even drive anymore—you do, or our college-student driver. And a little self-admiration isn't undesirable from time to time if you're feeling especially low on yourself, am I wrong?" and she said "I think it's fine; anything you wish; you deserve even more," and resumed talking to the people near her. The poet said to Gould "Thank you for reminding me of it, young man. That was extremely gracious of you. Do you know the quote of Samuel Johnson about the rare friend who will help you celebrate a good review? I like things to be brought back, especially acts like that. What do you do now, still a journalist?" when a woman stopped beside them and said "Bill, I wanted to say goodnight," and he said "Well, goodnight, and I guess I'll be seeing you at the Academy this year one time," and she said "The Academy? I've never been to it, so why would you think I'd see you there?" and he said "You don't go? You never went? I haven't seen you there any number of times? The Academy in New York, the one we've been members of so many years, of Arts and Letters and things," and she said "My goodness, I thought you meant the Maine Maritime Academy training vessel, so I thought 'Why on earth does he think I'd step onto that old tub?'" and he said "Perhaps because we both spent entire summers so close to it, you in the same town and straight up the street from the pier, in fact," and she said "Yes, but there's still nothing on there for me, can't you see that? So why must you insist on winning this misunderstanding instead of simply laughing at it?" and he looked at her, mouth open, stared at the ceiling a few seconds, felt around behind him for the chair arms, grabbed them and made a move to sit but then sprung up straight, kissed her cheek, and left the room, smiling as if he'd just exchanged some simple but satisfying pleasantries, and the woman said "Lucy, you have your hands full, I see; I didn't realize how much," and Lucy said "Don't tell me, dear, let me guess."

The second time Gould met him in Maine was a year later, over drinks at a little dinner party. Gould sat down next to him and said "So, how are you, sir, you're looking fine," and the poet said "I know you? What's the name?" and he told him and the poet said "Sorry, no bell struck. What do you do, young man?" and he said "It's nice to still be considered young, but now I'm a teacher though I was once a reporter," and the poet said "For whom?" and he said "You mean teaching?" and the poet said "I mean both, whom, what, where, when, all the journalistic questions," and he said "Well, many years ago I was a newsman in Washington when you were the Consultant in Poetry," and the poet said "Lucy, latch onto this; this pleasant young man was a reporter during my Washington consult-the-poet days, can you believe it?" and she said "I think I knew that," and Gould said "Not only that, sir—and I think we talked about it before, but at a crowded party in Castine and pretty quickly—but you gave me a lift once," and the poet said "I did, on one of the roads here—your car broke down, son?" and he said "I meant in Washington then, during a tremendous snowstorm, and you stopped for me and drove me to my office, something I was always grateful for. I mean, you didn't know me and just appeared when I needed help the most because of all the heavy gear I had on me—I was in radio news, did interviews, so carried my own equipment," and the poet said "Lucy, did you hear what I did for this young man years ago? Stopped in a snowstorm, didn't even know who he was or what he did, and gave him a ride to his office when he needed one the most," and she said "It was very nice of you," and to Gould "I can tell, after so many years, that you were quite appreciative," and he said "It was wonderful, one of the most selfless acts anyone's ever done for me, because I'm telling you, this was some snowstorm—a blizzard, knocked out Washington for several days," and the poet said "Good, I'm glad you survived it and are here today to recount it," and a couple of people in the circle of chairs they're in started laughing and the poet said "Did I say something that seemed to you unintentionally funny? Well good, it's summer, and we're supposed to be relaxed, so people should laugh."

It's in Maine at the old farmhouse they rent that Gould hears the poet's in a nursing home and his wife died the past year. He asked about him and the man who tells him it says "And as far as anyone knows, the old fool's on his way out too." The man's wife says "Now that's unkind," and the man says "I only meant he was once a fairly good poet and critic, and that two to three of his poems are among the best produced by any American the last four decades, which is something, but that he's been an old fool for more than thirty years, the longest period of addlement I've witnessed in a human being. Besides, with his memory failing for years, he'd become a menace to our entire cliff colony, forgetting he turned on a gas stove, leaving his suburban van parked on a steep hill with the hand brake unengaged, and things like that." "I'm sorry to learn of it," Gould says and the man says "We were too, but worse to observe it. Most of us haven't the kind of fire insurance to cover a completely burnt house. It's punitively expensive because of the local infatuation with arson on our peninsula; nor has been devised the type of body armor needed to withstand a ramming from a megaton van into one of us or our grandkids," and Gould says "Excuse me, but I meant I was sorry to hear about his wife and illness and confinement and so on. What a pity, for what a nice man." "Excuse me, and Dolores will no doubt rebuke my pitilessness to this moribund old guy, whom we both like, mind you, enormously, and as I said, admire. But to be honest, a greater egotist, braggart, social manipulator, and literary operator never walked so assuredly through the fields of poetry, and I've run across some lulus in my time. An example, and this also of his idiocy, for it didn't start when he first became senile, you know—" and his wife says "Now that's enough," and he says "No, let me finish, since I never could make any sense to Bill on this score, simply because he refused to see anything he'd done as wrong, no matter how inappropriate, ill-considered, or just plain dumb it was. Once, an anthologist was putting together a book of poems by poets under forty. When our poet hears this, and he has his ears screwed into anything he thought could help his career, he contacts the anthologist and says 'Why haven't you asked me for any poems?' 'Because you're over forty,' the anthologist says; 'you're sixty-two.' This was a number of years ago, of course, though he never changed. And Bill's answer? 'So what? If you're compiling an anthology of contemporary American poetry I'd think you'd want my work in it, because who cares what age a poet is when you read his poems?' Does that make any sense to you? Are we talking of a truly great self-effacing un-finagling realistic guy?" and Gould says "He's, well yes, it doesn't make much sense—but still, and maybe this'll seem silly to you, but he once did something so wonderful for me that it's hard to think anything bad of him." He starts to tell the Washington story and the man says "I know, I was at some home up here when you gushed all over him in recapitulating it, but you must know that everyone has his three to four involuntary magnanimous acts to his credit, and Bill probably has a few more than that, and not just because he's survived past ninety, but listen to this," and he reels off a number of stories showing the poet manipulating people and institutions, "and I'm only going back fifty-some years, which is how long I know him," and Gould says "Still, you can't see what I'm saying? I'm sure there was this other good side to him. Not so much involuntary or momentarily magnanimous but downright selfless and big-hearted and generous. Going out of his way for a stranger when most people in the same situation—a blinding snowstorm, which also meant he couldn't have recognized me as the fellow who interviewed him months before. Ten inches on the ground, maybe another fifteen expected, and you're in your warm car with your warm pipe and you want to get to your warm home fast with maybe even a fireplace going? Risking your life, you can almost say—that's not so farfetched. The snow was piling up a couple of inches an hour and the car could skid, when if he didn't stop for me and take all the time it took to load my equipment up and drive me to my office, he might be able to make it home safely . . . anyway, the chances of it would be better. But . . . what did I start out saying? This other good side of him that I caught immediately from that one situation and which I don't hear anything of in what you're saying about him over fifty years. And the interview he granted me when I first met him. That's what I meant about that he didn't recognize me at first. He didn't have to give it. I was a shrimp of a reporter and the news service I worked for was small too. And I should've got his press conference on tape when the other radio and TV guys did, if any of them—I forget—thought there was anything potential there to even attend it, but I asked him for an interview right after. I might even have given him some cock-and-bull story that my tape jammed. I did that then to get solo interviews—lied, finagled, cajoled, et cetera, all the things you said he did," and the man says "Sure he gave you an interview. For the fame, not because of your cajolery. When Bill saw a newsman's tape recorder and mike, he saw an audience of millions and possible book buyers and poetry reading invitations and so forth. I bet you even had him read a few of his poems for radio," and Gould says "I think I did; it's what I normally would have done for an interview like that with someone in his position," and the man says "That's my point. The regular press conference was what came with the turf of being introduced as the new poetry consultant, but your solo with him was gravy that made him giddy. You showed him individual attention that also had a good chance of being on radio for a lot more time than a news report of the pro forma press conference," and he says "But if I remember, he told me to come back anytime for a coffee and chat but not to bring my tape recorder. So if that's the case—" and the man says "Ah, come on, he was only trying to show he was more interested in you than what you could do for him. But you probably would have brought your tape recorder and he would have seen it and somehow worked you around where he ended up gladly giving you another interview," and Gould says "No, I'm not getting through to you and you really can't change my initial opinion of him, though you have opened me up to him a little, mostly because I didn't know him. Anyway, he did a wonderful thing for me and I just wish everyone would do things like that for people in similar situations, and I also feel lousy about the condition he's in now," and the man says "That's not the question; we all do."

————

Stephen Dixon is the author of nineteen books of fiction, the last one, *Gould,* published in 1997. *Thirty,* in which "The Poet" appears, will be published in spring 1999. Dixon has published around 450 short stories, has been anthologized in *The Best American Short Stories, Prize Stories: The O. Henry Awards, The Pushcart Prize,* and other places. He lives in Baltimore and teaches in the Writing Seminars at the Johns Hopkins University.

I was working in Washington, D.C., about thirty-five years ago and got caught in a blizzard. A man stopped in his car—I don't know how he even saw me, the snow was so thick. Maybe he thought I was a snowman and he had a deep freezer in the trunk and wanted to bring me home to his children. He smoked a pipe, had a tweed hat, was about the age I am now, and didn't mind that the snowman sat in the front seat with him and the melt coming off of it was already flooding the floor.

It was a slow drive because of the snow and we talked about poetry and philosophy along the way; politics and weather never came up. He wasn't Robert Frost or Richard Eberhart or Daniel Hoffman, but he could have been. For the entire trip my eyes remained mostly frozen shut and the ice only snapped off of them when I got out of the car.

Wendy Brenner

NIPPLE

(from *Five Points*)

In the cafeteria fourth period Lori said she had her Uncle Bert's nipple in an envelope. We were all like, What are you talking about, and she was like, I'm not kidding, his nipple fell off and I got it and he doesn't even know I have it. We were all like, screaming, except Meghan, who was like, Right, I'm sure your own nipple falls off and you don't even notice. Lori was like, It's in my locker, I'd be delighted to show you if you don't believe me, and Meghan was like, Woo, *delighted,* well excuse me, Miss Manners, why don't you send out embroidered invitations and hold a ceremony? Then she stood up and left, because she had to make up dissecting a fetal pig from when she had mono. Lori was like, What's *her* problem.

The rest of us were like, Just ignore her, so how did you get his nipple, and Lori goes, I found it in the shower, stuck in the drain thing, I almost stepped on it. Andrea was like, In five seconds I'm going to throw up. I was like, How do you know that's what it is, how do you know it's not a scab, or something, like, else? And Lori was like, Well, he visits every year from Canada and he always walks around without his shirt on, 'cause in the morning he does, like, the Canadian Air Force exercises or something, so every year I've been like *noticing* that his one nipple looks like it's hanging on a thread. It wasn't like bleeding or anything, it was just like, not *attached* all the way. The other one was fine, but that one was like, falling off. I've been waiting for it to fall off for like, three years.

Why was it like that, I asked her. Was he born with it that way or did something happen? Did he get it caught in something, like a zipper or a stapler or something?

Andrea stood up and was like, Excuse me, I am literally going to throw up now. We watched her leave, but she was heading toward the vending machines, not the bathrooms. She's like in love with Junior Mints. Lori was like, I have no idea how it got that way but I knew it was going to fall off eventually.

All of a sudden, Michelle was like, Wait, oh my God, remember, weren't you telling us that time about how your uncle got hit by lightning on a totally clear day playing horseshoes at a wedding and how now he's thirsty all the time and he never gets cold and he knows stuff before it happens? Well, maybe it happened when the lightning hit him, maybe it hit him exactly on his nipple, or even if it hit him on his back, wouldn't that be strong enough to make his nipple fall off?

But Lori said no, that was her other uncle. Michelle was like, Oh. Then she stood up and said she had to go because she had a conference with Mr. Sternad, the new guidance counselor who's like never brushed his teeth in his life, and we were like, Bye, don't forget your gas mask.

So then it was just me and Lori sitting there, waiting for the bell to ring, and I was like, So are you going to mail it to him in Canada, and Lori just looked at me like, *Okaay,* and I was like, *What?* And she goes, *Mail* it to him? Are you feeling okay? And I was like, Well you said you put it in an envelope, so I just figured you were going to send it to him.

She just gave me this total look and was like, I don't *think* so— are you, like, mental? Then he'd know I had it, and he'd think I, like, *wanted* it or something. God, Jenny, I can't even believe you just said that! Plus, it's not that kind of envelope, it's one of those little wax-paper ones from the orthodontist, you know, that your rubber bands come in? God, though, Jenny, I still can't believe you just said that. I swear, sometimes I think you are seriously mental. She sat there staring at me with her mouth open.

I was like, Well excuse me for living on planet earth—but I didn't say anything. I was just like, Whatever. Because that's the whole thing about Lori, she never lets anything drop. It's just like the nipple, it's like, no matter how small or totally irrelevant a thing is, if she's there, forget it, she'll get ahold of it somehow, and keep bringing it up for all eternity. She's like if you had to look into one of those lit-up Revlon magnifying mirrors that make your face look like a mountainous terrain, for like twenty-four hours a day.

And, incidentally, I know I'm not the only person who feels that way, because for like six months after that, every time Meghan passed Lori in the hall, she'd wave her fingers in Lori's face like she was doing voodoo or trying to hypnotize her or something, and go, *Woo, delighted, delighted.* So Lori basically stopped talking to Meghan altogether, but the whole thing about Meghan is that ever since the whole thing with the minister at her church hitting on her, she doesn't exactly care.

Wendy Brenner received her MFA from the University of Florida and currently teaches at the University of North Carolina at Wilmington. Her stories and essays have appeared in *Mississippi Review, New England Review, Southern Exposure, Ploughshares, The Oxford American, Travel & Leisure, New Stories from the South: The Year's Best, 1995,* and elsewhere. Her first collection of stories, *Large Animals in Everyday Life,* won the Flannery O'Connor Award in 1997.

I wrote this piece to give to a friend who was attempting to put together an anthology of short prose and poetry about adolescence, inspired, she said, by the movie Welcome to the Dollhouse. *"We want a lot of sex and violence," she said, "but don't tell anybody I said that." While I was writing I was thinking of my own adolescence in suburban Chicago in the early 1980s, when my friends and I had a simultaneous disgust and fascination with the bodies and hygiene habits of our parents. A bunch of us, all girls, sat together at lunch every day in the high school cafeteria and gleefully tried to outdo each other with grotesque anecdotes.*

Tim Gautreaux

SORRY BLOOD

(from *Fiction*)

The old man walked out of Wal-Mart and stopped dead, rec-
ognizing nothing he saw in the steaming Louisiana morning. He tried to step off the curb, but his feet locked up and his
chest flashed with a burst of panic. The blacktop parking lot spread
away from him, glittering with the enameled tops of a thousand
automobiles. One of them was his, and he struggled to form a picture but could not remember which of the family's cars he had
taken out that morning. He backstepped into the shade of the
store's overhang and sat on a displayed riding lawnmower. Putting
his hands down on his khaki pants, he closed his eyes and fought
to remember, but one by one things began to fall away from the
morning, and then the day before, and the life before. When he
looked up again, all the cars seemed too small, too bright and
glossy, more like fishing lures. His right arm trembled, and he regarded the spots on the back of his hand with a light-headed embarrassment. He stared down at his Red Wing brogans, the shoes
of a stranger. For a half hour he sat on the mower seat, dizziness
subsiding like a summer storm.

Finally, he got up, stiff and floating, and walked off into the grid
of automobiles, his white head turning from side to side under a
red feed-store cap. Several angry-looking people sat in hot cars,
their faces carrying the uncomprehending disappointment of

boiled shellfish. He walked attentively for a long time but recognized nothing, not even his own tall image haunting panels of tinted glass.

Twice he went by a man slouched in a parked Ford sedan, an unwashed thing with a rash of rust on its lower panels. The driver, whose thin hair hung past his ears, was eating a pickled sausage out of a plastic sleeve and chewing it with his front teeth. He watched the wanderer with a slow, reptilian stare each time he walked by. On the third pass, the driver of the Ford considered the still-straight back, the big shoulders. He hissed at the old man, who stopped and looked for the sound. "What's wrong with you, gramps?"

He came to the window and stared into the car at the man, whose stomach enveloped the lower curve of the steering wheel. An empty quart beer bottle lay on the front seat. "Do you know me?" the old man asked in a voice that was soft and lost.

The driver looked at him a long time, his eyes moving down his body as though he were a column of figures. "Yeah, Dad," he said at last. "Don't you remember me?" He put an unfiltered cigarette in his mouth and lit it with a kitchen match. "I'm your son."

The old man's hand went to his chin. "My son," he said, like a fact.

"Come on." The man in the Ford smiled only with his mouth. "You're just having a little trouble remembering."

The old man got in and placed a hand on the chalky dash. "What have I been doing?"

"Shopping for me is all. Now give me back my wallet you took in the store with you." The driver held out a meaty hand.

The other man pulled a wallet from a hip pocket and handed it over.

In a minute they were leaving the parking lot, riding a trash-strewn highway out of town into the sandy pine barrens of Tangipahoa Parish. The old man watched the littered roadside for clues. "I can't remember my own name," he said, looking down at his plaid shirt.

"It's Ted," the driver told him, giving him a quick look. "Ted Williams." He checked his sideview mirror.

"I don't even remember your name, son. I must be sick." The old man wanted to feel his head for fever, but he was afraid he would touch a stranger.

"My name is Andy," the driver said, fixing a veined eye on him for a long moment. After a few minutes he turned off the main highway onto an unpaved road. The old man listened to the knock and ping of rock striking the drive shaft of the car, and then the gravel became patchy and thin, the road blotched with a naked, carroty earth like the hide of a sick dog. Bony cattle heaved their heads between strands of barbed wire, scavenging for roadside weeds. The Ford bumped past mildewed trailers sinking into rain-eaten plots. Further on, the land was too soggy for trailers, too poor even for the lane's desperate cattle. After two miles of this, they pulled up to a red brick house squatting in a swampy two-acre lot. Limbs were down everywhere, and catbrier and poison oak covered the rusty fence that sagged between the yard and cut-over woods running in every direction.

"This is home," Andy said, pulling him from the car. "You re-member now?" He held the old man's arm and felt it for muscle.

Ted looked around for more clues but said nothing. He watched Andy walk around the rear of the house and return with a shovel and a pair of boots. "Follow me, Dad." They walked to a swale full of coppery standing water which ran along the side of the prop-erty, ten feet from the fence. "This has to be dug out, two deep scoops side by side, all the way down to the ditch at the rear of the property. One hundred yards." He held the shovel out at arm's length.

"I don't feel very strong," he said, bending slowly to unlace his shoes. He stepped backwards out of them and slipped into the oversized Red Ball boots.

"You're a big man. Maybe your mind ain't so hot, but you can work for a while yet." And when Ted rocked up the first shovelful of sumpy mud, Andy smiled, showing a pair of yellow incisors.

He worked for an hour, carefully, watching the straightness of the ditch, listening to his heart strum in his ears, studying the awful lawn that was draining like a boil into the trough he opened for it. The whole lot was flat and low, made of a sterile clay that never dried out between thunderstorms rolling up from the Gulf. After four or five yards he had to sit down and let the pine and pecan trees swim around him as though they were laboring to stay upright in a great wind. Andy came out of the house carrying a lawn chair and a pitcher of cloudy liquid.

"Can I have some?" the old man asked.

Andy showed his teeth. "Naw. These are margaritas. You'll fall out for sure if you drink one." As an afterthought he added, "There's water in the hose."

All morning, Andy drank from the pitcher, and the old man looked back over his shoulder, trying to place him. The shovel turned up a sopping red clay tainted with runoff from a septic tank, and Ted tried to remember such poor soil. The day was still. No traffic bumped down the dirt lane. The tinkling of the ice cubes and the click of a cigarette lighter were the only sounds the old man heard. About one-thirty he lay down his shovel for the twentieth time and breathed deeply, like a man coming up from under water. He had used a shovel before, his body told him that, but he couldn't remember where or when. Andy drew up his lawn chair, abandoning the empty pitcher in pig weed growing against the fence. The old man could smell his breath when he came close, something like cleaning fluid, and a memory tried to fire up in his brain, but when Andy asked a question, the image broke apart like a dropped ember.

"You ever been beat up by a woman?" Andy asked.

The old man was too tired to look at him. Sweat weighed him down.

Andy scratched his belly through his yellow knit shirt. "Remember? She told me she'd beat me again and then divorce my ass if I didn't fix this yard up." He spoke with one eye closed as though he was too drunk to see with both of them at the same time. "She's big," he said. "Makes a lot of money but hits hard. Gave me over a hundred stitches once." He held up a flaccid arm. "Broke this one in two places." The old man looked at him then, studying the slouching shoulders, the patchy skin in his scalp. He saw that he was desperate, and moved back a step. "She's coming back soon, the bitch is. I told her I couldn't do it. That's why I went to the discount parking lot to hire one of those bums that work for food." He tried to rattle an ice cube in his empty tumbler, but the last one had long since melted. "Those guys won't work," he told him, pulling his head back and looking down his lumpy nose at nothing. "They just hold those cardboard signs saying they'll work so they can get a handout, the lazy bastards."

Pinheads of light were exploding in the old man's peripheral vision. "Can I have something to eat?" he asked, looking toward the house and frowning.

Andy led him into the kitchen, which smelled of garbage. The tile floor was cloudy with dirt, and a hill of melamine dishes lay capsized in the murky sink water. Andy unplugged the phone and left the room with it. Returning empty-handed, he fell into a kitchen chair and lit up a cigarette. The old man guessed where the food was and opened a can of Vienna sausages, twisting them out one at a time with a fork. "Maybe I should go to a doctor," he said, chewing slowly, as if trying to place the taste.

"Ted. Dad. The best job I ever had was in a nursing home, remember?" He watched the old man's eyes. "I dealt with people like you all day. I know what to do with you."

Ted examined the kitchen the way he might regard things during a visit to a museum. He looked and looked.

The afternoon passed like a slow, humid dream, and he completed fifty yards of ditch. By sundown he was trembling and wet. Had his memory come back, he would have known he was too old for this work. He leaned on the polished wood of the shovel handle and looked at his straight line, almost remembering something, dimly aware that where he was he had not been before. His memory was like a long novel left open and ruffled by a breeze to a different chapter further along. Andy had disappeared into the house to sleep off the tequila, and the old man came in to find himself something to eat. The pantry showed a good stock of chili, but not one pot was clean, so he scrubbed the least foul for ten minutes and put the food on to heat.

Later, Andy appeared in the kitchen doorway weaving like a drunk. He led Ted to a room that contained only a stripped bed. The old man put two fingers to his chin. "Where are my clothes?"

"You don't remember anything," Andy said quickly, turning to walk down the hall. "I have some overalls that'll fit if you want to clean up and change."

Ted lay down on the splotched mattress as though claiming it. This bed, it's mine, he thought. Turning onto his stomach, he willed to remember the musty smell. Yes, he thought. My name is Ted. I am where I am.

In the middle of the night his bladder woke him and on the way back to bed he saw Andy seated in the boxlike living room watching a pornographic movie in which a hooded man was whipping a naked woman with a rope. He walked up behind him, watching not the television but the back of Andy's head, the shape of it. A quart beer bottle lay sweating in his lap. The old man rolled his shoulders back. "Only white trash would watch that," he said.

Andy turned around, slow and stiff, like an old man himself. "Hey, Dad. Pull up a chair and get off on this." He looked back to the set.

Ted hit him from behind. It was a roundhouse, open-palm swat on the ear that knocked him out of the chair and sent the spewing beer bottle pinwheeling across the floor. Andy hit the tile on his stomach, and it was some time before he could turn up on one elbow to give the big man a disbelieving, angry look. "You old shit. Just wait till I get up."

"White trash," the old man thundered. "No kid of mine is going to be like that." He came closer. Andy rolled against the TV cart and held up a hand. The old man raised his right foot as though he would plant it on his neck.

"Hold on, Dad."

"Turn the thing off!" he said.

"What?"

"Turn the thing off!" the old man shouted, and Andy pressed the power button with a knuckle just as a big callused heel came down next to his head.

"Okay. Okay." He blinked and pressed his back against the television, inching away from the old man, who seemed even larger in the small room.

And then a tall, bony face fringed with white hair drifted down above his own, examining him closely, looking at his features, the shape of his nose. The old man put out a finger and traced Andy's right ear as if evaluating its quality. "Maybe you've got from me some sorry blood," he said, and his voice shook from saying it, that such a soft and stinking man could come out of him. He pulled back and closed his eyes as though he couldn't stand sight itself. "Let the good blood come out, and it'll tell you what to do," he said, his back bent with soreness, his hands turning to the rear. "You can't let your sorry blood run you."

Andy struggled to his feet in a pool of beer and swayed against the television, watching the old man disappear into the hall. His face burned where he'd been hit, and his right ear rang like struck brass. He moved into the kitchen where he watched a photograph taped to the refrigerator, an image of his wife standing next to a deer hanging in a tree, her right hand balled around a long knife. He sat down, perhaps forgetting Ted, the spilled beer, even his wife's hard fists, and he fell asleep on his arms at the kitchen table.

The next morning the old man woke up and looked around the bare bedroom, remembering it from the day before, and almost recalling something else, maybe a person. He concentrated, but the image he saw was something far away, seen without his eyeglasses. He rubbed his thumbs over his fingertips and the feel of someone was there.

In the kitchen he found Andy and put on water for coffee, watching his son until the kettle whistled. He loaded a French drip pot and found bread, scraped the mold off and toasted four slices. He retrieved eggs and some lardy bacon from the refrigerator. When Andy picked up his shaggy head, a dark stink of armpit stirred alive, and the old man told him to go wash himself.

In a half hour Andy came back into the kitchen, his face nicked and bleeding from a month-old blade, a different T-shirt forming a second skin. He sat and ate without a word, but drank no coffee. After a few bites, he rummaged in a refrigerator drawer, retrieving a can of beer. The old man looked at the early sun caught in the dew on the lawn and then glanced back at the beer. "Remind me of where you work," he said.

Andy took a long pull on the can. "I'm too sick to work. You know that." He melted into a slouch and looked through the screen door at a broken lawnmower dismantled in his carport. "It's all I can do to keep up her place. Every damn thing's broke and I got to do it all by hand."

"Why can't I remember?" He sat down with his own breakfast and began eating, thinking, *This is an egg. What am I?*

Andy watched the old man's expression and perhaps felt a little neon trickle of alcohol brightening his bloodstream, kindling a single BTU of kindness, and he leaned over. "I seen it happen before. In a few days your mind'll come back." He drained the beer and let out a rattling belch. "Right now, get back on that ditch."

The old man put a hand on a shoulder. "I'm stiff." He left the hand there.

"Come on." He fished three beer cans from the refrigerator. "You might be a little achy, but my back can't take the shovel business at all. You've got to finish that ditch today." He looked into the old man's eyes as though he'd lost something in them. "Quick as you can."

"I don't know."

Andy scratched his ear and, finding it sore, gave the old man a dark look. "Get up and find that shovel, damn you."

Andy drove three miles to a crossroads store, and Ted wandered the yard, looking at the bug-infested trees. The other man returned to sit in the shade of a worm-nibbled pecan, where he opened a beer and began to read a paper he had bought. Ted picked up the shovel and cut the soft earth, turning up neat, sopping crescents. In the police reports column was a brief account of an Etienne LeBlanc, a retired farmer from St. Mary Parish who had been visiting his son in Pine Oil when he disappeared. The son stated that his father had moved in with him a year ago, had begun to have spells of forgetfulness, and that he wandered. These spells had started the previous year on the day the old man's wife had died while they were shopping at the discount center. Andy looked over at Ted and snickered. He went to the house for another beer and looked again at the photograph on the refrigerator. His wife's stomach reached out farther than her breasts, and her angry red hair shrouded a face tainted by tattooed, luminescent-green eye shadow. Her lips were ignited with a permanent chemical pigment which left them bloodred even in the mornings when he was sometimes startled to wake and find the dyed parts of her shining next to him. She was a dredge-boat cook and was on her regular two-week shift at the mouth of the Mississippi. She had told him that if a drainage ditch was not dug through the side yard by the time she got back, she would come after him with a piece of firewood.

He had tried. The afternoon she had left he bought a shovel on the way back from the liquor store at the crossroads, but on the second spadeful he had struck a root and despaired, his heart bumping up in rhythm, his breath drawing short. That night he couldn't sleep; he left the shovel stuck upright in the side yard like his headstone. Over the next ten days the sleeplessness got worse and finally affected his kidneys, causing him to get up six times in one night to use the bathroom, until by dawn he was as dry as a cracker and drove out to buy quarts of beer, winding up in the Wal-Mart parking lot staring out the window of his old car as if by concentration alone he could conjure someone to take on his burden. And then he had seen the old man pass by his hood, aimless as a string of smoke.

Two hours later, the heat rose up inside Ted, and he looked enviously at a cool can resting on Andy's catfish belly. He tried to remember what beer tasted like and could sense a buzzing tingle on the tip of his tongue, a blue-ice feel in the middle of his mouth. Ted looked hard at his son and again could not place him. Water was building in his little ditch and he put his foot once more on the shovel, pushing it in, but not pulling back on the handle. "I need something to drink."

Andy did not open his eyes. "Well, go in the house and get it. But I want you back out here in a minute."

He went into the kitchen and stood by the sink, taking a glass tumbler full of tap water and drinking it down slowly. He rinsed the glass and opened the cabinet to replace it when his eye caught sight of an inexpensive stack of dishes showing a blue willow design; a little white spark fired off in the darkness of his brain, almost lighting up a memory. Opening another cabinet, he looked for signs of the woman, for this was some woman's kitchen, and he felt he must know her, but everywhere he looked was cluttered and smelled of insecticide and seemed like no place a woman should have. The photograph on the refrigerator of a big woman holding a knife meant nothing to him. He ran a thick finger along the shelf where the coffee was stored, looking for something that was not there. It was bare wood, and a splinter poked him lightly in a finger joint. He turned and walked to Andy's room, looking into a closet, touching jeans, coveralls, pullovers that could have been for a man or a woman, and then five dull dresses shoved against the closet wall. He tried to remember the cloth, until from outside came a slurred shout, and he turned for the bedroom door, running a thumb under an overalls strap that bit into his shoulders.

The sun rose high and the old man suffered, his borrowed khaki shirt growing dark on his straining flesh. Every time he completed ten feet of ditch, Andy would move his chair along beside him like a guard. They broke for lunch, and at one-thirty, when they came back into the yard, a thunderstorm fired up ten miles away, and the clouds and breeze saved them from the sun. Andy looked at pictures in magazines, drank, and drew hard on many cigarettes. At three o'clock the old man looked behind him and saw he was thirty feet from the big parish ditch at the rear of the lot. The thought came to him that there might be another job after this one. The roof, he noticed, needed mending, and he imagined himself straddling a gable in the heat. He sat down on the grass, wondering what would happen to him when he finished. Sometimes he thought that he might not be able to finish, that he was digging his own grave.

The little splinter began to bother him and he looked down at the hurt, remembering the raspy edge of the wooden shelf. He blinked twice. Andy had fallen asleep, a colorful magazine fluttering in his lap. Paper, the old man thought. Shelf paper. His wife would have never put anything in a cabinet without first putting down fresh paper over the wood, and then something came back like images on an out-of-focus movie screen when the audience claps and whistles and roars and the projectionist wakes up and gives his machine a twist, and life, movement, and color unite in a razory picture, and at once he remembered his wife and his children and his venerable 1969 Oldsmobile he had driven to the discount store. Etienne LeBlanc gave a little cry, stood up, and looked around at the alien yard and the squat house with the curling roof shingles, remembering everything that ever happened to him in a shoveled-apart sequence, even the time he had come back to the world standing in a cornfield in Texas, or on a Ferris wheel in Baton Rouge, or in the cabin of a shrimp boat off Point au Fer in the Gulf.

He glanced at the sleeping man and was afraid. Remembering his blood pressure pills, he went into the house to find them in his familiar clothes. He looked around the mildew-haunted house, which was unlike the airy cypress homeplace he still owned down in St. Mary Parish, a big-windowed farmhouse hung with rafts of family photographs. He examined a barren hallway. This place was a closed-up closet of empty walls and wilted drapes, and he wondered what kind of people owned no images of their kin. Andy and his wife were like visitors from another planet, marooned, childless beings enduring their solitude. In the kitchen he put his hand where the phone used to be, recalling his son's number. He looked out through the screen door to where a fat, bald man slouched asleep in a litter of shiny cans and curling magazines, a wreck of a man who'd built neither mind nor body nor soul. He saw the swampy yard, the broken lawnmower, the muddy, splintered rakes and tools scattered in the carport, more ruined than the hundred-year-old implements in his abandoned barn down in the cane fields. He saw ninety yards of shallow ditch. He pushed the screen door out. Something in his blood drew him into the yard.

His shadow fell over the sleeping man as he studied his yellow skin and pasty skull, the thin-haired, overflowing softness of him as he sat off to one side in the aluminum chair, a naked woman frowning in fear in his lap. Etienne LeBlanc held the shovel horizontally with both hands, thinking that he could hit him once in the head for punishment and leave him stunned on the grass and rolling in his rabid magazines while he walked somewhere to call the police, that Andy might learn something at last from a bang on the head. And who would blame him? Here was a criminal, though not an able or very smart one, and such people generally took the heaviest blows of life. His spotted hands tightened on the hickory handle.

Then he scanned again the house and yard that would never be worth looking at from the road, would never change for the better because the very earth under it all was totally worthless, a boot-sucking, iron-fouled claypan good only for ruining the playclothes of children. He thought of the black soil of his farm, his wife in the field, the wife who had died on his arm a year before as they were buying tomato plants. Looking toward the road, he thought how far away he was from anyone who knew him. Returning to the end of the little ditch, he sank the shovel deep, put up his hands and pulled sharply, the blade answering with a loud suck of mud that raised one of Andy's eyelids.

"Get on it, Ted," he said, stirring in the chair, unfocused and dizzy and sick. The old man had done two feet before Andy looked up at him and straightened his back at what he saw in his eyes. "What are you looking at, you old shit?"

Etienne LeBlanc sank the blade behind a four-inch collar of mud. "Nothing, son. Not a thing."

"You got to finish this evening. Sometimes she comes back early, maybe even tomorrow afternoon." He sat up with the difficulty of an invalid in a nursing home, looking around the base of his chair for something to drink, a magazine falling off his lap into the seedy grass. "Speed up if you know what's good for you."

For the next two hours the old man paced himself, throwing the dirt into a straight, watery mound on the right side of the hole, looking behind him to gauge the time. Andy got another six-pack from the house and once more drank himself to sleep. Around suppertime the old man walked over and nudged the folding chair.

"Wake up." He put his hand on a pasty arm.

"What?" The eyes opened like a sick hound's.

"I'm fixing to make the last cut." Etienne motioned toward the ditch. "Thought you might want to see that." They walked to the rear of the lot where the old man inserted the shovel sideways to the channel and pulled up a big wedge, the water cutting through and widening out the last foot of ditch, dumping down two feet into the bigger run.

Andy looked back to the middle of his yard where the water was seeping toward the new ditch. "Maybe this will help the damned bug problem," he said, putting his face close to the old man's. "Mosquitoes drive her nuts."

Etienne LeBlanc saw the strange nose which had been broken before birth and looked away with a jerk of the head.

The next morning it was not yet first light when the old man woke to a noise in his room. Someone kicked the mattress lightly. "Come on," a voice said. "We're going for a ride."

He did not like the sound of the statement but got up and put on

the clothes he had worn at the discount store and followed out to
the driveway. He could barely hear the ditch tickle the dark and was
afraid. Andy stood close and asked him what he could remember.

"What?"

"You heard me. I've got to know what you remember." The old
man made his mind work carefully. "I remember the ditch," he said.

"And what else?"

The old man averted his eyes. "I remember my name."

Andy whistled a single note. "And what is it?"

"Ted Williams." There was a little bit of gray light out on the
lawn, and the old man watched Andy try to think.

"Okay," he said at last. "Get in the car. You lay down in the backseat." The old man did as he was told and felt the car start and turn
for the road, then turn again, and he hoped that all the turning in
his head would not lead him back to a world of meaningless faces
and things, hoped that he would not forget to recall, for he knew
that the only thing he was was memory.

They had not driven a hundred feet down the lane when a set of
bright lights came toward them and Andy began crying out an
elaborate string of curses. The old man looked over the seat and
saw a pickup truck in the middle of the road. "It's her," Andy said,
his voice trembling and high. "Don't talk to her. Let me handle it."
It was not quite light enough to see his face, so the old man read
his voice and found it vibrating with dread.

The pickup stopped and in the headlights Etienne saw a woman
get out, a big woman whose tight coveralls fit her the way a tar-
paulin binds a machine. Her hair was red like armature wire and
braided in coppery ropes that fell down over her heavy breasts.
Coming to the driver's window, she bent down. She had a big
mouth and wide lips. "What's going on, you slimy worm?" Her
voice was a cracked cymbal.

Andy tried a smile. "Honey. Hey there. I just decided to get an
early—"

She reached in and put a big thumb on his Adam's apple. "You
never get up before ten."

"Honest," he whined, the words squirting past his pinched vocal cords.

Her neck stiffened when she saw the old man. "Shut up. Who's this?"

Andy opened his mouth and closed it, opened it again and said with a yodel, "Just an old drinking buddy. I was bringing him home."

She squinted at the old man. "Why you in the backseat?"

Etienne looked into the fat slits of her eyes and remembered a sow that had almost torn off his foot a half century before. "He told me to sit back here."

She straightened up and backed away from the car. "All right, get out. Some kind of bullshit is going on here." The old man did as she asked, and in the gray light she looked him over, sniffing derisively. "Who the hell are you?"

He tried to think of something to say, wondering what would cause the least damage. He thought down into his veins for an answer, but his mind began to capsize like an overburdened skiff. "I'm his father," he said at last. "I live with him."

Her big head rolled sideways like a dog's. "Who told you that?"

"I'm his father," he said again.

She put a paw on his shoulder and drew him in. He could smell beer on her sour breath. "Let me guess. Your memory ain't so hot, right? He found you a couple blocks from a nursing home, hey? You know, he tried this stuff before." The glance she threw her husband was horrible to see. "Here, let me look at you." She pulled him into the glare of the headlights and noticed his pants. "How'd you get this mud on you, pops?" She showed her big square teeth when she asked the question.

"I was digging a ditch," he said. Her broad face tightened, the meat on the woman's skull turning to veiny marble. At once she walked back to her truck and pulled from the bed a short-handled, square-point shovel. When Andy saw what she had, he struggled from behind the steering wheel, got out, and tried to run, but she was on him in a second. The old man winced as he heard the dull ring of the shovel blade and saw Andy go down in a skitter of gravel at the rear of the car. She hit him again with a half-hearted swing. Andy cried out, "Ahhhhh, don't, don't," but his wife screamed back and gave him the corner of the shovel right on a rib.

"You gummy little turd with eyes," she said, giving him another dig with the shovel. "I asked you to do one thing for me on your own, one numbskull job," she said, emphasizing the word *job* with a slap of the shovel-back on his belly, "and you kidnap some old bastard who doesn't know who he is and get him to do it for you."

"Please," Andy cried, raising up a hand on which one finger angled off crazily.

"Look at him, you moron," she shrieked. "He's a hundred son-of-a-bitching years old. If he had died we'd of gone to jail for good." She threw down the shovel and picked him up by the armpits, slamming him down on the car's trunk, giving him open-handed slaps like a gangster in a cheap movie.

The old man looked down the gravel road to where it brightened in the distance. He tried not to hear the ugly noises behind him. He tried to think of town and his family, but when Andy's cries began to fracture like an animal's caught in a steel-jawed trap, he walked around the back of the car and pulled hard on the woman's wrist. "You're going to kill him," he scolded, shaking her arm. "What's wrong with you?"

She straightened up slowly and put both hands on his shirt. "Nothing is wrong with me," she raged, pushing him away. She seemed ready to come after him, but when she reached out again, a blade of metal gonged down on her head, her eye sockets flashed white, and she collapsed in a spray of gravel. Andy lowered the shovel and leaned on the handle. Then he spat blood and fell down on one knee.

"Aw, God," he wheezed.

The old man backed away from the two figures panting in the dust, the sound of the iron ringing against the woman's head already forming a white scar in his brain. He looked down the lane and saw her idling pickup. In a minute he was in the truck backing away in a cloud of rock dust to a wide spot in the road where he swung around for town, glancing in the rearview mirror at a limping figure waving wide a garden tool. He drove fast out of the sorry countryside, gained the blacktop, and sped up. At a cross-roads store, he stopped, and his mind floated over points of the compass. His hands moved left before his brain told them to, and memory turned the truck. In fifteen minutes he saw, at the edge of town, the cinder-block plinth of the discount center. Soon, the gray side of the building loomed above him, and he slid out of the woman's truck, walking around the front of the store without knowing why, just that it was proper to complete some type of cir-cle. The bottom of the sun cleared the horizon-making parking lot, and he saw two cars, his old wine-colored Oldsmobile, and next to it, like an embryonic version of the same vehicle, an anony-mous modern sedan. Etienne LeBlanc shuffled across the asphalt lake, breathing hard, and there he saw a young man asleep behind the steering wheel in the smaller car. He leaned over him and stud-ied his face, saw the LeBlanc nose, reached in at last and traced the round-topped ears of his wife. He knew him, and his mind closed like a fist on this grandson and everything else, even his wife fading in his arms, even the stunned scowl of the copper-haired woman as she was hammered into the gravel. As if memory could be a decision, he accepted it all, knowing now that the only thing worse than reliving nightmares until the day he died was enduring a life full of strangers. He closed his eyes and called on the old farm in his head to stay where it was, remembered its cypress house, its flat and misty lake of sugarcane keeping the impressions of a morn-ing wind.

––––––––––

Tim Gautreaux is the author of a novel, *The Next Step in the Dance,* and a collection of stories, *Same Place, Same Things.* His fiction has appeared in *The Atlantic, Harper's, GQ, The Best American Short Stories,* and *New Stories from the South.* He teaches creative writing at Southeastern

Louisiana University in Hammond, Louisiana, where he lives with his wife and two sons.

I came out of Wal-Mart one hot Louisiana day and faced the parking lot, completely forgetting where my car was, or even which car I was using. Then this story came to me, more or less. I wondered what I would do if I lost my memory. What people would do to me. Would I change if I never got it back?

A great deal of what we become as adults is determined by the temperament we are born with. In writing this story I was thinking of a person who has little seizures and temporarily forgets who he is for a minute or a week. Memory is a rudder. Without it, will either what he has been taught or what he carries with him from the womb determine whether he does good or ill? And what basic thing is left in the memory-less person that lets him judge the actions of others? These are two of the questions "Sorry Blood" approaches.

Enid Shomer

THE OTHER MOTHER

(from *Modern Maturity*)

Sheila works for $5.5ð an hour at Dillard's department store, in her first paying job. For two weeks now she has sold Finer Apparel. Finer than what? Not finer than the dresses she left in Mobile. Not finer than her grandmother's wedding gown, enlarged with gores of satin and lace so that she could wear it when she married Selwyn. Not fine enough for her daughter, Royal, fifteen, who sports a ring on every finger, like her mother. It's killing Sheila that Royal didn't run away from Mobile with her. "My heart is in splinters," she told the crisis hotline from a pay phone on University Avenue in Gainesville, a college town red-roofed with Pizza Huts and motels. "I had to leave my daughter behind," Sheila told the crisis counselor. "She didn't want to come with me just yet. She's adopted." At least Royal wasn't living with Selwyn.

Sheila works in vertical merchandising, meaning that she freshens the racks pawed over by customers and touches up wrinkled blouses with a steamer. All the blouses are white, identical except for price and small details indistinguishable from a distance: shawl collar, tuxedo pleats, princess seaming. Eventually the French cuffs will fray. Eventually the blouses will age into rags.

Sheila herself is like a piece of fine fabric that has been shredded. For three weeks she's been on the run. That's how she thinks of it, though she has come to a dead stop on the floor of her nephew's apartment where she sleeps on an air mattress, covered only with a sheet.

Three is her lucky number. When she left Mobile she grabbed three skirts, three pairs of slacks, three framed photographs of Royal. The counselor on the hotline had asked her if she was thinking of killing herself. "Not until you mentioned it just now," Sheila said, perfectly serious. The counselor gave her another phone number, urged her to call anytime. "Use a pseudonym," the counselor added. "Gainesville isn't that big a town."

If Sheila were Catholic, she would confess her sin every day, willingly accept a harsh penance, hope for a portion of forgiveness. But she is Presbyterian, spiked with brimstone Baptist. There is a hell, and she and Selwyn are going there.

Sheila had watched birth videos before they adopted Royal. All those grimacing little boys and girls, their newborn faces pressed flat. Babies looked so much alike except for hair and skin color. A few days later their faces plumped back up. Royal must have looked like that after she was squeezed out with love and pain from the other mother's body, before she was handed to Sheila, who had been waiting to adopt for years.

As Sheila moves through her day in Finer Apparel, she keeps mental track of Royal's routine. Now Royal is slamming her locker shut at high school in the clamor before classes start. Now her hands are fluttering above her food as she talks to a boy in the cafeteria. Royal didn't want to change schools. She is living with Sheila's mother in a seniors' condo where potted palms froth up in the lobby beneath huge ceiling fans. Sheila's mother is a thin, stylish woman held together with hair spray, Chanel No. 5, and Rebel Yell bourbon. She has trouble ordering from menus and doesn't watch the evening news or read the paper. Sheila never could confide in her mother without worrying about wounding her. Sheila's mother is selfish, not from arrogance, but from weakness. She is too frail to shoulder anyone else's problems, even someone she loves.

Sheila is a better parent, she is sure of it, though she now believes that she had sometimes been a touch careless, turning her back on Royal in her carriage, letting go of her pudgy hand in shopping malls and restaurants. She tries to recall every instance of imperfect vigilance: in the homes of friends, on her back porch, in the yard. And even at the airport, just like the other mother. Sheila imagines the other mother constantly now: sitting at a table with her back to Sheila, her shoulders rounded, her body drooping in motionless curves. Sheila moves closer, but she cannot picture the woman's face. The face has been eroded, washed away by anguish.

The day before Sheila ran away, Win came home from work at one in the afternoon, headed straight to the bedroom, and began drinking bourbon. When Sheila walked in, he was lying on the bed, staring at the ceiling. The radio was on and people were phoning in their many opinions of President Nixon, who had just died. He weakened the Presidency. He invented dirty tricks and changed the course of politics forever, Sioux City said.

"What's wrong?" Sheila asked.

"Everything," Win said.

Nixon was a lesson in perseverance. He paid for his mistakes. (How? Sheila wondered. Why didn't he go to jail?) He outlived his own shame until it aged into something finer, something called courage, said Austin, Texas.

"But what specifically is wrong?" How was today different from yesterday? Sheila wondered.

"I'm going to leave you," Win said. He looked remorseful.

"Oh God, Win. You can't. It'll break Royal's heart." That really was the first thing Sheila thought. Sheila would be okay. She'd join a singles group, get a job—any kind of job—place an ad in the Heart to Heart classifieds: *DWF ISO sincere WM, 40–50, for real commitment.*

"Don't bring Royal into it. She'll get over it. A lot of kids' parents get divorced."

"But not twice."

The call-in show was heating up: Nixon was either a criminal or a saint. Win switched off the radio. "We're not married, remember?"

Selwyn was slick. Selwyn was smooth, his body glossy as the inside of a shell, each muscle sleek, the skin slipping over it. In high school, his friends nicknamed him "Win" and it stuck. His signature made a dashing, cavalier impression on the page, like a stylishly tipped hat. *Love and kisses, Win. Thinking of you, Win,* as if cheering her to some victory.

They had met in Mobile, at a reunion for the Trewsdale Academy, a stronghold of castle-like buildings and wide lawns canopied with live oaks. They were both Trewsdale graduates, but hadn't known each other during their school days. Six months later they married.

Win depleted his inheritance in a succession of showy, volatile businesses. Broker of yachts and berthage. Importer of parrots from Suriname and alabaster from Turkey. When his fortune eroded to half a million, he bought into a silver- and copper-mining company. He worked out of one of Mobile's courtly Painted Ladies converted to offices. Headquarters was in a scrappy old building farther downtown, near the port. In return for his investment, he was put in charge of Asian operations. He flew to India, where the mines were small and backward. He suspected the translators of intentionally making him look like a fool.

Win kept Sheila on a cash allowance for the house and food. For everything else, she had two gold cards, both canceled now. The day after she left Win, she was as poor as a sparrow. It made her feel noble and desperate at the same time. Money could do that—sweep you up and drop you like a tornado. Most of Sheila's life it was a given. Now she feels its lack at every turn in surprising, humiliating ways that make her feel spoiled and unworthy. Her hair, for example, was frosted just before she left Mobile. Now she'll have to use drugstore color. Her head will be all one shade, like a wall.

Sheila misses the exquisite moments of pleasure that money bought. Her beaded minidress like granulated gold, the antique

lorgnette for a necklace. They were going to a gala benefit for the
Children's Society. Downstairs, Win waited in his classic jet tuxedo, a silhouette of corners tapering to points. Two rooms away,
in her crib, Royal slept her moist, perfumed sleep. Sheila primped
at her vanity, the smoke of her cigarette climbing the air in slow
spirals. A glass of good Scotch sat beside the cosmetics tray, a sky-
line of lipstick tubes and assorted wands. She took a last glimpse
in the mirror as she pushed the chair back along the dense wool
carpet and caught herself, nearly unawares, nearly someone else.

The car was clean and waxed. She slid into her leather seat. It
wasn't true things couldn't make you happy. Things had made her
happy for fifteen years. When she clothes-shopped in September
and March, the salesgirls brought in sandwiches and lemonade on
folding tables, always with nice touches—straw flowers in a vase,
a fanciful glass stirrer. She never thought of them as bootlickers.
Their behavior was natural. You would be nice to someone who
was going to spend a lot of money.

Sheila retreated to Watermelon Lake most days after work before returning to her nephew's. Located on the campus of the agricultural college, the lake was fringed with live oaks and caught the
sunsets in its golden clasp. It was beautiful and safe; the university
police patrolled it twenty-four hours a day. No one had ever disappeared from its shores despite alligators thrashing the water and
vagabonds spilling out like human refuse on the lawns. She could
think there, think in short bits, like breathing. She could hold her
breath over the worst parts.

She and Win had tried for six years to have a baby, practiced positioned, passionless sex according to a calendar. Win blushed, left
alone in a doctor's cubicle with *Playboy, Hustler,* and a plastic cup.
His sparse sperm wagged across a glass slide. He took vitamins
and worked out. He took vitamins and rested. He switched from
jockeys to boxer shorts as the doctor advised.

They went to Houston for in vitro fertilization. Several slow
tadpoles pierced eggs that had been surgically removed from

Sheila, but the eggs did not divide. They sat like small dented basketballs under the bright gaze of the microscope. The doctor tried to be comforting. It was probably a blessing in disguise, he claimed, a sign of incompatibility. If an egg had developed it might have been terribly deformed.

They signed up to adopt a baby, but the waiting list was long. They wanted a white baby, a baby that looked like them. Win explained to Sheila that Mobile wasn't ready for a mixed baby.

Nevertheless, they went to look at a light-skinned biracial infant. When Sheila stared into his unflinching brown eyes, her insides felt like they were flopping around. The baby's hair curled like gift ribbon from his perfect skull. "He's beautiful," Win admitted, "but his hair's too frizzy. He'll always be hassled." He handed the infant back to his caretaker. "I can't change the world."

Sheila was quiet.

"We're going to get a baby," Win insisted. "I promise you, we're going to have our own baby."

The list of infertile couples grew longer, babies scarcer. Someone at a houseboat party passed them a card with the name of a clinic in Mexico, but of course a Mexican baby would still stand out. They threw the card away.

And then, one day, Win came home from work ebulliently bearing a sheaf of delphiniums and irises, the stems so long he held the bouquet away from his body, like a torch. He'd heard of a doctor in Georgia who managed a lot of private adoptions.

It probably wasn't entirely legal, but Sheila didn't care about that anymore. She stood in the kitchen snipping the stems, inserting them into floral foam to create a spiky globe. If some girl in Georgia was desperate enough to give up or sell her baby, Sheila was going to take it.

Royal was perfect. She looked like Win, her eyes the same hazel wheels with flecks of gold in them. Win insisted on going to get the baby by himself. Sheila didn't question him. *Mommy,* Sheila thought. *Mommy and Daddy.* After Win brought Royal home, Sheila drove downtown to Posh Baby and paid for the opulent layette she had reserved the week before in both pink and blue. When Royal was six, they would tell her she was adopted. All the official records would be sealed under the weight of time, like a pharaoh in his tomb.

They never talked about the adoption again. Win gave me a baby, Sheila thought. That is how she always thought of Royal— as a love child.

If Sheila ever met Royal's natural mother, what could she say to her? *Possession. Possession is nine tenths of the law.* Sheila would do anything for this unknown woman, anything except give Royal up. *I'm so sorry,* she rehearses. *Ashamed. Kill me. Go ahead and kill me, I'd understand. But of course it would be terrible for Royal. I'm the only mother she knows.*

Win began smoking and drinking heavily. He had always been a social drinker, but now he got smashed every day. Some nights he didn't come home.

A silent rage possessed Sheila, expressing itself in more perfect meals, more expertly applied makeup, evenings out with women friends several times a month to give the illusion of greater independence. Sheila expected Win to leave her, but he didn't. She decided to wait it out rather than confront him. She believed he'd come around.

They stopped sleeping together. Sheila considered having an affair, but no one suitable came to mind. She and Win focused on Royal and extravagant distractions. At Christmas, they bought real gold tinsel for the tree. At Easter, the three of them vacationed in Austria.

It was the evening after their nineteenth wedding anniversary, the table laid with imported cheese and wines. Expensive food brought out their best manners, camouflaged painful dinnertime silences as mere formality. Royal had brought her date home. Now, she and the boy were in the den choosing CDs to listen to.

"I don't like the look of him," Win said. They had been arguing about the boy ever since he arrived. "It isn't a matter of trusting Royal, it's a matter of trusting a stranger with more than hands in his pockets."

Sheila set down her wine goblet. "I trust Royal's *judgment*. She knows this boy from school."

"You knew me from school," Win pointed out sarcastically.

"And now you don't like the look of me either!" She spit out the words like bitter medicine. "Win, I never thought you'd stop loving me."

"I still love you," Win protested. "I do."

She looked at him with surprise, her face burning. "Then why don't you want to make love to me?"

"I'm sorry," Win said. "I can't talk about this. I'll never be able to talk about it."

The divorce went smoothly. The only thing Win insisted on was joint custody, which Sheila agreed to. Win adored Royal. He'd protect her with his money and his life. She wanted Royal to have that affection and security.

Four months after the final decree, Win approached Sheila about borrowing money on the house. Once they began to talk about finances, about survival, a comfortable familiarity returned. They mortgaged the house to the hilt to save one of the teetering mines in India, and celebrated the risk by making love all night. Toward dawn, Sheila lay face down on the bed and Win lay on top of her, in a position he always called "the stationary massage." His naked body pressed against hers; she sank into the deep contours of the featherbed. Her chest heaved against his weight, as if she'd traveled to a planet where the atmosphere had the density of flesh. He'd never meant to stop wanting her. If it happened again, he'd see a counselor or sex therapist. His tears dripped down her shoulders. The effort to breathe against the weight of his body and his grief was satisfying.

He moved back in. Royal was elated. They celebrated their reunion with a vacation in the Caymans. It was terribly expensive and Sheila worried about Win spending so freely.

The bliss of the reunion faltered, deteriorating after four months into the pattern that had led to divorce—Win drinking heavily again, staying out all night. This time, Royal took it all in. And though she said nothing to her mother, Sheila sensed Royal's sadness and fear at the breakfast and dinner table as Royal's gaze shifted from her mother's passive face to her father's empty chair.

Win finally told her the truth on that last day before she left Mobile. They were in the bedroom, the place where they argued now instead of making love. The phone-in program was heating up, the one in which Nixon was either criminal or saint. That was when Win announced that he was going to leave her again. "A lot of kids' parents get divorced," he was saying.

"But not twice."

Win switched off the radio. "We're not married, remember?"

Of course, Sheila thought. It only *felt* like they were married. Still, something must have changed, something invisible and terrible had twisted Win's heart again. "Win, I love you," Sheila begged. "Whatever it is, we can work it out. We can."

"No. We *can't*," Win corrected her.

The next part of the conversation eluded Sheila whenever she tried to remember it precisely. Win had nothing but contempt for her. He couldn't stand the sight of her. The next clear words came from Sheila. They were "our Royal."

"Our Royal?" Win laughed bitterly.

"You know Royal isn't really ours." He lit another cigarette.

"Well, of course I know that. She's adopted."

"You're so dumb. I think you choose to be dumb."

"What are you talking about?"

"I've got a new girlfriend. Weren't you even suspicious?"

"No. I wasn't."

"Royal's not adopted," Win said. He watched Sheila's face.

"I'm not so dumb," Sheila said. "It occurred to me that somehow you might have—" She paused to find the least painful word.
"Somehow you might have *negotiated* for her."

"You mean bought her?"

"I don't know, Win. I don't know what you did."

"I didn't buy her." Win inhaled deeply from his cigarette and
held his breath until his face reddened.

"Oh, thank God. I figured you found some sleazy doctor who
told a poor girl it was legal to pay more than her medical—"

"I stole her."

The muscles in Sheila's body tightened all at once, as if someone had pulled a drawstring.

"That's right. She was kidnapped." Win was completely drunk
and talking fast now. Tears coursed down his cheeks. "I didn't per-
sonally do it. I hired a couple of guys. I told them what kind of baby
to look for and left the rest up to them. They took her from a rest-
room at Memphis Airport. One of them dressed in drag to do it."

Sheila collapsed into the wing chair in the corner of the bedroom. "The mother went into a toilet stall and left Royal parked
outside in a stroller a few feet away, in front of the sinks. No, not
the sinks." Win struggled to paint the scene. "In front of a counter
where women were combing their hair. It happened fast."

At seven-thirty it is still light out. Sheila drives to Watermelon
Pond, unfolds herself from the car and crunches down the gravel
path to a picnic bench. The wind is blowing the azalea petals off
the bushes. In a few weeks, she'll have enough money to rent a
place. Her mother and Royal will visit, her mother's head held stiff
and high above the rising water of Sheila's life, Royal appalled by
her mother's mingy quarters. Sheila will flap loudly between them
for two or three days, like a broken screen door.

"If you loved me, really loved *me,* you'd have been suspicious instead of selfish," Win had screamed. "You'd have shared the guilt."
He'd spared Sheila all those years, and now he hated her for it.

Win was a criminal. Maybe he kept it secret because he thought she wouldn't have gone along with it. Maybe he thought she might use it against him someday. Sheila's mind can't track all the possibilities. She wants Royal beside her now. Royal, please God, biting the polish off her nails, lobbying for a cashmere sweater from J. Crew, threatening to go to New York City instead of to college.

The sun drops into the lake, the water fades from molten red to rust. There's only the sound of dark waves probing the shore. She'll go back to Mobile, it's just a matter of time. A year, maybe less. To spare Royal, the rest of Sheila's life must be a lie, a lie that fills her chest like a heavy, dead second heart. She can never tell anyone. The lie is a kind of eternity that will outlive everyone who suffered or profited from it. She must teach Royal humility. Royal is already showing signs of privilege, expecting too much from life, just as Sheila used to.

She rises from the bench and heads back towards the path. Normally, she walks around the lake at least once before going home. But the moon is barely a sliver tonight and the way is hard to see. She reaches for the pine straw of the path with her foot, her arms held out to the sides like a tightrope walker, embracing the empty air.

Enid Shomer's stories and poems have appeared in *The New Yorker, The Atlantic, Poetry, Tikkun, The New Criterion, Best American Poetry 1996, The Paris Review, Boulevard,* and others. She is the author of three books of poetry, most recently *Black Drum,* and of *Imaginary Men,* which won the Iowa Prize and the LSU / *The Southern Review* Prize, both given annually for the best first collection of fiction by an American author. Shomer, who has lived for most of her life in Florida, has received two grants from the NEA. In 1997, she was Florida State University's first Visiting Writer. She has also served as writer in residence at the Thurber House.

I accompanied a friend to her first meeting of a support group in Gainesville, Florida, my hometown for many years. One participant, an attractive middle-aged woman dressed unusually well, had just run away from home. She emitted the heat of extreme distress like a hot coal. Since she didn't divulge the nature of her trouble and never returned to the group, I began to imagine a life for her, one that included the fact that she was a Southerner of privilege on her own for the first time. The story itself is completely fictional and evolved over a long period—a year or more.

Molly Best Tinsley

THE ONLY WAY TO RIDE

(from *Prairie Schooner*)

They had married in May, in the midst of a premature hot spell that withered the azaleas almost the minute they bloomed, the kind of weather, Nan thinks now, that makes people do crazy things—lean on car horns and shout obscenities and panic at the emptiness of their lives.

She'd hardly known him. There had been three dinners, then a comfortable weekend together, after which Will had flashed that ready smile of his—appreciative, condescending, heedless—and proposed. "If you're going to do something," he'd said, "you ought to do it right."

"I don't know about right," Nan said. Will was too handsome, too outgoing, too old; he had been married too often. They had nothing in common but the endodontist in whose waiting room they had met—she was facing a root canal for the first time, he had just survived one. Besides, Will had a problem—a daughter, Angela, who kept canceling Will's plans to see her, whom he talked about constantly. Had Nan been disarmed by his desperate concern for the girl? Flattered by his faith that she, Nan, could help him with her? In her next breath she had conceded, "But maybe it's time."

Nothing in her life had ever happened so fast. Two weeks later, she and Will drove straight from the county courthouse out to one of the further suburbs, to the tract of pastel town houses that had sprung up on the ruins of an old farm, where Angela lived with her mother, Terri.

Will and Nan were made to stand too long on the narrow stoop, he in his brand-new suit, she in an unbleached muslin dress, the sun like a huge scorching spotlight exposing the vanity of it all. With her eyes, Nan tried to tell Will that she wanted to leave. Will gave an absurd, mechanical laugh. "Don't hold this against me," he said. "I never could walk away from a mistake."

The woman who finally answered the door was only a little older than Nan. She wore velour shorts, a tank top, and a deep suntan, except for her face, which, framed by waves of dark hair, looked tired and faded, like a *before* picture in one of those articles about cosmetic makeovers. There was a little tuft of cotton between each of her toes and the nails on one foot were a glossy red. "Fancy meeting you here," Terri said to Will, sweeping Nan out of the picture with a disdainful glance. "Did you think she'd be sitting in the foyer waiting? I'm beside myself. I don't care if I never see her again. You—"

But Will had Nan by the arm and was guiding her back to the car. He was breathing loudly, a flush had darkened his features, muddled their confidence. And through the blur in her mind, Nan wondered what she'd gotten herself into.

After almost an hour of random, sometimes reckless cruising from one new shopping strip to another, they found her in a 7-Eleven parking lot: Angela attended by half a dozen friends, all sheathed in black despite the heat, leaning against an old Mustang with a cloudy finish, smoking cigarettes. Nan had faced classrooms full of these malcontents every day for years, even managed to teach them a few things about thesis statements, personification, tragic flaws. Then why was she so anxious and weak in the knees?

Pale makeup, blue-black eyeliner, and grape lipstick couldn't hide Angela's perfect features or her shock when she recognized the tall, gray-haired man in the suit as her father. Will approached slowly, murmuring greetings. Nan sort of shuffled behind him in her Guatemalan folk dress, drenched now with sweat, clutching the last-minute bridal bouquet of narcissus and forget-me-nots. The funereal lineup froze and went silent. Nan could feel their fear.

"I've got something to show you," Will said, his voice unexpectedly calm, firm.

Angela threw Nan the same dismissive look her mother had.

Will chuckled indulgently. "This is Nan. We've both got a surprise for you, if you want to hop in the car."

Angela's friends were watching her. The spiked mane of her hair fell in front of her face as she looked down at her pointed boots, shuffled them on the hot, oil-stained asphalt, shifting her weight. Nan found herself wanting to cry out, *Believe him, trust him, help him, help us all.* Instead she took a step forward, extending the flowers. Angela peeked up through her hair, then almost as though she couldn't stop herself, her arms reached for the bouquet while her eyes quizzed her father's.

"Something else," he said again, shaking his head. And then it happened. A stiffness in the girl broke, went slack. She let her father put his arm across her shoulders, she went with them. Will winked at Nan over his daughter's head.

What Will and Nan had done was buy Angela the palomino Brandy and arrange to board it on a surviving farm only minutes from her house. As a child Angela had gone through a horse stage, read horse books, collected horse figurines; she had taken riding lessons too, until her parents, in the confusion of splitting up, began forgetting to drive her there. The plan now was to interest Angela in riding again, provide an outlet for her energy.

In the car, Will asked Angela questions about school which she answered automatically, with no particular regard for the truth. When they pulled into the farm, Angela had to be coaxed from the car, teased out of her lethargy long enough to cross the lawn to the barn, but as they started down the row of stalls, glimpsing in their dim shadows the contours of horses, her face began to twitch. She finally gave in to a smile that seemed to Nan almost smug. Soon the girl was giggling like a child and offering up the tender heads of Nan's daffodils to Brandy's dark, mobile lips.

After that Will was in heaven, setting up riding lessons, replacing his daughter's black stretch jeans and torn shirts with suede-trimmed britches, a snappy green jacket. Sundays Angela abandoned her friends, removed the jumble of earrings from each lobe, wound her own chaotic hair into a prim French braid and sat up stunningly straight in the saddle. After only a month they were towing the horse in a rented trailer to one local show or another. By the time school started in the fall, they'd won their first ribbon. If Nan never saw any real point to all that scrubbing and grooming and trotting around in the sawdust, she was still amazed. Riding, Angela seemed transformed. Her sullenness settled into concentration; her apathy became in the saddle a lovely centered nonchalance.

That year of weekends seems almost like a dream to Nan now— the three of them like the family she'd never had as a child, and never let the grown-up woman hope for. Will and Angela fussed over Brandy, then Will and Nan waited and watched, sipping from a thermos of steaming coffee or a jug of lemonade once the weather warmed again. Wherever they parked the horse trailer, they pitched their brief camp, and Nan unpacked sandwiches, muffins, fruit, and it never bothered her that everything tasted faintly of leather and dung. Thinking back, Nan wonders if she'd really expected such times could last.

Angela became almost vivacious, if too polite. She complimented Nan on outfits picked straight out of L.L. Bean, asked her about her students. Nan got the feeling that Angela used their conversations to practice various facial expressions—respect, solicitude, disbelief.

"You know, you don't have to take care of me," Nan mustered the courage to say one Sunday, when Will had gone off to check the scores and they had lapsed into silence. "It's all right with me if you aren't always *on*. You can just be."

For a moment Angela looked offended, then she smiled with

compassion. "I feel sorry for teachers," she said. "Kids are so out of control."

Nan said she didn't think control was necessarily so all important.

"What is?" Angela asked, breaking open a muffin and picking out the raisins to nibble one by one.

"How about being who you are?" Nan thought she saw a flicker of yielding. "It's hard to keep hiding what you really think and feel."

All at once there it was, what Nan was looking for, what she feared—Angela's eyes squeezed shut, her face got all pinched up, she shook her head slowly, then opened her eyes. "I hate English," she said, her voice trembling. "You've always got to write what they want you to write if you want a good grade."

Nan tried to give a good-natured laugh. "I've heard that often enough that I believe you, it must feel that way."

"No," Angela said fiercely. "It's not the way it feels, it's the way it is." Their eyes locked for a long blank moment, then Angela's face brightened as though she were remembering a miracle. "This guy I met, Kiser, says to write stuff like how it *feels* when your dad gets killed in a car accident, then they give you an A. He's already graduated so it's like he knows."

"But if your dad didn't—"

"Or you can make it cancer. Pisspot gave me an A-minus for a brain tumor. Kids call her that," she explained, her tone encouraging tolerance. "Her real name's Nesbitt or something."

"I suppose good writing is good writing," Nan said.

Angela's aggressive smile went blurry for a moment, as though she were testing that equation for insult. "I still hate it," she said, but not as loud. Her fingers sifted through the pile of muffin crumbs in her palm. "I mean, writing that stuff just makes you feel guilty. What if it happens afterwards in real life and you already wrote it, it's like maybe you made it happen." She glanced at Nan and scowled when their eyes met. When Nan thinks about Angela now that Will's gone, when her nerves flare at the prospect of seeing her again, she remembers that transparent scowl, the wishful, guilty child underneath.

That afternoon in early fall, Angela recovered quickly. "Kiser doesn't even know what his dad looks like, except for one picture," she told Nan, with a toss of the head. "Well, I did get a good grade. Maybe next time I'll do you. I'll even let you pick how you want to die."

If that was the first time Angela mentioned Kiser, Nan hardly noticed. If Angela began showing up with rusty blotches along her throat, if she seemed jumpy sometimes, sometimes a new sort of remote, if there was an interim report now and then from Kennedy High School, if there were scabbed initials knife-scratched on the insides of her arms, if Kiser was steadily insinuating his life into theirs, Will and Nan just didn't notice, absorbed as they were with what pranced before their minds' eyes—Angela on Brandy.

And then the Sunday after Angela's eighteenth birthday, Nan and Will drove out early to pick her up and she wasn't home, had never come home. All Nan remembers after that is Will frantic, Will furious, Will obsessed, Terri tranquillized but still oozing accusations. Trips to the police station, appointments with lawyers, psychiatrists. If you were going to get your daughter back, you ought to do it right.

Although they finally traced Angela to an apartment she and Kiser had rented in the northern reaches of the county, there was no legal way to budge her from it, or even get her to open its door. Nor was there any way to keep her from going back to it after she finally did show up at her father's house in the middle of a muggy August night, enormously pregnant, a bloody towel over a gap in her upper front teeth. She and Kiser were dancing, she said, and she tripped and fell against the wall.

The next day she gave birth to Megan Michele.

Two weeks later in a transaction that included Brandy, Will acquired Simone, a prize-winning Percheron draft horse the color of storm clouds, and her antique cart and harness trimmed with silver and red.

* * *

The last time Nan saw Angela came as a surprise. It was Saturday morning and she barged in on Nan, riding Megan Michele on her back. Angela was wearing pink shorts with a bib front, a T-shirt from Diggity's, where she waited tables, pink padded high-top sneakers, and a pink diagonal slash across each cheek. The baby was dressed all in pink to match.

"I didn't think you'd be here," she said to Nan, who might have told Angela the same thing.

Extending her arms in the direction of Megan Michele, Nan asked instead, "Where else would I be?"

Angela turned Nan the shoulder with the diaper bag, then slid the baby around and down to the floor, where she sort of draped herself over her mother's Reeboks. The back of her mother's T-shirt said, *We put the meat between the buns.* "I thought my dad said he had to go somewhere."

"He probably did. He spends a lot of time with that new horse of his." They brushed looks. Angela had the advantage of mascara, liner, and two shades of eyeshadow. "I guess I should be thankful that he's not trying to *ride* her," Nan said with a breezy laugh. "You could break your neck falling off a horse that size. But it's still awfully strange."

Megan Michele was rocking on her hands and knees. Both women gazed down at the wispy curls that fringed the back of her head. Then Nan heard herself saying, "You haven't seen his full beard, or the black frock coat and top hat. He looks like some turn-of-the-century undertaker, standing up there on his fancy cart, cracking his whip. He isn't really himself. At least I hope not?"

Angela shrugged. "He said it was OK if I used your phone." Will had pleaded with his daughter to put in a phone. Finally she'd said she and Kiser had no cash for the deposit, and Will had given them a check. That was ages ago.

"Feel free," Nan said, then brightly, impulsively, she asked, "How's your new tooth?"

Angela's hand flew up to her mouth. She frowned—couldn't imagine why Nan should ask such a question—then she dropped into a squat. "Look at Megan Michele's," she said, wedging a finger between the baby's lips to reveal four white chips. Megan Michele tried to squirm away but Angela held her by the soft, indented nape of her neck, kept the glistening teeth exposed with her finger, looking up at Nan as if offering proof that all was not lost. "I don't guess I got any phone calls yet?"

"Calls here, Angela?"

"I put the truck in the paper," she announced rising. "With this number. Kiser keeps coming into the restaurant and threatening to take it. He says a truck should go to the man, and I get *her.*" She budged the baby by lifting one foot. "Besides, I'm tired of paying on it *and* the Visas."

The truck was a sky blue Silverado with a rollover bar and giant tires. Kiser had to have the truck. The check Will gave them to finance a wedding became the down payment. Kiser was on the stocky side with a snub nose and no apparent neck. Angela had to have him. He walked with a swagger, fell into bad moods, and quit jobs. Megan Michele was large for nine months, and though sticky in places and speckled with heat rash, apparently healthy. They had to have her. The way other babies smiled, she puckered her mouth into an O — an odd little reflex — maybe she was sucking in air to sooth her teething gums, maybe she was trying to say, *If you only knew what I've seen.* But what Nan wanted to know long looks at the child would never reveal: the depth of Kiser's imprint on her cells?

Such are the facts Nan assembles in her mind now, facts that should have made it impossible for Angela to say she was tired of anything. But they didn't, and she did. Kiser had left for bigger bucks on the Eastern Shore. The truck was up for sale. "It's over," was all Angela said that Saturday, and Nan had to bite her own fist.

How could Angela have known so definitely what she had to have, Nan wonders. How could she have done with such certainty and then undone without a trace of shame? It had taken Nan almost forty years to get up whatever it was you had to get up to get married. And always, whenever Nan had tried to compile reasons for bearing a child, her mind had gone blank. Almost forty years to do part of what Angela had done in eighteen, and Kiser twice in his twenty. As Will and Nan sat up through the night in the hospital waiting room while Angela labored with Megan Michele, Kiser had appeared with his mother, a woman with blue pouches under her eyes and thin hair that wouldn't stay in its rubber band. She'd drawn Nan aside and told her that Kiser's luck must be changing, praise the Lord, because he'd gone through all this before with another girl up in Mt. Airy, and the baby was born dead.

Nine months later Nan fixed tuna salad for Angela and Megan Michele while somewhere Will hitched the magnificent Simone to her museum-piece of a cart and drove her for one more blue ribbon. Nan can only guess why, if he knew Angela was coming, he couldn't have arranged to be there. She tried to explain to Angela how much her father missed her, and Angela, with her bitter clarity, called that *bullshit.* "I was the weak link," Angela said. "I didn't use the crop enough, or I didn't hold the reins tight enough, or I forgot about my goddamn thumbs."

"You weren't a weak link, you were wonderful," Nan told her.

"You never did know anything about any of that stuff," Angela said.

Later Nan remembers leaning out the side door to call Angela to the phone. She was perched on the back corner of the truck bed waving the hose in her hand. Water hit the waxed blue floor in long dollops, and Megan Michele, stripped to her plastic diaper, clung to the other corner, curls plastered to her scalp, enjoying the splash. Round bellied and swaybacked on sturdy legs, she gripped the sides. Her bare feet slipped on the slick bottom, and her mouth O tightened to a kiss.

"Be careful she doesn't fall," Nan said.

"I know," Angela replied. "I was going to fill it up and make a little pool for her but like it all leaks out the back here." Then she hooked one arm around the baby and scooped her up in fierce embrace. "She'd never fall," she said.

Seven years later Nan isn't ready to deal with Angela. She needs more time to compose herself, return to original intentions, let shame and sorrow settle into relief. She needs to understand first why desire wells up and then falters. Why one night in the dark her husband, whose decisiveness and raw need once captured her, convinced her to give up a life of sleeping alone, this husband left her side for the daybed in the den.

If only Will could have admitted that Project Angela had failed, if only he'd let himself grieve after Angela took off for the West Coast and, eventually, the change of address cards stopped coming. If only Nan could have brought herself to mention that it hurt her, the amount of time he spent decorating and driving that horse.

But then one day, when she thought she had grown past caring, Nan awoke to the surprise of a man's touch, Will stretched beside her again, guiding her hand to where he was hard. It was like a silent dream, strangely impersonal. She suspected that it was the doing finally of a tape she had glimpsed in his desk drawer, *Self-Hypnosis and Sexuality,* but such suspicions seemed trivial, she would not let them interfere. Dreamlike, impersonal, it might never occur again.

But it did. Week after week. Until she suspected desire had succumbed to sheer assertion, pleasure to proof, and her suspicions began to interfere. One morning, when he was finished, his body rolled away from hers and his eyes went dark with surprise. He muttered something she could not make out and as she leaned across his chest to hear more clearly, his eyes looked far beyond her. She thought he said, "Give me a hand," and then his own hands closed and opened on air.

Nan felt she needed to understand all this before she tried to find Angela. But Angela found her first.

Coming through the arrival gate from Phoenix, Angela is tinier than ever, in a short black dress, a maroon suede jacket with fringed arms, high-heeled cowboy boots, and a rhinestone in the flange of her nose. Marching a step ahead of her mother, a loaded backpack slung over one arm, Megan Michele looks large for her eight years, large and sturdy. She is wearing a baggy sweatshirt over a denim jumper and waffle-weave long johns under it to protect against December in the East. A bushy tail of hair spouts from over one of her ears and her forehead seems permanently flexed to entreat. The child stops in front of Nan; they exchange stares: *who are you?* each wants to ask.

"The spitting image of Kiser," Angela says, not proudly. The time for hugging each other, if they were going to hug, has passed. "Acts like him too, stubborn little know-it-all."

"No," Nan says. "I don't see any connection." The last she and Will heard, Kiser had landed where he belonged, in jail.

Angela rummages through the huge leather sack that hangs from her shoulder, pulls out a bronze horse key ring, a broken comb, two white plastic bags, packed tight and knotted, a wad of charge receipts, finally a pack of cigarettes. "This is all the luggage we brought," she says, as she lights a cigarette then holds it down behind her back like a secret. "More like all the luggage we've got." There are brown spots on her teeth; tobacco stains or decay, she is not taking care of them. "I can't believe it's happened."

"That's totally normal," Megan Michele says, folding her arms across her waistless middle. "We had this unit in school on death and dying."

Angela takes a deep drag of smoke. "Can't we, like, see him one last time?"

Nan shakes her head. "If I'd known how to reach you, I—"

"Some people have to see the body," Megan Michele explains.

"You'll just have to trust me," Nan says. "For once." Angela blows smoke over her shoulder. "One minute he was with me," Nan says. "The next minute he was gone."

"What about CPR?" Megan Michele asks with a slight whine once they are in the car. "We had this unit in school on CPR."

"My heavens," Nan says.

"Didn't you do it?" The girl has bounced forward to poke her round, sunburned face between the seats.

"Megan Michele, buckle up, it's the law," her mother says.

"I'm going to be a paramedic," Megan Michele says. "I like saving people. I sort of like seeing blood."

"Your grandfather had a massive stroke," Nan says, feeling suddenly old, the next in line.

Megan Michele flops into the corner of the backseat, out of sight. "You could still do CPR," she says.

What is Nan going to do with them? Angela has taken over Nan's fisherman's sweater and the den, where she stays up half the night watching TV and filling the room with cigarette smoke. And every time Nan turns around, there is Megan Michele, who keeps bringing up the subject of CPR, her mouth puckering in remonstrance. When she isn't trying to stir up guilt, the child hovers in the kitchen, asking questions, opening the refrigerator, the oven, poking her blunt little nose into every bowl and pot— she doesn't really care for anything made from scratch, she explains. It's just that she's used to her own cooking, the tastes that come in boxes and foil packets and plastic trays you can put in a microwave.

Though it has been weeks since he died, Angela is obsessed with seeing her father one last time. She stares at the framed snapshots on the mantel—Will in a wet suit, Will with ten-foot wings strapped to his back, Will in gray pinstripes, standing beside Nan and the daffodils in that too-youthful cotton dress.

Angela used to accuse Nan of *getting heavy* on her, and why not give her what she expects? "His spirit lives on in each of us," Nan tells her. It's what Nan's own mother promised, her face all puffy and alarmed like someone roused from sleep, when Nan's father didn't survive his last binge. Nan never denied it aloud, never told her mother no, no spirit that weak and sentimental was ever going to live on in her—not in her mind, not through her body.

Angela takes down a five-by-eight of a black horse in profile, its enormous size and strength mocked by the high, pointed collar, the patent leather bridle and harness, all encrusted with fake rubies and rhinestones, and the red ribbons woven into its mane and binding its tail. At its rear is hitched a dark, silver-studded chariot; facing the camera, legs planted apart, arms folded over his chest, Will grins through a full gray-white beard. She holds the picture out to Nan.

"He had presence, your father," Nan says.

"So that's the horse?"

"Simone," Nan says with an attempt at gaiety. "I don't know what he saw in her."

"Mid-life crisis," Angela says. "It wasn't his first."

"What are we going to do with her?" Another complicated question. This gigantic creature whom Nan has resented when she couldn't ignore—finally, she is in her hands. "It costs three hundred dollars a month to board her. The cart and harness are worth thousands. He kept adding things, getting fancier and fancier. He couldn't stop."

Angela just squints off through a puff of smoke.

Megan Michele plants herself in front of her mother. "Did you ask her what's in his will yet?"

Angela yanks her daughter into a hug, presses the girl's face into Nan's sweater. Bits of cigarette ash land on the child's head, more drift down to the carpet.

"Will didn't leave a will," Nan says with a silly giggle. "I don't think it ever occurred to him that he would die."

Angela buries her mouth in Megan Michele's hair. The two of them begin rocking from side to side, sort of like disaster victims waiting for relief, Nan thinks, or lost children. Maybe they are asking her to make a place for them. How can she, when all she wants is her old life back, separate and whole?

"As far as I'm concerned," Nan says, "Simone belongs to you, Simone and everything that goes with her."

For the first time ever, Nan seems to have caught Angela by surprise. Megan Michele wrenches away from her mother's grip and contrives an upward slap of Nan's palm. Angela looks afraid.

"You could get a lot of money for her," Nan goes on. "Enough to buy another horse for you and maybe a pony for Megan Michele. I've wondered whether you ever miss—"

"Not," Angela says. "What good would it do for me to start missing stuff?"

"Even the three hundred dollars a month. You could have that too. Till you got your feet on the ground."

Angela grimaces: how could Nan still be given to such dumb ideas? She begins rubbing her eyes until they appear to be melting down her cheeks.

"I think your father would have wanted you to have that much," Nan says.

Angela looks like someone about to jump from a high place, about to be forced to jump. "I don't want anything from him," she says, her voice cracking.

"Yes, she does," Megan Michele says, moving right under her mother's bowed head, looking up into her mother's face.

"Your father thought the world of you, Angela."

"Is that why he sold my horse?"

Yes, Nan thinks, but the word seems too complicated to speak.

"How could he just take it away"—Angela's closed eyes ooze darkness—"after he gave it?"

"He was angry. And hurt."

She pinches her face shut again, then relaxes it. "Well, maybe I am too."

"This is totally normal," says Megan Michele, patting the small of her mother's back.

"You stay out of it," her mother tells her.

Nan says, "He didn't know what to do."

"You think I did?" She throws Nan a look of such scorn that Nan has to remind herself that she, Angela, once seemed to know everything. "Why did he have to do anything?"

"That's a good question," Nan admits.

"It's sick, the way you try to understand everything," Angela says. "The way you're always trying to *communicate.*"

Her conviction smothers Nan, the way conviction in other people always has. "You don't know me, Angela," Nan manages to gasp, but Angela is busy with a Kleenex, reshaping her eyes.

Nan will probably never know Angela. But Megan Michele keeps seeming familiar. Nan looks in on her in the guest room from the doorway, this mystery child who has sprung up between the crisp floral sheets, wearing one of Nan's flannel nightgowns, the sleeves rolled thick around each wrist, her hands clutching a book. Her loose hair is fanned on the pillow like a tangled head-dress; her plump cheeks shine. Spread around her on the flowered comforter are other books from her backpack, some of the very books Nan loved as a girl. As Nan used to, Megan Michele has read them each four and five times. She's told Nan, "I like it better when I know what to expect."

Tonight she says, "My mom's upset, but she'll get over it. I mean, we need that money. That's what we came here for."

Nan nods. Does she wish the child were less honest, or that the situation were less simple—pay Angela off and she and Megan Michele will go away?

"What are you going to do with the money?" Nan asks.

Megan Michele shrugs.

"What would you *like* to do with it?"

"I don't think we can go back where we were."

"But school will be starting up for you again soon."

"I sort of like school," Megan Michele says.

"Where do you think you'll go next?" Nan detests prying, yet she keeps on asking questions. It's as if she craves the sound of the girl's voice answering, slightly plaintive, but absolutely candid, like a memory that won't quite come clear.

"She doesn't tell me," Megan Michele says. "She sort of doesn't like having a plan."

"What would *you* like?" Nan asks again. Maybe she is prying, looking for a cue.

"To meet my dad." Nan reaches for the doorjamb and takes a breath. "Did you ever know my dad?"

Nan nods. "Not very well."

"Is he really a heartbreaker?"

Nan backs away from the threshold, puts a hand to her mouth, but doesn't blow a kiss. "You could probably call him that."

Now that she has offered, it seems obvious to Nan that everything to do with Will's horse must be sold and the money returned to Angela, finally and unconditionally—no prying, no interference. Yet the next afternoon, as she drives mother and daughter out to the farm, doubt comes over her, as it always does.

They are all three bundled in Nan's clothes. Angela has belted the fisherman's cardigan like a kimono over her black, skintight stretch pants; Megan Michele wears an extra kneelength sweatshirt over her own. Nan leads them down the narrow passage beside Simone's empty stall, shows them the strips of silver bells, the whip, and the elaborate harness—a crisscross of patent leather straps that bind the horse's dark strength to the wooden hitch and cart that gather dust in another shed. When Nan tries to explain to Megan Michele how it all worked, this hobby that absorbed Will in his last years, the child just gazes at her skeptically, suspiciously, as though Nan is holding something back.

They catch up to Angela, who is already heading out toward the open, rolling fields. The horizon sinks and rises in front of them; the sky looks thick and gray. "Do you think it's going to snow?" Megan Michele asks. "I sort of like seeing snow, but I can't remember if I ever did."

Nan reaches for her cold bare fist and rubs it for a minute between her gloves before the child pulls away, runs ahead up a hill. The ground is frozen, lumpy, and Angela wobbles along in her high-heeled boots. Then from the crest the three of them spot a small herd of horses—mostly chestnuts, one paint, shaggy in their winter coats—and in their midst, Simone, huge and dark. Having gotten wind of humans, the horses pause in their grazing, heads raised, forelegs braced.

As Angela approaches the herd, it begins to drift along the fence, casually, carelessly, yet keeping constant the space between it and her. Simone seems to be coaching the others in this—to ignore the carrot, sugar, even their own names, because each is only prelude to the bit. After a few minutes of it, Angela halts. "All right, you guys," she shouts to the horses. "That's enough, goddamn it." She marches toward them again at as brisk a pace as her boots will allow.

They look away from her indifferently, but they slow their drift and she gains on them. She stops and screams at them again, and this time, when she starts toward them, they don't move. Then she shouts back, "What are you waiting for?" So Megan Michele and Nan advance, pretending indifference also.

Angela reaches the horses. Heads toss and snort. Muzzles poke at her, and she shoves each away with the heel of her hand, opening herself a trail into their center. They close ranks around her and she is lost. Megan Michele and Nan exchange a look of suppressed panic, then stumble stiffly forward. The paint swivels away from the group and ambles out to meet them, nibbles around Nan's hips and up the arm of her jacket, turns and ambles back.

Soon they too are surrounded by restless shoulders, flanks, swishing tails. The air seems warmer, steamy with mingled breaths. Megan Michele is clutching Nan's hand and Nan is clutching back. "If we just stay calm," Nan tells her.

"I am calm," she says. Her cheeks are a raw red and she keeps sniffling. "I sort of like how they smell."

There is a shift of bodies, and Angela appears, her right arm stretched straight up so she can hang on to the noseband of Simone's halter. "Here she is," she says, yanking on the band, pulling the mare's head down from its great height until the muzzle rubs her cheek. With her free hand, she gropes in her shoulder bag and comes up with an offering of Rolaids. Simone's black lips part to reveal teeth as big as piano keys.

Megan Michele strokes Simone's velvet nose. Nan is thinking that the nostrils are just like the word sounds—large, open, sensitive. Nan is thinking how wary and lonely the eyes are, with their drooping lashes, each fated to its separate one-sided view. Nan is thinking so many crazy things—about insurance money, enough to buy a place in the country, and give it over to grazing horses, and maybe have Megan Michele come and live with her. They would never ride the horses, but only watch them and walk among them, and maybe somehow their presence would erase all trace of Kiser in the child.

Angela is saying that bareback is the only way to ride, the only way to become one with the horse. Her dad always tried to discourage it, said it set a bad precedent—a horse who wasn't too crazy about the girth or the bit might get the wrong idea, might think it had options. Besides, Angela might hurt herself. But when her dad wasn't around, Angela used to forget the saddle and take off down the trails on Brandy, her hands full of mane.

"It's real easy," Angela says, "much easier than messing with reins and stirrups and stuff." When she tries to lead Simone closer to the fence, the mare jerks her head up, whinnying, and lifts Angela right off the ground.

Why doesn't Nan discourage this, not for Will's pragmatic reasons but for her own? Why, even when the darkening sky seems to drop down on them and a chilly wind starts? Maybe because she never feels she has a right to, she is only a witness. Maybe because she sees they are made for each other, Megan Michele and the horse, created to some special, heroic scale.

Angela hands over the halter to Nan to hold—no more than she ever asked of Nan with Brandy. Then like a child herself, she scrambles up the slats of the fence, grabs at Simone's mane, and throws herself onto her. The mare seems not to even notice that someone is wiggling herself up to straddle her back. Now Megan Michele is crouched on the top slat of the fence with one hand gripping Nan's shoulder. Angela reaches, encourages, the child lunges for the curve of space in front of her mother. The horse shifts her hooves; her ears twitch. With all the authority she can muster, Nan gives the halter a firm tug.

Angela is offering directions—legs loose, hips loose, seat deep. "Pretend you're sinking in," she says. Megan Michele closes her eyes, puckers her mouth, sort of slouches down. Then Angela's boot kicks back, Simone takes a quick unbalancing step, and Megan Michele falls forward, clutching at mane.

"Don't fight the motion," Angela advises. "Roll with it."

Megan Michele rights herself and now her body absorbs the jolts and the three are off. Simone's walk is uneven, slow, but they are moving away from the rest of the herd, which starts to follow halfheartedly, then returns to cropping the meager grass. Megan Michele looks back at Nan, her mouth in a wide-open smile, and jerks a thumbs up, which throws her off balance again. Angela, her gaze on the distance, doesn't seem to notice. *Sink in,* Nan whispers, as the child wobbles herself back into line, shoulders over hips.

Simone follows the fence which angles off across the hilly field. As they climb the first rise, mother and daughter lean forward over the mane, and when they reach the crest and start down, they lean back toward the rump. Then comes another rise and then a slope that drops much deeper than the first, and they sink out of sight. When they appear again, it is not where Nan expected, but on the other side of a fence, farther away than seems possible.

That is when it does start snowing. Large, soft flakes swirling like paper ash. Though Megan Michele's cheer falls faint on Nan's ears, Simone must have heard it as a command to trot. Nan worries that the child will be shaken to pieces, but Megan Michele is a natural, bouncing there in her mother's embrace, rolling with her, both of them become one with the horse.

The snow is falling faster now, beginning to stick to hair and shoulders. Nan wishes she could slow the riders down, make them stop, make them wait for her, wait with her—across the hills she hears Angela laughing—but she can't, and by the time she calls out to them that it is getting late and they had better go home, they are too far away to hear, and the snow has shrouded them so completely that Nan can't make them out, though it must melt around such heat as Simone's, who holds her dark ground against the billows of white.

Molly Best Tinsley, whose stories have appeared widely in literary quarterlies and anthologies, recently fled the Washington, D.C., area for the mountains of Ashland, Oregon. She has published a novel, *My Life with Darwin,* and is at work on a full-length play, *Group,* and a memoir, *Continuing Care.*

It took a couple of years for "The Only Way to Ride" to reveal its layers and assume its final form. It began with Angela's visit to Nan, the baby Megan Michele in tow, then unfurled in all sorts of unwieldy directions. Whether the third-person point of view and the anchoring present tense bring things under control is for someone else to decide. For me this became the story honoring horses I'd wanted to write for a long time.

BRIDGE

(from *Story*)

R ay and his wife had rented a house that looked down onto a small town piled into a narrow, gray valley. All the houses Ray could see, including his own, were built of the same rust-colored brick. The great river for which the valley was named flowed north; downstream was up on the map, while home, south, lay upstream, facts of geography Ray found disconcerting.

Ray had been a newspaper reporter until he began to forget how to spell. First, he lost track of the number of r's in "sheriff," then he lost the f's. "Commission" began to look right no matter how he spelled it. His wife found a job teaching computer science at a small, Christian college, and they packed up and moved for it. She was serious and pale, unashamed to pray out loud in restaurants. Ray stopped going to church with her about the time the letters in the word "Episcopalian" flew apart as if they had been held together by springs. He could still spell "God," but found that he no longer cared to.

Mornings, after his wife went to school, Ray lay on the couch and tried to think up ways to make his day seem constructive. Afternoons, he walked down the hill into the town, where the square, the buses, the restaurants, and barber shops were filled with old men waiting to die. The old men had once made steel for bridges. This is what they talked about while they waited. The steel they had made. They built the bridge that leapt from the town square out over the river. It was green and intricate, held high above the water by four tall, delicate-looking towers.

Ray could see the bridge from his kitchen window. He sneaked into the kitchen forty, fifty, maybe a hundred times a day to look at it, to make sure it was still there. He did not actually expect the bridge to disappear, but still took a kind of giddy, secret pleasure in keeping watch. Sometimes when Ray looked at the bridge he could feel himself falling toward the river, a sensation he tried to control. He had been told by a trained professional, his wife's idea, that he was in danger. Ray, however, did not feel as if he were in danger. Recently he had begun to feel very light, unencumbered, almost invisible. He sat among the old men in the square and they never looked at him. He startled them when he spoke. What was dangerous, Ray thought, was paying some stranger one hundred and twenty-five dollars an hour to tell him he shouldn't be allowed to drive his car, that he might suddenly decide to drive it into oncoming traffic. What the stranger didn't realize was how much he loved his car, even though it was old. He changed the oil every 2,500 miles; his tires were new, French, religiously rotated, precisely inflated.

One evening, after talking to the stranger, Ray told his wife he was feeling better. She smiled and suggested he walk down the hill and return a videotape they had watched. It was an Italian movie set on a Greek island where nothing bad ever happened. Ray removed the tape from the machine and promised his wife he would be good. Because he had not intended to lie, he was surprised and a little embarrassed when he dropped off the tape and headed immediately for the bridge. He knew he would get in big trouble if he got caught anywhere near it, so he hurried. The streetlights were blinking on. He looked down and away from the headlights of the approaching cars.

Ray began to smile as he turned the corner at the square and started toward the river. The thought of seeing the bridge up close made him happy. What he liked about the idea of falling—he had no intention of *jumping*, he was sure of that—was that shortly after hitting the water he would be somewhere. Not just in the river, which wouldn't matter, but someplace else. Ray had no idea where that place might be, or even if he would like it, but the existence of so many possibilities living so near his house intrigued him. The bridge was a gate, a wardrobe, a looking glass, through which he could travel. Ray also knew that his thinking of the bridge as metaphor would worry just about everyone he could think of to tell, so he decided to keep it to himself. Most people, Ray thought, were satisfied with simple ideas: bridge as bridge, road as road.

The bridge seemed alive when Ray approached, resting, breathing, capable of sudden movement. The hair stood up on his arms. He couldn't see the river, only the ancient steel curving out over it. The towers were taller than he had imagined. Ray walked through a wall of cold air and noticed that he could smell the water. He inched forward and reached out and put his hand on the bridge's cool, green flank. The steel vibrated beneath his palm. He said, "Shh," as if talking to a large, nervous animal. The bridge wanted him to walk out on it; he could feel it. That's why the old men had made it.

What stopped Ray from walking out to have a look was the husband's thought that his wife might be coming any minute in the car to find him. That was a scene he wanted to avoid. He could easily picture his old car stopped in the middle of the bridge, holding up traffic, while his wife shouted for him to get in. Ray hated loud noises; he couldn't stand shouting, horns blowing, the thumping cars of teenagers, the clack of a printing press, jets passing over his house, and the only thing worse than loud noises was being responsible for them. Ray patted the bridge, gently, acknowledging the secret regret they shared, and turned and faced the line of headlights moving toward the river from the square. Beyond the square, he could see more headlights snaking down the hill on which he lived. One of the cars could be his, his wife driving, leaning out over the wheel, her head filled with God and binary codes and concern. Ray jogged until he reached a place at which he could explain his presence. He considered himself a good husband, a man of responsibilities, a right-thinking man.

When Ray got home, his wife was making supper. She seemed glad to see him, but not alarmed that he had been gone too long. She did not suspect him of sneaking off to the bridge because he had promised her he wouldn't. Ray was touched by her simple trust. He considered himself the recipient of a small gift, a seashell, a marble, a stick man made of pipe cleaners. He smiled and gave his wife a kiss. He could look at the bridge again tomorrow. She would never know. Ray asked what was for supper. He glanced briefly at the thin reflection staring at him from the kitchen window. It did not look entirely familiar; it grinned in a way he could not explain. Ray hated it, if for no other reason than it kept him from seeing down into the valley, the line of headlights crossing and crossing the dark bridge. He set the table, drew two glasses of water from the tap, and joined his wife in the dining room. She bowed her head and over their married meal offered an earnest prayer, to which Ray neither paid attention nor believed.

———————

Tony Earley is a native of Rutherfordton, North Carolina, and a graduate of Warren Wilson College and the University of Alabama. His collection of short stories, *Here We Are in Paradise,* was published in 1994. He is currently at work on a novel. His fiction and nonfiction have appeared in *Harper's, Esquire, The Oxford American, Story,* and *Granta,* which named him to its "Best of Young American Novelists" list in 1996. He lives with his wife in Nashville, Tennessee, where he teaches writing at Vanderbilt University.

"Bridge" was originally part of an article I wrote on ghosts for The Oxford American, *with the idea in mind that ghosts could just as easily live in memory or imagination as they could in a haunted hotel in New*

Orleans. The editors at the magazine chose—wisely, I think—to cut all
the fictional elements in what was basically a travel piece. I realized several
weeks later that one of the parts I had cut from the original article looked sus-
piciously like a short story. So I guess you could say I found it in a trash can.
To all the people who say, after reading this story, "How are you?" I want to
say that I am fine. Ray didn't jump, and I didn't either.

Nancy Richard

THE ORDER OF THINGS

(from *Shenandoah*)

The Bigler girl had known it would happen again, so she was not alarmed when she emerged from Touchet's Grocery to find her mother had scaled the Chinese tallow tree behind the store. For a woman of her size, the girl observed, her mother was uncommonly graceful. And quick. When the girl called out, her mother settled in on one substantial branch before she answered. She may have been picking up the thread of an old conversation.

"It's the only real escape," she said, addressing some invisible listener, "from the rising waters of time's bitter flood."

Yeats again, the girl thought. Yeats and the hospital.

Old Mr. Touchet, whose breath already sang of whiskey, clutched the girl's arm. "I'm not responsible," he insisted, "if something happens. If your mama falls." He seemed overcome by the sight of Myrtle Bigler in his tree and returned almost immediately to his store. "I don't have no insurance for that," he announced from behind his screen door. "Only if it falls on my store in a hurricane. Nothing else."

If a small crowd had formed behind her, the girl scarcely heard their voices or the gravel beneath their feet as they gathered, milled about, and left. Soon a stout, fair young man appeared and remained alongside her as if this were his custom.

At first she paid him no notice. The sun was getting hot, and though Myrtle Bigler usually descended her perch within a couple of hours, her daughter knew there could be no rushing things.

Because for a time neither said anything, the girl merely watched her mother and listened to his breathing, a labored wheezing she could not ignore because he stood so close. She had seen him before, cleaning the store windows, pushing a broom, the whistle from his lungs a solemn accompaniment to his monotone humming. Soon he left her side and within moments returned, carrying two chairs. He set them in the shade of the Chinese tallow, directed her to one of them, and sat beside her.

"Your mama, I hear she does this often."

"Often enough," the girl said. Her mother had long ceased to pay attention to anything below. She might have dozed off.

He withdrew a handkerchief from a back pocket and wiped his forehead and upper lip, then the back of his neck. His wheezing had climbed in pitch.

"You don't have to sit here," the girl said. "Sometimes she takes an hour, sometimes all day. She'll come down when she's ready. Don't you have something else to do?"

The sun had climbed from behind the tree so it now glared without relief from nearly overhead. The girl wished she'd brought a hat. Her mother looked down at last and waved but said nothing.

"You want me to go get the priest?" The young man seemed to think she would welcome his idea for the ultimate solution it was.

"Why? Does he have a ladder?" The girl wondered why he thought a priest could talk her mother out of a tree. Or perhaps he feared she might jump and therefore be in need of some final words.

"I don't think so. But Father Mike, he makes things seem not so bad. Like in confession, he says 'Okey doke' when you finish. Your sins, they don't sound so bad when he says that. I can go get him if you want."

The girl tried to imagine her mother talking to a priest: *Sometimes,* her mother might say to him, *everything, everyone gets too close. I can't see the order of things.*

Okey doke, the priest would say.

"No," she said. "Thanks just the same."

They sat in silence while the girl regarded her mother, who stirred little except to swing her crossed ankles. So the girl sat and waited, the young man beside her, until just past dark, when Myrtle Bigler descended the tree.

That night her mother slept fitfully, the girl not at all. She drank coffee to stay awake, in order that she might watch and listen. She was watching when the sun crept into their dark kitchen, when her mother's breathing slowed to the comforting rhythm of sleep. Early on Monday morning the girl walked into Catalpa, and from the telephone at Touchet's Grocery, called the state mental hospital again. Then she bought their bus tickets.

Two days later, the girl woke before dawn to find her mother had already packed her bag.

"How many times is this?" She stood in the kitchen, facing the window where the sun announced itself every morning.

"I'm not sure," the girl said. "Six or seven, maybe?"

Her mother's gaze had not left the east horizon. "Oh, it must be more than that," she murmured. "I could remember that many." She ran water into the sink, let it run over her finger, turned it off. "We don't have to leave before sunrise, do we?"

"No," the girl said. "We have plenty of time."

Her mother turned finally to look at her. "Good," she said. "I want to watch the sun come up. I don't want it to happen behind my back. Not today."

In Touchet's Grocery, from behind the array of Daily Special signs, they watched for the bus. Her mother was checking the contents of her bag for the third time, though there was little to pack. She owned few clothes, a single pair of shoes, which she wore for the occasion—*You never know what's on the floor of a bus*—her collection of Yeats's poetry—*Maud Gonne was crazy, too, but she was beautiful so nobody cared*—a half dozen prescription bottles.

"Is it still Wednesday?"

The girl nodded. As she had seven names, arranged alphabetically, her mother kept track of them according to the days of the week. Myrtle had named her daughter after women she'd known in state hospitals. The drugs steal away parts of your memory, she explained to her daughter: the names hold them fast.

"There's something important I meant to say, Hattie," her mother went on, "and I'm telling you this so you'll know." She seemed to have been distracted by the clutter in her bag. She moved her hairbrush to the opposite side, checked the cap on her shampoo, and repositioned the Yeats. The front cover was missing. The girl had recovered it from a box of discards on the parish bookmobile, where the librarian had seen her but had pretended not to.

"What, Mama? What should I know?" She secured the latches on her mother's bag and checked the pocket of her dress for her own return ticket.

"Every time it starts," her mother said, without moving, "I think this time I won't let it. This time I'll hold on and I won't worry you. It is as if someone had rearranged the furniture in a familiar room and then turned the lights off. It is all disarray."

The girl saw the bus approach, took her mother's arm, and led her toward the grocery's exit. "I know, Mama," she said. "Let's go; we'll miss the bus."

For the next several weeks, or maybe it would be months, the girl would live alone, but she didn't mind; she had a fireplace, a cistern, a big washtub on her back porch. A couple of days a week she sold her produce from a roadside stand along the parish highway. On Friday nights she wrote a letter to her mother. On Saturdays she walked to Catalpa.

One Saturday morning in midsummer, instead of Mr. Touchet, the young man met her at the back door of the grocery. His gaze was clear and direct as a child's.

His name was Claude Joseph Doiron, he said. She could call him T-Boy. He stood in the doorway and stared at her.

"My vegetables," the girl said, "I bring them every Saturday. For the rent. When it's paid I get cash."

"I knew that," he said. "I'm the Saturday manager now. I knew that."

She crossed the store and made her way toward the annex where the Touchets ran the town's post office. He followed and stepped behind the counter. The girl was suddenly conscious of her mass of tangled hair, her bare feet, the size of her hands. "Any Bigler mail? And a stamp, please."

He shuffled through the stack of General Delivery. "Your name is Grace?"

"This week," she said, and took the envelope. Her mother had run through her names alphabetically, week by week; with her last letter she'd begun again with Alma.

"What you mean this week? Your name, it's going to be something else next week?"

"I have seven," she said, "seven names."

"Like the days of the week," he said, "and like that poem about Monday's child has a fair face and one of them works hard for a living." He studied her patiently, while from deep in his chest came a thin, high whistling, like a small mournful bird's.

"Yes, something like that," the girl said.

She pushed the wheelbarrow, which held her few purchases, from the back of the store around to the front and onto the shoulder of the highway. Though she avoided turning around, she knew he was watching.

"I never knew nobody with so many names," he called and, "You come every Saturday?"

At home she read the letter:

July 30

Dear Grace,

Old Mrs. Guidroz is back, the one whose dead child visits her dreams now and then. So's the boy with the scarred wrists. The routine hasn't changed. They won't let me read past ten, though sometimes I think the fire in my head is enough light to read by. I miss our vegetables; such curious food for a healthcare facility.

They tell me it's been nine weeks, but I always lose time in here. There's nothing to make one day any different from any other, except when somebody checks in or out. They tell me I will get used to these drugs, that soon I will be able to tell one day from another, one memory from another.

I have dreams, but I can't remember them. They wake me up, and they're gone. A kind of hit and run. What's left is all "testy delirium and dull decrepitude." How could Yeats have known? Did he get those words from poor Maud Gonne?

Your mother

The following week the young man appeared at her roadside stand. One morning he bought tomatoes and peppers. The next, all her eggplants. How did she manage to carry all this? he wanted to know. Could he give her a ride home? he asked.

The Bigler girl said, "I have a wheelbarrow," and, "No, thanks."

That Friday night the sky was violet, the moon a broad Cheshire grin. The girl sat on her front porch in the dark and watched the rabbits move about in the moonlight. When they scattered suddenly into the overgrown pasture, she looked up to see him walking toward her, at the far edge of the darkness, following his moonshadow. She went inside and from her window saw him stop at the edge of the blackness that was the woods and stand just beyond the fenceline, where the posts listed north and south, silvery in the moonlight. The rabbits had disappeared; she pictured them huddled and watchful among the thistles, waiting.

He carried a shovel. With one hand he withdrew something from a pocket in his trousers, stooped, placed it on the ground, and began to dig. One spadeful, two. Then he took the object, dropped it into the hole, and buried it. When he'd tamped the dirt into place with the back of the shovel, he turned and made his plodding way across the light-bathed pasture toward the railroad tracks.

She waited until he was gone, until the midnight freight had chuffed its way past, toward the river crossing and Baton Rouge, and she could see only the glow of the lantern that hung at the

door of the caboose. Then she retrieved her own shovel from beneath the back porch and unearthed the thing he'd buried. It was
a small black crucifix which trailed an inch or so of fragile silver
chain. She dropped it into the pocket of her dress. *There's plenty
of strangeness in the world. Mary-Margaret,* her mother might say
on a Friday. *Pay it no mind.*

The next morning she took her produce to town as usual. He
met her at the back door and collected her fine green and red peppers and a basket of zucchini. The girl ignored his stares and questions, picked up her letter and left.

August 6

Dear Hattie,

They think I'm making fine progress. Beginning to Cooper-
ate is how they put it. They have found a combination of drugs
that let me see past breakfast and I must be giving the right answers in Group. As many times as I've done this, you'd think I'd
have got the hang of it by now.

A new patient arrived yesterday, an old man here to dry out.
Mr. Badeaux. He's gone blind, and his daughter thinks he's Not
Taking It Well. I asked her how she thought he was supposed to
take it. She said I shouldn't be so hostile. A person can take only
so much, she said. I said yes, I could certainly understand that,
the "stir and tumult of defeated dreams" and all. She warned Mr.
Badeaux he should watch who he spends time with. She whispered, but I heard.

M.

The next week the young man pulled up to the Bigler girl's stand
and bought all the okra. "Your hair," he said, "in the sun it's three
different colors. You knew that?"

She said, "You'll want some tomatoes to cook with the okra."

Late that night, as the girl drew water from the cistern and filled
the washtub on her back porch, the train announced itself in the
distance. The whistle sounded in Maringouin, and the light on
the engine came into sight at the mill. She thought about Claude

Joseph Doiron. He stared at her, as if whatever she might say was exactly what he'd hoped to hear, even if she never answered his questions. He was slow and fat and he wheezed. But he didn't look at her in the way she had come to expect: *Poor girl her mama's a little funny, calls her a different name every day, it's no wonder she's shy.* And he saw colors in her hair.

That night there was no moon, and in the blackness that cloaked her garden, the pasture, the woods, it was easy to believe herself alone in the world. The lantern she'd set on the porch cast shadows that danced to the nightmusic she loved: the hum of treefrogs and cicadas, the clacking of the eastbound freight. She imagined she could hear the bayou lapping at its banks, the slap of a gar's tail on its surface, but soon the girl heard what she knew to be the young man's voice. Claude Joseph Doiron stood out there in the darkness, singing to her: "Grace, sweet Grace."

She went to the end of her porch. "What do you want?" she called into the night. "Why are you here?"

Soon she heard a rustling and the movement of large, heavy feet. His voice came from just beyond the glow of her lantern. "Don't be mad," he said. "It's not safe, being by yourself all the way out here. I just wanted to check up on you."

She held the lantern high and squinted but couldn't see him. "I'm just fine, I never asked you to come out here and check up on me. Please go away," she said. "I'm fine."

"You sure are pretty," he said.

She was already awake when the sun's first light found her kitchen. She went out into the garden and picked fat, red Creoles, rinsed and dried each one, and set the baskets into the wheelbarrow. Pushing past the house, she spotted a small mound of dirt directly before her front porch. This time her shovel found a small creased card bearing the image of a saint. "Saint Jude," the printing on the back said, "patron saint of lost causes."

She walked alongside the highway. The sun on the back of her head was already hot, the nape of her neck damp beneath her hair. When she accompanied her mother to town on Saturdays, they talked. Sometimes it was about important things, like why the egg-plants were stunted this year. Sometimes it was about other things, like why Mrs. Touchet had a moustache, why Mr. Touchet smelled like whiskey at seven in the morning. She wished for her mother, wondered when she might be well enough to read this in a letter. What does it mean, Mama, what?

It's just more strangeness, her mother might say, or, *Hospitals don't have room for all the strangeness there is, Alma. Pay it no mind. On a Monday or any other day.*

When Touchet's Grocery appeared, the girl turned her wheel-barrow and headed back home. It didn't have to be Saturday, she thought. She could take her produce any day. On Friday morning. Or Tuesday. He couldn't work all the time; she would find out when he was off, and she would never have to see him again. The next morning when she went out onto her front porch with a cup of coffee, she found a letter from her mother stuck into the frame of the screen door.

August 13

Dear Katherine,

I'm making you a present in Art Therapy. I have painted some dreadful pictures, but my pottery isn't too bad. Comes from working in the mud, I guess. I've already messed up two of them, but this one looks like the potter was both awake and sober. Which Mr. Badeaux is now, though he says being blind hasn't much to recommend it, being sober, less. Says he liked it better when the edges of things felt the way they were begin-ning to look.

That's white flies on the eggplant. Tell Mr. Touchet you need the Thiodan. Regards from Mr. B. and me,

Your loving mama

On Monday the girl walked toward town and got close enough to Touchet's to see his truck in the parking lot. On Tuesday his truck was not there, so she delivered her produce and hurried home, where she filled her wheelbarrow again and set up her roadside stand. She was prepared to ignore him when he came by, but he did not. On Friday night she sat and watched for him from her front porch. She fell asleep there and woke with the sun. Later, between her garden and back porch she unearthed from a long narrow trench a palm leaf. It was brittle, and when she brushed a finger across the tip, it drew blood. Sunday morning another letter appeared on her front door.

August 20

Dear Mary-Margaret,

I read Mr. Badeaux the paper every morning, front to back, even the classifieds. What people buy and sell, what they find and lose. What they're willing to give to get it back. Evenings I read him Yeats. Why shouldn't an old man be mad, he said over his eggs this morning. Why not, when the end never lives up to the beginning? You got no quarrel from me, I said.

Are you talking about that retarded boy? What do you mean he's burying things around the house?

Don't let the okra get woody.

Your soon to be sprung,

loving mother

The rain began on Sunday night, loud and violent at first, and then by Monday afternoon, slow and steady. Except for odd lapses at dawn and dusk each day, the rain continued all week. The girl lifted tomatoes from the sodden ground, straightened bean poles, rebanked two rows that had begun to wash away. A leak in the kitchen got worse and she set her washtub beneath it. At night she lay awake and imagined her little house an ark. The bayou would flood, she would wake and find herself floating over the railroad tracks, down the highway all the way to the Basin, and out to sea. Every pot in her kitchen was full of vegetables, the refrigerator and its tiny freezer were both full of vegetables, and she knew how to fish. No one would visit. No one to bury strange things in her yard. No one to look at her with pure delight, whether she answered his questions or not.

I am not like my mother, she thought, listening to the rain. *My mother would like this.*

Before she was fully awake on Sunday morning she heard his truck, then his step on her porch. When she'd dressed and reached her front door, a letter waited.

August 23

Dear Sophie,

   Mr. Badeaux died yesterday. I was reading to him from the Merchandise for Sale: Appliances, and before I could get to "Excellent condition, make offer," he took one deep breath—I thought it was a sigh—laid his hand on my arm, and didn't breathe again. I picked up a poem he liked and kept on reading, just in case he was still listening. Then an aide showed up and asked couldn't I tell he was dead? I said I thought some of us took our leave slower than others, and I wanted him to have some company. I wouldn't be surprised if this didn't set me back some.

   Be careful with that man. There's patients here who talk like that. Colors in your hair. Really.

Yours in experience,
Mama

Over the next three days there were more and longer spells when there was no rain and she was able to patch the hole in the roof. She was shelling peas on her front porch at midday on Wednesday when his truck crested the railroad tracks. The girl crept through her garden, her shoulders brushing okra leaves, and stepped behind the oak tree to watch the truck bounce across the rutted fields. She grabbed hold of the lowest limb, swung one leg over and then the other, and made her way to the place where she'd seen her mother sit.

From the tree the girl watched him step from the truck and onto her porch. He disappeared from view for a moment, and when he reappeared he hopped from the porch and headed through her garden, his blue-and-yellow plaid shirt a moving patch of light among the cornstalks. When he emerged from the garden he hesitated briefly and then strode toward her tree.

"Grace," he called.

She imagined herself part of the tree, quiet and still enough for a bird to trust.

Presently he began to wave.

I should have known, she thought, I am too large to hide anywhere. Now he will go away, he will think I am like my mother, and he will leave me alone.

He moved a step closer and she could now discern his face. It was a face, the girl realized, that never anticipated disappointment. No doubt he had been the brunt of rejection. But he seemed not to expect it.

"It's because of my mother, isn't it? You think I'm just like her, and so of course I would be sitting in a tree."

"There's a saint used to climb trees."

"I don't think my mother's a saint."

"You never know," he said.

"Who was she, the one who climbed trees?"

"Christina," he said. "Saint Christina the Astonishing. She climbed mountains and cathedrals, too."

The girl imagined her mother perched atop St. Basil's, another bus ride to the hospital. "Why did *she* do it? The saint."

"She could smell people's sins, so she climbed things. To get away from the smell of sin."

"Not much to recommend it," she said. "Being a saint."

"That depends," he said, "on who you get close to." He stepped forward a little and moved from the sunlight into the shade. "A letter from your mama came this morning. Maybe it's important." He drew the envelope from his shirt pocket and held it up.

"You didn't have to do that," she said, taking the letter. "I can get my own mail. Is that all you came for?" She opened the envelope and read.

August 30

Dear Theresa,

Come on the 6th. I'm going to be sprung, as they think I've
learned some Coping Skills. They still talk like that.

Ma

"I don't mean to criticize," he said, "but sometimes you can be
a little rude. How's your mama?"

"Just because you ask a question doesn't mean I have to answer
it. If it was any of your business how my mama was, I'd tell you."

"For her letter to come in the middle of the week, I figure either she's better, or she's worse. Tell her hey for me. If you feel
like it."

"She gets out on Saturday," the girl said. "She's fine."

"Your figs," he remarked, "they ripe. You don't pick them, the
birds will."

"Where does your mother think you are when you're here? Late
at night, hanging around in Mr. Touchet's pasture."

"I'm thirty years old," he said. "I told my mama, I said, I'm
thirty, Mama, and I got my driver's license and I have me a friend
and I'm going to go visit when I want."

"What'd she say?"

"'*Mon Dieu*,' she said, 'it must be a girl. You be careful, Claude
Joseph. Don't matter how old you are, you can't be too careful
about things like that.'" He turned and gazed briefly in the direction of her house. "What you did with everything?"

"With what?"

"The things I buried. They're blessed articles. You can't throw
them away. You have to burn them or bury them. I put them here
so your mama, she'd get better. And to keep you safe."

"They're in the house," she said. "I was going to give them back
to you. We're fine. We don't need you to bury things for us."

"I know," he sighed. "You don't need nobody to do nothing for
you. I know why you don't come on Saturday no more. I told my
mama you were mad at me. She says I been too pushy. Women

don't like that, she said. So I won't come back. I won't bother you no more."

From her spot in the tree the girl saw him now as part of the landscape she knew: the tiny shotgun house, the garden, the pasture where the rabbits lived. The day had brightened with his arrival, but now he turned to go, and she became aware he carried the brightness with him.

"Wait," she called, "you're right about the figs."

"I brought some buckets," he offered. "They in my truck."

Later she watched the truck top the railroad crossing and disappear over the other side. She went round to each window in her house and tried to examine her reflection, but there was too much light. That evening she filled her washtub early and stared into the surface of the water. She saw a round, dark face framed by too much hair that gave off no color at all. I don't know what he wants, she thought. What does he want?

On the following Saturday the girl woke to humming and dressed quickly. It was not yet dawn, but T-Boy Doiron was already there, sitting on her porch. He was eating biscuits from a brown paper sack. He wiped his hands on his trouser legs and removed a letter from his shirt pocket. "It's a letter from your mama. It came yesterday." There were crumbs around his mouth and down the front of his shirt. "How come you look like that when you just woke up?"

"Like what?"

He stood and wiped his mouth with the back of his hand. "Like you didn't just wake up."

"My hair," she said. "What about the colors? What three colors is it?"

"Come stand in the sun," he directed. She joined him in the patch of light which had found her porch through a clearing in the trees. He took into his hands a broad fan of her hair and splayed it out into the early light. "Red," he whispered, "and copper. And gold. I never saw hair like this." Then suddenly he'd leaned into it and closed his eyes. "And it smells like the earth," he added.

She thought about the smell of her garden, humus and peat and fertilizer. Insecticide. "What does that mean?" she demanded. "I wash it every night."

"No, like the earth. Like what grows: sweet olive, magnolias, lantana. Like that."

He smelled of fresh-baked bread and aftershave. The cowlick on the crown of his head stuck straight up. She took the bag he offered and inhaled its warm goodness.

"My mama, she made these for us. I tried not to eat too many."

There were two left. "Come into the kitchen," she said. "I'll make some coffee." Facing her kitchen window they watched the sun clear the treetops and illumine the wet pasture. "She gets out today. I'm taking a bus to go get her."

"I'll meet you at Touchet's tonight," he declared, "when you get off the bus. I know you can find your way home even in the dark. I just want to. You don't want that other biscuit?"

She handed him the bag, and when she noticed he wasn't drinking his coffee, she added more sugar and milk. "Is this how it will be?"

"Yes," he said, "if you want."

She said, "My mother wasn't always unhappy. But she's always been . . . different. You musn't ever get a funny look when she does something odd."

He shrugged. "I can't say what's odd. Everytime you turn around in this town, somebody's doing something I wouldn't do. It's not for me to say."

His coffee was untouched. She poured it into a glass, added still more milk and sugar and handed it to him. "I eat vegetable sandwiches," she said, "and we hardly ever wear shoes and in the morning my hair is real knotty."

"I think you're perfect," he said, and drank the entire glass of coffee milk. He set the glass onto the ring where his cup had been and cleared his throat. "When it's like this I think people get married. If they want?"

"I don't know how this is." She studied his hand, which lay between them on her table. She thought about touching him but didn't. "I don't know how it is to be married."

"Neither me," he said, "but if we get married you have to be Catholic. Are you Catholic?"

She cleared the table and took their things to the sink. "I don't know. I don't know what I am."

"If you were Catholic," he said, "you would know."

"Maybe I was and I forgot." She ran water into his glass and watched it fill, murky as summer fog.

"No," he said, "that's not something you forget. If you're Catholic, you know it. All the time."

She rinsed the glass twice more until the water ran clear, picked up her bag and moved to the door. "We'll see," she said.

"About getting married?" The bird in his chest was singing.

She thought about her mother, who was no help sometimes, when her daughter's pain got absorbed into her own. But there were more times when her mother could gaze down over the surface of things and see the pattern and make sense of it. It's what comes of sitting in trees, she'd said.

T-Boy Doiron cleared his throat again. "About being Catholic?"

She pulled the front door shut behind them. "About anything," she said. "About everything. We'll see."

He said, "I'll talk to Father Mike."

She said, "Okey doke."

At Touchet's he refused to leave until her bus had arrived and she had boarded and the bus had made its way toward the river. She found a window seat and opened her mother's letter.

September 3

Dear Alma,

I packed this morning and intend to live out of my suitcase till you arrive. Last night they admitted a girl they put in the bed next to mine. When the night nurse found her under the bed for the third time she tied her in and sedated her. How do you hold on, daughter, looking after me and "my own great gloom"? The goddess had her ugly blacksmith. Choose who you will, and I will keep my mouth shut. I will try to hold tight and work our garden. I do not think I can stay out of trees.

Do you mean marriage?

Take a fast bus. The food here is beginning to look okay.

Good dreams (which I am now having),
Mama

The girl gazed through her own reflection in the bus window, down at the Mississippi. As a teenager who had come here from other cities and from across other rivers, she'd thought it wide as the earth itself, broad and strong and brown, something which would separate the two of them from the very world. Now she was crossing a river that seemed not so wide. To get her mother and bring her home. To fill grocery sacks with sad paintings and misshapen pottery.

There is a man, she'd written her mother. He is slow and he wheezes, but he thinks I'm beautiful. He sees no strangeness he cannot love. He thinks he wants to tell his mother, though I am sure she knows. Just as you would know. And when you are home, you will hear him come at midnight on Fridays and stand in the moonlight when there is a moon, and in the utter darkness when there is not, and sing to me: "Grace, sweet Grace." Like that was my real name.

Nancy Richard's fiction has appeared in several literary journals, including *Shenandoah, The Greensboro Review,* and *Prairie Schooner*. A native of Lafayette, Louisiana, she teaches English and creative writing at Delgado Community College in New Orleans. She lives with her husband, two sons, a beagle, and three cats.

"*The Order of Things*" is one of a cycle of stories: T-Boy had appeared in three earlier ones, and it was inevitable, I think, that he would fall in *love. I tried to tell him he was in over his head, that surely there was a simpler girl, with a simpler life and a conventional mother, a girl he would not have to search the treetops to find. But he was not to be dissuaded. Myrtle's affinity for Yeats gave me the language I needed to impose some semblance of order on this extraordinary chaos.*

George Singleton

THESE PEOPLE ARE US

(from *Apalachee Quarterly*)

The trouble started when my wife admitted that she dreamt
regularly of shallow graves. Maybe it wasn't as much trouble as it was truth. We started getting to the root of our problems
when she got to Question 11 of the At-Home Marriage Repair test
we'd bought off of one of the channels. There was a guarantee stat-
ing that if the results didn't come out that we should either split
or remain together, then we'd get our money back. Besides the
hundred-question test and dual answer sheets, there was a teacher's
manual explaining what all the various answers meant, and a graph
to chart out our progress or lack thereof. There was even a 1-800
number to call in case we got sidetracked or confused.

Alexis did all right up to Question 11. She'd not had any trau-
matic childhood problems, she'd not felt teased as a child, she
didn't think her spouse—that would be me—gave her an inferior-
ity problem, ever. She didn't trouble with the way I dressed, or
the way I ate my food either.

My problem cropped up right at Question 1, so we pretty much
had me figured out. Question 1 was "At any time in your life did a
family member do anything that drew attention to you in such a
way that the entire community in which you lived would later
think of you as a leper, loser, heathen, or un-American?" At least
that was the gist of it, I swear.

I had to answer yes, but I never thought of the event as so detrimental to my overall psyche that it'd ruin my marriage. I was eight years old, and only two or three months into living in South Carolina. My father'd lugged my mother and me here from California. It was 1966, and he'd already survived a bout with cancer, overexposure to radiation, a forty-five-foot fall into the empty hold of a merchant ship, fifty-seven broken bones including both hips, back, knees, ankles, and so on. We moved to South Carolina because my father was disabled, but his father agreed to take him on as an under-the-table employee at the textile supply company my grandfather owned.

So there we were suddenly, trying to fit in. We went to the Baptist church my grandparents attended, Sunday mornings and Wednesday nights. I shuffled off with the other kids for Sunday school classes and did my best to stay in between the lines coloring pictures of Jesus. I'd never even heard of the guy up until this point in my life. I'm not saying that my parents were un-Christian or immoral or anything. I think they just didn't like fighting the traffic on Sundays.

When I think back to this point in my life in a cause-and-effect kind of way, I owe the church everything. Because we went to church, I had to get a suit. Because I got a suit, I started noting how I looked like this tap dancer on the Lawrence Welk show, except I was white. Because I started secretly tap dancing down in our cement basement, I assume I took an interest in the arts, which later followed me throughout school, which kept me from being scared of writing, which ultimately came in handy when I went into that field. What I'm saying is, without the Baptist Church I wouldn't be the scholarly researcher that I am today.

My first book will be an annotated, nonscholarly, human interest bibliography on Job. I know every work ever written that mentions Job somehow.

Anyway, on one of those Wednesday nights the preacher decided to have a Q and A session with the congregation. Some old lady asked when the choir could get new robes—there was an

Andy Griffith episode just like this—and some other old woman asked everyone to pray for some other old woman who had gout. No one mentioned Vietnam or other global issues.

The civil rights movement did pop up, though, and that's what got me treated like a leper, heathen, loser, un-American for the rest of my stint in the town. Some man stood up and said "What do we do if a black man comes into our church?" except he didn't quite use the term "black." He didn't use the term "Negro," and this was long before the notion of "African-Americans" came into being, of course. He didn't even soften up and say "a colored fellow." He used that racist term my father told me to never use, right before first grade at a multicultural elementary school in Anaheim, along with words I'd picked up from a guy named Frenchie when I got to visit my father on the ship when it came to unload its cargo at the dock down in Long Beach.

This guy at the church asked the question, and someone else stood up and said, "Ignore him and hope he doesn't come back." Everyone laughed and applauded.

Except my father and mother. I can't say that I didn't laugh, because I did. To tell the truth I wasn't really paying all that much attention, but I'd learned to kind of do as everyone else around me did. I learned to say "Amen" with the rest of the congregation at the right time. So when everyone laughed and clapped, I laughed thinking it was appropriate.

I'd stopped by the time my father jerked me off the pew, right there beside his father and stepmother. He still used crutches at this point, three years after falling into the hold and two or three years before going through a succession of replacement hip operations. I remember my mother slipping her arm through his elbow as we walked down the aisle and out of the place, and I remember being on the other side with my father's index finger holding my wrist right up against the rubber knobs where his hands fit on those wrap-around-the-forearm-style of crutches.

People turned around and stared, I'm sure. I just kept looking down at the wooden floor. People took notes, said things like,

"Those are them Sheltons from up North," I feel certain, what with the way I got treated between second and twelfth grade by every kid except those who'd also moved with their parents from other exotic heathen places like New Jersey and Georgia.

I do know that my father made an awkward multishuffled pirouette when we got to the front door of the church, turned to the congregation, and said, "Ignore this," and gave everybody the finger. Even my mother, of all people, let out this little squeak not unlike a gerbil or chipmunk being squeezed too hard—her way of saying, "Up yours."

I know that for a while my father and I dressed up in black and revisited the same church on Saturday nights for a couple years so he could paint Coca-Cola around the door frame and front steps, so that on Sunday mornings the congregation would have to enter through a swarm of yellow jackets, if they had the faith.

Somehow I'd forgotten to tell Alexis about the church incident, so after I explained Question 1 to her she said, "I think this explains some things about our marriage." She said, "Don't think I've not noticed how you always swipe the Gideon Bible out of hotel rooms when we're on vacation."

I said, "I just do it to be funny. If someone thinks he or she has the right to force religion on me, I feel I have a right to take it away. Simple."

She said, "I'm no psychologist, but it's pretty apparent that you have this enigmatic sense of duality," or something like that. She said, "I find it amazing that you grew up in a Christian-paranoid household and ended up trying to write a book on Job." No, Alexis wasn't a psychologist. She worked directly with the garment industry as a buyer. That's why she didn't have problems with the way I dressed. She pretty much knew the ins and outs of fashion.

I said, "Uh-huh. If you want to add on to that, I'm kind of glad that my father's dead. He'd kill me if he knew."

It's not that Alexis and I had that big a problem with our marriage. It's not like I was out whoring around, or she couldn't find herself suddenly. It's not like she had to go to Al-Anon. We both liked kids even though we didn't have any. Basically we wanted to find out why she went to sleep crying oftentimes, and why she woke up in the middle of the night in tears, and why I kept making scenes in public unknowingly.

I didn't quite get past Question 2, either, which was "Have you ever had a relative frighten you so much that you didn't know how to react?" Alexis said, "My aunts and uncles and grandparents are normal. I have a cousin who acted odd as a child, but she ended up being a violist. She just didn't talk much."

I said, "Oh fuck," when it was my turn.

I knew I didn't have the time to tell Alexis about how my grandfather later showed up with a gun to shoot my father after we walked out of church, and how my father ended up getting fired from the under-the-table job. I knew I didn't have the time to tell about how I got summoned to the office over the intercom in the seventh grade so the secretary could tell me that my grandfather would be picking me up from school—which ended up being a kidnapping ploy that failed when I asked to use the phone, called my mother, and she came and got me out of school right then. I only said, "My father's biological mother was kind of odd."

My grandfather and my father's real mother divorced in 1941. My father was sixteen, and he ran away from Dallas to join the merchant marines. He told stories about his escape, usually with different reasons, endings, road stories, and so on. When I was about sixteen and complaining in my snot-nosed way about Hungarian goulash for supper again, my father told about how his parents were so poor they ate grass soup. When I brought up the grass soup incident again a few years later, he said I was nuts, that I must've dreamt it, that he never ate grass soup in his life.

He told me he bought a duffel bag of marijuana for ten dollars one time back before anyone knew what it was, but that he quit smoking the stuff because he got too hungry and thought he'd fall off the deck of the ship.

Anyway, we drove from California to South Carolina in this

cool red-and-white Oldsmobile, with mostly my mother driving seeing as how my dad's hips hurt and he'd vowed to quit morphine. We stopped in Dallas to see his mother, a woman who played a honky-tonk piano in a bar once owned—I found out later—by Jack Ruby. She played honky-tonk, and she wore purple dresses and a stole. Her name was Nelta, and she caked white makeup on her face and wore lipstick as deep red as thin blood.

This was the beginning of August, understand. I got out of first grade sometime in mid-June, and my parents flipped coins whether to move or not. Social Security and the Sailors Union of the Pacific provided my father something like $300 a month all together, which wasn't quite enough to keep a household together, even if my mother went back to work for Western Union. Without morphine, my father needed bourbon. Without bourbon he needed cigarettes, and the doctor'd already made him quit smoking what with the cancer a few years earlier. A fifth of bourbon a day cut into $300-a-month living expenses, even in 1965 dollars.

We packed up what we owned and moved, stopping outside of Phoenix to see a friend of my parents who gave up and moved into a trailer so they could look for copper. We maybe stopped another night I don't remember. I recall El Paso at 110 degrees in the shade, and I remember stopping at an apartment building to meet my father's mother. She wore *purple* and had hair dyed the same color as her lipstick. She said, "Little Enloe, the Easter bunny knew you were coming and he left something off for you."

She didn't have a piano in the apartment. She had a couch with stuffing coming out of the upholstery at both arms. She didn't own a cat. My biological grandmother wore high heels and went into the kitchen. She opened the refrigerator and pulled out this hollow chocolate bunny in a box with the cellophane window. It'd turned white, and the head had been eaten off.

My father said, of course, "What do you say, Enloe?"

I know what I wanted to say. I knew I wanted to say, "This is stale," or "My parents told me not to take candy from strangers," or "The Easter bunny must get really tired by the time he makes it to Texas."

My grandmother Nelta said, "You don't have to thank me, honey. Come here, and sit down on Grandma's lap, and let me sing you a song."

I knew I didn't get the "thank you" out as fast as I should've and had no choice but to do what she wanted. I swear to God she took me over to the couch and sang me a song about a woman named "Softhearted Sally Tucker," a song she said she wrote herself for the club where she worked.

I knew what the words meant, too. I'd heard the words from Frenchie, remember.

I am not lying when I say Alexis moved her chair back from me inch by inch subconsciously as I explained the answer to Question 2. I noticed it the way a person watching a movie notices how the victim keeps stepping backwards as the attacker wearing a mask nods a knife up and down.

We went through questions 3 through 7 together on a par. I'm not sure what they meant, but they were easy, and graphing the answers—we cheated by looking at the Teacher's Manual—we ended up side by side: "I tend to wear blue more than brown," "I like dogs more than cats," "I'd rather read a book than cut the grass," "At night voices call out my name and it bothers me," and "I like to travel to distant cities," all with yes or no answers.

Alexis and I felt pretty good about our chances of mending the marriage for about two minutes. She even scooted her hardback chair back towards me halfway. We sat in the den face-to-face, like the opening instructions said we should do. We drank water.

"Do you want some supper?" Alexis asked me. She said, "I'm hungry. I can go outside and mow the grass so we could have some grass soup."

I said, "You're funny." I said, "Let's get this over with. I want to get to the bottom of whatever it is we're going through." Alexis and I'd been married half a decade and I still liked her looks. She

wore a thin skirt and kept her legs open when I told the stories of
my childhood. I could see right up there, is what I'm saying. I said,
"I'll fast a day if it'll fix you from crying and me from standing in
the middle of the Canned Meat section of Winn-Dixie singing out
the lyrics to Johnny Mathis and Tony Bennett songs."

Alexis said, "It's the George Jones that has everybody thinking
you're just drunk out of your mind."

I said, "What's the next question?"

She held the booklet. We kept separate answer sheets and short
pencils that came with the package, pencils that looked like they
came straight from a miniature golf course. She said "For the next
question, I answer 'No.'" She said, "Question 8: 'Did one of your
parents ever force sex on you?'"

I said, "Yes!" right away. I didn't take the time to think about
how ambiguous the question was. I didn't think about how it
could've sounded like your parent tried to rape you, or how he or
she just tried to set you up with a member of the opposite sex,
which is how I interpreted it.

Alexis stood up and said, "You shouldn't've told me about the
tap dancing! You shouldn't've told me about the tap dancing!"

I understood what she thought I meant. I said, "No, no no!" I
said, "What I mean is, my father wanted me to go to bed with this
Waffle House waitress!"

My father stayed at his father's business long enough to figure
out how to make replacement aprons, which were leather belts
that went on spinning frames. He figured out better ways to make
them, and started up a business in my mother's name seeing as
he was so-called disabled. My dad made me work weekends and
summers, but mostly we just drove around. I mean, we'd go to
work and tinker for an hour or so, then go out back and shoot a
pistol or two at whatever we decided looked like a good target—
a roll of butcher paper, a gross of unfolded die-cut boxes, a spare
tire he thought wasn't needed, a poor dying sweetgum tree out off
the highway.

When we didn't shoot, we drove. When we didn't drive, we

stopped and drank coffee. My father always said he'd pay me five bucks an hour, and at seven o'clock that night in the kitchen I'd say things like, "You owe me sixty dollars," to which he'd relate to me how we only worked in the shop an hour and drove around, drank coffee, and shot a pistol for the rest of the time.

When we stopped off for coffee, we stopped at this Wafffle House on business 25 in town, and always—always—some pimple-faced twenty-year-old woman with three kids and no wedding band would serve us, and my dad would say, "You ain't married?"

She'd say, "Was."

And he'd say, "This is my son Enloe, Jr. He ain't got no girl-friend." He'd turn to me and say, "Whyn't you ask her out?" The waitress would always smile, and shake her head from side to side, more than likely thinking about how she needed a high school sophomore in her life about as much as she needed only one finger on each hand thus keeping her from being able to pour from the pot.

I'd turn as red as the plastic tablecloth and look away, outside, way past the city limits. I'd look outside and see a land where only my cast of buddies from outside South Carolina came from, and how we could all live in peace, not worrying about what other kids our age had to say about us being un-American heathens.

Well, maybe I just looked out the window. Maybe I just turned red and kicked my father under the table and muttered, "Dad, please shut up," under my breath.

After the woman left, my father would say something like, "She liked you, son. I could tell by the way she was looking. She wants you. She wants to take you home when her kids are gone and play a game of ring-toss, you know what I mean."

Of course I knew what he meant, seeing as Frenchie called sex "ring-toss." I knew what my limping father meant because more than once he'd say things like, "Those Baptists pretend to be so goddamn superior to everyone else, but I bet you there's more ring-toss going on between the congregation than there is at a kindergarten field day."

I usually kept pretty much quiet around my father. I knew what he could do with yellow jackets. By this time, too, he'd had a couple hip replacements and could walk only using a cane. A quick cane to the back of the thighs is something a son remembers.

Alexis said, "I don't know if we can get through all these questions." She said, "Do you mind if I skip around to what kinds of food you'd rather eat or cars you'd rather own? Do you mind if I go on towards Question 100? I'm not sure I can take all this. Why didn't you tell me before?"

We'd gotten married by a notary public. Instead of a honeymoon we just held a party for friends. We didn't have a china pattern. People brought us paper plates. My mother made a toast. She didn't really mention anything that happened when I was being brought up.

Alexis and I married late. We married, probably, out of nothing else to do. I'd already worked in an ad agency for a year, gone to graduate school, taught college, and tried writing fiction before settling on applying for yearlong grants so I could work on annotated bibliographies. She'd gone to college, and worked as a social worker, and modeled when someone discovered her, and gotten the job as a buyer through a guy named Bernie Sachs up in New York. We'd already gone to bars and art gallery lectures thinking we'd meet people who'd be compatible. I met Alexis when I was thirty-one, and she was thirty. We both needed tune-ups, oddly. Some religion professor or massage therapist could go on and on about the symbolic and ironic implications of the event, but the simple truth is we sat in opposite chairs at a Lube-World, waiting for mechanics to get the job done.

She owned a Toyota wagon, and I had a big Chevy pickup for no real reason.

We sat there reading old magazines. I asked her if she minded if I smoked. She asked me if I could smell her perfume—she thought she'd put on too much. I said I liked the smell of perfume better than oil. She told me her name and held out her hand. We shook. I am not lying when I say I didn't really make eye contact at the time. There was a glass partition between us in the waiting room, and the shop. I could see my truck and Alexis' Toyota, going up and down the hydraulic lifts, randomly like pistons, like sex between two pessimists.

It didn't take that long a courtship, and it didn't seem like all that long a marriage before we sat there across from each other answering the questions. Alexis said, "Do you trust people who don't drink?"

I said, "Not always. I'm sorry to say I don't always trust them. I hate to say those kind of people who always brag about how they're on a natural high or whatever also seem to be the kind of people who're either really boring or who want me to be exactly like them for some reason. Like there's an exclusive club. People who brag about not drinking are just like people who brag about living in gated communities near Asheville." But I added, "People who don't drink and just live without mentioning anything, I respect."

Deep down I figured I shouldn't tell the truth, but Alexis and I'd made an oath to each other. She said, "I feel the same way!" all excited. She said, "Question 10's easy—'Does your spouse ever seem to be more interested in inanimate objects than you? Does your spouse ever seem to care more about the garden, or the eaves, or the car?' I want to answer first, Enloe. I want to say 'No!'"

I said, "I've always thought you cared more about me than you did about lawn ornaments or farm implements."

I penciled in "No" on my answer sheet and assumed Alexis did the same. She didn't respond to me, though. Alexis put down the booklet, and her pencil. She walked back towards the kitchen and I swear I heard her let out this little noise that I'd only heard her make right before she cried in the middle of the night.

I said, "Is the pollen bothering you?" That's how much I had the situation figured out.

She said, "I want to know what you have to say about Question 11. Pick up that booklet and tell me what you think."

The questions was, "In your dreams, have you ever noticed any kind of symbolism you could interpret as wanting to hurt your spouse?"

I said, "While you're in there, could you get me a beer?" I said, "Oh, wait—that was some kind of reflex. I forgot we agreed to drink water while doing this thing."

Alexis came back with a good cup of vodka, straight, one ice cube floating in the top of the glass. She brought the same for me, plus the can of beer. Alexis said, "I have some theories. I'm not sure it has to do with you. I've been thinking," she said.

I said "You're dreaming of killing me?" like that. I couldn't believe it. When we first met she kept a sawed-off shotgun under her bed, but took it away once I told her how it made me feel uncomfortable.

Alexis said, "I don't think I've killed anyone in my dreams." She didn't make eye contact. Right away I knew something was up, and at first I kind of felt good about it, I hate to admit. After having to spill out all the things about my chocolate bunny without a head and whatnot, I felt like Alexis was about to start catching up with me.

I said, "What did you dream, honey—you got real mad at me and stepped on my foot or something? You spank a dog that you think is symbolic of me? What?"

Then she told me about the shallow graves. Alexis said, "I keep having this nightmare. In the dream I'm walking down a path in the woods, and then I'll come to a clearing where there's a cemetery. I walk through the cemetery looking at all the headstones— really nice headstones, too. But then I keep walking back into another part of the woods further ahead, and finally I get to this shallow grave with a hand sticking out, or a piece of a flannel shirt. A couple times it was hair sticking out from the dirt."

I said, "When did you start drinking straight vodka? This is terrible," and put my glass down.

"All that crying in the middle of the night is from this dream, Enloe. Every time I have the dream I say to myself in it, 'I need to go get some fill dirt and cover the body?' I promise I don't ever say, 'I better cover up Enloe,' or 'I better cover up my husband?' I just know that I've done something very wrong, and I don't want to get caught."

She still looked away from me. She didn't reach out her hand for me to hold, like in the movies right before the psychoanalyst makes his unethical move on a patient. I said, "So I guess you'll be entering a 'Yes' on your answer sheet."

Alexis got up and said, "I can't finish this tonight."

I told her it was okay. I told her we could get back to it whenever she wanted, that we had time. I tried not to think about synchronicity, about how if I'd never taken such an interest in Job I'd've never been able to show such patience.

Of course I didn't sleep that night and neither did my wife. I couldn't sleep on purpose, and Alexis couldn't sleep because I kept pumping her full of coffee. I lied. I told her about watching a fascinating and timely documentary on how large amounts of coffee have been known to purge human beings of visions. We sat together in the den, apart.

Alexis said, "It's all me. There'd be nothing wrong with our marriage if I wasn't involved," pathetic-like.

I said, "Well, true, if you weren't a part of this marriage I doubt we'd be talking about what's wrong." I tried not to laugh. I tried not to think about getting a third shift job so I'd be gone from the bedroom when Alexis dreamt.

Alexis said, "Maybe I need to go to a real psychologist before we can go on with the test. Maybe I have some problems stemming from deep in my own psyche I need to resolve before we can even think about getting our lives together back on track."

I said, "I don't want to sound like an ingrate or anything—I'm proud of you for wanting to get everything in order—but I have about the least amount of confidence in psychology as a science. I'd just as soon we went up in the mountains and have some woman place gemstones on our nerve endings. Honey, if you think that psychology's going to solve your dreams, then I can tell you right now what your problem is."

Alexis said, "I know."

I said, "There is no hope. Listen, when I get through with the book on Job—and it should be really soon—I'll go back and get a real job. When the grant money's gone, I'll get out of the house more often. That'll cure things I bet." I said, "I love you," and got up to kiss her.

Alexis said, "I love you too," and grabbed the channel changer away from me. It was four-thirty in the morning, and she wanted to see the news. She said, "What do you mean there's no hope?"

On one of the twenty-four-hour news channels a guy stood in a small workroom somewhere in the midwest. He told about how he had these solar-powered engines that could provide electricity for the entire country if only the government would give him a large chunk of the Mojave Desert.

I said, "This is a perfect example of what I'm saying. Let's pretend the government gives this guy all that land. And let's say that his solar-powered engines are such a hit that somehow every nation is able to use them so we don't have to suck oil and coal out of the earth anymore. Pretty soon the whole entire center of the world will be filled with oil, and it'll creep closer and closer to the surface, and then one day some jackass will throw a cigarette butt out his window, which will catch some of the oil on fire that's seeped through the surface, and the entire planet will explode from the inside out." I said, "I think there's something about that towards the end of the Bible but not so detailed."

Alexis just looked at me. She handed me back the changer and went for more coffee. From the kitchen she said, "Don't get weird on me, Enloe."

I flipped over to watch bowling on the sports channel. I flipped over to watch an old movie where the shadow of the microphone was visible at the top of the screen. I turned to that infomercial channel that advertised the booklet we bought on how to repair a marriage.

Alexis came back in with her cup and I said, "Look."

There was a blue-suited motivational speaker-host talking to various people in the audience about their addictions to home shopping networks. One couple from Mesa, Arizona, told how they went into bankruptcy after she'd bought every doll ever advertised. A man from Columbus, Ohio, stood up and said, "I had this dream that when I retired I'd open up a small woodworking and baseball card store. I bought every drill bit and table saw advertised, plus autographed baseballs and bats and 8 × 10 photographs, not to mention complete sets of cards from the fifties up until now. Well, I retired, and then I rented a little place in one of our strip malls. To make a long story short, I couldn't sell any of the memorabilia for half of what it cost me, and I cut off my thumb trying to make an armoire."

He showed his left hand. Alexis said, "Who *are* these people?"

The host came running back down to the stage and said, "I've heard these stories all across the country where I give my seminars. Peer pressure, last straws, and that old notion about the Great American Dream is running all of us into the red." He walked over to a table and picked up a book and said, "And that's why I want to tell you about my new book, *How to Stop Buying Useless Quick Fix-Its Off Late-Night Television.*" He said, "I know what I'm talking about, and I have documentation to prove it."

At the bottom of the screen it read, "Dr. Barnes is a direct descendant of Franz Mesmer, the father of Hypnotism."

I didn't want to sound melodramatic or anything, but I said, "These people are us."

I turned off the TV. Alexis and I sat in the dim light of the room. I wondered about questions 12 through 100, and knew that somehow both of us would have to bring up our college years, of things we'd done, of things it'd be better not knowing. I thought of Job's seven sons and three daughters, and wondered if there was any way possible to research our family trees so one day Alexis and I could go on that channel with my book and plug the concept of Patience. I wanted a subtitle under my face saying, "Enloe and Alexis are direct descendants of Job, the father of Patience."

Alexis moved to the couch. I scooted way over. She kind of laughed and said if I rubbed her feet, she'd promise not to kill me and dump my body in a two-foot grave. I thought of that poor woodworker without the thumb. My wife and I mentioned nothing. Eventually it got light outside, again, like it had for my parents, and theirs.

George Singleton grew up in Greenwood, South Carolina, and is a graduate of Furman University and the University of North Carolina at Greensboro. He has published short stories in *New Stories from the South: The Year's Best, 1994; Writers Harvest 2; Playboy; The Georgia Review; Shenandoah;* and elsewhere. He divides his time between Dacusville, South Carolina, and Skyuka Mountain, North Carolina.

I'm doing something wrong-headed. I keep hearing writers talk about how their works started off as poems—"I wrote a haiku, and then it became a sonnet, and then it became a villanelle, and then a sestina, and before I knew what was going on the thing became a full-fledged short story, and then miraculously, I had a novel"—like that. "These People Are Us," like most of my stories, started off as a novel. I got stuck and quit at five thousand words.

If I ever have a collection of stories come out, it'll be called something like These People Are Us—And Other Aborted Novels.

Seriously, I have a deep fascination with psychology. I am particularly intrigued with the concepts of "enabling" and "denial" and "projection"—especially "projection." More than anything else I like to get into a conversation with a mere stranger and have that person use those terms out of nowhere, in a this-is-free-psychoanalysis kind of way. Sometimes, if no one brings up those terms in a twenty-four-hour period, I feel like attending a "grief therapy" session.

I imagine "These People Are Us" came out of hearing someone talk about some MMPI-like test that he or she took in the back pages of one of those magazines. Honestly, I don't remember.

Stephen Marion

NAKED AS TANYA

(from *Epoch*)

They were laughing. Her eyes would settle on him, and
soften, and they would laugh, their bodies rising and thud-
ding down, shuddering forward and back. Taft was unaware of
what she was saying. The school bus was noisy, and he was unaware of what passed outside, except that it was a blue-and-green
blur, and there was all the air pouring in through the windows,
and his heart would fall each time she punched at Scott or allowed
him to touch her on the shoulder or to grab at her hair, which
flapped in the pouring air. He had a vague feeling of evil and of
secrecy, but he had entirely forgotten why. Every few minutes he
had a pang of fear, thinking they had passed the stop, and that he
didn't know where he was. She was in the middle. Her shoulder
pressed against his, and he felt her movements, and when she
lifted her right hand to put back a strand of hair he felt it, and the
side of her leg, her thigh, and the bone of her ankle against his.
She had led them straight to the backseat, the back-most, wheel-
bouncing seat, where the smokers and nun-chuck carriers resided,
peering unflinchingly through the dust-written sliding windows,
the whole narrow gullet of the bus before them with its little head
of a driver.

Why had he told Scott? That was his idiot mistake. Scott took
the key, which, though it was steel, seemed vulnerable in his palm.

His fist closed round it, and he started walking in a march down the hallway, where lockers banged and there was the hum of combination locks.

Hot damn, Taft heard him say. He knew where Scott was headed, revving up her name again like a chainsaw. Why had he ever turned loose of the key? Now it seemed to fall farther and farther down the well of Scott Woody's mind. Alone at her locker, with her back to them, she seemed not to hear. She had on a striped top which showed the back of her shoulders, and ripped jeans, and some kind of hat. Scott held the key up in front of her eyes, which had grown larger and more colorful yet didn't register anything, and informed her that they had wheels. The two of them exchanged a look of distaste and subdued enthusiasm, such as Taft had seen in married couples, and then she sighed and pushed the locker door shut.

The bus dropped them off in an afternoon fully formed, in the air excited by the color and smell of leaves, and the great height of the October sky. Grasshoppers still made their shimmering waves of sounds in the weeds along the road, after the bus had faded away, backfiring. Tanya had no love of Scott. Did she? She didn't like smoking either, but she did it.

This is a nice place, Taft, she said, standing in the exact center of the road, lighting a cigarette with a pink butane lighter. All she had was a small leather purse. Is there anything else?

Scott had picked up a handful of gravel to throw. The car, Defaro, he said, popping one off Taft's arm.

Leave Taft alone, said Tanya. He's going to show us. Right, Taft?

Taft wasn't sure if she liked him or just liked to scold other people. He just started down the gravel lane. Behind him a big rock smacked the mailbox.

Drop the rocks, said Tanya. Please.

One whizzed overhead.

The feeling in Taft's stomach was like hunger. He liked the way Tanya walked beside him. Her walk had a glide to it, unlike a girl's, more like a cat's, independent and balanced, with smoothed-over caution. She had a kind of deep giggle, which seemed to keep on pouring out like water through a very small leak, and she smelled like menthol cigarettes. It was difficult, however, to take pleasure in any of this with the gravel flying overhead, and the possibility that his grandmother might not only be home, but outside.

Hot damn. They heard Scott's gravel drop. There she is. They had just topped the hill, with the river below them, its trees leaning out over it from each side, seeming almost to touch in the middle. The Corvette sat astraddle the lane in front of his uncle Tony's trailer.

Son of a bitch, said Scott.

Tony's girlfriend Clarice was mowing the yard. The white river rocks had been moved from around the birdbath and piled up, and then he heard the sound of the engine, faint, moving around the other side of the trailer. Clarice had on jeans and a white T-shirt instead of her bikini, which she usually wore when she mowed the yard.

Tanya rearranged the purse strap on her shoulder. She said, There's got to be something we can do till dark. Think, Taft.

Taft thought.

They cut through the woods behind his grandmother's house. Tanya's face, in the twenty different ways it looked at him, seemed more actual than any idea of time. She managed to keep her hat on, even with the low tree limbs. They must have gone a good distance, but Taft had no memory of it. In his mind he fixed the smell of cut grass with Tanya, and with the movements of her body, however small. Her statements, even the ones which trailed off without meaning, had more presence than anything he saw. Other things, squirrels rippling, seemed to occur in the past. When a briar ripped across his ankle it felt okay, even though it stung until they reached the clearing along the river, where the air suddenly grew cool and damp beneath the great strands of ivy closer to Indian Cave.

They had stopped saying anything in the woods. Scott, subdued, started picking his beggar-lice off, but Tanya didn't. Taft was itchy all over, but Tanya didn't seem to itch or even notice. They walked past the dance barn, which was quiet and damp, and then came to the concrete sluice which ran from the cave, and then the mouth of the cave with its iron gate. Scott ran up and hollered, Hey! into the cave, but it was too big, and swallowed up his voice completely. Tanya surveyed the whole place with her colorful eyes, and then sat down, crossing her legs, directly in front of the cave mouth, and said, Let's talk.

Taft watched her take out a vial of lip gloss and start rubbing it on. He wished he could kill Scott. He wished he could shake the gate, where Scott, smelling of sweat and aftershave, had already climbed up ten feet, and fling him off, onto a rock. Or knock him out, and then dump him in the river, where the green water would escort him away forever. Instead, he sat down on the soft grass a good distance away from her.

Some place, Taft, she said, shutting her eyes for a second.

Taft agreed that it was. But he didn't much feel like he was here.

Let's go back in the cave, Scott called from atop the gate. Let's go to the very back.

Let's not, answered Tanya.

There was a thud and then a rolling sound in the leaves as Scott obediently struck the ground.

Taft, said Tanya, will tell us what's inside. Won't you, Taft?

The shit he will, said Scott.

You watch him. Tanya opened her compact and took out a wrinkled cigarette with twisted ends. She lit it with the pink lighter and held in the smoke for a few seconds and then coughed it out. Then, as if he had asked, she handed it over to Taft, and he dropped it on the grass. Without speaking, or even smiling, she picked it up again, flicked open the flame of the lighter, and this time she held his wrist steady with her other hand, as carefully as she might hold a baby's. Taft lifted it to his mouth, and the paper was sticky from her lip gloss, and he sucked in the smoke.

It didn't do anything.

Taft looked out at the river, which continued to flow at the same speed, and then at Tanya, who was taking another draw. She leaned back and let the smoke come out of her throat on its own.

I like to get stoned so much more than drunk, said Tanya, handing him the joint again.

This time Taft looked at the glowing end for a second. He smelled the smoke, and it smelled less official than tobacco smoke.

Not me, said Scott, who had kneeled down right next to Tanya. Ain't nothing on God's green earth better than a cold beer. He looked up through the trees, which were releasing yellow and brown leaves. Pardon me, God, he said. Hurry up, Taft.

Taft held the smoke down in his lungs the way Tanya had, and then Scott grabbed the joint out of his fingers. When it grew too small to hold, Tanya took out a little alligator clip and they held it with that. This went on for a long span of time, longer than the whole day, probably the whole week, had lasted. Taft noticed that Tanya was smiling, and that she needed a filling between two of her upper teeth, and he was smiling back, not with his lips but with his entire body.

Scott asked Tanya where this came from. Her hat was askew.

It grew, she said.

Taft smiled.

Taft's mother grew it.

Taft's mama is growing more than that.

I know, said Tanya. Isn't that great? But she did. She grew this.

She did not.

Did so.

Where?

Tanya grew serious. Her garden. I planted it for her.

Taft laughed. The laugh continued for several minutes.

Let's take the Vette to the ball game tonight, said Scott.

Right, said Tanya, losing her good humor. I want to watch a bunch of faggots pile all over each other. I got other plans. So does Taft. Right, Taft? Taft is the boy, right Taft? You're the boy. He has other plans.

Uhuh, said Taft.

Scott lay back on the grass. Like what?

Like you'll see what. Tanya stood up. Her knees popped, and

she acted like she was holding up the hem of a long dress. Cindy Mindy is escorted by Dirk Longprod, she said, walking on her tiptoes. Cindy is a sophomore and the daughter of Mr. and Mrs. Bank President. She is a member of the pep club, glee club, and nothing has ever come even remotely close to her groin area.

Yay, Cindy, Taft said.

Cindy enjoys horseback riding, listening to music, and fellatio.

Being with friends, said Taft. She enjoys being with friends.

What the hell is fellatio? said Scott.

Really being with friends, she said.

It ain't done it.

Look it up.

Do you see a dictionary?

I think there was one next to that tree.

Scott stood up to look. Tanya sat down in Taft's lap. She was heavy, smelling of menthol cigarettes, and he felt pain somewhere far off, as if he were remembering it. Pretend I'm Cindy, she said, her smoky breath in his face, and laughed for such a long time that he thought she would cry. Finally she calmed down to sporadic tremors. He realized that he was laughing too. She shouted, Did you find one yet? loud enough to make his ears ring, and they heard Scott's feet crashing in the dry leaves, but he didn't answer. Tanya kissed him on the mouth, pressing against him so hard it mashed his lip, and then moved a few feet away.

A baby, she said. I'm so jealous. Then she said, But you *are* still the boy, aren't you?

Taft tried not to feel his lip to see if it was bleeding.

Tanya just lay back on the grass and said, Be quiet. After a while Taft lay back too. His mouth burned and there was electricity all over him. He began to hear the river whispering and he felt the air breathing out from the cave, not saying anything, just breathing.

Do you know anything about the mines? said Taft.

Sure, said Tanya.

Some of the rooms are taller than that tree, said Taft. There are rivers like this one.

Really.

Taft wanted to tell her that the smell of oil on Tony had been that of rock he had mined underground, but he wasn't able to speak. He wanted to tell her that he was with Tony before they took him to jail, and he knew things. But all she recognized was that Taft had stolen the spare key to Tony's car.

Are you about ready? she said, sitting up with a sound that seemed to flow down his spine.

Ready for what?

To tell us what's in there. She motioned with her eyes toward the cave. It was a long time before Taft comprehended the words, because they were only objects at first, and he had to wring out their meaning, as if he were in first grade. Hey, Mr. Dictionary! she called. He's ready!

Scott came moping back, kicking leaves. Tanya started looking hard into Taft's face. Her own face was less sharp, but still as newly beautiful. From certain angles she seemed ready to cry. Tell us, she said.

Taft started talking. The words came out exactly as Tanya's had, as things, and he completely lost the idea of what they were saying. However, he noticed that Tanya and Scott still watched him closely, nodding every few seconds, and their eyes kept twitching and widening and narrowing, as if they understood. This gave him confidence. During the time he spoke to them, he allowed himself to think of all they didn't know about. He thought of the hay stuffed up to the windows in his mother's old house. And his grandfather's airplane, and the runway, which was no longer present, and the wire, growing thinner and thinner, in the air over the river where the ferry used to run. These occurred to him not as places, or things, but simply as words. It relieved him to know that all this was meaningless to them. After a while Taft realized he was speaking in Moody's voice. Once the largest electrically lit cavern in the world, he had said. And he remembered other statements, too. There are seventeen man-made bridges, and the room of the Seven Sentinels, all natural stalagmites. Cave pearls and cave diamonds, and the stoke marks of Indian torches still on the walls above the actual ashes. The long tube extending from the ceiling in one room was the well casing from a Baptist Church two miles from the river. Of course the interesting thing about all of this is that it exists in total darkness, the most total, perfect darkness imaginable, in which it is absolutely impossible to see.

Later, Taft saw that he had finished, because Tanya and Scott were standing up to stretch their legs. He stood up too. His mind was clear as sunlight now, and he felt embarrassed, because it seemed that he had missed the greater portion of this incredibly long afternoon. He also felt as if one of the Indians had stoked a torch in back of his throat, which was dry and scratched from smoke. His tongue was burned too.

Scott shook his fist at the sun, which was still over the trees. Go down damn it, he shouted. Get dark.

Tanya said she was going down to the riverbank and started off by herself. The bank was steep with only a skinny path, full of tree roots, and they saw her stumble two times and then fall. She jumped up quickly, but there was mud on the back of her jeans. She cussed, Taft could tell, not in the blatant way she usually did, but out of anger at her own self. The word, fuck, was barely audible over the sound the river made. By the time she reached the water, which was carried over a gravely shoal, Taft had to get up on a rock with Scott in order to see her. Tanya took off her tennis shoes and a pair of white socks and laid them down in the weeds. Scott, arms folded over his chest and head laid to one side with a squint in his eye, showed absolutely no emotion when she unbuttoned her jeans and took them off, stepping her whitened legs out into the sunlight, and then up to her ankles in the water. Taft didn't feel surprise either. She bent down and splashed water on the jeans and rubbed them with a tissue from her purse, which stayed on her shoulder. The mud had not gone through to her white panties.

Too bad she didn't get her shirt dirty, said Scott.

Taft watched Tanya in the way a person watches directions to a complicated place or the way parts of a machine go together. Yet with a helplessness approaching sorrow he knew his memory would fail him, utterly, as it always did when pressed, and it would yield him nothing more than a faintness or an absence. His grandfather, who had probably stood on this exact rock, would have remembered, due to a mechanical mind and an appreciation for women's legs, and so would probably Tony, who inherited both. Taft, however, felt the one single emotion for her he did not want to feel. Here was Tanya Mayes, the same one of fifteen minutes ago, on the riverbank in her panties. Light from the water, he imagined, was sometimes visible between her legs. But she was was so absorbed with the mud on her blue jeans that she seemed no longer to notice herself, sticking three fingers onto her tongue for moisture, and Taft quit watching even as he watched. Instead, he turned aside and pushed Scott, who went careening backward with a shocked look in his eyes, much farther than Taft had expected. Instead of jumping up to attack him, Scott lay wheezing on the ground until Taft had decided he was injured. Gradually he saw that it was a laugh, one so heavy, or so mild, that it barely made a sound. He kept on laughing that way, no matter what Taft said, as if he knew better than Taft what he was thinking, and already saw the humor in it.

When she returned, Taft could see that Tanya had washed her face in the river. The ends of her hair were dark with it.

That water is nasty, Scott told her. Taft's granddaddy is in it.

Tanya smoothed down her clothing. So is yours, she said.

On the way back, in the dusk, which settled quicker now that it was fall, Tanya was different. Spiderwebs hung between all the trees, and sometimes simply in the air itself, and she acted afraid of them, grabbing Taft's arm with a fierceness that scared him too. Their bodies were light from hunger. All the smells, tree bark and water, dead leaves, and finally the heavy mown grass, smelled of hunger. His headache crept back as if someone had pulled a drain plug. Tanya kept saying she had some cough drops they could have. Taft laughed at her. Whatever she said seemed absurd and superfluous to him, not richly so as in the daylight, but only so. He helped her climb fences, and she clung to him there too, whispering things to herself. Once Scott ambled up to him, swinging a big stick, and threw his arm around Taft's shoulders and said, She's a crazy bitch, ain't she. Taft didn't respond, and he wasn't even certain what Scott said, but it seemed true, and the tomato smell of his breath was oddly comforting.

It's only about lilac dark, said Tanya, keeping her arms folded and watching the ground under her shoes. The sky *was* lilac, with red at the bottom. Meadowlarks were stretching their thin whistle notes across the field. Scott put his arm around Taft and pointed at the two houses, each of which had a lit window. Lights are on, he said. That means they can't see out. He started running, or trotting really, and Taft felt stupid following him, but he still did. Tanya never quickened her pace. When they reached the Corvette she had not even crossed the last gate.

Scott ran his fingertips along the red metal body, which was still warm. Out of breath, they were standing in the smell of cut grass, also still warm, but growing damper. The old boy is in the big house, huh, he said. Sold his soul up the river. Out here in the open Taft felt naked as Tanya with the water going over her feet. He was trembling. Scott stuck in the key, and creaked open the driver's door, and the inside gave up its smell of oil and metal.

Stephen Marion works as a newspaper writer in the East Tennessee county where he grew up. He has a MFA in fiction from Cornell University, and his fiction has been published in *Epoch*. He is at work on a novel.

Years ago on a canoe trip down the Holston River we stopped at Indian Cave. The mouth of the cave struck me as enormous, maybe seventy-five feet tall, opening before the river. Once it actually was the largest electrically lit cavern in the world, but now it holds only the largest feeling of abandonment in the world.

I wrote "Naked as Tanya" because I think the landscape exists inside the people who live in it.

Scott Ely

TALK RADIO

(from *The Southern Review*)

I'm having a great night. Folks from all over the Carolinas are dialing me up, filling the air with their howls, like a bunch of ancient warriors gathered about a campfire, working themselves up into a killing mood. Bob, the station manager, as if he knows what I'm thinking, dances a war dance outside the booth, what he always does when I'm really rolling. Peggie, who sells advertising, shakes her head, but she knows that tomorrow will be a good day for her, that she won't have to wiggle her ass or shake her tits to make those sales.

We're talking about gun control. They're calling in from mobile phones as they drive into our signal on the interstate; they're calling from bars and bedrooms and phone booths. I imagine all that hate pulsating through the night like colored gas in a tube.

"Guns could disappear," I say to a caller. "The Japanese did it in the seventeenth century. Tokugawa Ieyasu halted the production of guns, and the country returned to the sword for 250 years. He lopped off a few heads, and folks came around to his way of thinking."

"I got a made-in-America .357 right here in my truck," he says. "I got it loaded with Teflon-coated rounds. Go right through a flak jacket. I just hope somebody tries to carjack me. I just hope they do."

In North Carolina it's legal to carry a handgun in a car, and you can carry it on your person if you have a permit. All you have to do to get a permit is prove you don't have a criminal record or haven't spent a few months in a mental institution. And take a course in gun safety, and pay a small fee. It's easy.

I wonder what some of the callers would say if they knew I don't own a gun of any kind. Once Bob had us do a show from a pistol range that caters to women. The sign advertising the place shows a woman in a two-fisted firing stance, filling a male torso full of holes. They had me shoot a few rounds at one of those torsos, but I didn't do well at all, even though I'd qualified with a .45 when I was in the army. Bob told me he was shocked at my ineptitude.

Then the caller becomes inarticulate. He snorts like a wild hog, makes sounds that are half words and half snarls. I let the listeners enjoy a little of that before I cut him off.

We go to a commercial break.

"Ease up a little on the intellectual stuff," Bob tells me. "Ease up. This isn't public radio."

I had enjoyed my job with public radio, where I hosted a talk show devoted to the standard liberal causes. Sometimes I long for the slower pace of that life, but I don't hold it against them for firing me. I came to work drunk one too many times. They did me a favor. Now I'm making plenty of money. I still drink, but I haven't come to work drunk a single time. I do that at home. I've got it under control.

"But I'm hot," I say.

"Back off a little."

"Everybody loves me. All those truck drivers and mill hands and hog farmers. You've seen the mail."

"That's right, Luther. Remember that."

I live in the two-story white house I grew up in on one of those oak-lined Charlotte streets. My father is dead. My mother is in a nursing home. I go to see her every Sunday, and she has no idea who I am.

With all the money they're paying me to be a local radio personality, it was no problem to put in a tennis court, the kind surfaced with brick dust like at Monte Carlo and Roland Garros. It's the only red clay tennis court in the city, and probably in the whole of North Carolina.

I pick up the phone for the next call.

"Every man, woman, and child in the United States should be given an AK-47," a voice says.

I know who it is, although I can hardly bring myself to even think his name. It's a voice I remember well, coming out of the night, wrapping itself around me just as it's doing now. If I speak, I imagine some spell will be broken and that voice will be gone, spinning off into the night, lost out there amid the clamor of the mob.

"Is that you, Thac?" I ask.

I know that voice from when I was in a radio research company in Vietnam. We monitored radio traffic from a base camp near Pleiku. With the help of interpreters, we tried to identify individual units down to the platoon level. That way we could keep track of the movements of regiments and divisions. Everyone in Saigon was worried about losing a provincial capital like Pleiku to the enemy; they all remembered Dienbienphu. It was in the back of command's mind, some bad dream that might come true.

"Where are you, buddy?" I ask.

"Roland Garros," he says.

We often talked about playing a match at Roland Garros after the war was over. Thac had spent time in Paris as a student at the Sorbonne.

I transfer the call to another line, so I can talk off the air, and go to an unscheduled commercial break. Bob is outside the booth, looking at me strangely, probably wondering if I've started coming to work drunk.

Thac says he's staying at a hotel. I agree to meet him in the morning. I tell him that I have to get off the line and back to the show. We hang up.

Thac was my counterpart on the other side, a brother officer. He appeared on our tactical frequency one night, asking to speak to anyone who knew how to play tennis.

We became friends in the same way that soldiers in the trenches at Vicksburg became friends, or Germans and British soldiers in World War I. Later they would kill each other. Thac and I would have done that if we had met in the jungle, but we only met over the radio.

The talk about AK-47s stirs the audience into a frenzy, makes listeners reach for their telephones. Soon I'm having a conversation with someone who argues that no child under six should be issued a rifle. Bob has returned to the booth with the engineers. He sits there with a satisfied look on his face.

Bob started the show with Jack Perkins, but Jack quit one night, announced on the air that he was going to live in Alaska, that he didn't think much of anyone stupid enough to listen to his show. Told his listeners that he didn't much care for Charlotte, that city of trees and churches. Said he wanted to live somewhere where he was not necessarily at the top of the food chain. Bob told me that Jack is up in Anchorage, doing the midnight-to-six shift, broadcasting the music of the '60s to army guys and trappers and Indian villages. I was drafted as a temporary substitute. To everyone's surprise, I was wildly successful.

"Who was that?" Bob asks. The show is over, and I'm preparing to go home.

"Some guy I knew in Vietnam," I say.

"A tennis player?"

"Yeah."

Bob worries about me making references to tennis on the air — or classical music or jazz or books. He says elitist talk is bad for advertising.

During those long nights in Vietnam, Thac and I talked about exceptionally good Wimbledons or Paris Opens. He had learned to play tennis in France and claimed to have served once as a ball boy at the French Open. His interest in the game was frowned upon by his superiors, who regarded it as a bourgeois sport.

In the morning I drive to the hotel. I call from the lobby, and Thac tells me to come up to his room.

When he opens the door he's about what I expect to see, a small man whose hair is turning gray around the temples.

"Come in, Luther," he says as he shakes my hand. "I heard your voice and knew it was you. Let me make you a drink. Whiskey and water?"

"Sounds good," I say. I notice right away that he walks with a limp.

"Bullet through the ankle," he says. "I can run, but I can't jump."

He explains that he is here on business. He wants to import pharmaceuticals into Vietnam, so he's been up around Durham talking with those big companies. That's where he first heard my voice on the radio. I'm surprised, because our signal doesn't usually reach that far north.

We had been talking to each other for a couple of months when abruptly he disappeared. I had promised to play him a new Jimi Hendrix tape. He was playing me *The Magic Flute*.

Major Wallace, who ran the operation, thought I was a little strange, but he didn't take my eccentricities seriously. After all, I was just a reserve officer, and he was a West Point man.

Under his direction we looked for deviations from standard radio procedure, individual idiosyncrasies that would help us identify the operators. But it had been difficult, because their discipline was excellent. I told Thac how our South Vietnamese interpreters had made fun of their northern accents, the same way that Major Wallace, who was from New York, had made fun of my Savannah accent: "It's *room*, Luther," he used to say. "Not *rum*. Jesus, but you talk strange."

"What happened to you?" I ask.

"My superiors discovered that I was having those conversations," Thac says. "They did not approve. I was put in command of an infantry platoon."

"No more Mozart," I say.

"No, we had difficult times."

I think of Thac wandering around in the jungle with his platoon, all because of his conversations with me. It makes me sad thinking that happened to him, and I tell him so.

"I was fortunate," he says. "A B-52 strike got our bunker. Everyone was killed. I would have died if I had been there."

"Saved by Jimi Hendrix," I say.

"Do you listen to him now?"

"No."

"I still love Mozart."

"We'll go to my house and listen to Mozart. Why don't you have dinner? Spend the night."

Thac says he will, so I call Verna at work to let her know I'm bringing someone home. She moved in with me about six months ago. She works at a health club, where she teaches aerobics. I suppose you could say that she's Miss Hardbody. One of these days I'm going to think more deeply about why she's with me, a man who prefers his women soft. Maybe it's her big breasts that attracted me. Verna dislikes them. She'd rather be much smaller, more athletic.

No woman like her, beautiful and twenty-five, would ever have taken up with Luther Watkins, the public radio disc jockey. On the air I'm called "The Professor." Bob came up with that name. What the audience likes, Bob says, is to listen to a liberal like me espousing conservative causes. It's like they are watching me being born again every afternoon on the radio. They take a sort of joy in my denigration, I once observed. And Bob said I was exactly right—that was what he had in mind, he just didn't have the words to express it.

Verna says she's dying to meet Thac. She does tend toward hyperbole. I know that simply means it's OK with her. We'll eat shrimp. I volunteer to pick some up on my way home.

We go to the grocery store and buy two pounds of king-sized shrimp, fresh from the waters off Charleston, the kid behind the counter tells us. Thac puts a couple of six-packs of German beer in the buggy. I buy a chocolate amaretto cake at the bakery. Verna won't touch that, but I can eat whatever I want.

Thac is impressed with the house. He doesn't say anything, but I can tell he is. He looks everything over carefully.

"They pay you well for insulting people on the radio?" he says.

I haven't told him about the court, which I've saved as a surprise. He sees it through the kitchen window when we bring in the groceries.

"*Terre battue?*" he says.

"That's right," I say. "If there's another one in North Carolina, I don't know about it. We'll play that match before you leave. You still play, don't you?"

"Yes," he says. "Whenever I can."

I put *The Magic Flute* on the player and make us drinks. Thac begins to explain to me what is going on in the music. He knows about it; he knows about the libretto. He never did that in Vietnam, probably thought it wasn't worth the trouble, but now I can see that he really wants me to understand it, to appreciate it in the same way he does. The rest of the morning we listen to it, playing sections of the disc over and over until I can feel that music in my bones.

I order us pizza for lunch, and we drink the German beer with it. We eat half of the cake. After lunch we give Mozart a rest. Thac puts *Carmen* on the player. After *Carmen* we play *Tristan und Isolde.* Every now and then I ask a question, and he always has the answer. Thac knows those operas backwards and forwards. For some reason I haven't listened to opera in a long time. Verna likes New Age stuff, which I can't stand.

When Verna comes home from work, we are in the middle of *La Bohème.*

"I could hear that out in the driveway," Verna says.

I turn down the sound and introduce her to Thac. She's dressed in a spandex exercise suit. Thac looks at her with fascination, as if he has never seen a beautiful woman before.

"So you knew each other in Vietnam," she says.

I explain how we talked on the radio, how we never saw one another, and how Thac had suddenly disappeared. Verna was asleep when I came home after my telephone conversation with Thac and was gone before I woke. I had considered waking her to tell her about Thac but decided against it.

"We lived like animals in the jungle," Thac says. "We ate such food as pigs eat."

"Tell me about it," Verna says.

Neither Thac nor I has said a word about Vietnam all afternoon.

"I ate steaks," I say.

It was true. We had it easy in base camp. Occasionally the enemy would lob a few mortar shells into the camp or drop a rocket in on us, but mostly it was pretty quiet.

Neither of them laughs at my comment about the steaks. They ignore me.

"They hunted us from the air," Thac says. "My men died from bombs and malaria and dysentery. We had little medicine."

Thac goes on talking about the six months he spent in the jungle. He tells the story in great detail. I'm not that interested, but Verna is riveted. That surprises me. He describes how he was shot in the foot, how he was evacuated back to Hanoi for treatment. He spent the rest of the war directing the repair of a bridge that American planes blew up at least once a week. Thac brags that his men had trucks running across it within two hours of each attack. His wife died in a B-52 raid on Hanoi.

All this flows out of Thac, who speaks it to Verna and not to me. It's like I'm not in the room, or that he assumes it's a story I already know. But we never talked about the war on the radio. I get fresh drinks for Thac and me; Verna doesn't drink. Thac takes one sip and puts it down. He talks while I watch the ice cubes in his drink melt. He talks on and on. I expect that Verna will get impatient with him and make some excuse to break off the conversation, for Verna is not a good listener. The war was over when she was still a baby, and I can't imagine her having any interest in it. But she sits on the floor with her legs crossed and listens intently, every now and then asking a question. An hour goes by, and he's still talking.

* * *

I want a cigarette. At Verna's urging I stopped smoking those, but she likes the smell of cigars. I get one for myself and offer one to Thac, who accepts. He's stopped talking. He sips his drink. I offer to get him some ice, but he says he doesn't need any.

We light up. There's nothing I want to ask Thac about his life in the jungle. He's told it all to Verna. He sits on the couch beside me and leans his head back and blows a smoke ring toward the ceiling. I don't know why I find that amazing, but I do. I tell him I do.

"I was a great smoker of cigars in Paris," he says.

Verna says that she's going to do something with the shrimp, that we should sit and talk.

"Y'all reminisce," she says.

Thac surely cannot have anything more to say about the war, nothing to add to that litany of disease, starvation, and violent death.

"We'll play tennis in the morning," I say. "Maybe you can wear a pair of Verna's shoes."

"I have shoes and a racket," he says. "I have played every day for a week."

"Do you play in Hanoi?" I ask.

"There are courts in Saigon," he says. "We play on them during the monsoon. Everyone calls us amphibians." He tells me that balls and strings are difficult to obtain and expensive. He is the number one player in Saigon. "The level is not high if an old man who cannot jump can be number one," he says.

At dinner we switch to wine. Verna has put chopsticks at our places instead of knives and forks.

"I'll get a fork," I say. "I'm not very good with these things."

I know that Verna is even worse than me. Thac shows her what's wrong with her technique, and soon she's handling those chopsticks like an expert. I stick with my fork.

I begin to tell Verna about my year with the radio research company. I know that my experience is bland compared to Thac's, but once I get started I can't help myself. And Verna seems interested. Thac concentrates on his food and the wine. Soon we're into a second bottle.

I tell Verna about listening to the war at night, of all that radio traffic from companies and platoons, of men calling desperately for evacuation helicopters and the calm, professional voices telling them they had none to send. We were eavesdropping on the war, those transmissions sailing across mountains and rivers and savannahs. The tropical night was alive with them.

We have ice cream for dessert, and then coffee. Afterward I serve brandy. Thac and I smoke another cigar. Verna excuses herself and goes off to bed.

I turn on the player, and we listen to *La Traviata*. When Thac goes to sleep toward the end, I turn off the player and wake him. After he heads off to bed, I drink a beer and listen to the rest of the opera. Then I go to bed.

Verna doesn't stir. She sleeps through thunderstorms. Last year when the hurricane came, she slept through that.

As I drift off, I think of Thac wandering about in the jungle, watching his men die. The army could have sent me anywhere. I never asked for radio research. I have nothing to feel ashamed about.

When I wake to the sound of Jimi Hendrix, it isn't light yet. Verna is gone. I get out of bed and walk into the hallway. The hall is in darkness and so is the room below, but in the glow from the streetlights outside I can see Verna kneeling before Thac with her head between his legs. He is seated on the sofa. I know his head is thrown back, because the red tip of his cigar is pointed at the ceiling.

I go back to bed and lie there, listening to my heart pounding. It's not that I am completely surprised, but if it happened I expected it would be with one of those young studs at the health club.

I decide to say nothing to Verna or Thac. Thac will be gone

tomorrow, and I'll never see him again. In a few weeks I'll start some quarrel with Verna. It will be easy to get rid of her, and I'll be left alone and at peace. Charlotte is filled with women who like the sound of my voice in the night.

Though I try to go to sleep before Verna comes back to bed, I can't. When she does return, she smells of cigar smoke. I pretend to be asleep. Soon she dozes off, and I lie there listening to the regular sound of her breathing. I try to imagine that I can smell Thac on her, underneath the cigar smoke, but all I can detect is the sweet scent of the soap she uses.

Then I sleep too.

In the morning Verna wakes me. I avoid looking directly into her eyes.

"I made you breakfast," she says. "Thac is already up."

When I go downstairs, Thac, dressed in tennis clothes, is seated at the kitchen table eating eggs and bacon. Verna has gone to work.

"Eat," he says. "We can play. I must be on a plane to Atlanta at two o'clock."

It's eight o'clock. We have plenty of time. I sit down and eat. I wonder what I will be thinking the next time Verna has her head between my legs.

Instead of talking to Thac, I concentrate on my breakfast. He smokes a cigarette while I finish.

After I dress we cross the dew-wet grass to the court. It is already a very hot day, but I imagine that Thac is as acclimated to the heat as I am.

When we start to warm up, I see why he is the number one player in Saigon. If it weren't for that shattered ankle, I wouldn't stand a chance. But his lack of mobility is going to be the difference, I tell myself. That and the fact that most of his play has been on fast surfaces. On concrete, in Saigon.

We both play sluggishly at first. Thac doesn't have much of a volley and can't jump for overheads, so on important points I bring him in and lob him. Most of his smashes go into the net. I win the first set easily.

I think play has gotten rid of my anger, but toward the end of the second set it returns as blind rage. I net a couple of easy shots. I have a chance to hit Thac with an overhead, but I miss. Now I wish we were boys on a football field. I would take much pleasure in hitting Thac with a hard tackle.

Thac looks like he's tiring. Perhaps, I think, he is still jet-lagged, and staying up half the night with Verna couldn't have helped. I give him a point here and there until the score is even. We agreed not to use tiebreakers, so by the time he wins the second set, the score is 14–16.

And the third goes better than I could have expected. Though I don't give him any points, he jumps out to a three-game lead, which I manage to close. Then it is six all, and we begin to trade games. I'm hoping he'll cramp up. I want to see him writhing on the clay.

At ten all I can tell he's close to cramping. He lifts his left leg and pulls it up behind him to stretch the muscle.

"I am obliged to retire," he says.

"We'll call it a tie," I say.

We drink some water together at the net.

"Sit down and rest," I say.

"No, if I sit I will cramp," he says.

I wonder why I've done this to Thac. I never pretended I was in love with Verna, and the only thing she loves is her own body. I think about saying these things to Thac but decide not to.

"You have time to sit in the Jacuzzi," I say. "We'll get some fluids into you."

We walk back to the house. Thac has taken off his shirt. A shrapnel scar wanders under his right nipple.

He showers and then gets into the Jacuzzi. I fix myself a drink and give Thac a quart of Gatorade. I sit in a rocking chair and smoke a cigar. Verna likes to make love in the Jacuzzi, to cavort as if we are a pair of porpoises.

Thac and I have leftover pizza for lunch, and the rest of the German beer. Then I call him a cab.

When the cab arrives and Thac starts out the door, I offer him the Jimi Hendrix disc.

"No," he says. "I have no way to play it."

There's not the slightest hint, no tremor in his voice, that would let me know that he knows I know.

I walk out to the cab with him, and we shake hands.

"Call me the next time you're in town," I say.

He smiles. "Come to Ho Chi Minh City and play on my courts," he says.

Then he's gone. I go back inside. I call Verna, but she's at lunch. I sit on the couch and have another drink and think about tonight's show. We're going to talk about busing.

I kick off my shoes and put my feet up. I set my drink on the table.

Then I close my eyes and think of those nights when Thac's voice would appear, how I'd listen and wonder what the man was like who was sitting in a bunker outside Hanoi, both of us plugged into the war, listening to the heartbeat of battle. I hear the confused babble of those voices from the past, a great chorus of pain and despair, rising out of those forest-covered mountains, sweeping over the coastal plain, and sailing out above the South China Sea. I sit very still and attentive before my memory, searching for individual voices, as if I am trying to identify the singer of an aria on a faulty disc.

I imagine playing tennis with Thac in Saigon during one of those days of the monsoon, the warm wind steady off the sea, the clouds low and thick over the city, the air filled with a fine mist. The concrete courts are slick. The balls are heavy with water. We move carefully, as if we are playing on ice, but I know that neither of us is going to fall. We are safe.

I wonder if Verna considers herself safe, protected by her perfect body. Maybe she was born safe, could have wandered through that jungle with Thac and never received a scratch. I imagine touching her, running my hands over those beautiful breasts and thighs. To my surprise, instead of being moved to anger or disgust

by thoughts of her and Thac, I imagine something entirely different, something I cannot quite name. All I know is that it will be a
good feeling. Then I realize that she will be a connection with
Thac, like his voice on the radio.

I am not going to drive her away. I am going to hang on to her
for as long as I can.

———————

Scott Ely received an MFA from the University of Arkansas. He has published two novels and one short story collection. His work has appeared
in *The Southern Review, The Gettysburg Review, Shenandoah,* and *Playboy.*
He has received an NEA fellowship and a Rockefeller fellowship to
Belagio, Italy. He teaches at Winthrop University in South Carolina.
His most recent collection of short stories, *The Angel of the Garden,* will
be published in spring 1999.

*When I was in Vietnam, a unit in our base camp was responsible for
monitoring enemy radio traffic. I carried the radio on a six-man recon
team. Over the border in Laos, an NVA unit was surely listening to our
team's transmissions. I guess I always wondered about that guy down in a
bunker at some NVA base camp, who in the early hours of the morning
might be listening to my request for artillery, or illumination, or my reports
on enemy troop movement.*

APPENDIX

A list of the magazines consulted for *New Stories from the South: The Year's Best, 1998,* with addresses, subscription rates, and editors.

Agni
Boston University Writing Program
236 Bay State Road
Boston, MA 02215
Semiannually, $18
Askold Melnyczak

Alabama Literary Review
253 Smith Hall
Troy State University
Troy, AL 36082
Annually, $10
Theron Montgomery, Editor-in-Chief

American Literary Review
University of N. Texas
P.O. Box 311307
Denton, TX 76203
Semiannually, $15
Fiction Editor

American Short Fiction
Parlin 14
Department of English
University of Austin
Austin, TX 78712-1164
Quarterly, $24
Laura Furman

The American Voice
Kentucky Foundation for
   Women, Inc.

332 W. Broadway, Suite 1215
Louisville, KY 40202
Triannually, $15
Frederick Smock, Editor
Sallie Bingham, Publisher

The Antioch Review
P.O. Box 148
Yellow Springs, OH 45387
Quarterly, $35
Robert S. Fogarty

Apalachee Quarterly
P.O. Box 10469
Tallahassee, FL 32302
Triannually, $15
Barbara Hamby

The Atlantic Monthly
745 Boylston Street
Boston, MA 02116
Monthly, $17.94
C. Michael Curtis

Black Warrior Review
University of Alabama
P.O. Box 862936
Tuscaloosa, AL 35486-0027
Semiannually, $14
Christopher Chambers

Boulevard
4579 Laclede Ave., Suite 332

St. Louis, MO 63108-2103
Triannually, $12
Richard Burgin

Carolina Quarterly
Greenlaw Hall CB# 3520
University of North Carolina
Chapel Hill, NC 27599-3520
Triannually, $10
Fiction Editor

The Chariton Review
Truman State University
Kirksville, MO 63501
Semiannually, $9
Jim Barnes

The Chattahoochee Review
DeKalb College
2101 Womack Road
Dunwoody, GA 30338-4497
Quarterly, $16
Lamar York, Editor

Cimarron Review
205 Morrill Hall
Oklahoma State University
Stillwater, OK 74078-0135
Quarterly, $12
Fiction Editor

Columbia
415 Dodge Hall
Columbia University
New York, NY 10027
Semiannually, $15
Lori Soderlind

Confrontation
English Department
C.W. Post of L.I.U.
Brookville, NY 11548
Semiannually, $20
Martin Tucker, Editor

Crazyhorse
Department of English
University of Arkansas at Little Rock
2801 South University
Little Rock, AR 72204
Semiannually, $10
Judy Troy, Fiction Editor

The Crescent Review
P.O. Box 15069
Chevy Chase, MD 20825-5069
Triannually, $21
J. Timothy Holland

Crucible
Barton College
College Station
Wilson, NC 27893
Annually, $6
Terrence L. Grimes

CutBank
Department of English
University of Montana
Missoula, MT 59812
Semiannually, $12
Fiction Editor

Double Dealer Redux
632 Pirate's Alley
New Orleans, LA 70116
Quarterly, $25
Rosemary James

DoubleTake Magazine
Center for Documentary Studies
1317 W. Pettigrew Street
Durham, NC 27705
Quarterly, $24
Robert Coles and Alex Harris

Epoch
251 Goldwin Smith Hall
Cornell University

Ithaca, NY 14853-3201
Triannually, $11
Michael Koch

Fiction
c/o English Department
City College of New York
New York, NY 10031
Triannually, $20
Mark J. Mirsky

Fish Stories
3540 N. Southport Ave., Suite 493
Chicago, IL 60657
Annually, $12.45
Amy G. Davis

Five Points
GSU
University Plaza
Department of English
Atlanta, GA 30303-3083
Triannually, $15
Fiction Editor

The Florida Review
Department of English
University of Central Florida
Orlando, FL 32816
Semiannually, $10
Russ Kesler

Gargoyle
c/o Atticus Books & Music
1508 U Street, NW
Washington, DC 20009
Semiannually, $20
Richard Peabody and Lucinda
    Ebersole

The Georgia Review
University of Georgia
Athens, GA 30602-9009
Quarterly, $18
Stanley W. Lindberg

The Gettysburg Review
Gettysburg College
Gettysburg, PA 17325-1491
Quarterly, $24
Peter Stitt

Glimmer Train
812 SW Washington Street, Suite 1205
Portland, OR 97205-3216
Quarterly, $29
Susan Burmeister-Brown and Linda
    Davis

GQ
Condé Nast Publications, Inc.
350 Madison Avenue
New York, NY 10017
Monthly, $20
Ilena Silverman

Grand Street
131 Varick St., Room 906
New York, NY 10013
Quarterly, $40
Jean Stein

Granta
250 W. 57th Street
Suite 1316
New York, NY 10017
Quarterly, $34
Ian Jack

The Greensboro Review
Department of English
University of North Carolina
Greensboro, NC 27412
Semiannually, $8
Jim Clark

Gulf Coast
Department of English
University of Houston
4800 Calhoun Road

Houston, TX 77204-3012
Semiannually, $12
Fiction Editor

Gulf Stream
English Department
Florida International University
North Miami Campus
North Miami, FL 33181
Semiannually, $7.50
Lynne Barrett

Harper's Magazine
666 Broadway
New York, NY 10012
Monthly, $18
Lewis H. Lapham

Habersham Review
Piedmont College
Demorest, GA 30535-0010
Semiannually, $12
Frank Gannon

High Plains Literary Review
180 Adams Street, Suite 250
Denver, CO 80206
Triannually, $20
Robert O. Greer, Jr.

Image
P.O. Box 674
Kennett Square, PA 19348
Quarterly, $30
Gregory Wolfe

Indiana Review
465 Ballantine Ave.
Indiana University
Bloomington, IN 47405
Semiannually, $12
Fiction Editor

The Iowa Review
308 EPB

University of Iowa
Iowa City, IA 52242-1492
Triannually, $18
David Hamilton

The Journal
Ohio State University
Department of English
164 W. 17th Avenue
Columbus, OH 43210
Semiannually, $8
Kathy Fagan and Michelle Herman

Kalliope
Florida Community College
3939 Roosevelt Blvd.
Jacksonville, FL 32205
Triannually, $12.50
Mary Sue Koeppel

The Kenyon Review
Kenyon College
Gambier, OH 43022
Quarterly, $22
Fiction Editor

The Literary Review
Fairleigh Dickinson University
285 Madison Avenue
Madison, NJ 07940
Quarterly, $18
Walter Cummins

The Long Story
18 Eaton Street
Lawrence, MA 01843
Semiannually, $9
R. P. Burnham

Louisiana Literature
P.O. Box 792
Southeastern Louisiana University
Hammond, LA 70402
Semiannually, $10
David Hanson

Lynx Eye
c/o Scribblefest Literary Group
1880 Hill Drive
Los Angeles, CA 90041
Quarterly, $20
Pam McCully

Mid-American Review
106 Hanna Hall
Department of English
Bowling Green State University
Bowling Green, OH 43403
Semiannually, $12
Robert Early, Senior Editor

Mississippi Review
Center for Writers
University of Southern Mississippi
Box 5144
Hattiesburg, MS 39406-5144
Semiannually, $15
Frederick Barthelme

The Missouri Review
1507 Hillcrest Hall
University of Missouri
Columbia, MO 65211
Triannually, $19
Speer Morgan

Modern Maturity
601 E Street, NW
Washington, DC 20049
Six times a year
John Wood

The Nebraska Review
Writers Workshop
Fine Arts Building 212
University of Nebraska
  at Omaha
Omaha, NE 68182
Semiannually, $9.50
Art Homer

Negative Capability
62 Ridgelawn Drive East
Mobile, AL 36608
Triannually, $15
Sue Walker

New Delta Review
English Department
Louisiana State University
Baton Rouge, LA 70803-5001
Semiannually, $8.50
Erika Solberg

New England Review
Middlebury College
Middlebury, VT 05753
Quarterly, $23
Stephen Donadio

The New Yorker
20 W. 43rd Street
New York, NY 10036
Weekly, $36
Bill Buford, Fiction Editor

Nimrod International Journal
The University of Tulsa
600 South College
Tulsa, OK 74104-3189
Semiannually, $17.50
Francine Ringold

The North American Review
University of Northern Iowa
Cedar Falls, IA 50614-0516
Six times a year, $22
Robley Wilson

North Carolina Literary Review
English Department
East Carolina University
Greenville, NC 27858-4353
Semiannually, $17
Alex Albright and Thomas E.
  Douglas

Northwest Review
369 PLC
University of Oregon
Eugene, OR 97403
Triannually, $20
John Witte

The Ohio Review
290-C Ellis Hall
Ohio University
Athens, OH 45701-2979
Semiannually, $16
Wayne Dodd

Ontario Review
9 Honey Brook Drive
Princeton, NJ 08540
Semiannually, $12
Raymond J. Smith

Other Voices
University of Illinois at Chicago
Department of English
   (M/C 162)
601 S. Morgan Street
Chicago, IL 60607-7120
Semiannually, $10
Fiction Editor

Oxford American
P.O. Drawer 1156
Oxford, MS 38655
Bimonthly, $24
Marc Smirnoff

The Paris Review
541 E. 72nd Street
New York, NY 10021
Quarterly, $34
George Plimpton

Parting Gifts
March Street Press
3413 Wilshire Drive

Greensboro, NC 27408
Semiannually, $8
Robert Bixby

Pembroke Magazine
Box 60
Pembroke State University
Pembroke, NC 28372
Annually, $5
Shelby Stephenson, Editor

Playboy
680 N. Lake Shore Drive
Chicago, IL 60611
Monthly, $29
Alice K. Turner, Fiction Editor

Ploughshares
Emerson College
100 Beacon Street
Boston, MA 02116-1596
Triannually, $19
Don Lee

Prairie Schooner
201 Andrews Hall
University of Nebraska
Lincoln, NE 68588-0334
Quarterly, $24
Hilda Raz

Puerto del Sol
Box 30001, Department 3E
New Mexico State University
Las Cruces, NM 88003-8001
Semiannually, $10
Kevin McIlvoy

Quarterly West
317 Olpin Union Hall
University of Utah
Salt Lake City, UT 84112
Semiannually, $12
M. L. Williams

River Styx
3207 Washington Avenue
St. Louis, MO 63103
Triannually, $20
Richard Newman

Salmagundi
Skidmore College
Saratoga Springs, NY 12866
Quarterly, $18
Robert Boyers

Santa Monica Review
Santa Monica College
1900 Pico Boulevard
Santa Monica, CA 90405
Semiannually, $12
Lee Montgomery

Shenandoah
Washington and Lee University
Troubadore Theater
2nd Floor
Lexington, VA 24450
Quarterly, $15
R. T. Smith

Snake Nation Review
110 #2 W. Force Street
Valdosta, GA 31601
Triannually, $20
Roberta George

The South Carolina Review
Department of English
Strode Tower Box 341503
Clemson University
Clemson, SC 29634-1503
Semiannually, $10
Frank Day

South Dakota Review
Box 111
University Exchange

Vermillion, SD 57069
Quarterly, $18
Brian Bedard

Southern Exposure
P.O. Box 531
Durham, NC 27702
Quarterly, $24
Pat Arnow, Editor

Southern Humanities Review
9088 Haley Center
Auburn University
Auburn, AL 36849
Quarterly, $15
Dan R. Latimer

The Southern Review
43 Allen Hall
Louisiana State University
Baton Rouge, LA 70803-5005
Quarterly, $20
James Olney

Southwest Review
307 Fondren Library West
Box 750374
Southern Methodist University
Dallas, TX 75275
Quarterly, $25
Willard Spiegelman

Sou'wester
Dept. of English
Box 1431
Southern Illinois University at
  Edwardsville
Edwardsville, IL 62026-1438
Semiannually, $10
Fred W. Robbins

Story
1507 Dana Avenue
Cincinnati, OH 45207

Quarterly, $22.00
Lois Rosenthal

StoryQuarterly
P.O. Box 1416
Northbrook, IL 60065
Quarterly, $12
Diane Williams

Tampa Review
Box 19F
University of Tampa Press
401 W. Kennedy Boulevard
Tampa, FL 33606-1490
Semiannually, $10
Richard Mathews, Editor

The Threepenny Review
P.O. Box 9131
Berkeley, CA 94709
Quarterly, $16
Wendy Lesser

TriQuarterly
Northwestern University
2020 Ridge Avenue
Evanston, IL 60208
Triannually, $24
Reginald Gibbons

The Virginia Quarterly Review
One West Range
Charlottesville, VA 22903
Quarterly, $18
Staige D. Blackford

West Branch
Bucknell Hall
Bucknell University
Lewisburg, PA 17837
Semiannually, $7
Robert Love Taylor

Whetstone
Barrington Area Arts Council
P.O. Box 1266
Barrington, IL 60011
Annually, $7.25
Sandra Berris

William and Mary Review
College of William and Mary
P.O. Box 8795
Williamsburg, VA 23187
Annually, $5.50
Forrest Pritchard

Wind Magazine
P.O. Box 24548
Lexington, KY 40524
Semiannually, $10
Charlie G. Hughes

Yemassee
Department of English
University of South Carolina
Columbia, SC 29208
Semiannually, $15
Stephen Owen

Zoetrope
126 Fifth Avenue, Suite 300
New York, NY 10011
Triannually, $15
Adrienne Brodeur

ZYZZYVA
41 Sutter Street
Suite 1400
San Francisco, CA 94104-4903
Quarterly, $28
Howard Junker

PREVIOUS VOLUMES

Copies of previous volumes of *New Stories from the South* can be ordered through your local bookstore or by calling the Sales Department at Algonquin Books of Chapel Hill. Multiple copies for classroom adoptions are available at a special discount. For information, please call 919-967-0108.

New Stories from the South: The Year's Best, 1986

Max Apple, BRIDGING

Madison Smartt Bell, TRIPTYCH 2

Mary Ward Brown, TONGUES OF FLAME

Suzanne Brown, COMMUNION

James Lee Burke, THE CONVICT

Ron Carlson, AIR

Doug Crowell, SAYS VELMA

Leon V. Driskell, MARTHA JEAN

Elizabeth Harris, THE WORLD RECORD HOLDER

Mary Hood, SOMETHING GOOD FOR GINNIE

David Huddle, SUMMER OF THE MAGIC SHOW

Gloria Norris, HOLDING ON

Kurt Rheinheimer, UMPIRE

W. A. Smith, DELIVERY

Wallace Whatley, SOMETHING TO LOSE

Luke Whisnant, WALLWORK

Sylvia Wilkinson, CHICKEN SIMON

NEW STORIES FROM THE SOUTH: THE YEAR'S BEST, 1987

James Gordon Bennett, DEPENDENTS

Robert Boswell, EDWARD AND JILL

Rosanne Coggeshall, PETER THE ROCK

John William Corrington, HEROIC MEASURES/VITAL SIGNS

Vicki Covington, MAGNOLIA

Andre Dubus, DRESSED LIKE SUMMER LEAVES

Mary Hood, AFTER MOORE

Trudy Lewis, VINCRISTINE

Lewis Nordan, SUGAR, THE EUNUCHS, AND BIG G.B.

Peggy Payne, THE PURE IN HEART

Bob Shacochis, WHERE PELHAM FELL

Lee Smith, LIFE ON THE MOON

Marly Swick, HEART

Robert Love Taylor, LADY OF SPAIN

Luke Whisnant, ACROSS FROM THE MOTOHEADS

NEW STORIES FROM THE SOUTH: THE YEAR'S BEST, 1988

Ellen Akins, GEORGE BAILEY FISHING

Rick Bass, THE WATCH

Richard Bausch, THE MAN WHO KNEW BELLE STAR

Larry Brown, FACING THE MUSIC

Pam Durban, BELONGING

John Rolfe Gardiner, GAME FARM

Jim Hall, GAS

Charlotte Holmes, METROPOLITAN

Nanci Kincaid, LIKE THE OLD WOLF IN ALL THOSE WOLF STORIES

NEW STORIES FROM THE SOUTH: THE YEAR'S BEST, 1989

NEW STORIES FROM THE SOUTH: THE YEAR'S BEST, 1990

Tom Bailey, CROW MAN

Rick Bass, THE HISTORY OF RODNEY

Richard Bausch, LETTER TO THE LADY OF THE HOUSE

Larry Brown, SLEEP

Moira Crone, JUST OUTSIDE THE B.T.

Clyde Edgerton, CHANGING NAMES

Greg Johnson, THE BOARDER

Nanci Kincaid, SPITTIN' IMAGE OF A BAPTIST BOY

Reginald McKnight, THE KIND OF LIGHT THAT SHINES ON TEXAS

Lewis Nordan, THE CELLAR OF RUNT CONROY

Lance Olsen, FAMILY

Mark Richard, FEAST OF THE EARTH, RANSOM OF THE CLAY

Ron Robinson, WHERE WE LAND

Bob Shacochis, LES FEMMES CREOLES

Molly Best Tinsley, ZOE

Donna Trussell, FISHBONE

NEW STORIES FROM THE SOUTH: THE YEAR'S BEST, 1991

Rick Bass, IN THE LOYAL MOUNTAINS

Thomas Phillips Brewer, BLACK CAT BONE

Larry Brown, BIG BAD LOVE

Robert Olen Butler, RELIC

Barbara Hudson, THE ARABESQUE

Elizabeth Hunnewell, A LIFE OR DEATH MATTER

Hilding Johnson, SOUTH OF KITTATINNY

Nanci Kincaid, THIS IS NOT THE PICTURE SHOW

Bobbie Ann Mason, WITH JAZZ

Jill McCorkle, WAITING FOR HARD TIMES TO END

Robert Morgan, POINSETT'S BRIDGE

Reynolds Price, HIS FINAL MOTHER

Mark Richard, THE BIRDS FOR CHRISTMAS

Susan Starr Richards, THE SCREENED PORCH

Lee Smith, INTENSIVE CARE

Peter Taylor, COUSIN AUBREY

NEW STORIES FROM THE SOUTH: THE YEAR'S BEST, 1992

Alison Baker, CLEARWATER AND LATISSIMUS

Larry Brown, A ROADSIDE RESURRECTION

Mary Ward Brown, A NEW LIFE

James Lee Burke, TEXAS CITY, 1947

Robert Olen Butler, A GOOD SCENT FROM A STRANGE MOUNTAIN

Nanci Kincaid, A STURDY PAIR OF SHOES THAT FIT GOOD

Patricia Lear, AFTER MEMPHIS

Dan Leone, YOU HAVE CHOSEN CAKE

Karen Minton, LIKE HANDS ON A CAVE WALL

Reginald McKnight, QUITTING SMOKING

Elizabeth Seydel Morgan, ECONOMICS

Robert Morgan, DEATH CROWN

Susan Perabo, EXPLAINING DEATH TO THE DOG

Padgett Powell, THE WINNOWING OF MRS. SCHUPING

Lee Smith, THE BUBBA STORIES

Peter Taylor, THE WITCH OF OWL MOUNTAIN SPRINGS

Abraham Verghese, LILACS

NEW STORIES FROM THE SOUTH: THE YEAR'S BEST, 1993

Richard Bausch, EVENING

Pinckney Benedict, BOUNTY

Wendell Berry, A JONQUIL FOR MARY PENN

Robert Olen Butler, PREPARATION

Lee Merrill Byrd, MAJOR SIX POCKETS

Kevin Calder, NAME ME THIS RIVER

Tony Earley, CHARLOTTE

Paula K. Gover, WHITE BOYS AND RIVER GIRLS

David Huddle, TROUBLE AT THE HOME OFFICE

Barbara Hudson, SELLING WHISKERS

Elizabeth Hunnewell, FAMILY PLANNING

Dennis Loy Johnson, RESCUING ED

Edward P. Jones, MARIE

Wayne Karlin, PRISONERS

Dan Leone, SPINACH

Jill McCorkle, MAN WATCHER

Annette Sanford, HELENS AND ROSES

Peter Taylor, THE WAITING ROOM

NEW STORIES FROM THE SOUTH: THE YEAR'S BEST, 1994

Frederick Barthelme, RETREAT

Richard Bausch, AREN'T YOU HAPPY FOR ME?

Ethan Canin, THE PALACE THIEF

Kathleen Cushman, LUXURY

Tony Earley, THE PROPHET FROM JUPITER

Pamela Erbe, SWEET TOOTH

Barry Hannah, NICODEMUS BLUFF

NEW STORIES FROM THE SOUTH: THE YEAR'S BEST, 1995

New Stories from the South: The Year's Best, 1996

Robert Olen Butler, JEALOUS HUSBAND RETURNS IN FORM OF PARROT

Moira Crone, GAUGUIN

J. D. Dolan, MOOD MUSIC

Ellen Douglas, GRANT

William Faulkner, ROSE OF LEBANON

Kathy Flann, A HAPPY, SAFE THING

Tim Gautreaux, DIED AND GONE TO VEGAS

David Gilbert, COOL MOSS

Marcia Guthridge, THE HOST

Jill McCorkle, PARADISE

Robert Morgan, THE BALM OF GILEAD TREE

Tom Paine, GENERAL MARKMAN'S LAST STAND

Susan Perabo, SOME SAY THE WORLD

Annette Sanford, GOOSE GIRL

Lee Smith, THE HAPPY MEMORIES CLUB

New Stories from the South: The Year's Best, 1997

PREFACE *by Robert Olen Butler*

Gene Able, MARRYING AUNT SADIE

Dwight Allen, THE GREEN SUIT

Edward Allen, ASHES NORTH

Robert Olen Butler, HELP ME FIND MY SPACEMAN LOVER

Janice Daugharty, ALONG A WIDER RIVER

Ellen Douglas, JULIA AND NELLIE

Pam Durban, GRAVITY

Charles East, PAVANE FOR A DEAD PRINCESS

Rhian Margaret Ellis, EVERY BUILDING WANTS TO FALL

Tim Gautreaux, LITTLE FROGS IN A DITCH

Elizabeth Gilbert, THE FINEST WIFE

Lucy Hochman, SIMPLER COMPONENTS

Beauvais McCaddon, THE HALF-PINT

Dale Ray Phillips, CORPORAL LOVE

Patricia Elam Ruff, THE TAXI RIDE

Lee Smith, NATIVE DAUGHTER

Judy Troy, RAMONE

Marc Vassallo, AFTER THE OPERA

Brad Vice, MOJO FARMER